ACCLAIM

"Crystal Grant has created an engaging new epic fantasy in *Shadowcast*. Seria—whose charm, kindness, and joy make her a memorable and fun character—dreams of someday becoming a healer. When she discovers a wounded soldier near her home, she nurses him back to health, having no idea she has aided one of the enemy in disguise. *Shadowcast* beckons readers into a world with complex characters, a desperate conflict, and a compelling allegory of light versus darkness. This book is a great choice for fantasy readers looking to delve into a promising new series. I'm looking forward to the next installment!"

—JILL WILLIAMSON, Christy Award-winning author of *By Darkness Hid* and *Thirst*

"*Shadowcast* gripped me from beginning to end. I couldn't stop thinking about the story long after I turned the last page. Crystal Grant has a way of creating characters that stay with you—I fell in love with Mason from page one! A five-star read that's sure to leave readers begging for a sequel."

—SARA ELLA, award-winning author of the *Unblemished* trilogy, *Coral*, and *The Wonderland Trials*

"Grant presents a strong fantasy novel with themes of light versus dark and the constant struggle between. Intriguing worldbuilding and characters make for a page-turning read that will call to readers of allegory and adventure alike."

—C. M. BANSCHBACH, award-winning author of *The Wolf Prince*

"Drenched in political intrigued and the neverending war between good and evil, *Shadowcast* highlights how one decision-whether good or bad-can change the course of another's life. Yet the reader learns that although we may feel cornered by the darkness, there is always a light to be found."

—V. ROMAS BURTON, award-winning author of the *Heartmaker* trilogy and *Fortified*

"A beautifully compelling tale of the consequences of light and dark, good and evil. *Shadowcast* had me hanging on the edge of my seat!"

—AJ SKELLY, bestselling author of *The Wolves of Rock Falls* series, and *Magik Prep Academy* series

"Like its title, *Shadowcast* weaves themes of hope and light into the tapestry of a dark world torn apart by the ongoing battle between good and evil. The sweet romantic tension between a grumpy, reluctant hero and a brightly resilient heroine kept me turning those pages! Throw in a conflicted prince, a lot of secrets, and Grant's thoughtful magical worldbuilding, and *Shadowcast* truly becomes an epic adventure full of spiritual truths with a love story worth rooting for."

—KRISSI DALLAS author of the *Phantom Island* series

SHADOWCAST

Other Writing By Crystal D. Grant

Anthologies
What Darkness Fears
Fool's Honor
Sharper Than Thorns
Casting Call: Havok Season Six
Tales of Many
The Sun Still Rises

SHADOWCAST

Quill & Flame
PUBLISHING HOUSE

CRYSTAL D. GRANT

Shadowcast

*Dedicated to all those who have ever thought it too late
to see their dreams realized.
Believe me. It's not.*

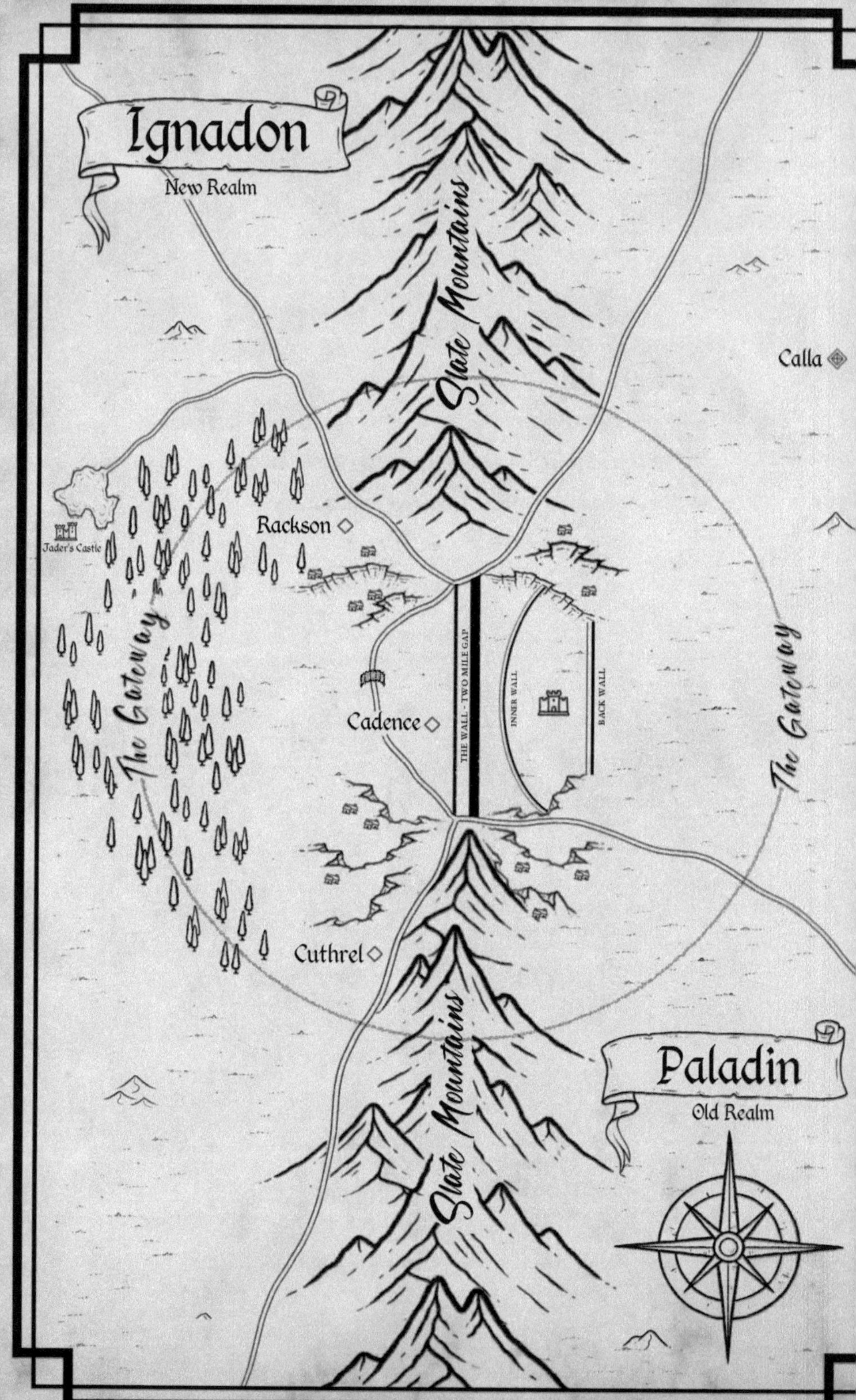

Ignadon
New Realm
Slate Mountains
Calla
Rackson
Jader's Castle
The Gateway
Cadence
THE WALL - TWO MILE GAP
INNER WALL
BACK WALL
The Gateway
Cuthrel
Slate Mountains
Paladin
Old Realm

Cast of Characters

Mason Grey – scout in the Dark Army

Seria Gayle – washerwoman in Cadence

Eric Passion – prince of Paladin

Aden Passion – king of Paladin

Uralis Faunt – Grand Marshal of the Steward Army

Braylee Wright – Captain in the Steward Army

Dudley Nells – Captain in the Steward Army

Jervis Planks – Captain in the Steward Army

Draven Kilton – Lieutenant in the Steward Army

Ollen Knavis – Sergeant in the Steward Army

Lionel Percy – Sergeant in the Steward Army

Gus Chesney – knight in the Steward Army

Graulik Jader – Emperor of the New Realm

Bruin Pralus – Commander of the Dark Army

Shon Larson – scout in the Dark Army

Dreeya Faybe – scout in the Dark Army

Feegan Hames – Captain and Shadowman in the Dark Army

Lyoth Unt – Shadowman in the Dark Army

Areem Kanen– student of Mason's

Liam Grey – Mason's brother

Crue Vancer – servant boy of the Dark Army

Gayner Leynus – Head Councilman in the Gateway Stronghold

Luron Furvor – physician in the Gateway Stronghold

Byron Jayes – peasant boy living in Cadence

Lena Carwright – baker in the Gateway

Ira Dankton – former client of Seria's

The Massacre

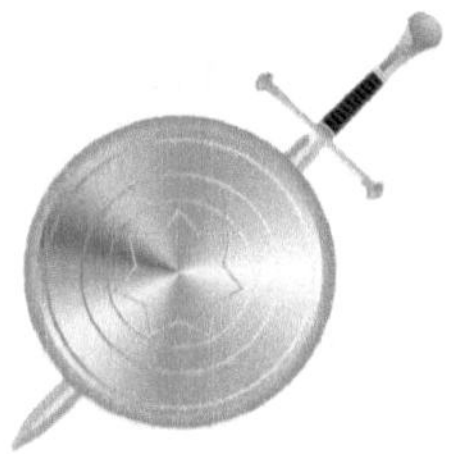

"You mark my words, Mason. Those Steward Knights are dangerous."

Mason Grey bit back a chuckle and worked to keep up with his guide. "You always say that."

Admonition darkened Baris's tone as he led the way through the midst of the color-splatted forest. "Wait and see, they'll show their hand someday. And with the way they're prancing about in the New Realm, bold as you please, I wager it won't be long."

"Liam says they're trying to keep the peace." Mason brushed a skinny twig aside. Liam knew a lot about the Stewards of the Old Realm, had even dreamed of becoming one, until he lay that dream aside to look after Mason.

"I know your brother likes to find the sunshine, but clouds have a way of covering it. And then the rain falls."

Mason didn't respond. Liam always joked that Baris thrived on his own pessimism. But the young man had befriended Mason, despite their ten-year age difference, so Mason tolerated his cynical outlook.

"Hmm. Speaking of rain." Baris squinted through the canopy of leaves above them.

Mason hid a sigh as he dropped back to follow the man through a thick strand of trees and vines. Did Baris never tire of his negative outlook?

But this time, he was right. Dark, heavy clouds bunched up around the rising autumn moon. "That won't stop us." Mason pushed confidence into his voice. Liam had promised this hunt would take place, rain or shine. At twelve, Mason was finally old enough to join the older boys, and not even a little rain could dampen his excitement.

"We'll see."

The path opened up, and they once again walked side-by-side. Baris sent Mason a smirk. "Think you'll kill anything today?"

Mason fingered the crossbow hanging at his side. "I'd better, or the other boys will hound me into next year. This is—"

"The first step into manhood. I know; I've heard it before." Baris chuckled. "But don't worry, this is your big day. You're the best shot in the group."

Mason straightened his posture and met his gaze. "You think so?"

"You're not trying to read my mind, are you?"

He barked out a laugh. "You know I can't do it most of the time."

Baris grinned. "You'll learn how to control it someday, and then you'll have a Gift beyond anyone's imagination. It'll make you great!"

Mason scoffed at the idea. Sometimes, he wished he had obtained a different Gift of the Moon, something a little less complicated. His Gift had done nothing but drive him and his brother from house to house after their parents died until Liam had secured a place for them at

Handan's Home for Boys. Here, Mason felt almost normal, even though he could read his friends' thoughts with a single look. Sometimes.

Baris smacked Mason's arm. "Remember when you sent Lewie to sleep in the barn last year?" He snickered. "Next morning, he had no idea how he got there. What a riot!"

"I thought Handan was going to expel me on the spot." If Liam had not convinced their benefactor it was a harmless joke, they would have both been sent back to the streets.

"Aw." Baris waved a wand. "Handan doesn't appreciate what you're capable of."

Liam hadn't appreciated it, either. His warning still rang in Mason's ears. *"You've got to control that Gift of yours, Mason, or you'll end up in a heap of trouble."*

The distant drum of hoofbeats broke the stillness of the forest, and Baris drew up short. "Wait."

A tendril of uncertainty swirled through Mason at the fierce lines crossing Baris' forehead. "What is it?"

"Something's not right." Baris moved ahead, slower now.

Shouts and screams ascended from the clearing ahead—where Liam and the other boys waited. Mason's heart lurched, and he took off running.

"Mason, wait!"

The woods seemed intent on holding him back. Branches slapped at him, and low-lying shrubbery grabbed his feet. Cold droplets pelted his face. At the tree line, Mason slid to a stop. Horror and shock wrapped themselves in a tight noose around his neck, robbing him of the oxygen his desperate lungs sought. His knees shook, and he braced himself with one hand on a gnarled trunk.

Through the mist, a party of knights on horseback circled the Handan boys in the middle of the large glade. Their scarlet breastplates flashed as they aimed long, deadly swords. In the same hand that held their reins, they grasped short, crystalline rods that lit up the glowering sky with brief flashes of white brilliance.

Beacons. *Stewards*.

Mason's breath lodged in his windpipe. What was happening?

Beside him, Baris cursed. "The beasts! They're killing them!"

That snapped Mason out of his stupor, and he bolted for the clearing. Baris caught him and hauled him back. "Nay, Mason! You'll be killed!"

Mason's heart thundered against his ribcage as he pulled against Baris, unable to drag his eyes from the sight. With their secondhand hunting gear, the boys stood no chance against the highly trained Stewards. Some had already fallen.

BOOM! Thunder roared, and a torrent of rain fell, veiling the nightmare from Mason's view. Baris tugged him back, away from the deadly scene and into the safety of the woods. But Mason's stunned mind jerked to his brother, and he dug his heels into the dampening ground.

The Stewards' Beacons cut through the gray vapor like a knife, offering brief snatches of visibility. Liam stood in the middle of the circle, his bow raised up to his stark-white face, though he did not shoot. A rush of relief swept over Mason.

Then a Steward advanced, his sword aimed and ready.

"Liam!" Mason struggled against Baris. "Let me go!"

"It's too late! We can't do anything!"

The rain rolled back its curtains long enough for Mason to see the Steward stop before his brother and pierce the sword through his body. Liam stood stock-still for a brief moment, his mouth open in shock, before he slumped to the ground in a lifeless heap.

"Noooo!" The cry ripped from Mason's throat, snatched away in the wind and rain. Everything in him shattered. His big brother, protector, and friend. The only family who cared enough to stay with him, gone. His life snuffed out. By a Steward.

Mason's pulse tripled in strength, and red-hot fury surged through him. He swung around and stared Baris down in one last-ditch effort to gain control. "Let. Me. Go!" When that didn't work, Mason hooked his arm around Baris' elbow and swiveled, breaking his hold.

"Mason, stop!"

He darted for the open area, gripping his crossbow with white knuckles. He slid to a quick stop and launched a shot. His target: Liam's killer. The Steward tumbled from his horse.

His first kill in the hunt.

A thick haze of pain and darkness fell over him, shoving out everything but hatred for these knights who attacked with no cause. His trembling lips flattened against his teeth. He would kill them. All of them.

The air chilled, wrapping icy fingers around his limbs. Spots danced before him, and his movements slowed, but he fired again and again. He stumbled to his knees, still squeezing the trigger on his now-empty crossbow.

Black fog drifted in and out of his head, trying to suck him in. At a strangled cry, Mason looked behind him, swaying against the spinning world. Baris lay face down in the mud, mere feet from where Mason knelt.

A jolt of fire struck Mason's upper body, knocking him back. He rolled to his side and looked down at the arrow sticking out of him. Blood spurted from the hole by his sternum, pounding in his ears.

The screams echoed in his head. The smell of blood, rain, and mud mixed in his nostrils, turning his stomach. Shock chilled him.

So dark. So much pain. Hard to breathe.

Liam. Dead.

Stewards. Must. Die.

Mason sucked in one last desperate breath and lost himself to the darkness.

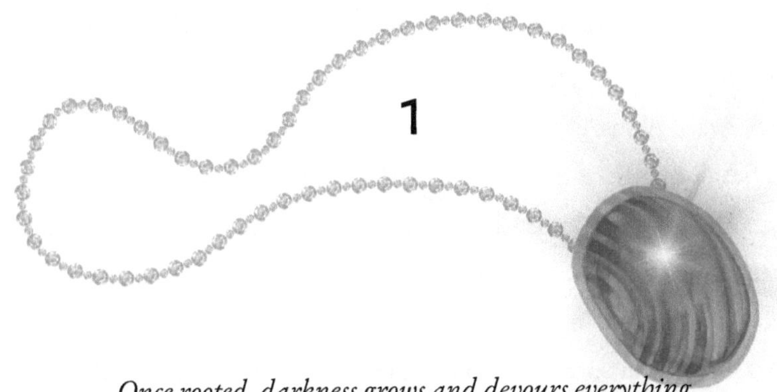

1

Once rooted, darkness grows and devours everything
in its path, satisfied by nothing but its own hunger.
-The Sacred Code

Ignadon, New Realm
Twelve years later

The cold hole within would soon consume him and leave nothing but a shell behind. Unless he could fill it with the vengeance his soul sought.

Mason sat deep in the saddle and rode hard, despite the dusk falling over the forest, his sword bouncing lightly at his side. His gelding snorted, its sides warm beneath the leather girth. The familiar path they traveled was nothing more than a dirt line cut in the terrain, blanketed with rotting leaves. Mason stared straight ahead, consumed with his destination.

Everything was about to change. His orders were forthcoming—orders which would take him far from this place that had become his home.

Surely, this call would put him en route to becoming a Shadowman.

That long-held pursuit had kept the growing void at bay most nights, but the desire alone was not enough. He needed the Shadowstone, the matchless purple gem that would inject a trace of the emperor's dark power into his broken soul and stitch it back together with the threads of justice and purpose. It was all Mason wanted. No more pain. No more loss. Nothing but a clear-cut vision of the end goal: the annihilation of the Steward Army.

The silhouette of the massive castle lay ahead, nestled among jagged bluffs and framed against the fading sky. The front tower stood tall like a beckoning finger. Constructed of dark stone, Ignadon's castle stood huge and ancient.

Mason rode under the ivy-lined archway of the curtain wall into the lower ward, then past the guardhouse and across the upper ward to the steps of the main hall. The walls cast everything in shadows.

His horse relaxed its long-legged stride at a slight tug on the reins. Mason swung out of the saddle before they came to a complete stop. He patted the sweaty roan's neck and handed the reins to a groom. "Treat him well."

"Aye, Sir Mason."

Though Ignadon was not the largest or most recent of the New Realm conquests, Mason knew it to be Emperor Jader's proudest. It held the most influence, thus compelling the last of the independent kingdoms to bow readily to his will. And now, the last thing that stood between Jader and the Old Realm was the Slate Mountain Range and the single passage through them.

Mason swept the travel dust from his black vest and trousers as a doorman bowed and motioned him to follow. They hastened through dim, dank rooms, their footsteps echoing on the cobbled floor, while servants tiptoed up and down the halls. Jader's gray and black banners, emblazoned with blood-tipped spears, hung in every room, a boastful reminder of who now reigned. Tables and benches of black wood stood against the cold walls. It was a bit dark and dreary for Mason's taste, but it suited the emperor.

The doorman stepped inside the throne room and called out, "Sir Mason Grey has arrived." Then he slipped away without another sound.

Emperor Graulik Jader sat tall on the high-backed throne, watching as Mason entered another wide archway. Mason stuffed his fervor at being called this unusual hour behind a stoic expression and gave a smart bow. "Emperor."

Jader acknowledged him with a slight nod. He cut an intimidating figure with sharp features and shoulder-length, russet-colored hair brushed straight back off his thin face. Dark whiskers lined his upper lip and chin. A vicious scar ran down the right side of his face over his eye, skirting his mouth, and into the hairs of his chin. It left a black streak across the pale, unmoving iris of his eye. The sight of it always aroused Mason's curiosity, but he stifled it out of respect for the man who took him in so many years ago.

"You look well, my friend." Jader's voice was smooth, almost soothing.

"I've fared well."

"Master Bruin tells me your latest recruits have been placed in their permanent units."

"Aye, sir." Mason straightened his shoulders.

Jader's face held the trace of a smile. "Congratulations. You took the progeny of mindless rabble and transformed them into worthy fighters. You are well on your way to becoming an influential leader."

Mason inclined his head. The flattery was nice, but he was not here to discuss his recruits. His ears strained to hear the word, that promise of power.

The Shadowstone.

"I have dispatched a troop to the town of Rackson."

Mason blinked. "Rackson, sir? Isn't it—?" He took a step back. "Forgive me, Emperor."

"Come, Mason, there is no need for such formalities between the two of us." Jader folded his hands on his lap. "Is it insignificant? Aye, it is. I care little for Rackson's existence and need its patronage even less. However, reports of insurrection have emerged, and that cannot be tolerated. It will not take long to deal with the problem."

"I see." Mason gave a deflated nod. For a speck of a town like Rackson, punishment would be swift.

Fortunately, Jader seemed oblivious to his letdown. "However, Rackson's sins are not the singular motivation for this move."

"Sir?"

Jader stood, smoothing the folds of his black surcoat as he descended the stairs. His dark gray cloak, woven with red and black threads, flowed regally down his back to the floor. "You are aware Rackson rests near the border of the Gateway, so carefully guarded by Aden's Stewards."

"Aye, sir." What did this have to do with him?

A smile stretched Jader's features, and he placed a thin hand on Mason's shoulder. "For one so perceptive, I can see I have lost you."

"Forgive me, sir."

"In order to enter the Old Realm, we must break Paladin and its weak-hearted king. When Paladin falls, the rest of the kingdoms will follow as the New Realm did." Jader's white eye twitched. "How long do you think it will take for the Passions to hear of Rackson's situation?"

It hit Mason then. "You're trying to get their attention."

"In part, yes." Jader released him. "It is time the Stewards know we will not back down. By its actions, Rackson has proven disloyal. But the Stewards will not see it that way, and we both know what they are capable of, do we not?"

Heat climbed up Mason's spine. No answer was needed to confirm the Stewards' brutality. He still saw it in his dreams. The chasm inside him writhed at the reminder.

"It is time the rest of the world know as well." Jader's intonation tightened. "But to rid this land of their hold and their archaic book of laws, we must breach that valley."

"Am I to be a part of Rackson's judgment?"

"Not exactly. We both know you have set your sights on a higher goal than one town's sentence. I believe the time has come."

His fingers tingled. Finally!

"The Stewards will no doubt interfere," Jader said. "They have laid claim to the entire valley, as well as the surrounding territories, and it takes very little to provoke them."

Mason gulped. Aye, the Stewards were certain to be provoked by Jader's actions.

"Master Bruin will move his troops to the forest at morning's first light. The sentence is to be carried out at nightfall. You have a special mission. When the time is right—you shall know when it comes—you are to slip past them. Weaken their defenses at Rackson to give our men the advantage; while they're distracted, move on to Cadence and infiltrate the fort." Jader gave a soft laugh. "Do what you do best but gather as much information as you can about the layout of their stronghold. And when finished, report back to me."

"Aye, sir." Mason tapped his fist against his thigh.

"This is the first step in getting through the Gateway and seeing the Aged Realms once again united," Jader said. "I trust this task to no other. Nothing but your exceptional Gifts will grant you access. No one's mind can stand up to the power of yours. I attribute my victory in the New Realm in part to your prowess on the field, as well as behind the lines.

You have served me well, but I waited until certain you were ready for this assignment. The thirst for vengeance boils inside of you, ready to spill over."

Mason's neck tightened, and he slowed his breathing. It would not do to let Jader see how close to the surface his emotions raged.

"I know you will not disappoint me." Jader turned to dismiss him. "Or yourself."

An usher appeared to escort Mason to his chambers, but that void in his spirit drove him to make a hasty exit outside. He needed to clear his head, needed to think.

It was getting hard to see in the evening shadows, but Mason plunged on. He climbed a grassy incline with ease, his swift, sure movements borne from years of familiarity. Not until he reached the top did he pause to catch his breath and pay heed to the scene before him, memorizing it one last time.

The dark waters reflected the moon, casting its dim light throughout the ripples. Rolling hills rose and fell in the distance. The woods stood tall and black against the deep indigo of the sky. A few brave stars sparkled like diamonds on a velvet cloth.

This land had become his home, a place of refuge ever since he found himself alone in the world. How long before he saw it again? Jader had said little of Mason's personal aspirations, but the implication remained. The Shadowstone would soon be his.

The last picture of his brother with his teasing smile hung before him. Mason squeezed his eyelids shut and let the memories take him back until the serenity of the moment was overtaken by flashes of memory.

Swords. Rain. Screams. Blood. Liam falling. And those accursed Beacons. The cries shrieked through Mason's ears, and he gritted his teeth against the torrent of fury locked inside.

Anger was the one emotion he seemed to feel these days. Sometimes that worried him. Other times, he embraced it. All would be made right when he wore the Shadowstone around his neck.

Mason lifted his chin and embraced the cold night, drawing peace from it while he still could. A night owl swept down over the lake, catching a fish in its talons. A black fox trotted along the edge of the waters, casting furtive looks in every direction. Fireflies darted back and forth, their golden lights flickering constantly. The intoxicating scent of the night rose drifted from a nearby bush.

The scene brought a measure of tranquility. The heat faded from his veins. His muscles softened, chasing away the tension clinging to him. Darkness never intimidated him like so many others. Rather, he found solace in its power. The nocturnal flora and fauna drew him. They were creatures of the night, sharing a bond in which they found the light harsh and uncomfortable. It was safer, freer in the shadows.

Mason filled his lungs with the cool, cleansing air. It was unfortunate that it was not so easy to fill the dark hole in his soul, but for that, he needed the Shadowstone. Until then, the sharp focus of vengeance would carry him. His fingers clenched around the hilt of his sword.

He would soon see justice for Liam.

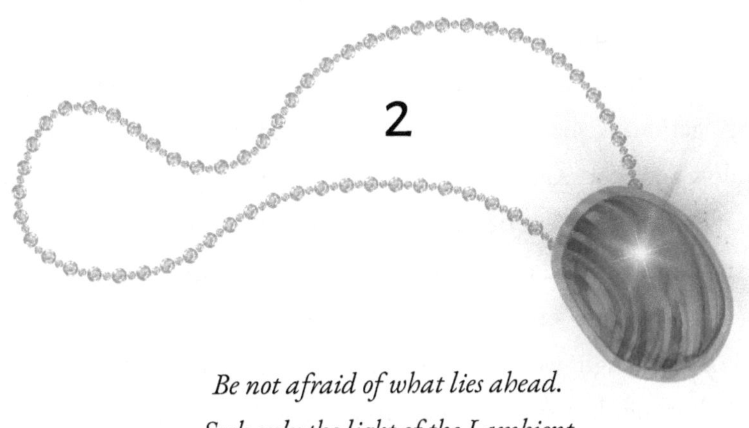

2

Be not afraid of what lies ahead.
Seek only the light of the Lambient
and He will guide your way.
-The Sacred Code

Paladin, Old Realm

Screams split the air, cutting through the soul of anyone unfortunate enough to hear. Soldiers advanced in every direction—Shadowmen with black breastplates, Stewards with red—all wielding blood-stained swords. Fear hung thick and rancid, an almost palpable cover. Sinister shadows clung to the sky, choking the dawn and all hope. Little by little. Moment by moment. Until, at long last, the light was snuffed, and the valley plunged into an endless void.

Eric Passion shuddered and tried to block out the presentiment, only to see it played out in the canvas of his mind.

"Are you all right, son?"

The soft question drew Eric's attention to the white-haired man across the room. To their people, he was King Aden of Paladin, wise ruler of the greatest kingdom of the Old Realm. But to Eric, he was his dear father and last remaining family.

Evading the question, Eric straightened and surveyed their desolate surroundings. Whitestone benches sat in half-circle rows, but with no congregation. A shard of weak sunlight sliced through a stained-glass window and exposed the tufts of grass poking through the cracks in the paved floor. An ancient building, empty and forsaken.

And in the middle of the chamber stood a wooden platform with a large, glassy sphere—the timeless, yet forgotten Beacon Orb.

"I never thought we'd see another Steward Hall closed," Eric said.

"At least not hither in Paladin." Aden sagged beneath his blue tunic. "At one time, people revered the Lambient. But so many have fallen away."

"There are multitudes who still honor the old ways. We mustn't let this discourage us." Eric waved his hand at the vacant hall. "The Steward Army is still the strongest army on both sides of the Slates."

"That may be, but it does not change what's happening." Aden caressed the Beacon Orb with a worn hand. The glass lit beneath his fingertips—a soft, dim light, as though the Orb itself was tired.

The glow beckoned to Eric, calling him to draw from its source—so strong that he took a step forward. But he looked away, breaking the connection, and instead voiced the concern hanging over his mind. "Jader's army grows stronger."

Aden gave a slow nod. "With the New Realm now firmly in his grip, he'll set his sights on the Gateway."

They needed no missive to accept the truth of the warning. Theirs was an almost omniscient premonition passed down through the ages, borne of their shared heritage and bloodline. A sixth sense: the Passion intuition.

Aden spoke again, still running his hand over the knobbed surface of the glowing globe. "Not so long ago, those kingdoms were much like

Paladin—pure, good. But Jader's message of darkness turned the people from the Code, and they still cling to his shallow promises and his lies." He gave a soft grunt, his stare distant. "As if the Sacred Code is to blame for all the devastation befallen them."

The deteriorating platform buckled, and the Beacon Orb tipped. From across the room, Eric stretched out his arm to stop it from hitting the floor. Energy from his Gift—pure and light—flowed down his arm to his hand. The sphere hovered in midair.

Aden nodded once and rubbed his hands together. "I suppose that says it all."

The words smacked at the stubborn optimism Eric held. He guided the Orb onto one of the tall chairs up on the platform, where in years past, young cadets were granted entry into the Royal Steward Army. Eric had stood in a hall much like this when he withdrew his own Beacon from the Orb and heard the famous commencement speech given by Grand Marshal Uralis Faunt. The marshal then spent many months training Eric for the command of the army.

Eric turned for the open door. "Come. We should head back before dark."

"We'll have the Orb moved to Calla for now. Mayhap this Hall will open again someday, and it can return to its rightful spot."

There was his father. Always clinging to hope—hope that was becoming harder to believe, evidenced by the deepening lines on his face.

They stepped outside into a meadow splashed with golden sunshine. Their ten-man mounted guard waited a few yards away. Eric's dappled gray stallion nickered in greeting. "You ready to go, Oakley?" Eric stroked the horse's muscular neck and mounted. When his father made no move to mount, he glanced over. The old king stared out at the green hills and fields that made up the vast part of their dominion. Peaceful and serene. Safe.

For now.

Eric's attention shifted to the peaks in the distance. The Slate Mountain Range stood steep and vertical, the impassable divider of the Aged Realms. A two-mile gap marred the ridgeline like a broken tooth, the one valley for leagues and so narrow it couldn't be seen from some angles. The Gateway was supposed to be neutral ground, but for how long?

"Have you heard from Marshal Uralis?" he asked.

"Aye." Aden hauled himself up on his horse and gathered the reins. "The Fourteenth Battalion has been relieved and is due home anytime. Uralis says Cadence has turned into quite a lovely little town. I think he's rather enjoyed his first day at the fort."

"And why not? With his favorite captain along for the ride, this is nothing more than a holiday for the both of them." He lightened his tone to mask his growing uneasiness.

"True." Aden let out a chuckle. "Captain Braylee's ethics would never allow him to petition for a maintenance commission, but I think he was pleased when Uralis requested him. That pair works together like a well-trained team of horses."

His smile warmed Eric. "'Tis no wonder, the years they've served together."

They turned their horses to the north, towards Calla, their cherished capital city. Their escort fanned out around them.

An iron band tightened around Eric's torso, in spite of the shift in conversation. His fingers curled around the reins. Something was not right. Fear for Uralis and the Stewards at the fort formed a rock in his gut. But it was more than the threat of war that yoked him. A hidden menace he could not define but sensed just the same kept him awake at night.

A shout from an approaching rider jolted Eric, and he jerked on the reins. Oakley tossed his head in protest. The guards spurred their mounts ahead, forming a shield before the king. Eric recognized the rider as a messenger from the castle. The man pulled his lathered horse to a stop and spoke to the lead guard in low tones.

"What is it, Jervis?" Aden called.

The captain rode back to his side, his dark face drawn tight. "Troops approaching Rackson, Sire. The Dark Army. Uralis requests aid."

Eric's mouth dried. "How many Stewards are with him?"

"He took two platoons."

Eighty men, with a mere hundred or so militiamen based at the fort. Eric's eyes slid shut. If trouble arose, Uralis would not run. And Captain Braylee and the rest of the gallant knights would all ride at his side without question.

Aden covered his face with a trembling hand and shook his head. "What can he do with so few?" Never in all of Eric's thirty-two years had his father looked so old.

"Captain Dudley is preparing a brigade now," Jervis added.

Aden turned his face to Eric, his piercing blue eyes pinning Eric to the saddle, transforming him back to the young boy who used to trail the king all over the castle. Urgency pressed him, making it difficult to breathe. Sweat broke out on his brow. It was too soon. They were not ready for this. *He* was not ready.

"'Tis time, son."

The brief statement shattered his wall of resolve. "Father—"

Aden moved his horse closer. "There is something more at play here, Eric. Something darker. You feel it, too."

Mercy, he did. And the angst of what he must do held him in a steel grip.

"You can do this, son."

Eric gulped, his conscious pricked. What did it say of him as a ruler, if he was unwilling to fight for his kingdom? He unclenched his jaw. "I will ride with Dudley for Rackson straightaway." The words rasped past the clamp on his dry throat.

Aden straightened, as though a little of the weight he carried had been lifted. He reached down and unstrapped the belt around his waist. "Then you must take Lavrynth."

"But that's your—"

"'Tis bound to be yours soon enough." Aden extended it out to him. "It will serve you well, as it did for our fathers over the ages since the day it was handed down from Lambient Himself."

Eric hesitated before wrapping his hand around the leather and slowly withdrew the silver blade partway from its scabbard. Etched diamonds and stars glistened in the gold hilt.

Indecision swamped him. Stepping out would rip the scab off the mistakes of his past. Could he lead again, dare to take the command back from Uralis? Nay, but he could not dismiss the heavy feeling that Uralis would no longer lead the Stewards after this night.

Aden pressed his weathered hand over Eric's clenched one. "Lavrynth was forged for this very darkness we face, laced with the power of the Lambient and the blood of our ancestors. It is linked to you, son. And when the time comes, it will be enough."

Eric gritted his teeth and slid the sword back in its casing with a soft thud. War was upon them. Jader would use all the dark power he possessed to his fullest advantage to alter the future of the Gateway. Beyond that, the Old Realm lay before him, ready to fall as the New Realm did.

His father spoke the truth. The time had come.

Aden squeezed Eric's shoulder, bequeathing some of his own strength, and gave him a long look, fraught with shared emotion and memories. Then he turned to follow Jervis back home.

Eric glanced back at the granite Steward Hall, tucked in a small grove of trees by the meadow's edge. A pleasant picture if not for the evening shadow stretching its long fingers over it. The door hung open to the empty, black void within. Eric reached out with his hand and mind to pull the door shut against the darkness. As he turned away from the scene, that familiar dread settled over him again, smothering him with its closeness.

Night would soon descend on the land.

3

Regard the pure.
-The Sacred Code

Just outside Rackson, the Gateway

"The best fishing occurs at sunset."

Seria Gayle spoke her father's oft-repeated words aloud as she relaxed on the low bank of the giggling creek with a line in the cool water, moments before the spring sun kissed the western horizon. The gurgling currents swept out of reach of her slippers, and the clean scent of wet grass permeated her senses. "He certainly knew what he was talking about, didn't he?"

A snuffle met her ears, drawing her attention to her geriatric donkey nibbling at the tender grass lining the creek.

"Not interested in fish, huh?" At his snort, she chuckled. "Fine, Sanjo. Eat up. You earned it."

He replied with a flick of a long, gray ear.

Seria readjusted her position and checked her line. Her cart sat close by, piled high with wild melons that grew around the bank. In the water hung her net, which already housed several plump fish—a testament to her father's knowledge. She would wait until it was time to leave before hooking them to her line.

The fishing trip didn't happen as often as she liked, though this particular location sat but a few miles north of Cadence. It was easier now that she had Sanjo, but the trek through the unbroken meadows and then back to her little cabin on the outskirts of town still took a good part of the night, even with the shortcut through the bluffs.

Not for the first time, Seria considered fishing closer to home. This creek ran all the way to Cadence, almost to her doorstep. But this was the best spot, where she was almost guaranteed to catch something. And she could not find a wild melon patch anywhere but in this slight curve of the Slate Mountains.

But you shouldn't go so far from home by yourself, especially in the dark. Her father's voice echoed in her mind, and she answered him aloud. "True, but who would come along?" Some of the town children might be happy to join her, but the walk was too long and strenuous for short legs. And the few adults she claimed as friends were busy with their own lives. Fulfilling their own purposes.

She straightened her spine. "In any case, it's nice to get away from the washbasin." The town got a bit lonely now and then.

Something tickled her elbow, and she glanced down. "Ooh! Sorrel grass!" She plucked a few sprigs of the purple-tinged leaves and slipped them into the pocket of her hemp apron. They were the last ingredients she needed to make a soothing balm to smear over scraped knees or smashed fingers.

It was a far cry from what she wished to do with her healing skills, but at least a few of the children had begun to trust her. Now if only their parents would see her as more than the town laundress. To them, she was naught but a girl, a peasant. Or worse, a washerwoman, the lowest rung of the societal ladder.

The pole bowed, and she tightened her grip. With an experienced tug and twist, she pulled up another silvery trout.

"Got another one, Sanjo!" Her smile stretched across her face. There was enough to last a few meals. "My best catch this year. I might actually have enough to trade."

Releasing the fish from her line, she dropped it in the net with the others and tilted her head back to check the sky. Behind her, the sun sat low over the Scarps Forest, ready to drop behind its wooded screen, but the moon was full and bright. Across from the forest, the Slate Mountain Range towered above her, a black, stone curtain in the gathering dusk. From where she sat, she couldn't see the narrow gap in the Slates known as the Gateway, where Cadence would soon be bedding down.

She tried to gauge how long before nightfall then shrugged. "If worse comes to worst, we can always camp out under the trees." It wouldn't be the first time. She had her oil lantern with her; she would get by. Besides, she felt a little freer outside her four dingy walls.

One more catch. Then she would head home.

Seria dropped the hook back in the water and made herself comfortable again. A soft rip met her ears. "Not again." Sure enough, a new tear gaped at the waistline of her gown. "Argh!" The worn garb would never do to be seen in public anymore. She frowned. Who was she kidding? This dress was good for nothing but the rag pile.

And that was where it would go when she got home. The hip-length tunic was drab and hung on her like a sack. The brown dress was faded and threadbare, the hem long worn through.

She frowned as she fingered the frayed edges. "Mayhap it's time to buy another one." She glanced at Sanjo. "What do you think?"

He sniffed.

Seria chuckled. "Exactly. With what? A few smelly fish?" Whatever she managed to catch tonight would not be near enough.

Nay, her job did not afford her many luxuries, and that included new clothes. She was fortunate to have enough to fill her stew pot and keep Sanjo fed, but washing other people's fine garments seemed a cruel twist of fate. Colorful wimples and scarves. Long, flowing dresses. Fitted tunics with leather belts.

Seria's spirit sighed. While she appreciated having work, she had no desire to be a launderer for the rest of her life, not when her hands and heart itched to practice the healing arts her mama had taught her. Her back ached at the mere thought of lugging bags of laundry for months more, much less years.

She inhaled through her nose and raised her chin. "I'll do whatever I need to do as long as necessary, Sanjo. I'll make Mama and Papa proud by working hard and seeing after our own needs." She would be a burden to no one. But someday, she would prove she was more than a peasant launderer.

A distant rustle in the dark behind her cut into her thoughts. Sanjo jerked his head up, clumps of grass sticking out of his wrinkled muzzle. Seria twisted around to peer through the shadows and listened for what had disturbed the quiet dusk.

She set her pole down and headed for the small rise nearby, patting Sanjo's rump as she passed. The hill tucked her in safe, but it also hid her view of what was out there. If a bear or wolf—or worse, a horned grizlon—approached, she, at least, wanted to know what would have her for a late dinner. She took her father's old, rusty sword from the cart. It would do her little good if she was forced to use it, but it offered a sense of security.

Gathering the ratty folds of her skirt, she made the careful climb up and crouched down when she reached the top. She pushed aside the short, brushy shrubs and peeked through.

All was quiet and still. The terrain was rockier and wooded beyond her vantage point, sloping sharply down to level ground. The small town of Rackson lay down the hill on her right to the north, close enough to see people moving about in the lantern light. To the west, about a hundred feet away, were the woods. Above them, the sun cast a red-gold light over both the town and the hill where she crouched. Black shadows edged the glow of the setting sun, creeping closer and closer to Rackson.

Something flashed in the trees. Torches. Metal. Muffled shouts and calls. Then the sound of marching disturbed the quiet, growing louder as they drew nearer to her spot.

Men on horseback. Soldiers in black mail. Swords. *Darkmen.*

Instinct pressed her flat against the cold ground. Bits of grass and twigs and dirt stuck out through the clenched fingers of her fists. Her breath hardened in her lungs.

What was the Dark Army doing here so close to the Gateway? And why were they attacking a small town like Rackson? What could the New Realm emperor possibly gain from such a move?

There was no time to warn the civilians of the village. A deep trembling started in Seria's core and spread through her limbs. Rackson was oblivious and helpless to its impending doom, and she could do nothing but watch.

Someone gave a shout. "Charge!" She slapped her hands over her mouth as the Darkmen surged forward, their faces and blades aimed for the sleepy little town down the hill.

Oh, Lambient, help them!

4

In the waiting camp, Mason crouched on the balls of his feet under the shelter of the silent trees and stared up at the steep mountain range of the Slates. The sun had already disappeared, bathing the region below in deepening shadows. In the distance, screams and shouts rang out. One platoon of Darkmen had already initiated their objective. The rest waited on the call to move out. The Shadowmen would follow them.

It could be hours away, but Mason's whole body—coiled and tense—craved to move. The sky darkened with every second, and sounds of the conflict carried in the night breeze. He tightened the bracers covering his forearms.

Next to him, his longtime accomplice shifted his weight. "Word has it you got a special mission from the emperor."

Mason hesitated. He called no one friend anymore—not after so much loss and betrayal—but Shon was the closest he'd had in a long time.

"I don't expect all the details, Mason."

"You could say I've got a specific job to do." *Weaken their defense. Get into Cadence. Infiltrate the fort.*

Shon nodded, his unkempt, red hair falling across his face. "Will it get you closer to the Shadowstone?" When Mason gave an evasive shrug, Shon let out a chuckle. "I hope it's worth all the time and work you've invested."

A feminine voice cut in. "You ready, handsome?"

Mason grinned. "Do you have to ask?"

Shon nudged him with an elbow. "How do you know she's not talking to me?"

Dreeya Faybe disengaged from the shadows, hidden by the dark, imperceptible cloak standard to all the scouts. Beneath the mantle, she wore the same black shirt and trousers as Mason and Shon. Her long hair was slicked back in a tight bun, but the sultry brunette could still turn heads.

She flashed Mason an alluring smile as she knelt on his other side. "I wanted to hear it from you."

Mason slanted her a look. "I'm always ready."

Shon leaned forward. "Nice to see you, too, Dreeya."

Dreeya waved her fingers at him, then turned her focus back on Mason. Shon sent Mason a wink and moved to give them space.

She slid her hand up Mason's arm. "Want to celebrate when this is over?"

"You act as though we've already won."

Her brows arched. "You have doubts?"

"Not a one."

"That's what I thought," Dreeya said with another smile.

A small squeal cut through the night behind them.

"What was that?" Mason asked.

"One of the boys caught a squirrel, and they were entertaining themselves. I guess they finally got bored with it."

He folded his arms. "Fools."

"Oh, you always get cross when the boys play." She smoothed back a loose strand of hair. "So, how about it?"

"How 'bout what?"

"Oh, really, Mason."

He let out a short chuckle. Dreeya was nothing if not persistent. "Let's focus on what tonight holds. I might be held up for a while."

Dreeya's pout let him know her thoughts on the matter without any trouble. "One of these days, Mason Grey, I'm going to wear you down." She traced her finger down his jawline.

For an instant, Mason leaned into her. His mind was consumed with the task ahead, but the turmoil in his spirit churned, desperate to be filled with anything that would stop the chasm from overtaking him. He tightened his fists and turned away. This was not the night to lose his head.

Dreeya pushed against him and pressed a kiss against his clenched jaw. "I'll save it for later." Her hand slid back down his arm. "Be careful tonight, handsome."

Mason nodded once. "Always. You, too."

"Commander's coming." Shon's whisper cut through the conversation, and Mason stood tall as Commander Bruin Pralus strode into view with long, purposeful steps through the rocky outcroppings. Dreeya stepped in line with Mason and Shon and assumed the same position—hands behind their backs and heads lowered.

"Scouts, get ready to move."

The words sent an exhilarated rush through him. He was so close, on the brink of the first step toward the promise he had spoken at twelve.

Bruin stopped before Mason and stared down at him. With his height and broad physique, emphasized by his dark gray cloak, the leader of the Dark Army could be quite imposing. "Are you ready, Sir Mason?"

"Aye, Commander." Mason held the other man's probing scrutiny, though Bruin's Shadowstone prevented Mason from reading what thoughts he hid behind those cool gray eyes.

Bruin nodded once, a satisfied smirk twisting his face.

Another knight hurried over, wiry and seasoned from years as Bruin's captain.

"Everything in place, Captain Feegan?" Bruin asked.

"Aye, Commander. We're ready for the second wave. Rackson will soon fall like so many other insignificant towns before it. Every man, woman, and child."

Mason caught Shon's amused expression and looked away lest he let a grin slip. Feegan was known for his dramatic flair for words.

But Bruin did not look amused and glowered when Feegan glanced up at the darkening sky. "Something bothering you, Captain?"

Feegan snapped his head back down. "Nay, sir. But I was wondering if you're sending us in a rainstorm."

Bruin waved a dismissive hand at the sky. Dark, bulging clouds materialized in the distant south, responding to the summoning of his Gift. "Just enough cover for our Shadowmen without hindering the Darkmen."

"Aye, sir." Feegan fingered the dark stone that hung around his neck.

Mason tightened his jaw as the stone gave off a dim, purple glow. He itched to touch it, savor the weight of it. But it was not simple enough to wear the stone. He had to earn it, meld with it. One day, it would be his.

Bruin's jaw shifted, his eyes glittering with anticipation. "The Stewards will no doubt arrive any moment. Everyone knows their job. Get ready to move."

He moved on then, with Feegan on his heels. Dreeya squeezed Mason's hand before slinking back to her position. Shon let out a soft chortle, but Mason faced forward. Dreeya was a temptation, especially on the lonely nights when his inner vat threatened to consume him. But tonight, nothing would turn his focus. Too much was at stake. Not just for Emperor Jader's rule, but for Mason's personal mission as well.

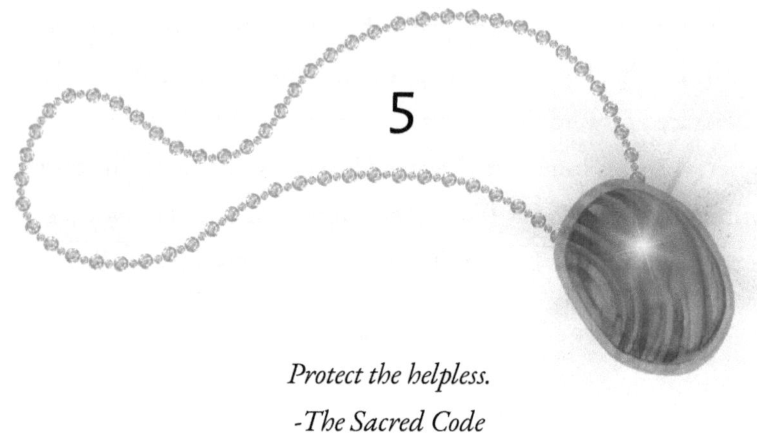

5

Protect the helpless.
-The Sacred Code

Rackson, the Gateway

Captain Braylee Wright dodged a Darkman's blade and took advantage of his opponent's unguarded side to thrust his sword. When the man fell, Braylee braced himself against a partially burnt wall and pulled his helmet off to brush the damp hair from his eyes. The flaming white sword on his crimson breastplate was streaked with dirt and blood. Sweat trickled down the sides of his face.

He chanced another look out into the street. It was calm for the moment, though the night echoed with a cacophony of hoofbeats, cries, and steel. Fire consumed much of the village, and smoke hid the clouded night sky. Rackson's civilians were nowhere to be seen, hiding in fear. Death filled the air.

Acrid smoke stung Braylee's nose and windpipe. Hungry flames licked at what was left of homes and businesses. The terrorized citizens' only hope of survival lay with the Stewards and faded with every minute.

At the sound of approaching shouts, Braylee ducked behind the wall and peered over. Darkmen stormed every direction, most of them on horseback.

Mere hours before, Braylee had ridden into Rackson behind Uralis, heads and swords held high. The carnage had already begun, but the Stewards plunged through the streets, their sights set on the black helmets and crests of the Darkmen. They had quickly gained the upper hand and drove the Dark Army out of the ransacked little town.

But a fresh troop ambushed them right outside of Rackson, forcing them into swift retreat. Outnumbered four to one, Uralis' battalion was overwhelmed, and the marshal was nowhere to be seen. Braylee feared the worst.

He risked another look, though he could barely see anything. The moon remained hidden behind thick clouds and smoke. One Darkman threw a fireball into a nearby house. Another lifted a heavy wooden beam with his bare hands and flung it, nearly crushing Braylee where he hid. His stomach soured to see Darkmen abusing their Gifts of the Moon for their operation of destruction. They were searching—not for him alone, but for any Steward who dared shine the light of the Lambient.

He ground his teeth. His faithful mount of many years was slain, his last arrow spent, and his company dwindling and scattered, but he would fight until he had nothing left in him. The people of Rackson deserved that.

Gripping his sword, Braylee shifted to the balls of his feet and prepared for one last effort. He would take down as many Darkmen as he could before he fell. At the least, his stand could give someone else a chance to escape.

Reaching for the Beacon on his belt, Braylee watched the clear glass rod light up in his fist. Such a small weapon, but so pure and powerful. He pressed it against his forehead. *This is how it ends.* He committed these last moments to the Lambient he had served for most of his life. There were no regrets, but how he wished for another moment with his family. His sweet, supportive wife and two beautiful daughters waited for his return home, but it was not to be.

Tightening his jaw, Braylee took hold of his helmet and calculated this final assault. Then the rod sparked and burned brighter, the whole length of it turning white. His body stiffened. What was happening?

The thunder of hooves shook the ground. Braylee raised his head, though afraid to look. Through the fog, the Prince of Paladin plunged into view astride his magnificent gray steed, his father's famed sword raised high. Behind him rode Captain Dudley and a throng of Stewards and militia.

It must be Braylee's exhaustion, creating fragmented visions of optimism.

The thick smoke lifted and disappeared with a wave of the prince's hand. Eric stretched his hand and lifted a barrage of debris—stones, wood, glass—flinging it at the enemy. Braylee stood to his feet.

The Darkmen were not the only ones utilizing their Gifts.

Eric's stallion carried him to the center of the village as Darkmen shielded themselves from the detritus, giving the Stewards room to pass farther into the town. His riders filled the main street.

At the sound of an approaching rider, Braylee turned. A burly soldier rode straight for the prince. Braylee stepped out and grabbed him by the arm and leg, pulling him off the saddle. The Darkman hit the ground hard but sprang to his feet, sword ready. A few strikes later, he lay dead at Braylee's feet. Grabbing the reins of the man's horse, Braylee swung up, drawing the prince's gaze.

"Captain, where is the marshal?"

Braylee shook his head. "I know not." His concern was reflected in the shadow that fell over Eric's face. But there was no time to reply, for the Darkmen had regathered at the end of the street and, with a blood-chilling war cry, charged.

Eric froze for a heartbeat as it became clear that, in the marshal's absence, he would be expected to command. Braylee gripped the reins. Would the prince resume the position he had once claimed?

But Eric's face hardened, and he reached for the light rod hanging on his belt. "Now, Stewards!" He raised the brilliant light over his head. Oakley reared beneath him. "For the Code!"

The men behind him lifted their rods, and light filled the street. Braylee joined in as other knights emerged, battered and bloody, but still standing.

The combined light grew until Rackson was awash with radiance, blinding every man and beast of the Dark Army. Dazed and bewildered, the enemy scattered. Chaos ensued as new strength filled Uralis' company.

"Spread out!" Eric directed the fresh horsemen behind him. "Vanguard and midguard, ride with me. Rearguard, purge the village and drive them out!"

Captain Dudley turned to the right, his company fanning out behind him as they infiltrated the dark streets with men and light.

Many of the Darkmen ran for the opposite end of Rackson, toward the black woods. Eric's Beacon threw a path of light before his horse. A growl started low in his throat and grew into a roar as he kicked Oakley's sides and charged after the enemy, not waiting to see if his men would follow.

For the first time in hours, despite his exhaustion and worry, a half-smile broke through Braylee's dry, cracked lips as he spurred his mount to join him. Victory blossomed in his chest.

The prince of Paladin had taken the lead.

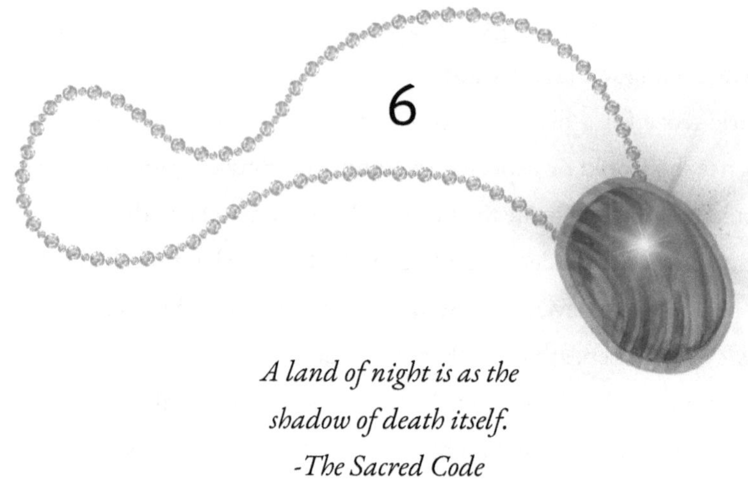

6

Complete darkness smothered the land as Mason skulked along the shadows of the woods. Flaming arrows whizzed in every direction, igniting small fires hither and yon. The skirmish had moved deeper into the woods, away from Rackson, offering more shelter for both sides.

Amid the bedlam, Mason kept his head low and wrapped his cloak close around him, thankful for its camouflage, but coveting the security the Shadowstone offered. Apart from the battle, his mind was consumed with his specific job.

Don't draw attention to yourself. Focus on your assignment.

Weaken their defense. Get into Cadence. Infiltrate the fort.

The flickering light from the flames lit the way for him. He paused for a moment, staring at the burning shell of Rackson to his left. The civilians would be hiding, seized with fear by the confrontation on their doorstep. Fear was a necessary and useful part of war; one he had utilized multiple times. Though not with the adept skill the Shadowmen held.

It wasn't pretty. War never was. But sometimes, it was necessary.

Mason turned his back to the ruins and started forward again. A Steward appeared before him, and he dodged a wild sword. Spreading his feet, he raised his weapon to meet the other knight's. They traded a few quick blows before Mason, with a quick thrust of his wrist, flipped the Steward's sword from his hand. Without hesitation, Mason sunk his blade into the opening of the man's armor under his arm. The Steward let out a guttural grunt before sliding to the ground.

Before Mason could move away, another came at him. With a move born of ease, Mason ducked, reached out, and grabbed the side of the man's neck through the opening in the plate mail and pinched. The man gawked as he stood frozen, unable to move a muscle. Keeping his hold on the nerve, Mason yanked the man's Beacon off his belt and tossed it. Then he locked eyes with his captive. "Where are the reserves?"

In an instant, the answer flashed through the soldier's mind and into Mason's, all without a word spoken.

When Mason had all he needed to know, he maintained eye contact and reached deeper into the man's mind, gaining control of the man's will with his Gift. "Stand still." He let go of the nerve, and the knight made no move to run or fight. Mason did a quick scan of the area. "Come with me."

"At once." Now compliant, the man gripped his sword and followed Mason.

They made their way around the reservists' hiding place and came up behind the rear line. The men hunkered low, waiting. There were at least two dozen—too many for him to gain control of, but none of these were Stewards, so Mason could still make his presence known.

He turned to the man with him and spoke low. "Go turn the horses loose. And when I give the call, start attacking from your position."

The man nodded and moved away.

Approaching the back row of soldiers, Mason tapped one on the shoulder. When the man whipped around, ready to fight, Mason stopped him with a whisper. "Quiet. Come with me." The man nodded and moved out of rank.

Mason went down the line, managing to gain a few more followers before too many of the reserves noticed a disturbance in the ranks. Time to make his move.

He stood tall and raised his sword. "Attack!"

The armsmen under his control ran at their allies, swinging their weapons. Pandemonium ensued. Shouts and curses rose as the soldiers tried to make sense of the surprise attack by their own men.

Mason took advantage of the confusion to take a few guards down, then moved on, always watchful for another opportunity to act.

A mess of Stewards and Darkmen appeared ahead, their swords criss-crossing rapidly. Mason's fingers curled at the so-called *brave* soldiers of the Stewardship. In his mind, broken fragments of another brutal encounter with the knights echoed. One that left his brother dead.

Bitterness entangled his thoughts and slowed his movements. He dashed the images away. *Focus.*

A dead Steward lay on the ground, his body twisted at an awkward angle. An idea formed, and Mason grabbed the body by the feet, pulling it in the nearby brush, out of view of the feuding soldiers.

"Thanks for making this easy, Steward." It took but a few minutes to take the breastplate and helmet off the body. He hurried to put the Steward's armor over his dark chainmail, though slipping it on felt like a betrayal. The white sword on the front mocked him. It was not a perfect disguise, but it would give him enough cover in the darkness. Maybe enough to get into the Gateway Stronghold without suspicion. No one would think to question him in the red breastplate.

He took the Steward's sword last, gripping it in his hand. The Beacon lay on the ground, and Mason scowled before kicking it farther into the bushes. He would never carry one of those, not even in pretense.

Now to get out of these woods without getting fired on by one of his own men.

The fight between the reserves and his accomplices was dying down. He would have to acquire more help, and the new armor would allow him to get close to his opponents.

A runaway horse burst from the brush, bumping into Mason and almost knocking him down. Then it stumbled and fell to the ground, an arrow protruding from its neck. The animal gave a shrill cry and tried to stand.

Mason gritted his teeth and circled around it. At another squeal of pain, he stopped. *Blast.* He turned back and covered the eye gaping up at him and pointed his sword at the soft part of its neck. "Easy, boy." A quick thrust of the blade, and it was done. Then he bent to clean his sword on the grass.

The ground rumbled beneath him, and he froze. Men on horseback burst from the woods on both sides, coming at each other with vengeance. He dove out of the path of a large steed and landed hard on his abdomen. Dust flew up in his face. Once he swiped his vision clear, he found himself surrounded by swinging swords, flying arrows, and kicking hooves. He stayed low and scrambled to get out from the midst. A small rise appeared in his vision, and he aimed for it. Blood raced through him, setting his pulse to thrumming.

An arrow shot forward and pierced his side, knocking him over. Agony exploded through his body and out his lips. His mind whirled as he tried in vain to pull the protruding object out. White-hot pain spread and blood flowed.

Safety was a few feet away, in the shadows of the hill and out of reach of the fighting around him. He crawled with one hand, every movement torture. His breaths puffed out in short bursts as sticks and rocks cut his palm and slashed through the knees of his pants. Before he could go far, another arrow thrust itself into his upper right leg.

"*Argh!*" He grabbed at his leg, still gripping his side with his other hand. Warm liquid seeped through his fingers. Shock dulled every other sense. For a brief, surreal moment, he slipped back to that similar scene years ago. The Stewards. The chaos. The arrow...

Nay! Mason clenched his teeth to keep from crying out. *Not again! Not now!*

The mounted horsemen were right on top of him. He rolled to his back to miss being trampled. Another horse moved in, rearing with a squeal. Mason gaped at the powerful hooves over his head, coming straight at him. He heard a dull thud before the crack shot through his skull.

The noise faded as the fighters moved on and left him alone. But he lay still, gasping and staring blindly up where the sky should be. His mind drifted back to when he was a boy, trailing Liam around in the woods.

Muted footsteps approached, and he flinched when a fuzzy form leaned over him, but he could not move. Hands touched him, moving over his body gently, avoiding the arrow wounds. A soft voice spoke to him, but he couldn't make anything out.

Just let me die. The pain in his body was sharp and consuming; but it was nothing against the agony raging in his spirit.

Once again, he had failed his brother.

7

"The time will come, Stewards, when you will be called to stand in the gap of the Gateway. Someday, you will be required to uphold the Sacred Code in the face of death."

-Commencement speech given by Steward Grand Marshal Uralis Faunt

The Beacon sent energy, pulsing and fervent, up Eric's arm and through his veins. His blood pumped steady; passion rolled over him. It had been a long time since he had wielded the rod in his hand. Too long.

A bright flash lit the entire region as the Stewards burst from the borders of Rackson and into the woods. As Eric expected, more enemy troops awaited them. In front, a gray-headed Darkman brandished his sword and shouted, "No mercy!"

More Darkmen responded with a loud cry and surged forward, encountering the Stewards in a brutal clash of swords and spears. Eric met the leader in the middle. They sat astride their horses, face to face for an instant, their stares hard and pierced. Eric shrank back at the purple gem around the older man's neck.

The Shadowstone. The Shadowmen had never ventured this close to the Gateway before. His insides quaked at the thought. How many more were here?

The Shadowman glowered. "You forget your place, Steward." He thrust his sword.

Eric deflected it and returned the blow without thinking. He held his Beacon and the reins in the same hand, ensuring his light filled the space between them.

The conflict around them continued as they parried strikes. Oakley spun and danced beneath Eric before other Darkmen joined their leader's side, ready to finish what he had started.

The Shadowman leered and grasped the stone with his bare hand. Darkness pressed in around the Beacon's radiance, cold and stifling. Eric clenched his jaw and gripped his light rod, but the gloom penetrated his skin and into his soul. Fear, swift and rank, wrapped around his mind.

What was he doing? He couldn't fight against Shadowmen. They were too strong. He should've stayed in Calla.

And then Uralis' company would have perished. Rackson would be destroyed. That truth pushed back against the panic, but a chill gripped him, silencing all but the fears and doubts. Paralyzing him. Oakley shuddered beneath him.

"Prince Eric!" Captain Braylee rode his horse from the shadows, his light splintering both the gloom and the web over Eric's mind. Braylee positioned himself between Eric and the Shadowman, drew his Beacon back and snapped it forward. Eric's jaw slackened at the whip of light that shot from Braylee's rod and cracked in the air. Embers scattered. The Darkmen yelled and dispersed, but two fell on the ground, dead before their bodies hit.

The Shadowman glared, his stone hissing and sparking. "Take them down!" Then he turned his horse and bolted for the nearby woods. As soon as he stepped outside of the Beacon's ring of light, man and beast vanished from view.

The vice around Eric lifted, and he slumped, bracing himself against Oakley's neck. Anger swept over him that he had allowed the Shadowstone to take hold of him.

A swarm of Darkmen moved in on Braylee, too many for the captain to hold back after exerting himself with the light whip. He was knocked off his horse but jumped back on his feet, sword in hand.

Eric lost sight of him when another opponent challenged him. After a brief scuffle, the Darkman fell to the ground, and Eric looked around for the captain.

There he was, struggling between three Darkmen. Braylee fell to one knee, his sword and light rod still flashing.

Eric urged Oakley to cut through them as Braylee had done for him moments ago. With Lavrynth in hand, Eric took one man out and turned to another. The match was quickly evened out, and the enemy soldiers lay dead.

Braylee stood and braced himself against his knees. "It's an honor, my prince."

Eric shook his head once. "Nay, Captain. I am the one so honored."

Shouts drew their attention, and Eric tugged on his reins. He heeled his mount as Braylee caught another horse. Adrenaline coursed through Eric's veins, and he lashed out repeatedly. Lavrynth held firm. The captain never left his side.

A brief pause allowed Eric to glance to the edge of the woods. Dudley would have the reserves in position now, cutting the Dark Army off from pushing farther into the valley. Now to force the enemy back into the woods from whence they came. But would they be enough against the Shadowmen?

Eric readjusted his grip on his sword, ignoring the aching muscles in his arms. "Drive them back!" He lifted his Beacon so that light flooded the area. It was their strongest defense against Jader's dark soldiers.

After what seemed like hours of nonstop fighting, Captain Dudley reined his horse in next to him. "They're retreating, Sire! You want us to pursue?"

Indecision stole Eric's words from him. Dudley waited for a reply, and Braylee watched from the side. Eric swallowed the knot in his throat and his pride. "Do you think we should?"

"I wouldn't advise it, sir. Our line of reserves broke down somehow, so we don't have a strong right guard. And we don't know how many Shadowmen are out there."

Eric glanced over at Braylee, who nodded. "It doesn't help that we're near grizlon territory."

The tight line between Eric's shoulder blades relaxed. "Very well. Let's gather the casualties and fall back to Rackson. We must find the marshal."

Dudley turned on his horse, already shouting out orders.

Weariness and sadness wrapped around Eric's limbs, weighed them down. The noise diminished as he rode back into the town with Braylee. Eric swiveled his head back and forth, in search of the marshal.

The destruction of Rackson was evident in every direction. Blackened skeletons of what had once been homes stood on both sides of the street. A few structures still smoldered, and soot coated everything. And the bodies. Too many bodies.

This could have been prevented. His posture wilted under the weight of the thought. If he had done his job in the beginning, maybe this tragedy would never have happened. On the heels of his regret, a wave of trepidation washed over him, chilling him. Something was amiss. As if he had stood mere feet from a growing threat and narrowly missed it.

Dudley appeared before him. "We've managed to take a few prisoners, Sire."

"Has anyone found the marshal yet?"

"Nay, sir."

Eric clenched his jaw. "I will speak to the prisoners." Time to get some answers on this looming menace.

Each prisoner's hands were bound and tethered to the horse of a militia reservist. There were no Shadowmen among them. Eric dismounted and stood before them, meeting their hard stares head-on.

"This is your one chance for mercy. If you denounce the ways of Jader's Dark Army and tell us what you know of his plans, your punishment will be lightened."

The men stared back at him.

"This is your last opportunity. It will be too late by the time you reach my father's court. There you face execution or imprisonment."

One pock-faced man thrust his chin out. "I look forward to seeing the great king of Paladin, so I might spit in his face."

Eric stiffened at the insult. Stepping forward, he met the man's smirk straight on, then backhanded him across the face. The Darkman stumbled back a few steps and glared at Eric.

"You will not speak of my father in that manner." He ground the words out through clenched teeth. "You've made your choice, and there's no going back. You shall be tried by the Council, and then sent on to face King Aden's judgment." Not awaiting a reply, Eric stepped aside and led Oakley away. Vindication tangled with regret at the looks of surprise he received from Stewards and Darkmen alike.

A Steward commander should be in more control over his emotions. The prince of Paladin even more so.

Eric spoke to his captains. "The people of Rackson are no longer safe here. Gather the survivors who wish to go to Cadence and ready the injured for the journey. We must leave, lest Jader sends another wave." He hesitated, hating what had to be done. "Tend to the casualties."

There would be no time to bury all the civilian dead, so the bodies would be laid to rest in what was left of the town hall and burned in a feeble attempt to honor the dead. It was all he could do.

Stewards and militiamen moved with purpose, despite the heavy cover of sorrow. The wounded were tended to. Women, children, and the elderly were given seats on the remaining wagons, many with nothing but the clothes on their backs. The Steward fatalities were wrapped and draped with care over their mounts to be taken back home to their families.

But there was still no sign of Uralis. Eric was about to despair of finding him when someone shouted out, "Captain Braylee! I've found him!"

A young Steward waved them over from a narrow alley. Eric and Braylee ran over. Weakness invaded Eric's limbs at the sight of the marshal propped up against a crate with multiple arrows piercing his upper body. The entire front of Uralis' shirt was soaked in blood. In one hand, he held his Beacon, still glowing.

"Marshal." Eric slid to his knees at the man's side. *Please, Lambient, save him.*

Uralis opened heavy lidded eyes and looked straight up at him. A tired smile lifted one side of his face, and he nodded once. "You came."

"I'm sorry I didn't get here sooner." Eric could hardly get the words out.

"You're here now. That's what counts."

The young Steward pulled his own cape off and tried to staunch the flow. Uralis sucked in a sharp breath and waved a weak hand. "Let me be, Sgt. Ollen."

Ollen's features blanched, and he shook his head. "Nay, sir."

"It is well, son." Serenity filled Uralis' expression, despite his obvious pain, and he patted Ollen's knee. "Thank you... Now, go fetch my horse."

Defeat broke Ollen's strong stance, but he put his hand over his heart and bowed his head. Then he averted his face as he left, pushing his way through a small crowd of sober Stewards that had gathered a few feet away.

Grief smote Eric hard, robbing his lungs of oxygen. Uralis was fading before him, and the marshal knew it.

Uralis winced and licked his lips. "You lead them on...from here, Prince." He spoke so quietly, so weak, so unlike the man who used to shout at Eric to raise his weapon and stand his ground. This man had shared so many lessons with Eric when he was a young prince, confident he had a firm grasp on the world.

Eric blinked rapidly. "I never finished my training."

Uralis closed his eyes briefly, then forced them open and looked to Braylee, who knelt on his other side. There was no missing the respect for his longtime captain that lit Uralis' countenance. "You...finish...for me."

"I'll never fill your shoes," Braylee answered, his voice thick. "But I'll do my best."

Eric braced an elbow on a knee and pressed the back of his hand against his mouth. Surely this was a nightmare. He was supposed to get here in time to help Uralis, not watch his beloved mentor die.

Soft light bathed the spot where Uralis lay. Eric looked up at the Stewards holding their Beacons before their faces in respect, some with tears coursing down their sooty cheeks.

Uralis gave them a faint smile before his head sagged against the crate, and he lifted his Beacon an inch to point at Eric. "The light within you..." He drew in a loud, labored breath. "Is greater...than the darkness without."

Unable to speak Eric nodded, his vision blurred.

Braylee rested a hand on the older man's shoulder. "May the Lambient guide your way into the Eternal Light, my friend."

Grand Marshal Uralis Faunt's eyes closed again, and he took one last breath. His Beacon glowed for a few moments, before it flickered, then went out.

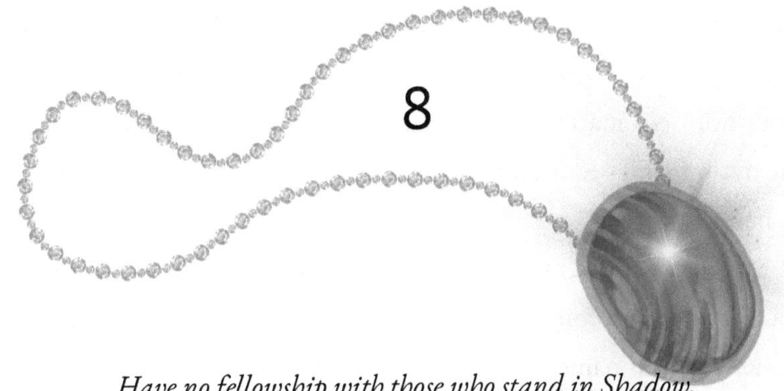

<h1 style="text-align:center">8</h1>

All was still and quiet...too quiet. Mason struggled to open his eyes, but the effort drained him. His head throbbed; his side and leg both burned like fire.

Where was he? What happened? Was the battle over?

At a touch on his head, he stiffened. Something wrapped itself tight around his temples. His first instinct was to fight it off, but he could not move to do so. It took every ounce of willpower to drag his eyelids open, but he still couldn't make out the blurry figure leaning over him.

"I'm sorry. I know it's uncomfortable."

The voice—muffled and completely unfamiliar—sent ripples of alarm through him. Confusion mounted as he strained to identify his surroundings. He moved his hand across the soft surface he lay on. The act sent a sharp streak through his right side, and a groan escaped.

"Easy now. Don't go moving around too much, or you'll pull those stitches." It sounded feminine. Dreeya?

"Can you tell me your name?"

He rolled his head back and forth, senses swimming. Not Dreeya. She would know his name. He blinked furiously, desperate to get a clear view of the stranger. But it was all muddled.

A cup touched his lips, and he sipped at the cool water, reluctant at first, then with growing thirst. He gulped, staring up at the hazy apparition. No matter how he tried, he couldn't get his vision clear. Frustration wrapped itself around him, pushing its way out in a grunt. "Where...?"

"Easy now," she went on. "We're a little ways from the fort. It'll be no trouble at all to get someone here for you. You're safe." She paused. "Can you tell me your name?"

He fought to shake the cobwebs. *Mason. My name is Mason. Who are you? What happened?* The words exploded through his head, but he couldn't tell if they made it out. A swirl of blackness swept over him, bringing with it another wave of pain. The indistinct voice mumbled again, but the words were lost as he sank back into oblivion.

Seria exhaled as the man succumbed again to unconsciousness. His breathing soon evened out, and he dropped deep into the bed. She finished tying the bandage around his head.

"Mason." She whispered his name; at least she managed to get that much out of him.

The poor man had roused twice but was unable to pull himself into complete wakefulness. Maybe that was for the best for now, uneasy as he was.

Seria pulled the blanket up over him and turned to the pile of blood-soaked rags on the floor. As she cleaned up the mess, the horrors of the battle again flooded her senses. The cries. The bloodshed. The death. A tremor passed through her. Her innocent trip to the creek for moonlight fishing had swiftly turned into a nightmare.

From her perch, she'd had a perfect view of the ambush on Rackson. At times, the fighting drifted to the base of her hill, leaving her horrorstruck with the sights and sounds that held her captive.

Another groan from the bed pulled Seria back to the present. Still asleep, the man pushed at the blanket. She stepped over and tucked his arms inside.

The loss of blood had weakened him. His skin was pasty white, except for a large, purple knot above his right eye, swelling it shut. The arrows to his side and leg had sunk in deep, tearing into muscle. He was not going anywhere for a while.

Her father used to regale her with stories of the Stewards' sacrifice, of their great chivalry and bravery in battle. Now, she had witnessed it for herself. She regarded Mason's cut-up face, a little breathless at the thought of being able to honor the Stewards in this small way.

A little thrill squiggled up her spine, despite her very real concern for the man. At last, she had a chance to use her healing skills to help someone. The town would see she was good for more than washing their dirty clothes. And who better to make that a reality than one of the king's Stewards?

"Mason." This man was a hero, a knight devoted to protecting the innocent. Rackson's battle had not been his first. She had seen the old scars, nestled among fresh wounds on his body. One prominent mark rode high on his trunk, under his collar bone. It looked to have been a serious injury once and opened her mind to unanswered questions as to its origin. But it was clear that he had fought before and survived. He was still a survivor. A Steward.

And all she knew about him was his name.

9

The Gateway Stronghold

A steady rain fell over the valley, washing away the ugliness from the night before. Eric stood under the cover of the north gate tower, the highest position of the inner wall of the Steward garrison. He looked out over the lower courtyard, his hands braced against the rough, gray stone windowsill.

The Gateway was well-named, a narrow gap slashed out of the Slate Mountains like an open door. Around both sides of the gap, clusters of steep bluffs crowded around, as though a giant hand had disturbed the straight, mountainous wall. Within the miles of bluffs were housed other Gateway towns like Rackson. The valley itself boasted of spring-fed streams and green meadows. On the outskirts, the immense, mountainous forest extended for leagues into the New Realm.

Eric shifted his scrutiny to the village of Cadence, sheltered in the center of the rain-soaked valley a few furlongs beyond the outer fort wall. It was a small settlement, consisting chiefly of refugees from the New Realm. He had visited but a few times in recent years and was impressed with its development. Dwarfed by the cities on both sides of the mountains, it still survived and flourished. For years, Cadence had enjoyed security and peace, resting in the shadow of his father's garrison.

He glanced behind him. The Gateway Stronghold nestled securely within the breach between the Slates, its thick, stone walls effectively blocking any passage, save through the gates.

Eric straightened to his full height and crossed his arms. Much had been done since Rackson's fall. Though unseen in the deluge, men were posted at all points. Extra guards patrolled the top of both walls. Lookouts watched the landscape with a critical eye. And more troops were on their way from Paladin. The stronghold had not seen so much activity in a long time.

Braylee joined him in the tower, his rain-splattered hood over his head. At a glimpse of his sober expression, Eric asked, "What is it, Captain?"

"I'm not exactly sure, Sire." He scratched his head. "It was reported to me that one of our fallen Stewards was found sans his armor. But there was a Darkman breastplate near the body."

The chill running down Eric's back did not come from the rain. Had someone taken the armor hoping to impersonate a Steward? He looked out over the fort. They could be here now.

Braylee spoke again. "All of our men are now accounted for, sir. Including the casualties."

Eric nodded, but it was not enough to ease his mind. He ran his hands over his damp hair and stared out at the nearby town through the downpour. Anyone could be hiding out there. Yet, how much trouble could one person cause?

Enough to warrant extra caution. "We need to be careful. Especially with those coming and going from the fort."

Braylee nodded. "Aye, Sire." He inhaled and crossed his arms over his broad chest. "Uralis' memorial will be tomorrow. Followed by your commencement."

His commencement. The official moment he would take the leadership of Paladin's armies. He swallowed back the fear that choked him, then caught something in Braylee's look. "Is there something else?" *No more bad news, please.*

"'Tis none of my business, Sire."

"I asked, Captain." Eric spoke over the pattering rain. "Feel free to speak."

Braylee rubbed the dark whiskers on his chin. "If you'll forgive me for saying so, Sire, it won't be easy, resuming the leadership of the Stewards after all this time, especially in the wake of Uralis' death."

A pang went through him. "Aye." Eric leaned against the wall, stared at the floor in front of his boots. "But there's no greater army I could ask to lead." Despite his apprehension, he meant it. The words bolstered him a bit, loosened the cord around his gut.

Braylee looked out the window, chewing his lip. "I've never served as captain under anyone but Marshal Uralis." He paused. "But you've already proven your courage when you put your life on the line for Rackson." He turned his dark eyes on Eric. "You saved my life in Rackson, and then again in the woods."

Eric put his hand up. "Captain, you delivered me from the hold of the Shadowstone. I let it get into my head, and had you not intervened, I would have been carried out, same as Uralis."

"Be that as it may, you have my full support, Prince Eric." Braylee raised his head high. "Despite your doubts and regrets, I believe you are what we need. You have the faith, wisdom, and skills to lead the Steward Army to victory. And as long as you will allow me, I will be at your side."

A ray of hope shot through the shadows of doubt in Eric's soul. The set of Braylee's wide chin made it clear the words were not spoken lightly. "Thank you, Captain Braylee." The acknowledgment was inadequate, but it was all Eric could offer.

Hours later, the rain still pounded the roof of the infirmary as Eric walked through the rows of cots, checking on his wounded men—a small step in assuming his role as Steward commander. He stopped at a cot and smiled. "How are you faring, Gus?"

The fifty-something-year-old veteran's eyes twinkled in his usual good cheer, even as he grimaced and patted the clean, white bandages over one arm. "Looks like I'll live to see another day, Sire. Should be out soon." His face sobered, and he looked Eric directly in the eye. "I'm glad to see you back where you belong, Prince Eric."

"Thank you, Gus." He moved to the next bed, where a man sat rubbing his head. "How are you faring, soldier?"

The man raised his head slowly and squinted up at Eric. A large bruise rested over his left cheekbone. "I don't know, sir. Feeling very strange."

Eric took a seat on the cot across from him. "What's your name?"

"Timothy, Sire."

"Do you need the physician?"

"I don't think so. My head is throbbing, and I've never felt so weak. But I'm more confused than anything."

"Can you tell me what happened?"

"I was in the woods, with my squadron. We were keeping the rear, as Captain Dudley ordered. Then this...Darkman appeared in front of me." He shook his head, then pressed his fingers to his temples. "I think he wanted to know where the reserves were hiding. And I told him."

Eric's brows went up. "You told him?"

The man exhaled and shrugged. "I thought I did." He didn't sound so sure now. "But I also have this crazy memory of attacking my own men before someone knocked me out. Then I woke up this morning feeling awful. I'm not sure of anything."

The head injury must have created some confusion, for Timothy's story made no sense. "I'm sure it'll come to you in time. You need your rest."

Eric stood and found the gray-headed physician washing his tools in a dented basin. "Luron, how are things looking?"

Luron greeted him with a nod. "Not too bad, considering, Your Highness. We haven't lost any more since the battle. Most of them will get out in another day or so, but a few will take longer to heal." He dried his hands. "I hear your commencement is tomorrow."

Another reminder. "Aye, it is." Eric gestured back at Timothy. "What's his story?"

Luron exhaled, the lines around his mouth deepening. "Not sure, really. From what I gather, there was a bit of confusion at one point, and some of our men were caught in the middle. I'm guessing he got hit in the head, became confused, and started fighting the wrong men."

The picture created a sick knot in Eric's belly. His own men fighting each other. "It was so dark. And with Shadowmen mingled with the Darkmen." He sighed.

"It's easy to see how it could've occurred," Luron said.

Eric shook his head. "It shouldn't have." He would have to find out what happened.

"That's the bad thing about war." Luron folded a rag and put it aside. "It matters not how much you plan; you cannot plan for everything. This was an unfortunate incident, but it's over now, and you must go on."

The wisdom was sound, if hard to accept. Eric thanked Luron for his work, then left the infirmary, his cloak wrapped around him to shelter him from the ongoing shower.

His Stewards were on the mend, but the few they lost still grieved him, especially those who might have been lost to their allies. How many more would they lose before it ended?

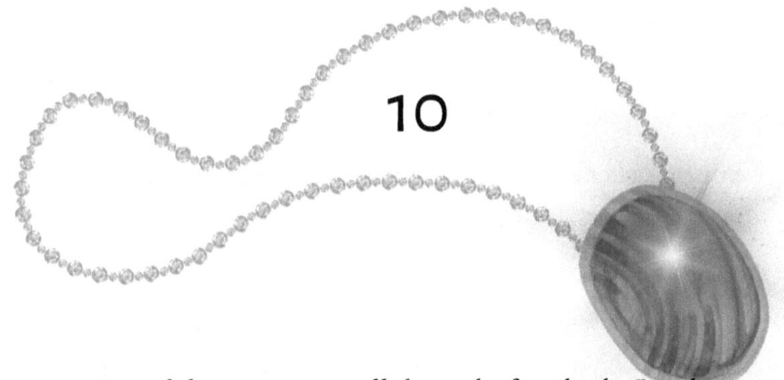

10

Pain and despair come to all those who forsake the Lambient.
-The Sacred Code

Cadence, the Gateway

A gray cloud fought to pull Mason back to the darkness, but he forced his eyes open. Ever so slowly, the room melted into a semblance of order, though still fuzzy.

The dying embers of the hearth cast a dim glow over an unfamiliar one-room cabin. A lump of blankets lay before the fire; log walls framed the circle of weak light. In the middle of the room stood a roughly cut table with two crooked chairs. A smaller table sat next to his bed. The gap between the window shutters hinted at a black world outside.

A fog still draped his mind and vision. Mason lifted his head and winced against the pain. The lump on the floor turned out to be a woman, best he could tell, wrapped up in a blanket and sound asleep if the slow, rhythmic breathing was any indication.

Who was she? Mason strained to see her clearly and tried to remember something—anything. It was all so hazy.

A voice, unfamiliar and feminine, drifted in his mind. *Fort. Stewards.*

The words cut through the confusion. She had threatened him. Her statement pounded through his head. *"No trouble at all to get someone here..."*

His pulse quickened. He might not get a better chance to go. Pain and fear mashed in his head, clouded his reasoning. All he knew was that he had to get out.

Gritting his teeth against any discomfort his movements might elicit, Mason jerked his blanket away and forced himself to sit up. He gripped the side of the bed and willed his head to stop spinning.

Take it slow. Hurrying would do nothing but hamper his efforts.

The floor tilted beneath him, and he closed his eyes until he could sit without swaying. The throb in his head nearly overpowered him but would not drive him back to bed. *Must. Get. Out.*

Mason put one hand on the bedside table, took a shallow breath, and pushed to his feet. Pain ripped through his side and stole the breath right back. Keeping his weight on his good leg, he stood motionless for a long moment. He could do this. One step at a time. He had survived worse.

Quick, heavy gusts of air burst through his lips, and sweat broke out on his forehead. His injured leg convulsed and shook, but he braced himself and took a tiny, halting step. As soon as his weight settled on the leg, it buckled, sending him sprawling on the floor. He grasped for the table and caught nothing but air; everything on top scattered and fell around him.

The woman sprang from the blanket. "Oh, gracious! What happened?"

Blades! The wound in his torso ripped at him, tearing him in half. Warm blood seeped through the bandage.

She hurried to the big table and lit a lamp. Then she crouched at his side and took his arm. "You're bleeding again. Let's get you back into bed."

He jerked away from her grasp, sliding lower to the floor. "I'm leaving."

"You can't! You'll make it worse!" Her high-pitched voice grated against his jangled nerves.

He steadied himself and moved to stand. A jarring pain rocked over him, and he hissed through his teeth.

She wrung her hands. "Please, let me help."

"Fine." He grabbed her wrist and glared into the blurry space where her eyes should be. "Get. Me. *Out of here.*"

"I'm sorry, Mason. I can't. Not yet anyway."

Mason dropped his hand. She had refused his order. Without hesitation. Sharp jolts streaked through his body and immobilized him. Blood pounded in his ears like a war drum. What was happening?

"Can I help you up now?"

He gave a short nod. What else could he do? Moisture oozed through the bandages on both his side and leg.

The girl put one of his arms across her shoulders and positioned herself to help him stand. She grunted under his weight, but with him supporting himself on the table, they managed to get him up and back on the bed, though his head went swimming for the pain.

"What were you trying to do?" She began unwrapping the dressing around his middle. "Kill yourself?"

Limp against the pillow, he tried to breathe, perspiration pouring down his face. His torso was wracked with agony, and he couldn't move on his own. On top of that, the girl somehow knew his name. But none of that alarmed him so much as what had transpired.

It hadn't worked. He had looked her straight in the eye and given his order. Sure, his vision was a little unclear, but he could still catch her gaze with his own.

It didn't matter. She had dismissed his demand without a second glance. And he could not read a single thought of hers. Nothing. Fear spiraled through him. What was wrong with him?

A stab darted through his temple. He reached up to press the bandage and flinched at a tender spot. *The head injury.* Hot air gushed from his lips. His Gift was inaccessible, and he was powerless.

So much for an escape.

The girl bustled above him, holding a rag against the hole in his side to stay the blood flow. "Your leg is bleeding, too, but we've got to take care of this first. You shouldn't have tried to get up."

He squeezed his eyelids shut. "I've got... to get..."

"Out of here," she finished for him. "I know, but, like it or not, you can't go anywhere for a while. Longer, if you push your limits like this." Her hands moved quick and sure as she worked, her hair hanging in her face. He still did not have a clear picture of her.

Too drained to argue, Mason let his head fall back, trying not to flinch at her touch.

She moved down to his leg to begin the process of staying the blood all over again. "My, you're a fine mess. It's a wonder you didn't decide to clobber yourself on the head again while you were at it."

"Do you ever stop—?"

"Talking?" She didn't bother to look up. "Sorry, but I prattle when I've had a scare. And you've definitely given me one. I saved your life in the middle of a crossfire. I'd hate to lose you in the middle of my house."

Her words arrested his attention. She had saved him from the cross-fire? He stared at her, straining to get a clear view of her face. "Who are you?"

"Seria Gayle."

The name meant nothing to him. He started to speak again, but fatigue hit him. Hard. He fought against the darkness that tugged on him. He had to stay awake, keep an eye on the girl. Who did she work for? Where had she come from?

Seria pulled the blanket back over him. "You need to rest."

"I don't ..." His words slurred in his exhaustion. "I want ..." Despite his resistance, he lost the fight and slipped back into sleep.

His ears hummed, and questions filled his mind as soon as he awoke again. How far was he from Bruin's camp? How would he get by without his abilities? And what would he do about—?

"How are you feeling?" Footsteps approached.

Mason's gaze shot to the girl. What was her name?

Seria.

He frowned. "I'm fine." With his vision still burry, he attempted another glance at her face. His jaw clenched. Like looking at a blank canvas. A distorted one, at that.

"Are you hungry?"

Food was the last thing he wanted, but he nodded to put some space between them.

As she bent to stir a pot hanging over the fireplace, he tried to study her. All he could make out was long, blonde hair tied back from her face and dull, brown clothing. How did a mere peasant girl have the gall to try bullying him last night?

Mason rubbed his pounding temples. What had she said? They were not far from the fort, where the Stewards had planted themselves. How far? Had she already notified them? The thought made him stiffen, sending a sharp jab through his side. He bit back a groan.

Aden's knights must be unaware of his presence, or they would have already ripped him from the bed and thrown him in a cell. Or to the executioner. But how much time did he have before this girl turned him over to the bloody Stewards?

Something else fought to get through the murk of his mind. She claimed she had saved him. But why?

He took a slow, careful breath so he could focus. His training and experience rose to the forefront of his mind as he considered his options. Which were limited.

Hearing footsteps, he looked over. The girl—Seria—held up a wooden bowl. "Think you can eat something?"

He stared up at her, straining to catch a glimpse of her thoughts. She cocked her head with a little smile. He turned away and clenched his teeth. It was no use. He was powerless.

"You'll probably feel better if you eat."

Nay. He would feel better leagues away from here. But, powerless or not, it was time for answers. "Who are you?"

"I told you once, but I suppose you don't remember. I'm Seria. Seria Gayle."

Not the answer he was looking for. "Why did you bother with me?" Especially if she planned on turning him over to the Stewards.

"I had to. I couldn't leave you out there. You were doing your duty against those..." She shook her head. "I refuse to call them knights. They don't deserve a title like that. When I saw you were still alive, I brought you here. I wasn't going to let them take you prisoner and have you die in a cell."

The pounding in his head made it difficult to follow her. "Didn't you threaten to turn me in?"

"Oh, no. I wasn't threatening you." She set the bowl on the table beside his bed and pulled a chair over, settling down for a good, long chat. "I was merely letting you know where you were."

He rubbed his hand over his head. Was he missing something?

"Here." She handed him the bowl. "Why don't I start from the beginning?"

This girl wore him out. He took the bowl and gave her a curt nod.

Seria checked that his mug was within his reach, then sat back. "I happened to be a short ways from Rackson when the fight broke out, doing a little late-night fishing. It's a guilty pleasure of mine." She waved a hand. "Anyway, boy, that fight scared the stuffing out of me! I watched it all happen from a little hill. I got down low and didn't move an inch."

He took a spoonful of the stew and worked it up, his hand already shaking with the effort.

"I saw you get wounded in a crossfire and couldn't let you lay out there and bleed to death. So, as soon as I could, I slid down the hill and pulled you out of the way. When I had the chance, I brought you here. I looked around first to see if I could help anyone else, but..." She fell silent.

So, they must not be far from Rackson. Was the town still standing, after all? Impossible.

"Anyway, Sanjo helped me get you back here."

Sanjo? Of their own volition, Mason's eyes darted around the single room. Who else was here?

"Sanjo's my donkey."

A donkey. He couldn't hold the sigh that exhaled from him.

"It's a wonder we made it without getting shot or trampled." Seria shivered. "It must've been the hand of Lambient Himself that kept us from being seen."

Mason paused in his eating. So, she was a believer in the Lambient. Wonderful. "Who else knows I'm here?"

"No one yet, I'm afraid." Her head turned to the shuttered window. "The rain has flooded the creek again. We'll be stuck for a few days."

The rain! The constant hum in his ears made sense now. His spine sank back against the pillows. He was safe.

For now.

But something still nagged him. Why had this girl risked herself? Emperor Jader still had a number of loyalists in the Gateway, though they seemed to be swallowed up by Steward enthusiasts. Could she be an ally?

The image of her feminine form dragging his dead weight out of harm's way passed over his mind's eye. Whoever she was, she was gutsy. But it didn't erase his precarious situation. The rain might hold them for a while, but sooner or later, someone would find out he was there. He had to be ready.

"Where's my sword?"

"I'm sorry, I didn't have time to grab it. But I do have your armor." She nodded to a corner. "Right over there with my father's old sword."

His armor? Mason turned his heavy head in that direction. A smear of red huddled in the corner, shaped like a breastplate. Just like the one he had put on in the woods. His heart jumped then dropped to his stomach.

By the moon. This feather-brained girl thought he was a Steward.

Jader peered down at Commander Bruin Pralus from his elevated spot on the throne. Bruin's longtime captain stood a few steps back, out of sight of Jader's bad eye. "You have not found his body?" Jader asked Bruin.

"Nay, sir." Bruin stood tall and proud, his black cape barely brushing the floor under his boots. "But he did not send word upon getting in, as was arranged."

Jader frowned and smoothed the folds of his robe. "That is no reason to consider him dead. It is early yet. Surely, you do not believe they could take him in? With or without the Shadowstone." He shook his head.

All the years spent waiting on Mason to be ready, all the planning and investing—there was too much to believe it was all for nothing.

Bruin scratched at the dark whiskers of his chin. "Do you want me to find out what I can?"

The idea was worth considering, as Bruin was nothing if not stealthy. "Nay. If he's inside, we don't want to risk drawing attention to him." Jader steepled his fingers. "We'll bide our time. You know as well as I do, Bruin, Mason is capable of taking care of himself."

Bruin nodded, then glanced behind him. "There is more. Captain Feegan brings news from Rackson."

The gray-headed soldier took a step into the line of sight of Jader's good eye and bowed at the waist. "Emperor Jader."

Jader gave the man a slight nod. "What do you have for me, Captain?"

Feegan straightened. "Prince Eric Passion himself led the defense of Rackson."

The surprise of the statement washed over Jader, and he had to work to keep it off his face. He sat motionless for a moment before speaking again. "Are you certain?"

Feegan elevated his head with importance. "Aye, sir. I faced him myself."

Jader tapped his fingers against the arm of the throne. "And did you kill him?"

The proud chin lowered. "I beg your pardon, my lord. He's still alive."

"I see." Jader turned to Bruin. "I must say, this is an unexpected move."

"What will we do, sir?"

Jader shot a quick look to the pompous fool of a captain, who stepped back at his boldness. "I mean, will we advance on Cuthrel as planned?"

"What kind of question is that?" Bruin asked. "One foolish, ambitious prince will not change Jader's course."

A slow smile spread over Jader's face as he ran his finger down the scar on his cheek, his mind jumping back in time, then ahead. Though his scarred eye saw nothing but darkness, the memories he carried were tattooed like paint stains on a canvas.

How convenient that the son of King Aden had put himself on the front lines. Jader slowed his mind down to consider the options. It would not do to get hasty. "Your commander is correct, Captain Feegan. Young Passion's decision to take up the sword will not affect the outcome. Though it may bring about a change of strategy." He turned his seeing eye back to Bruin. "I appreciate the prompt report, Commander Pralus."

Bruin gave him a smirk. "I didn't feel the Keeper of the Dark would appreciate being *kept* in the dark."

The attempt at humor elicited a rare chuckle. Or maybe it was the sudden prospects for his future. In any case, Jader's optimism for his impending ambitions blossomed. "Send me word as soon as you know the fate of my scout. In the meantime, let us proceed with our plans for Cuthrel."

11

The rain would not allow Eric's commencement to be held outdoors, for which he was thankful. The last thing he wanted was to be the focal point of attention for hundreds of soldiers. Instead, the ceremony would be held in the Council Hall, and the Councilmen would preside over it, rather than the king. But the end result would be the same. Eric would soon be the Grand Marshal of the Steward Army.

But first, he had to endure Uralis' memorial.

The very heavens wept as the beloved leader was carried from the Great Hall, wrapped in red velvet cloth. The rain stained the cloth dark crimson, too much like blood. The pallet was carried by six Steward heads, Captains Dudley and Braylee at the forefront. Knights stood in rows on either side of the road, silent and solemn as the gurney passed.

As they passed him, Eric pictured the marshal as he used to be. On the training fields, Uralis had been tough as Eric learned to use a sword. How he laughed when a young, arrogant Eric attempted a move he was not ready for during one of their duels and ended up flat on his back.

That laughter was gone forever, along with the many words of wisdom he had imparted to his Stewards over the years.

As Uralis was loaded in the back of a carriage, the Stewards all raised their Beacons, creating an arch of light over them. The young sergeant, Ollen, stood at one end of the line, his face set like stone.

Eric's grasp tightened on the light rod, and he clenched his teeth against the pain raking at him. Stand tall. Stand strong. It was the least he could do for the marshal who had stood strong for him so many times.

Captain Jervis Planks, who had traveled from Calla to see his marshal home, mounted and signaled to the cloak-shrouded carriage driver. He gave a nod to Eric and the soldiers, then tapped his horse's sides with his heels. The carriage began its slow journey from the fort, followed by the wagons carrying the rest of the slain Stewards and reservists. All headed home for the last time.

A mounted guard surrounded the caravan, ensuring a safe journey for their fallen comrades.

The back gate of the fort creaked loudly as it swung open, rubbing against Eric's raw emotions. He stared, motionless, as the wagons slipped through the exit with their silent passengers. Never to return.

Not a sound rose from the congregation. Even the civilian observers were quiet and subdued. No one paid any notice to the rain plastering their hair and clothes to their bodies. Every eye was riveted on the procession.

And then they were gone, to be received on the other end by King Aden, his armies, and the many other mourners. The finality of it devastated Eric, sucking his lungs dry. The gates closed, shutting the door on the past, and forcing them to face the future.

As was expected, Eric lowered his Beacon first. One by one, the others brought theirs down until Ollen was the last one. The light faded until finally, the cold gloom of the rain resided over all again.

It felt wrong to hold a commencement mere hours after sending Uralis to his final resting place. But it had to be done.

Eric stood in the debate room at the end of the Great Hall, ready to make his way to the Council. Butterflies made war with one another in his stomach. Memories of past mistakes, as well as future worries, wrapped themselves around his mind, much like the fur-lined cape wrapped around him, smothering him. His crown was back in Paladin, not needed to take his expected place as Steward Commander. As prince, this was his purpose. A purpose he had avoided for years. Uralis had been there to fill the gap the prince of Paladin was supposed to hold.

The double doors swung open before him, thanks to a pair of lieu-tenants—*his* lieutenants. He gulped back a boulder-sized knot and took the first step through. His knee-high black boots made no sound on the red and gold rug. Lavrynth, polished until it shone like glass, hung at his right hip, and his Beacon was snapped to the left side of his belt. His scarlet tunic concealed the sweat pouring down his back and sides.

And then he stood before the tall podium where Gayner, the head Councilman sat. The white-headed old man, much like Eric's own father, looked down at him. Wisdom and understanding reflected from his observation. Behind the podium hung the red banner with the flaming white sword—the Passion crest.

Braylee stepped to Eric's right side. His strong presence smoothed the tattered edges of Eric's nerves. Eric drew in a deep breath, slowing his heart rate. He glanced over and tried to thank the older man with a slight nod.

Captain Dudley moved to Eric's other side, tall, thin, and proud with his hands clasped behind his back. The seasoned veteran harbored no no reservation or concern on his weathered face. Eric drew comfort from that and forced himself to attend to the front.

This was it. There was no turning back now.

Numbness stole over his body as soon as Gayner started to speak. His mind froze while words faded in and out—familiar words from the Sacred Code. "To uphold... preserve... protect..."

He knew the oath well. As a mere boy, he had memorized the ancient creed spoken by generations of Stewards. And he meant it with his whole being. But at that moment, his movements and speech became automatic. Mindless.

"Are you well, Sire?"

Braylee's soft question broke through his stupor. Eric scanned around him. The Councilmen were talking softly amongst themselves. "What did I just do?" The whispered words slipped out before he could stop them.

A reassuring smile split Braylee's beard. "You became the rightful Grand Marshal of the Steward Army. Uralis would be honored."

Eric wiped a hand over his damp brow. "At least, I didn't make a fool of myself." He paused. "Did I?"

"You did well, Sire."

Dudley joined them and gave a slight bow. "Well done, Prince Eric. You make us all proud."

Eric reached out to shake Dudley's hand. "I thank you, Captain Dudley. And I appreciate your years of service. I'm afraid I shall rely on you and Captain Braylee much in the days to come."

Dudley's expression shone with sincerity. "And I will do my utmost to serve my new Grand Marshal. You will make a fine leader."

"What makes you sure of that, Captain?" The desire to know pushed him to humble himself.

"Because you are a Passion." The statement was fervent in delivery. "You carry the same astounding instinct and wisdom in your noble blood as your father and the many before him. Beyond that, you bring your own abilities to this position. You possess a Gift of the Moon, and your individual strengths will make you a bold commander. And your weaknesses will keep you humble enough to serve the Lambient."

Eric let out a chuckle that eased a little of the tension in his neck. But nothing could dislodge the heavy burden that perched itself on him.

A short while later—much too short—Eric looked out over the officers before him and suppressed the urge to gulp. Two captains and ten lieutenants stared back at him from around a long, wooden table in the mess hall after the dinner crowd had long gone. He was supposed to be discussing strategy with his senior officers, a battle plan for protecting the Gateway.

His mouth went dry. *Get it together, Eric. You've done this before.* He cleared his throat. "We all knew the day would come that Jader would launch his first assault against the Gateway." Though he had hoped against hope the emperor would be content with the control he had gained in the New Realm. "His hitting Rackson is but the beginning, and I fear he will target others, if only to make his point. We cannot leave them defenseless."

A couple of heads nodded, bolstering his confidence. Good. They were in agreement. He pressed on. "We need a squad on patrol for every few villages residing within the shelter of the gap. At the very least, they will be able to get word to us quickly if suspicious activity is going on." He did not like the idea of sending his men out closer to enemy territory, but it was the Stewards' duty to protect the civilians of the Gateway.

One man raised his hand. Lieutenant Draven—if Eric recalled his name correctly—was in Braylee's brigade and had ridden in from Calla with Eric. He looked roughly Eric's age but was broader and stockier, carrying himself with confidence, if not a little arrogance. "Won't that spread our men a little thin?" Draven asked. "There are over dozen villages hidden away here now."

Eric deferred the question to Braylee, who acknowledged the lieutenant with a dip of his chin. "Captain Jervis is organizing a battalion of militia reserves from Paladin. If and when the time arrives, they will be ready."

Dudley spoke up. "We feel it's important to keep a strong Steward presence in the Gateway—for those depending on us for their safety and for the enemy to see."

Eric began to relax as other men joined in the discussion, becoming an active part of the plan. This was good, what he wanted. Voices raised in collaboration and unity.

"Are we to search for the Shadowpit?"

The question snapped Eric's attention back to Draven even as his chest seized. "Nay."

Draven's brows rose. "With all due respect, Sire, if the Shadowmen are making their presence known, should we not stop their power at the source?"

Eric gave a quick shake of his head, working to keep from overreacting. "The Shadowpit is not our priority at this time. Building our resistance against the Dark Army is where we must focus our attention."

"Maybe we should at least consider it," another man spoke up.

"Didn't Marshal Uralis feel that we should be seeking out the pit?" Draven directed the question at Dudley.

Had he? Eric's father had never mentioned it before. Heat built up in the back of his neck.

Dudley scratched his grizzled jaw. "Aye. He believed it would be a good course of action. But he was not willing to go against the king to do so."

A brief silence fell as the men looked back to Eric. "I understand your stance, and I respect it. But too many lives were already lost in the search for the Shadowpit. I refuse to put our Stewards or anyone else in jeopardy to find something that may not even exist." Self-loathing pulled at him as soon as he finished speaking. Of course, the Shadowpit existed. It was where Jader drew his power to instill in his Shadowmen.

Draven's jaw shifted. Judging by the way the other officers glanced over at him, he held a measure of influence. Frowns and scowls appeared on several faces, but no one spoke any further of it. Dudley turned the subject to the matter of guard duty, and the discussion moved on.

But the mood had shifted, and a slight edge now hung over them. It pained Eric that he had lost some support in his decision, but that couldn't be helped. It did not matter if Uralis himself believed they should continue the search. Eric would not budge on this. The Shadowpit had already cost him too much.

12

Fear and deceit shall be the companions
of all who shut their eyes to the light.
-The Sacred Code

Seria slipped out of the house early in the morning while Mason still slept. She covered her head with an old shawl, but the rain licked at her face, and her bare feet were soaked by the time she stepped into the little shed behind her cabin where Sanjo was housed.

"Good morning, old boy. Hope you're staying dry."

The sound of dripping water drew her notice to a wet spot inside the door. "Well, dry enough, at least." She moved to the bin in the corner and pulled out some hay. It didn't smell so fresh anymore, but it was all she could offer for now. The grass around her cabin was sparse and thin, and the rain prevented her from staking him out in lusher pastures.

She patted his neck, stepping closer to draw in his warmth. "I'm sorry, boy. Someday, I'll get us a better place. I promise. And someday might be sooner than we both thought now that I have myself a patient."

Even if that patient was a bit tight-lipped. "He's certainly a strange one."

It had been three days since he awoke, and he remained a mystery, closed off and reserved. Every attempt she made for conversation fell flat with his short replies, and though he was polite enough when he had to be, his voice remained cool and distant. He didn't trust her, and he watched her when he thought she was unaware, as if waiting for...something.

It left Seria at a loss. She had always thought a Steward of the Old Realm would be a little more gracious.

Maybe she expected too much of him. With those deep wounds, every move he made had to feel like torture. Fortunately, he was over the worst, so long as he didn't do anything foolish like fall out of bed in the middle of the night.

"Maybe he's still in shock." She rubbed Sanjo's ears. "What do you think?"

The donkey continued munching, oblivious to her musings.

Seria chuckled and wrapped her shawl back around her head. "Fine, I get the hint. I'll leave you alone to eat."

Her shawl was soaked, and she was chilled to the bone when she stepped back inside her warm cabin. Even a drafty shack seemed comfortable during a cold mountain rain.

"Where have you been?"

Seria's head jerked around. "Oh! I didn't realize you were awake."

"Where were you?" The question came out thick and raspy.

"Out feeding Sanjo." She dropped her wet shawl by the door and handed him his mug of water. "I can't go anywhere else with the footbridge flooded."

Her answer did not ease any of the tension in Mason's body. He looked past her to the crimson breastplate in the corner, and his lips clamped shut.

Seria hesitated a brief minute before plunging ahead. "If I offended you by touching your armor, I'm truly sorry. My father told me a lot about Stewards, but if there's a rule about their armor, he never said."

Her words picked up speed. "But there was no other way to tend to your wounds without getting it off of you, and then I thought I should clean it off as best as I could. It might need a good polishing once you get back to the fort, but at least it's not all smudged with mud." She rambled to a stop.

For an instant, his pallid face hardened, sharpening the contours of his bruised, purple cheekbones. Then the moment passed, and he cleared his throat, swallowed twice. "Nay, you've been...very kind." His voice croaked, and he drank the rest of his water.

"Well, I'm glad I didn't ruin anything." She chuckled and dished him up some oats before turning to the pile of clean laundry on her table. Tending to Mason had made her clients' laundry long overdue, but the rain had given her a good reason for putting it off for a while. No one would expect her to deliver their laundry in the middle of a flood.

At least she hoped not.

She grabbed a large canvas bag and glanced back at her patient. "I'm sure this rain will let up soon. When the footbridge is clear, is there someone you want me to contact at the fort when I can get across?"

"Nay."

At his curt tone, she swiveled around. Mason's gaze again locked onto hers, hard and probing, a hint of panic in the amber depths. Goodness, he had a way of staring someone down. "I don't want you to contact anyone."

She frowned at his strange reaction. "Why not?"

His jaw clenched beneath the fringe of whiskers. "I wasn't supposed to be in that battle. I had an assignment elsewhere." He gripped the blanket. "I was heading out when I heard the fight break out and went back to help. If my superiors find out I disobeyed orders, I could get in a lot of trouble."

"But why? You were trying to help."

He shook his head, then squeezed his temples. "That's the way things are. They're very strict against disobedience, no matter the reason."

A ribbon of uneasiness swirled around Seria's stomach. "Won't they realize you're missing?"

"Not yet. My assignment was long distance." He glanced around the room.

Seria let silence fall. Her attention drifted to the Steward breastplate with its white sword pointing up like a Beacon, then to her father's old sword. It looked rather pitiful standing in the corner next to the finely crafted armor. But a farmer had little use for a soldier's sword.

Pulling her wandering thoughts back to the man on the bed, she considered his story.

He's scared. The realization made her heart ache. She had heard of men struggling with the trauma a battle left within. Not all scars were visible. Mason was helpless, tethered to a bed by his injuries, without his unit or his sword. Even his sleep was troubled at times. She had experienced Rackson from afar, and it had still shaken her. No wonder he was so ill-at-ease.

But there was more to his story than he was telling.

She chewed her lip. She did not know much about how Stewards did things.

He spoke again. "I figure as soon as I'm up to it, I can finish what I was supposed to do before I go back. Then at least..."

"You won't be in as much trouble." She turned to face him.

"Aye." He held himself tensely, his expression wary.

She hesitated, still trying to form the right words. "Your secret is safe with me. I'd hate for you to survive that fight and then get in trouble over it. Especially when you were trying to do the right thing." She gave him what she hoped was a reassuring smile.

Mason stared at her, his stoic expression frozen in hard lines.

She finished stuffing the clean clothes in the bag. "While you're here, you might as well take advantage of the time to rest and heal."

As she moved about in her tiny kitchen area, she sensed him watching her every move. And not because he found her captivating, what with her ratty attire and tousled hair. Not for a man of his caliber, anyway.

Nay, there was something more, something she couldn't quite put her finger on. He kept a thick wall up, determined to stay behind it. But why? What caused him to pull so far within himself?

What was he hiding behind that mask?

13

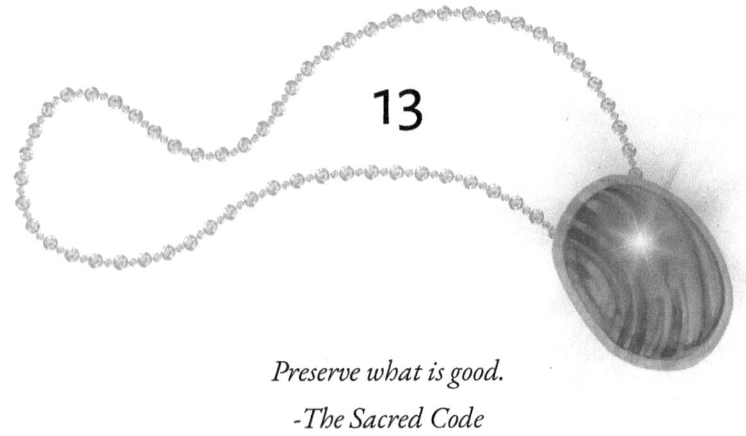

Braylee squinted against the bright morning sunlight as he rode atop a small knoll in the lower bailey. Having spent the last hour at the training grounds, he now rode through the back gates into the keep. The break in the weather afforded him the chance to see how the Gateway Stronghold had grown since the last time he was hither a year ago.

A pang struck him that Uralis had not been able to see it all before their visit had been cut short. How he missed his longtime friend. He reached down to pat the damp neck of the bay beneath him. Uralis' horse had been passed to Braylee since he lost his mount in Rackson, and Braylee appreciated having this one last connection.

Raised voices drew him from his deep thoughts, and he turned in time to witness two Steward sergeants trading blows. Heat rushed to his head, and he swung off the saddle and stalked to the wrestling pair.

Lionel Percy was one of the youngest officers, a little impulsive, but always dependable. Ollen Knavis was a couple of years older and already showed signs of great potential. Both were of exemplary character, well-built, and well-trained for combat. Even so, Braylee did not hesitate to step between them.

"What's the meaning of this?" He shoved them apart. "Two members of the King's Stewards fighting like schoolboys? And officers, no less!"

Both young men backed off and bowed in respect, their faces still cloudy.

"I want an answer."

Lionel's nostrils flared. "We disagree on the merits of the prince, sir."

Braylee turned to Ollen, who stared back, his jaw clenched.

"What have you to say?" Braylee demanded.

"I mean no disrespect to the prince, Captain Braylee. But I do not feel his place is here."

Braylee kept his feelings off his face. The Steward Army was unique from others in that its leaders did not dissuade honest discourse. "And why is that?"

Ollen raised his chin. "Marshal Uralis was a great warrior for most of his life and died in the line of duty. Prince Eric seems valiant, sir, but he's been raised behind sheltered walls. When it comes down to it, he has neither the experience nor the fortitude to lead the Stewards, or he would have been here before. Where was he these last few years while we defended the Old Realm?"

Lionel stayed quiet but watchful of Braylee's response. Ollen's question reminded Braylee of their age. There was so much he could say, but it was not his place, nor was this the time. Many of the Stewards stationed at the Gateway would be too young to recall the early days when Eric had briefly led the Stewards.

He bit back a sigh. Uralis was famed for his prowess on the battlefield. He never backed down and led his men with wisdom. In return, his men were loyal to a fault. A replacement would be met with mixed opinions, no matter who it was. And for Ollen, who was at Uralis' side in his last moment, it might prove to be more difficult.

"The prince is unwilling to venture out into the Gateway in search of the Shadowpit."

Braylee jerked back to Ollen. "Where did you hear that?"

The younger man faltered. "Some of the senior officers were talking."

Lionel spoke up. "Lt. Draven claims Marshal Uralis wanted to seek it out to destroy it years ago, but the royal family would not allow it."

Draven would get a visit from Braylee later for his wagging tongue. "Prince Eric has his reasons, and we have to stand by that."

Ollen frowned. "Meanwhile, Jader is strengthening his army."

"We are not sitting idle. Preparations are underway, but we cannot risk being hasty."

"We're risking our entire kingdom by waiting." Ollen's eyebrows lowered. "Does Prince Eric think the problem will go away if we ignore it?"

"Nay, he does not. We must be patient and trust in his intuition. He has Paladin's best interests at heart."

"He's not showing the kind of wisdom needed by a leader of Stewards. History has shown itself time and again. The marshals are men of action. They don't sit by and make preparations. They take it upon themselves to defend their kingdom, risking everything they've got. Prince Eric isn't willing to risk anything."

"After the way he fought for Rackson?" Braylee asked. "When he led our men to drive back the Dark Army's first assault on the Gateway? Have you forgotten that?"

Ollen's jaw shifted. "Not as quickly as you've forgotten the marshal, it would seem."

The insolence burned, and Braylee narrowed his eyes. Ollen blanched and took a step back.

Lionel scowled. "You forget your place, Ollen!"

"I'll handle it." Braylee reined in his anger and faced Ollen. "The fact remains, Sgt. Ollen, that the prince is the marshal of the Stewards now. So, you can put aside your reservations and trust he knows what he is doing, or you can turn in your Beacon and move on."

"I will never go back on my vow to honor the Code!"

"Then I suggest you spend less time criticizing the leadership and more time promoting unity within our ranks."

Ollen stared back at him for a long moment, as though he had more to say. Instead, he lowered his head.

"I understand your reservations, having served under Uralis for years. But your opinion gives neither of you reason to come to blows." His stern look encompassed both of them. "As officers, you are both above this. Uralis would not condone such action, and neither do I."

Remorse flashed across Ollen's countenance, and Lionel ducked his head.

"On the morrow, I want both of you to spend an extra hour on the training fields."

"You're right." Ollen's voice lost its edge. "I apologize to you both for my rashness."

"As do I," Lionel added.

"That's good to hear. But in the meantime," Braylee crossed his arms and held Ollen's stare with his own. "You can take John's shift in the barn. Be there in one hour."

Ollen's face flushed at the humble task, but he gave a single nod. "Aye, sir." His posture slumped in resignation at the penalty for disrespecting a senior officer. Lionel bowed once more before following Ollen to the barracks.

Braylee inhaled deeply and let it out slowly. Ollen would have to come to his own conclusion concerning Eric's ability to lead. But Braylee feared the young Steward did not stand alone in his judgment.

"So, you're getting the questions, too." Dudley appeared at his side, leading Braylee's horse. "Most of the reservations they carry have nothing to do with the prince's leadership, but in his silence over the years."

"The lieutenants wagging their tongues about the Shadowpit certainly doesn't help."

"Aye. I cannot blame the prince for his decision, but I understand everyone's frustration." He hesitated and looked at Braylee. "Do you think he can lead?"

Braylee rubbed the whiskers on his jaw. "I think Prince Eric is going to have to believe he's a leader before he can ever lead this army to victory."

14

By all appearances, Seria believed Mason's cockamamie story. But still, he couldn't relax, so he kept a wary eye on his hostess. When he could keep them open.

His body had betrayed him, binding him to a bed and pulling him into the black grip of unconsciousness, time and time again. Seria said he needed the sleep, but sleep was no ally to him. It brought with it faded images he had not had since he was a boy. Dreams of bloodshed and death.

The poor weather gave him some time to plan, and as long as it rained, he was out of harm's way. In the moments he was awake, he focused on coming up with a strategy to get out of this predicament.

A difficult task, with Seria's constant yakking.

The girl chatted nonstop until he wished he had lost his hearing with that blow to his head. Even when he contributed nothing to a conversation, she kept up an animated, one-sided dialogue. Did she ever stop to breathe? His chest felt like a horse was sitting on it, squeezing the life out of him, and she wanted to talk about laundry, Stewards, and her dumb donkey.

He lay back against his pillow, feigning sleep to steal a few minutes of peace. His insides writhed. How long had he been here? Four days? Five? It felt like forever. Mason had been in tough positions before, but he'd always had his full mental capabilities.

Could he trust her not to blab?

Nay. He could not. He learned long ago not to trust anyone who supported the Stewards. He needed to see her thoughts, to control her movements. But until this confounded beating in his head stopped and his Gift returned, he was stuck.

Masquerading as a pretentious bigot soured him, but he had no choice. He had heard of the so-called justice Aden of Paladin dealt out—death or life imprisonment for Jader's Darkmen.

He had no intention of accepting either.

Everything he knew about Stewards, aside from their obvious brutality, ran through his head. Knights who hid their cruelty behind professed vows of honor. Known for their compassion and chivalry, they waved their weak, pithy virtues in the faces of those too blind to see that they aimed to crush anyone who resisted their control. All in the name of their Sacred Code.

His blood heated, flaming his face. He swallowed back the bitterness and focused on the moment at hand. This charade was his only chance for survival. He had to play his part well, which would be harder than anything else he had ever done.

From across the room came a splash, then a soft swish.

She must be doing laundry again. How a girl who wore nothing but rags could have so much laundry was beyond him.

Opening his eyes, he strained for a clear view of the sparse cabin again. Though it was a little clearer, it was still a mix of tans and browns where the walls and furniture should be. Nothing stood out. Yet, even with his impaired vision, he could see that it was plain and sparse. Bruin's camp was a haven in light of her dwelling place.

Seria worked over a large pot in front of the fireplace in the far corner, her back to him. Her dress was the same color as her surroundings—dull. But it hung over her like a sack.

As if sensing his scrutiny, she looked over her shoulder. "I didn't wake you, did I?"

Act like a Steward. He forced a small smile. "Nay, not at all."

"Ready for something to eat?"

At his nod, she moved to get his breakfast. He grimaced as he pushed himself up. Every move sent fire shooting through his body.

"Here you go."

Mason had to hide his scowl before taking the bowl. His lips turned down at the mush. "Oats."

"You're welcome." She tittered.

He tipped the bowl in her direction. "Aye, of course. Thank you." He dug in. They were filling, despite their flatness.

"Did you ever remember your surname?"

He froze. "What?"

She pushed a strand of hair off her face and resumed her laundry. "You told me your first name, but I thought that whack on the head might've affected your memory. I never got your surname."

"Oh." So that was how she had known his name. "I ..."

"Don't remember it right now." She finished his sentence for him. "Head whacks can do that to you for a while. Don't worry. I'm sure it'll come back to you."

He gave her a stiff nod. This small talk was awkward and tedious, but if he had to live with her for now, it would help to know as much about her as he could, in case it came of use later. "Do you have family nearby?"

Her hands faltered in their scrubbing. "Nay. It's just me."

Good, at least he didn't have to worry about relatives barging in on him. "Are you from around here?"

She shook her head. "I used to live in Shadrin."

"In the New Realm?" What on earth would possess a young woman to leave her family in Shadrin to live in this valley alone?

"Do you hear that?" Seria's brows rose.

"Hear what?"

"Nothing. That's the point. It stopped raining!"

His body jerked as he looked to the window. Silence. So much for that cushion of security. *Stay calm. Act normal.* "Aye. It did."

She met his gaze. "But you don't have to worry. I meant what I said. No one will find out you're here."

He nodded, trying to glimpse into her thoughts. She returned his look without reserve. For once, he was the first one to look away. "I appreciate that." When she flashed him a smile and turned back to her laundry, he let out his pent-up breath, feeling it to his toes. Thank his lucky stars she wasn't any smarter than she was.

He had stew for lunch. Again. Did she know how to cook anything else?

Seria swung the door open; a wide ribbon of yellow light flooded the room. The wooden shutter was propped up, letting clean, fresh air in. "Look at that sunshine." She drew in a deep breath. "You eat that, and I'll be right back."

Before he could gulp down his food to reply, she sailed out the door. He set the bowl on the table and pushed himself up. A jagged streak jolted through him when he straightened, knocking him back against the pillow.

Blast. Would he ever stop hurting?

Several long minutes passed. He massaged a wrist, where his bracer should be. Then he heard her talking to someone. His pulse skittered. He strained to hear the other individual and stayed alert for the sound of approaching footsteps. When they came, Seria appeared in the doorway. Alone.

"Someone here?" he asked.

"No one but Sanjo." She announced with a grin as she shut the door behind her. "He's snug and dry. Well, not completely dry. Afraid that shed doesn't keep all the water out."

Weakness flooded his limbs, and he exhaled. That donkey would be the death of him.

"Something wrong with the stew?" Seria picked the bowl up and frowned at it.

"Nay. Trying to get comfortable."

"Oh, well, here you are, then." She handed the bowl back and went to dish her own up.

A loud knock gave him a violent start, and his half-filled bowl hit the floor, spilling its contents. On instinct, he dropped his hand to where his sword usually hung. He hissed as another sharp sting lanced through his side. *Blazes.*

Seria jumped up. "Oh! Don't worry, it's probably Byron."

Byron? He clenched the sheet in his fists.

Seria tossed her blanket over the breastplate in the corner and hurried to the door. A small figure stood at the threshold. Mason blinked in an attempt to clear his vision.

"Hello, Byron, good to see you," Seria greeted. "Are you enjoying the break in the rain?"

Mason couldn't make out the boy's reaction, but it looked like he had nodded. Then he spotted Mason and took a step backward.

"It's all right, Byron." Seria's voice was gentle, as though talking to a frightened animal. "He's a friend. Is your mama doing any better?" Seria asked.

The boy gave a tiny shrug. Through it all, his face stayed turned in Mason's direction. Mason frowned back at him.

Seria put her hand on Byron's head. "Thank you for stopping by. I'll have some work for you tomorrow."

Without a word or a backward glance, he turned and left.

Mason snorted. "Friendly kid."

Seria gave Mason an apologetic smile as she set about cleaning up the mess on the floor. "Byron doesn't take well to strangers."

"I noticed." He stiffened. "Hey, is he going to—?"

"Nay, he won't. Byron doesn't talk much anyway or bother with something that's none of his concern. His family moved to the area a few months ago. They've got five other kids and Byron's father hasn't been able to find steady work."

Mason could already picture the ragtag family. Scavengers. Parasites who lived off other people's hard work.

"Byron sort of works for me." She tucked another strand of hair behind her ear and stood. "At least, that's what I tell him. He's but eight years so there's not much he can do at his age. He fills my water basins outside and dumps them when I'm done with laundry, and he helps take care of Sanjo."

Gingerly stretching his aching leg, Mason asked, "Kind of a runt for eight." He shot her a quick look. Would she think the statement too harsh for a Steward?

"Not surprising, considering. His father suffers from a bad back and can't always work. So, needless to say, they go without a lot."

"I see." *In other words, they're riffraff.* He turned his head away, rolling his eyes. That beggar kid better keep his mouth shut.

She held up his bowl. "Do you want any more?"

"Nay. Thank you." He huffed a long-suffering sigh at the ceiling.

Seria resumed her laundry, and soon her soft mumbles mixed with the slap of wet clothes and gurgle of water. The smell of ash and lye rose from the area where she worked, irritating his already achy head. At a chuckle, he looked to see her holding a garment up.

"Isn't this fancy?" It looked like nothing more than a blob of yellow and blue to him. "Can you imagine wearing something like this?"

He squeezed the bridge of his nose. "I'm sure it is, if I could see it."

She dropped it on the table and approached. "You're having difficulty seeing? For how long?"

"Since I woke up here."

"Why didn't you tell me sooner? I didn't even consider that possibility. It's pretty common with head injuries. How bad is it?"

His tired brain tried to catch up. "I don't know." He squinted up at her. "I think it's a little better."

She leaned closer. "Can you see me better now?" When he shook his head, she moved closer. "How about now?" She continued moving until vivid green eyes hovered inches before his nose.

He drew back as far as the pillows would allow. "That's pretty clear."

She let out a giggle as she pulled away, her features lost again in a muddle of muted colors, and the contact was broken. "Sorry to invade your space like that."

Mason bit back a curse at the missed opportunity to control her. He couldn't very well ask her to come that close again without arousing suspicion. Not that he needed another clear picture. He could still see those green orbs of hers before his impaired vision like sunspots.

"I'm sure it'll come back in time," she said as she returned to her work. "My mother treated a few serious head injuries, and most recovered completely, and those that didn't were much worse than you are now. She was a master healer at one time. I used to think she must have a Gift of the Moon. I wanted to be like her and even prayed to the Lambient to give me that same Gift."

Mason ran his hands over his face, his insides tensing the more she talked.

"But Mama finally explained to me that her skills were not gifted, but the result of hard work and knowledge. And then, she proceeded to teach me all she knew."

She went on, but Mason closed his eyes and ignored her, ready to face the nightmares of his sleep rather than hear any more stories of her Lambient. He had learned long ago that Lambient did not answer the prayers of those who called on Him.

Because He didn't exist.

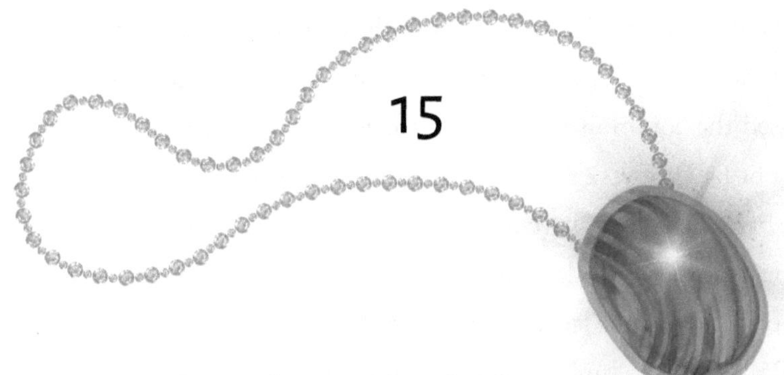

15

"This is a day of remembrance. A day of celebration. But it's also a day of solemnity.
This is the day you choose to commit to the cause of the Lambient.
This is the day you become a Steward, a member of the united Royal Army."
-Commencement speech given by Steward Grand Marshal Uralis Faunt

Eric stood on the edge of the training field under the rising sun and watched Braylee. The big man was alone, his eyes closed, his movements solid and sure. He swung his sword in decisive strokes, every motion a reflection of the calm and steady knight. Eric waited until the other man was done before he greeted him.

"Good day, Prince Eric." Braylee slid his sword back into his sheath.

"I have never seen anyone practice like that."

Braylee smiled. "It helps me focus when I shut out what I can see."

"Have you ever fought anyone like that?"

"Nay, but it is how I learned to harness the Beacon whip."

Eric's mind went back to the night Braylee stood between him and the Shadowstone, flinging his whip of light. "That is truly a magnificent display."

"It takes a lot out of a body; thus, rarely used more than once in the same setting. But it's powerful."

The two entered back into the fort through the back gate and retrieved their horses. The earthy scent of herbs and vegetables teased Eric as they passed the community garden in the lower courtyard, reminding him that he had not yet eaten. "My father utilized that weapon in his days on the battlefield, but I have never managed to wield it." Maybe because he had spent the last decade of his life shirking his duty. Maybe because he would never be the leader his father or Uralis had been.

Braylee's deep timbre cut through the doubts. "It will come. Do not let a few misgivings cause you to doubt yourself. Now, how about that tour?"

Ready to think about something else, Eric gave a short nod.

They left the fort to ride through Cadence. Eric had not been to the town for some time and wanted to familiarize himself with the layout and all that it contained. He witnessed several curious looks from the townspeople but doubted many of them realized who he was yet. Word would soon spread. But for now, he took advantage of his low profile to move about without restraint.

Cadence was quite charming, as far as refugee villages could be. It had the greatest advantage of all the Gateway communities in that it lay so close to the actual opening in the Slates. The main street was busy with vendors and herders. Eric enjoyed a pastry from a maiden's bakery cart and took in the medley of voices calling to one another. Children darted in and out of the side streets, necessitating a steady hand on Oakley's reins. This was a town full of businesspeople, but of families as well.

"Do you have a family, Braylee?" he asked as they passed back through the double gates of the lower courtyard.

Warmth filled Braylee's face. "I do."

Eric smiled. "Tell me about them. Where are they?"

"In Cassels. My wife and two young daughters, ages nine and thirteen. The most beauteous creatures you'll ever see."

"You must miss them." Eric could only imagine the pain of being separated from a wife and children.

"With everything in me," Braylee said with feeling, rocking with the rhythm of Uralis' horse. "It's been over a month since I've seen them."

"I look forward to meeting them someday."

At that, Braylee gave a short laugh.

"What did I say?"

Braylee ran a hand over his head. "Well, my wife and youngest would be flattered beyond words to meet the prince of Paladin. But their pleasure would pale in comparison to Ella's elation."

"Is that so?"

"Ella is every bit the romantic. She got a glimpse of you during a visit to Calla one day and now thinks you are the most divine man to ever walk the earth."

"So, she has good taste."

Braylee slanted him a look. "She used to say I was the most divine."

Eric chuckled. "I am sorry to be responsible for displacing you."

"No need to apologize. My other girl, Shayna, more than makes up for Ella's lack of enthusiasm. She told me the prince looked like mud compared to her papa."

Eric threw his head back and laughed out loud. "Your family sounds delightful, Braylee."

"I've always thought so." His face became pensive.

"I envy you. You have someone to fight for, someone to go home to. You are truly a blessed man."

They surrendered their mounts to the livery stable housing the officers' horses and made their way to the mess hall.

Dozens of Stewards and militia moved about the garrison as the two walked, and they all paused and inclined their heads as he passed. Ever watchful of the way the men interacted with each other, Eric responded and continued moving so they could go on with their daily tasks. As they drew nearer to the center of the courtyard, he uttered his growing concern.

"Why do I detect dissension among the Stewards?"

Braylee didn't look at him. "Dissension?"

"The men are on edge."

"Must be the uncertainty of the future." Braylee shrugged. "Knowing Jader could strike at any time has them all a little tense."

His tone came out a little too casual, prompting Eric to stop. "How about the truth, Captain Wright?"

Braylee let out a breath and faced him. "Many are struggling with Uralis' death, Sire."

A light dawned. *Of course.* "And his replacement." Uncertainty pricked, cracking the flimsy shield of confidence he had gathered. Was it the loss of their marshal they struggled with? Or the faults of their current one? He scratched his jaw, the near-resentful way some of the Stewards looked at him burning through his mind. "I can't say as I blame them."

Braylee stayed silent, his face sober.

Uralis was not a man who could be replaced, and his death still stung like a knife. "I know his men were devoted to following him. I can't expect them to switch their allegiance to me without a thought."

Braylee's jaw twitched. "Like I did?"

"Nay, not at all." Eric hurried to amend his statement. The last thing he wished to do was insult this great captain, whom Uralis himself had relied on many times over the years. "I've long been aware of your friendship with Uralis. Your promise to me means all the more because of it. But I cannot step in and inherit the men's trust and loyalty. I will have to earn it, as he did." Even if the very thought scared him witless.

"I've no doubt you can do so, Sire."

Eric let a sad smile slip. "Your faith in me is more than appreciated, Braylee." He slapped the other man's back. "What a shame we never had much time together in the past. I could have used your optimism many other times throughout my life."

The captain winced. "My optimism does not come so easily in the mornings, I'm afraid. A fact I'm sure you'll come to see sooner or later."

"I appreciate the warning." But even as he said it, Eric wondered how this big-hearted knight could ever be anything other than kind and generous.

They resumed their stroll, but this time, Eric was more sensitive to the feelings of the knights. No one acted in disrespect, but he felt their restraint. A few barely looked at him as they bowed. Others crossed the street in advance so they wouldn't have to encounter him. Why had he never considered the possibility that the Stewards would resist his command as strongly as he did? His own lieutenants had made it clear they did not trust his judgment. Why would anyone else?

He was not offended, but it did deflate him a bit. Something stirred within him, a resolve to be the kind of leader they would have no qualms following, the kind that Uralis had trained him to be. It would take a lot of time and discomfort, but the worth was greater. After all, no finer army could be found in all the Old Realm. Any man would consider it an honor to command King Aden's Stewards.

But what would it take to earn their respect?

16

"You going somewhere?"

Seria turned to the bed where Mason had awakened. "I have to make this delivery, then I'm going by the market." She still felt uncomfortable leaving him, and judging by the way he considered her through his lashes, he felt the same. But it couldn't be helped. If she didn't deliver this load of laundry, she would have some unhappy clients. "I won't be long. Do you need anything before I go?"

"Nay. Thank you."

She swung the heavy bag up and over with a grunt. "You rest 'til I get back."

Mason responded with a slight nod. Seria stepped outside, staggering under the weight of the bag. If only she could find another way to support herself. Alas, there were few prospects for uneducated, young women.

Someday, things will be different.

After the delivery was made, she made her way to the vendors with her usual hurried, gotta-get-there pace. She purchased a few simple items, then lingered at the carts of fresh produce and baked goods.

The tantalizing scent of honey and cinnamon teased her nostrils as she passed the last cart. Pastries and tarts beseeched her, but her work kept enough food on the table to keep her from starving. It did not allow for treats. Especially now that she had a guest.

"Smell good?"

Seria inhaled. "It smells heavenly! Is this another one of your creations?"

The petite brunette held a pastry out. "Aye. Would you like to try one?"

"Oh, Lena, I wish I could, but I can't this time."

Lena shrugged. "Take it as a sample. I need people to spread the word."

Seria looked up from the sweets. "How is your grandfather?"

"As independent as ever." Lena rolled her dark eyes. "The man is half-blind and insists he can live on his own." She grinned and held a platter out. "Come on. You know you want one."

Seria still hesitated. Her conscience would never give her any rest if she indulged in sweets while Mason got nothing but mushy stew. "I shouldn't."

Lena cocked her head. "Why not?"

"I have a guest. Actually, it's a patient." She couldn't stop the grin that slipped out.

"Really?" Lena's face brightened. "Is it anyone I know?"

Seria twisted her lips to the side. Lena and her mother lived inside the fort and knew almost everyone who lived in Cadence. "I don't think I should say too much, out of courtesy for my patient."

Lena nodded. "I understand." She squeezed Seria's hand. "But that's wonderful for you. It won't be long before others start realizing what a gift we have right here in the Gateway."

Seria warmed at her friend's faith in her. Surely, Lena was right, and Mason was only the beginning.

"Have you taken any more late-night fishing trips?"

Not since the last one that landed her in the middle of Rackson's assault and brought Mason into her life. "Not lately."

Lena leaned against the cart on her forearms. "One of these days, I'm going to have to go with you. I love the idea of sitting under the stars."

"It is lovely, but it's usually pretty late when I go. The gates would already be closed."

Her friend wrinkled her nose. "That wouldn't stop me."

Seria chuckled. "I've forgotten how you like to sneak out late at night."

"Someone's got to check on Grandfather since he refuses to join us in the fort." She leaned closer. "Did you hear the rumor?"

"What rumor?" Seria held her breath; Lena was not given to idle gossip.

"The prince is staying at the fort."

Seria's jaw slackened. "He is?"

Lena nodded. "Apparently, the assault on Rackson was enough to draw him away from Calla. Which is high time, if you ask me."

"Why do you think that?" Seria asked as her mind hovered over the wounded Steward in her house.

"Evidently, in times past, it was customary and expected that the king led the Steward Army until he could no longer do so. Then the leadership is supposed to be passed down to the prince. But Prince Eric led for a short time before he went back to Calla, leaving Uralis Faunt in charge. Until he was killed in Rackson."

Seria bit her lip. The Stewards had lost their commander? No wonder Mason was out of sorts. "Why hasn't the prince been leading?"

Lena shook her head. "I'm not sure, and I didn't want to pry. In any case, he has once again stepped into the leadership role that was supposed to be his. But I'm not sure how well he will be received after such a long absence."

News of the prince living in the fort was fascinating enough, but now Seria found herself wondering what Mason thought of it all. Maybe it would be better to keep what she learned to herself. She did not wish to cause any undue stress on Mason if the news was not supposed to be public outside of the fort.

"He bought one of my sweets yesterday."

Seria gaped at her. "You saw the prince?"

Lena gave a coy smile. Her hair looked sleek and neat in a knot twisted at the back of her head. Seria tried not to envy her long, emerald green dress without a tear or faded spot. "He was trying to keep a low profile, I think," Lena said. "But that's going to be hard for someone of his physique." She winked, then took two tarts out of her cart and wrapped them in a clean rag. "Here. I can afford to give away two samples. Especially if the prince starts recommending my goods."

Seria's mouth already watered at the thought of biting into her tart. "You keep doing that, and you'll never save enough money to open your own bakery."

"It'll happen in its own time. Tell me later how your guest likes them."

"I'm sure he'll love them." *Rats.* Seria slid a glance to see if Lena had caught her slip of the tongue, but she was busy rearranging her baked goods. Lest she keep talking and say too much, Seria thanked her friend and hurried back down the trail.

It was growing cool by the time she returned home. She glanced up at the sky, appreciating the gentle breeze. Spring had taken a firm hold, but the winds blowing down from the Slate Mountains chilled the valley at night.

Upon opening the door, she found Mason sitting up in bed, his feet on the floor. His coloring was a bit wan, but his chin jutted at a stubborn angle. Seria's first instinct was to scold him, but something told her he would not take to that.

"Well, look who's up. How does it feel?"

"Not bad." He looked winded, but not exhausted—a good sign.

"Don't push yourself too hard."

He turned to lean back against the pillow. Seria stepped over to lift his feet back on the bed. "You ready to eat?"

"I suppose. Thank you."

Seria pursed her lips. She would almost rather he forget being polite than sound so forced. Then she remembered the loss of the Steward commander and tapped her irritation back. Instead, she gathered the fixings for another stew and put it over the fire.

"Is stew all you know how to cook?"

Her face heated at the question, but she batted away any offense. "No, but it's filling and the best I can afford right now."

"Is that your way of saying I'm eating you out of house and home?"

She gave a glance around the single room. "Wouldn't take much, I'm afraid. This house is a bit smaller than the one I was raised in. But I did manage to get ourselves a little treat for after supper." She held up the tarts.

His expression brightened for an instant, and a smile almost appeared. She bit back a chuckle. Nothing like a little dessert to bring out the boy in a man.

17

A sudden noise jerked Mason from another sound sleep. How long had he been out this time? The days meshed into one long stretch of sleep or wakefulness. Nothing else.

Loud, insistent knocking echoed through his achy head and drew his gaze to where Seria hurried across the room. Probably Byron for a handout. Mason huffed and rubbed his face as she opened the door.

A brash, male voice thundered through the small cabin, flooding Mason's imagination with Stewards pouring in to take him away. Adrenaline shot through him, and he bolted upright in bed, ready to fight, though he had no sword.

But it was a lone man who pushed his way through the door, forcing Seria to back up a step. "Lemme in, wench!"

Mason almost laughed out loud at the short, heavyset man with a double chin and receding hairline. *That's no Steward.* The energy rush faded, and he fell back in the bed, drained. His side complained at the sudden movement.

The rotund man—no taller than Seria—wobbled as he walked. "I wan' my money, laun'ry girl!"

"I told you, Ira, I'm not paying you. Now leave me alone." Seria's tone was sharp and abrupt.

Mason blinked at the sudden change in her demeanor. Gone was the girl who welcomed life with open arms. She faced the man with stiff arms and clenched fists.

"You owe me for my tunic!" Ira leaned forward and almost tipped over.

Seria backed up a step to avoid him falling into her and spoke through a clenched jaw. "We've been over this before. It was a small tear, and I repaired it and washed it for free. That's all you're getting from me."

"I'm not leaving without *my* money." Ira's words slurred. "You're a thief!"

Seria's face reddened. She grabbed a small whip from the wall and raised it over her head. "No one calls me a thief in my own house, Ira, now you get out before I thrash you again!"

Mason's brows shot up. She stood like an enraged warrior with her stick held high, blonde hair flowing down her back like a cape. He detected a flush spreading across her cheeks.

Ira glowered at her and took another shaky step. "I will get my money." He jabbed a thick finger at her. "Or I'll turn you over to the authorities!"

"Get out of here!" She brandished the stick. Ira pulled back in time to avoid it. He gave her another dark look, then took his leave, mumbling incoherently and slamming the door behind him.

Seria hung the whip back in its spot.

"What was that all about?" Mason asked, and then put his hands up when Seria spun toward him. Even he could see the green fire snapping from her eyes. "Sorry."

She gave a shaky laugh and blinked the sparks away. "Oh, nothing. One of my former clients, Ira Dankton. His cloak ripped a little when I washed it. The material was so flimsy, it's no wonder, but I took responsibility for it. He got it washed *and* mended for free. He's usually harmless unless he's wanting another strong drink. Then he'll try to bully a few pence out of me. But I don't put up with it anymore, not after that first time, anyway."

Mason rubbed his head and tried to keep up with her rapid-fire explanation.

"He broke into my house and pushed me around a little. Scared me to death, then it made me mad that I let it happen. The next time he came around, I was ready." She flashed an unrepentant grin as she straightened his covers. "I didn't bother to wait for him to start talking. He ran off with welts up and down his face and arms. It was either that or hide every time he came around."

Mason shook his head, trying to picture the scene. He had thought her little more than a pushover, jumping every time he made a request and bending over backward for the little runt. *I guess there's more to her than I gave her credit for.* He somehow doubted she lost her temper often, but it was clear she would not let herself be pushed too far before pushing back.

Then a thought made his neck tighten. "What if he does go to the authorities?"

"He won't risk it. His standing in town is not very respectable. Don't worry, they won't find out you're here until you're ready for them to know."

Surprise flooded him at how she had read his concern. "Why haven't you gone to them yourself about him?"

She blushed. "Well, you Stewards are too busy for my petty problems."

Blazes. He had to be more careful with what he said. The Stewards were the authorities around here. He should know that

She went on. "You all have enough on your plates protecting the Gateway from Jader's Dark Army."

Mason bit his tongue. Whatever respect he had started to feel dissipated. This girl had no idea what she was talking about. Everything she said about the Stewards was so sickeningly besotted, that he wanted to slap her himself.

Maybe it was his irritation that pushed the next question out. "So, what made you decide to leave your family and home to live out here by yourself, anyway?"

Her smile slipped a little. "Well, my parents are gone... dead."

If he could have pulled his tongue out and stomped on it, he would have. Instead, he ran his fingers through his already disheveled hair to mask his discomfort. "Sorry."

"It's all right." Her tone lacked some of its usual cheer, but she did not look upset. "I didn't have any other family, so this seemed the best place to go."

"Why here?"

"It's a good town."

Something must have flickered across his expression because she laughed and put her hands up. "It's not perfect. We can be a little hard on each other. Most people here don't have much anymore, and we hang on to what bits of pride we have left like it's our last coin. Then we tend to judge others so we don't feel so small."

It was not lost on him how she included herself in with the townspeople, though she did not seem so inclined to be so proud and judgmental.

"So, when did you become a Steward?"

He jerked his head up. "What?"

"I admit, I've been a bit curious."

Oh, brother. Now she would take his questions as an invitation to dig into his personal life. But the difference was, he had nothing to share. "Ah, not long ago."

"It must be so exciting." She perched on his bedside chair, hands clasped in her lap.

"Sure," he mumbled.

"How does it happen?"

"Huh?"She shook her hair back. "How does it happen? I've always wondered."

Sweat began to form on his forehead. "Well, there's this big—"

"Ceremony." She jumped in. "Do they have music and everything?"

"Sure."

"Does the prince come?"

"Nay!" When Seria pulled back at his quick reply, he licked his lips and calmed himself. "He does not. Too busy."

"Oh." Her voice fell. "What happens then?"

Mason grew impatient. "They give you the stick, make a big cheer, and that's that."

"What happens after that?"

Enough was enough. "Actually, I can't remember it all." He pointed to his head. "You know?" *Please stop talking.*

She fell silent, which unnerved him more than her chatter. Her regard became pensive as if she was trying to figure him out. Then she shrugged. "I'm sorry. I didn't mean to make you feel bad."

Agitation churned when she tilted her head. He was starting to recognize that pose. She was not done talking.

"I remember a story my father used to tell me about a famous Steward named Seelas. Have you ever seen his statue?"

They had a statue of a Steward? Of course, they did. What better way to exploit their greatness? "I've never had the privilege."

"His story gives me chills every time I hear it told. Do you remember it?"

"Afraid not." The last thing he wanted was to hear her yammer on about a dead Steward he could not care less about, but maybe if she got it out of her system, he would get some peace.

Her face lit up, and she began. "Well, there was this big fire in the town where Seelas lived at the time. It consumed everything in its path—homes, businesses, barns. Seelas tried to get everyone else out before he thought of himself. And then he found out a baby was left behind." She paused with a frown. "I don't know what kind of mother could leave her baby behind, especially in a city-wide fire."

Mercy, this girl could ramble on. How long was this going to last?

Her movements became more animated in her enthusiasm. "But anyway, Seelas goes all the way back, gets the baby, and runs for the end of town, where everyone was waiting. His clothes catch on fire, and he has to put it out, but he never stops. He finally makes it to the baby's mother, hands him over, and then falls over on the ground."

She shook her head. "But it was too late for him. He died later that night."

What a hero. Mason closed his eyes and leaned back against the headboard.

She didn't get the hint.

"The town put up this big memorial for him, and his story's been passed down as an example of the Stewards' bravery and sacrifice. Doesn't that give you chills?"

More like nausea.

"I never get tired of that story. And I heard another one—"

That was it. "I'm sorry, but would you mind if I slept for a while? I'm not up to any more stories."

Seria sat back, her hands falling on her lap. "Of course. I'm sorry." She didn't make another sound.

Finally.

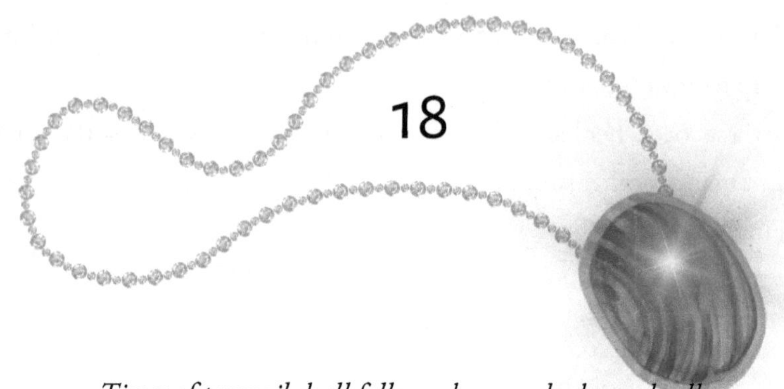

18

Times of turmoil shall follow wherever darkness dwells.
-The Sacred Code

Mason stretched gingerly, trying not to pull on his wounds, and massaged his clenched jaw. The tattered, scratchy blanket smothered him, and he shoved it off. Over a week in this stuffy little cabin. How he longed for the coolness of his tent. Even that was an improvement over his current living quarters.

Seria bustled in and out of the open door, doing what, he didn't care. Every time he was alone, he sat up in bed, desperate to build up his strength. It was torture, dragging himself upright, and at times, his heart pounded against his ribcage in exertion, but he pushed on, ignoring the exhaustion. He had to get out of here, despite his aching back and throbbing head.

A small figure appeared at the door while Seria was still outside. Mason let out another huff as he stretched back out on the bed, sensing the boy's scrutiny. Byron stared at him as if he had never seen a man before.

"What do you want, kid?"

He shrugged, pulling his stare from Mason to the fresh loaf of bread cooling on the table. "I fed Sanjo." His tone was dull, like everything else about him.

Mason scowled. The warm, doughy scent had teased him all morning. It would have been a welcome change from the pottage Seria had been feeding him, but she had made it clear the bread was to be Byron's payment. For feeding a donkey.

"There's your handout, kid, now get."

Byron spun on his heel and ran from the house, leaving the bread and almost knocking Seria over in the process. She gasped. "Mason! Why would you say that?"

Oh, boy. Not a good move. Mason clenched his teeth to keep from saying more he would regret. "His staring got the better of me."

"He doesn't know you, Mason. He's curious."

He bit back a scoff. "Are you sure he's not hoping for another handout?"

Seria shook her head with a dark frown. "He works harder in his eight years than most grown men have their whole lives, and he wouldn't think of asking for anything."

Stop talking, Mason. But frustration loosened his tongue. "You let him eat you out of house and home. No one should have to put themselves in the poorhouse to take care of a few beggars."

"That's hardly an attitude I would expect of a King's Steward."

Heat spilled down Mason's neck. He was tired of being laid up, hurting all the time, unable to do a thing. And he was fed up acting like a self-righteous, decorous Steward.

"And I suppose I ought to take the counsel of a *washerwoman*?" His voice splintered, burning his throat.

Seria's face flushed and she glared at him. Silence fell, heavy and thick, as he stared her down as well as he could with bleary eyesight. Then she spoke, low and strained. "You know what? I wish someone else would've found you." She stormed out, slamming the door behind her. The little cabin shuddered at the impact.

Mason stared at the door, rage coloring his compromised vision crimson. What an impertinent little wench. She had no idea who she was dealing with. Were he in control of his abilities, she would think twice before talking to him in such a manner.

A smirk tugged at a corner of his mouth. In truth, she wouldn't have the chance to *think* about it at all. He would take care of that as well.

"No matter." He jerked his pillow out and pounded it. Let her sit in the woods and stew about how unchivalrous he was. At the moment, he did not care if she ran and told the fort he was there. Sitting in prison had to be better than being laid up here.

Despite his resolve, sleep would not come to his stiff body. He kept listening for the sound of her footsteps, or worse, the stomping of soldiers' boots. On top of that, the heat surge from his anger had drained him, leaving him chilled and parched. Seria, of course, had not refilled his mug before storming off. "Thanks a lot, girl." He rubbed his gritty eyes.

The thirst clawed at him until he pushed himself up. His lungs constricted at the effort, and sweat popped out on his forehead. He fell back into the bed and clenched the blanket in his fists. It was no use. Despite how much he pushed, he was still too weak.

"You're an idiot." Seria covered her flaming face with her cold hands. She sat on a stump, surrounded by cold, silent trees, and continued her monologue. "You're no better than he is, flying off at him like that." Her mother had always warned her about her temper.

But his attitude and harsh words about Byron shook her. Did he believe charity shouldn't be offered to the less fortunate? How could a Steward feel such a way?

As she sat and wrestled with her anger, she fought the hurt that poked its way into her heart. *Washerwoman.* Her cheeks blazed. That was how everyone saw her. Including a member of the Stewardship.

Doubt wrapped around her until she felt as wrung out as an old rag. What had she gotten herself into? This man would not be on his feet for at least another week, but his recovery could very well stretch out over two or three more. Could she put up with his negative outlook much longer?

Aye, she would. Because it was the right thing to do. That's what healers did. They healed people, and that meant people of less-than-desirable qualities as well.

Besides, what if his attitude was fueled by something else? The thought drew her up short. *That's it!* She should have considered it long ago. The way he guarded himself made it clear. It wouldn't ease the tension that blanketed the room when he was awake, and it didn't make his attitude any easier to deal with, but there may be a reason he hid behind a thick wall.

She pushed herself to her feet and started the trek back through the darkening woods. Fine. She wouldn't fuss over him if he didn't appreciate it. And she wouldn't encourage any more conversations about Byron or their differing views on charity. But she would try to be a little more patient and understanding. It was the least she could do. He was, after all, a Steward. A wounded one, at that. There was no telling what terrible things he might have seen while defending the kingdom.

She paused and stuffed her hurt into a well of resolve before she pushed her door open.

Mason met her gaze with his wary one. His face was still red. "Decided to come back?"

She lifted her chin. *Don't let him rile you.* "It *is* my home, in case you've forgotten."

His jaw shifted. "Nay, I certainly haven't."

"Good."

"Do you think I could get some water? *Please*?"

It didn't escape her notice how he tacked on the last word. Avoiding his open stare, she took the pitcher and set it down on his bedside table.

Mason pursed his lips but said nothing. Seria turned away and busied herself preparing her pallet on the floor. When silence fell, she glanced over. Mason had the pitcher beside him, but the cup still sat on the table.

"I'm fine," he said at her questioning look.

She stopped herself from rushing in to do it for him. "Do you need some help?" At his short nod, she took the pitcher, poured some water, and handed him the mug. Without another word, she went back to her spot on the floor. As soon as he finished, she blew the candle out.

The darkness and silence pressed in on her. Would she ever feel comfortable in her own house again? Maybe not until Mason was recovered and gone.

The night held no sleep for Seria. She rolled over yet again and stared into the dying embers of the flame, unable to sleep. From the sound of the bed creaking, Mason was having a restless night as well. Was he upset by their argument, too? *Not likely.*

When a low groan drifted from Mason's corner, she sat up and peered in his direction. He shifted again and grunted. This was more than his usual unease. She stood up and plodded to the bed in time to see him shove the blanket away, then massage his temples.

"Mason?" She lay a hand over his forehead. His clammy skin burned against her touch, and his heavy, raspy breathing sent her pulse racing. *Oh, no.* She grabbed a rag from her cleaning supplies and dunked it in his pitcher. She soaked his face and neck for several long minutes, but still his face flushed with fever.

It was time to try her mama's special blend of tea. She rushed to heat a pot, but even in his sleep, he wouldn't lay still long enough for her to get more than a few drops in him.

Why had she not seen this coming?

Because you missed it while taking everything he said so personally. Her heart sank, remembering his flushed cheeks before bed. No wonder he had been so irritable. And instead of realizing the true cause for his mood, she had left him alone.

Some kind of healer she had turned out to be.

The night dragged on while Seria kept her diligent vigil at his bedside, bathing his face with cool water. But Mason's fever still raged. He tossed and turned, his clothes soaked with perspiration. In a short time, he was delirious and rambling in his sleep.

Seria chewed her lip raw as she watched over him, worry clawing at her. "This cursed, drafty shack." She cast a disdainful look around the one room. The nights were still quite cold, and the wind rattled at the shutters. It was no wonder he had fallen ill, especially with his body already weakened by his injuries, and with him pushing himself so hard, he had not given himself time to heal.

Mason moaned. "I gotta... get outta here."

"Shh." Seria exchanged the cloth on his head for a fresh one. He was talking out of his head, but she continued murmuring to him, hoping her voice would cut through his confusion.

His hand twitched. Seria tried to tuck it under the blanket, but he shoved it away, still mumbling.

"Gotta get... outta here."

She pressed a new rag to his forehead. "Come on, Mason. Stay with me, all right? You're going to get over this. You'll be back with your Stewards before you know it, and then you can take care of those Darkmen."

A grimace passed over his face. "Nay...Bruin...Jader."

Seria frowned. His words made no sense, and he grew more restless.

He gave a sudden cry. "Liam!" Shaking his head against the pillow, he grabbed at the blanket.

Seria fought the unease working its way up her chest. "Easy, Mason." What if he started thrashing about? There was no way she could hold him down. It was too dark and far to run to the fort for help from the Stewards. She could run and ask someone from Cadence, but the risk of leaving him alone at this point, even for a little while, was too great. She had to get some of the tea down him. But with the way he resisted, it was nearly impossible.

Pulling herself away from the bed, Seria pulled out some long pieces of scrap material from a basket under the window. Shoving away her distaste for what she had to do, she tied his feet down to the bed, then his hands. It was a difficult task with him tossing, but she managed.

Then, she mixed a pot of fresh tea. Her mother had taught her the recipe when Seria was thirteen. It was most effective when served hot and fresh, and it was her last hope of getting Mason's fever to break. As soon as the tea was at the right temperature so it wouldn't burn him, she poured some into a mug.

"Mason, I've gotta get some of this into you." She sat on the bed beside him, catching his head under one arm. Holding him as still as she could, she brought the mug to his lips. He struggled and tried to pull away, spilling some of the hot liquid on the pillow beside him. Seria set her chin and tried again, tightening her hold on him.

"Come on." She grunted as she used every ounce of strength to keep him from turning away. She watched in satisfaction as some of the tea made its way into his mouth. He coughed and gagged, and she waited for him to settle down before doing it once more. She managed to get half the cup down before she ran out of energy to hold him anymore. She would try it again in an hour.

Fighting off the weariness that came over her, she resumed sponging his face. Rest could come later. For now, Mason needed her. With every minute that dragged by, and his fever did not break, her anxiety heightened. Would the tea be enough?

Had she failed her first patient?

19

Seek not the praise of the fallible.
But seek to please the Eternal Light.
-The Sacred Code

The sun had begun its descent when Eric crossed through the back gates, headed for the training grounds. He glanced down at the green, oiled leather jumpsuit he wore—standard training attire for Stewards. His quiver was slung over his back, his bow held loosely in his hand.

It was warm, but not uncomfortably so. A breeze brushed over his bare arms. It was late to be practicing, but that was his intention.

Despite his best efforts, relations were still strained with the knights. If it wasn't for Gus, Eric would stop visiting the infirmary altogether. It didn't do any good. Some of the militia reservists took their cue from the Stewards. Though no one acted in disrespect, their resentment rubbed at him.

Maybe his father was wrong. Perhaps he should go back to Calla and appoint Dudley or Braylee to step into Uralis' role. They had the wisdom and experience to lead the army, and the Stewards trusted them.

In the meantime, Eric avoided crowds and kept to himself. He ate meals in his room and trained in the archery field hours after drills ended, feeling like a complete coward.

Squinting against the evening sunlight, he topped the slight hill. His steps faltered at the small crowd gathered around the practice range at the base of the hill. A crowd of knights. Stewards, to be exact.

He turned and tried to slip away unnoticed, but Lionel Percy, one of his faithful supporters, called out.

"Your Highness, come join us for a friendly game!"

Hiding the sigh working its way from his lungs, Eric waved and began the trek down to where they stood. He gave a collective nod, aware of the shifting mood.

Lionel spoke again. "Some of the officers have been at this for two hours. I was eliminated after the first round." His face shone with good sportsmanship. "I'm not the marksman some of these men are. Come throw your bow in."

Awkwardness invaded his body. But he heard himself respond with, "Of course."

A murmur rose and fell. Some of the men didn't look pleased, but others shrugged and readied their bows.

Draven Kilton began packing up. "I think I'll pull out now."

"Aw, stay, Lieutenant." Lionel's forehead wrinkled. "You're the last one left in our platoon for this round."

Draven sent him a crooked grin. "Best to pull out while I'm ahead then. Wouldn't want to embarrass myself in front of the prince. Or embarrass him."

A low rumble of laughter swept over the group. Dampness coated the inside of Eric's suit as he forced a weak smile. "I have no wish to infringe upon your game."

"No infringement. I was leaving anyway." But Draven didn't look at Eric as he gathered his things.

Eric stepped aside as the other man said his goodbyes and left. A few of his men followed his lead, as well as Sgt Ollen Knavis, who was not in his platoon. Eric had the crazy impulse to order them to stay, to assert his authority. Instead, he stood there and wished the ground would swallow him. Despite his excuse, Draven's actions were clear. He had no interest in fraternizing with his new commandant.

"Well, then, let's go on without them." Lionel's frown accentuated his words. "Prince Eric, would you like to lead this round?"

A path was cleared for him as he stepped to the spot. A faint ray of optimism attached itself to his spirit. This was his chance to prove himself. Eric had always excelled in archery, and he was confident in his ability. These men needed to see his capabilities, needed to be able to see him as a warrior and a leader. This could be the first step in earning their respect.

The target stood yards away in front of the mountain wall, looking quite small. He pulled out an arrow, its red feathers quivering as he set the nock against the bowstring. Bringing it up close to his face, he eyed the target. Then paused. The arrow shot forward, burying its head near the edge of the board. Nowhere near the center of the target.

His breath left him in a rush. A miss! Eric, the star of his archery class, had blundered his first shot in the most important match he had ever been in. Uralis would have given him the worst tongue lashing.

He could hear the mutters behind him. His face heated as he stepped back to let the next man take his turn.

Lionel was quick to wave it off. "Don't worry. Every man gets three chances. You'll get it the next time."

But he didn't make it the next round. Eric ground his teeth as he watched the arrow miss the board completely. What was wrong with him? What must these men think of him now? All he was proving was that he could not shoot straight. How could he lead them into battle?

Again, Lionel seemed to sense how much weight Eric had put into the competition. "It's not easy trying to outshoot your rivals. I never do well with this kind of challenge. I assume I'll be outmatched in the first round or so. Then if I last longer, I've exceeded my expectations." He chuckled.

Eric forced a smile. He appreciated the young man's attempt, but his neck tightened as his turn came around again. Gripping the bow, he focused on the target, tension paralyzing his arm muscles. Sweat poured and impeded his vision. His drive to impress was smothering his skill. He knew without trying that he would miss again. *Lambient, help me.*

He would not win these men by trying to best them at a game he was sure to lose.

Letting out a long exhale, he raised the bow and released the bowstring. Rather than letting the arrow shoot forward, his mind held it in midair for a brief moment. With an exaggerated move, Eric stretched his arm, pointing to the board. "Hit the target." The arrow made huge, sweeping circles until it landed dead center.

Eric dropped his arm and looked back at the men. "Does that count?"

The silence stretched like the tension between his shoulder blades. Then a snigger and a laugh. Chuckles swept over the crowd, but they lacked the sting of arrogance. The pressure lifted as the men exchanged good-natured laughs. A few even cheered. Lionel beamed like the whole thing was his idea.

Eric wiped the moisture from his face and shrugged. "Not my best day."

20

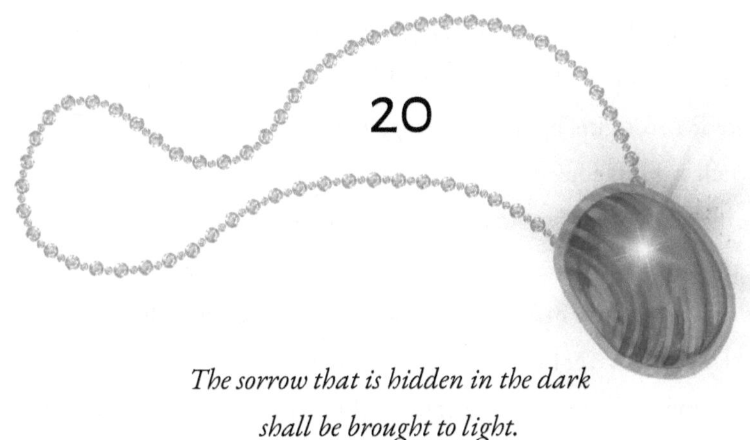

Mason rolled onto his back and blinked up at the ceiling. The cool, pale glow of dawn shone through the crack in the window shutters. He felt as weak as a newborn lamb, but why? Shouldn't his injuries be on the mend? He took inventory. His side didn't hurt as much, and for the first time since awakening in Seria's cabin, his head no longer ached.

It's about time.

The cabin was quiet. Too quiet. Raising on his elbows, he looked around and spotted Seria curled on the floor, sound asleep.

The action drained him, and he rested back on the pillow again. Why was he so tired? And why was Seria still asleep? She was always up and busy by the time he awoke, ready to launch into the first topic of conversation that popped into her mind when she spotted him.

The quiet wouldn't last for long. Once she was up, she would go on and on about the Stewards again. The prospect left him with a bad taste. What kind of fool risked her life to sneak in the middle of a battlefield to pull a no-good Steward from death's grip?

You thought it pretty plucky when you believed she had done it for a Darkman.

The thought drew him up short. Foolish or not, she still proved her mettle. And she had saved his life. How many young women would be so bold? Most girls her age were giggling, small-minded girls who relied on their parents for every need and want, until they found a man to take care of them. None would be able to survive on their own, much less care for an invalid. For one so young and foolish, she was capable.

But does she have to be so annoying? A long-suffering sigh deflated him. He glanced down at her on the floor again. His vision was clearer, though a slight mist still clung to it. But he could see her long blonde hair fanned out over the ratted blanket she had pulled up to her chin. Behind those lids hid green eyes that could snap like embers in a fire if she was riled. The dim morning light concealed the freckles that dotted her face.

He frowned. How on earth did he know that? His mind flashed back to her leaning inches from his face until he could see her features. Faint freckles sprinkled across her nose and cheeks.

The thought made his mouth twist with amusement. What a girlish attribute that most ladies despised. He doubted Seria even knew they were there.

Her chest rose and fell in a deep sigh. *Boy, she must be worn out.* No surprise, the way she made herself available and fussed over him because she thought he was a Steward. And all without a word of complaint.

Well, almost. Unless he said mean things about the beggar boy.

Their disagreement rushed to the forefront of his mind. Why did that feel so long ago? He could not remember anything past the moment she put the candle out. Other than Seria's constant presence throughout the night.

A soft moan caught his ear. Seria stirred and sat up, rubbing her cheek and still half-asleep. Her hair hung in a riot around her, and her dress was a wrinkled mess. A deep crease ran down one side of her face.

One word floated through Mason's mind as he arrested the smile threatening to break. *Adorable.*

After a long moment, her eyes cleared, then widened. She turned and froze when she saw him watching. "You're awake!"

"Aye." His voice sounded like gravel.

Seria jumped to her feet and reached for the mug of water on the table. "Here." She helped him take a sip. "How are you feeling?"

He pushed himself up with a loud exhale. "Like I've been trampled by a runaway team." He rubbed his face with his palms. "What happened?"

"You developed a bad fever last night."

No wonder he had no energy left. Sitting up alone drained him.

Seria let out a loud exhale. "You had me worried there for a while. You've been pushing yourself too hard, and then your body couldn't fight the infection. I couldn't get your fever down for a few hours. Finally tried one of my mother's healing remedies, dryweed root and daisy seeds. And it worked. Or at least it did once I forced some down your stubborn throat." She smiled. "I never met a man who pitched a bigger fit about taking his medicine. I had to tie you down."

His brows went up. "You tied me down?"

She gave him a teasing wink. "You want anything?"

He angled his head. "I'm a little hungry."

Seria smiled. "Even for oats?"

A weak grin appeared. "Beats starving, I guess." He leaned back against the pillows as Seria worked in the kitchen.

She was right. This was his own fault for pushing too hard, adding more strain to his tired, hurting body. He knew the importance of rest after a major injury so that the body could fully recover.

"Here you go." Seria offered him a heaping bowl of steaming oats. Then she took the chair again with her bowl. "You know how to keep a girl on her toes."

He took a big bite, his stomach hollow. Even the plain oats tasted good today. Had they grown on him? Mason shrugged off the notion as he chewed. Nonsense.

"I worried for a while I was going to have to send word somewhere that you had fallen ill."

He paused long enough to say, "I'm glad you didn't."

Seria studied him with an unreadable expression. "Well, it all worked out, so I am, too, now." She looked down at her bowl and stirred. "You certainly had a lot going on in that head of yours last night. You were going on about Darkmen and Stewards, and even Bruin at one point."

Mason's heart stuttered, then raced. His bite turned to tasteless goo, stuck on his tongue. How much had he shared?

Seria went on. "I've heard of Bruin. Isn't he one of Jader's generals?"

"Something like that." He struggled to maintain a casual tone as he realized again the precarious position he was in.

What if he had said too much? One wrong statement, spoken in his confusion, could have proven disastrous, and he might have awakened in a prison cell. His lungs emptied at how vulnerable he had been, how close he came to being exposed. Especially after their confrontation, when doubts could have been planted in Seria's mind.

His mouth went dry, and he gulped more water from his cup. It was time to ensure Seria's belief. He had to work harder to keep her trust, be more convincing, lest she suspect he was not who she thought he was. Something slithered in his gut at having to perfect his act.

"Who's Liam?"

The room tipped, and he jerked. "What?"

"You hollered for Liam at one point. Is he another Steward?"

"Nay." The answer shot out of him before he could stop it. "He's not." There was no way he would explain who Liam was. Doing so would open up a whole new set of questions he wasn't ready to answer.

Seria looked like she wanted to ask more but instead glanced down at her wrinkled dress. "My, I'm a mess. I've never slept so long. I slept like the dead. It's a good thing you didn't need me." Her words came in rapid succession, conveying her embarrassment.

Act like a Steward. He cleared his throat and his mind and launched into his ongoing charade. "I wouldn't have dared to wake you, after what you did for me." He grimaced. Did that come across as stiff to her as it did to him?

Her cheeks tinted, and she rubbed at her skirt. "Look at me," she murmured. "You're not supposed to wake up first and see me like this."

He smiled at the scolding. "I'm sorry."

She shot him a sharp look. "You don't look sorry."

He dropped the smile. "Believe me, I've seen worse in the morning."

"I can't imagine how." She picked her blanket up off the floor and folded it, a frown turning her lips down.

Feeling more relieved than hungry now, Mason set his half-empty bowl aside. "I'm starting to get tired; I think I'll—"

"Sleep a while. That's a good idea." Her back was to him as she continued to smack at the stubborn folds in her dress, and she sounded more annoyed than concerned.

For the first time in years, he was tempted to laugh.

As the day waned, however, he became aware of a shift in the atmosphere. After her initial relief over his recovery, Seria didn't fuss over him as she used to. In fact, she avoided talking to him when she could, though she muttered nonstop to herself.

The friction of their confrontation had eased, but a thin veil of tension still hung between them. And though it galled him, it was up to him to smooth things over. Because she expected it of him. Because he was supposed to be a Steward.

Bitterness sat on his tongue at what he had to do to keep the peace and Seria's trust. He glanced over to where she worked on another pile of laundry, folding each article and placing it in a large bag. "I..."

Seria paused in her work. "Did you need something?"

"I feel I owe you an apology." The words had to be dragged out. "I was wrong to speak to you that way."

"I appreciate that. Thank you."

Why did he get the feeling she expected more? His thoughts darted to and fro, trying to grab something else that would erase the taut lines in her face.

Oh. The beggar kid.

He gritted his teeth. "And I shouldn't have snapped at the beg—" He bit the word back before it slipped through. "Boy." Seria would doubt his sincerity if he called Byron a beggar.

Her stiffness melted into a soft smile. "I'm glad to hear that, but I don't think I'm the one who needs to."

Wait, was she implying he should apologize to the vagrant kid? He gripped the blanket in his fists. Was this act worth this kind of humiliation? "Aye, you're right. And I will tell him, first chance I get."

Another smile lit her face until her eyes sparkled. "I'm sure he'll be around soon. He won't let one bad exchange keep him away."

Sure, he wouldn't. Where else would he get free food?

"Byron absolutely loves Sanjo. He'll come back to see his little donkey friend."

Mason forced a smile.

Seria finished folding the breeches in her hands, tucked them safely away in the sack, and then took her seat at his bedside. Her smile was gone, and she sat for a moment, twisting her fingers. Mason tensed. Wasn't his apology enough?

She finally inhaled and looked up. "The fact is, Mason, I owe you an apology."

What was this? Mason hid a grin and leaned back against his pillow and gave her his complete attention. "Whatever for?" This would be interesting.

She hesitated. "I shouldn't have stormed off on you. To be honest, I was a little..." she grimaced, "put out with your outlook on life. You being a Steward, it took me by surprise, and I didn't handle our differences very well."

Mason gave a slow nod. This was good. Maybe she would say she was sorry for being so annoying, too.

"I knew better than to act like that," she said. "My parents raised me to accept people's differences, to respect them, regardless. I wasn't fair to you."

Her gaze was fixed on his face. Open and honest. He didn't have to read her thoughts to see her sincerity. Whatever gratification he had felt drained away. "Don't trouble yourself."

But she wasn't done. "There's always a reason people take on their beliefs, why they act the way they do. And it hit me."

A squiggle swam through his torso, and he scratched the back of his neck. An apology from her wasn't as much fun as he had thought.

"You must have seen something awful."

His breath snagged. "What?"

Her countenance darkened as she went on. "I should've seen it before now, a man in your position. But I do understand." Her shoulders lifted and dropped. "I may not know a lot. But I do know that life's not always fair." A shadow descended over her usual sunshine-and-roses demeanor. "Sometimes it knocks us down and completely changes us. And when that happens, it leaves us a little emptier. We see the world differently. We live differently. And sometimes we fight differently."

An image of swords and Stewards flashed through his mind as he stared at her. How did she do that? He was living a lie in front of her. She knew nothing about him. Nothing. But somehow in her naïve, short-sighted view, she had managed to make him feel more exposed and vulnerable than he had experienced in a long time. What exactly had he said aloud while sick and feverish?

She slapped her lap, startling him out of his reverie. "Anyway, I wanted to get that out there. So, am I forgiven?" And just like that, her features were lit with their usual sunny sentiment. While he was left in the dark. Which was where he wanted to be, wasn't it?

"Of course. You're forgiven." His words faded.

She smiled again. "Thank you. How 'bout we let this be a new start for both of us?" She held her hand out.

He gave a quick nod. "Sure. Sounds great." He reached up to shake her hand. She grasped his firmly and gave it a squeeze that traveled up his arm and into his chest.

"Now, how about some dinner?"

He must have responded, because she made a beeline for the kitchen, talking nonstop as she cut up the vegetables for another stew. Mason dismissed the memories that begged to be visited again. Seria couldn't know how close her words had made their mark. Because no matter how wrong she was in her beliefs about him, she was right about one thing. Maybe two.

He had seen something terrible. And it had changed him.

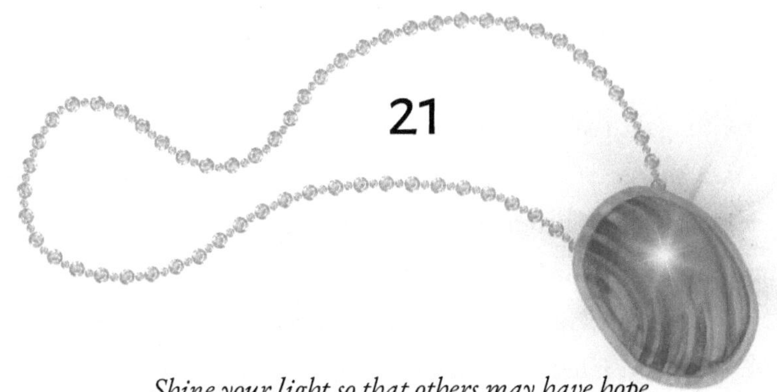

21

Mason shuffled to the window, careful not to put too much weight on his healing leg, and leaned against the wall. After being bedridden for two weeks, his strength was beginning to return, though walking across the room once still exhausted him. The wound in his side still throbbed and ached, letting him know he needed more time before he could get out of here. Before someone discovered his presence.

He wore plain, homespun clothing from Seria's trunk, his own too torn up to salvage. His arms felt bare without his bracers, but they were piled in the corner along with his boots and the blasted Steward armor that put him in this mess in the first place.

Squinting against the bright sunlight, he spotted Seria in the yard, bent over a large tub. His vision was clearing up as well, and he could make out her flushed cheeks and arms bare to the elbows as she scrubbed the clothes across the washboard. For someone so tiresome, she could be appealing to look at. Why had he ever thought her plain?

If he was honest, the last few days had not been so trying. Seria did not cater to his every whim like she used to, and whatever awe she felt for him seemed to be gone. How it happened made no difference to him, but at least she was trying not to get on his nerves. The tension of the first week had lifted.

Seria hung the last of the laundry on a piece of twine hanging between the shack and a tree and headed for the door. As soon as she stepped inside, movement outside caught Mason's eye. Byron emerged from hiding and approached the washtub. The boy put his hands against it and pushed with all his might, his feet sliding across the wet grass in his effort. With a great heave, he knocked it over, spilling soapy water on the ground.

"What're you watching out there?" Seria moved to stand beside him, her arm brushing against his.

He stepped back, out of reach. "Your little hired hand."

She smiled as Byron gave a suspicious look around, then plodded around the side of the house on dirty, bare feet, where Sanjo's shed stood. "He doesn't like me to watch. But he always knows when I'm finished, and he gets it done."

"And for that, you pay him a loaf of bread?"

"That's right."

"But why trouble yourself?" He turned to face her, careful to keep his tone neutral. "Why not make his family responsible for their own?"

She cocked her head as she looked up at him. "They are responsible for their own. They're hardworking, proud people that have run into a strand of bad luck."

"I don't believe in luck. People make their lives better or worse of their own accord."

"Mayhap that's the way it's supposed to work, but sometimes things happen beyond our control."

Mason waved his hand at the sparse living quarters. "You barely have enough for yourself."

"I do it because it's the right thing to do." Her tone was uncompromising.

"Did you ever think you might make things worse if you always step in to help those who need to look out for themselves? We're only required to take care of ourselves." Why did he bother trying to reason with her? What did he care about how she spent her time and resources?

"If I'd followed that line of reasoning, I would've spared myself a heap of trouble and left you lying in the woods." She cocked her head again. "But then again, you might have a point."

He slanted her a look. "Ha, ha, funny."

She flashed him a smug grin and flounced away.

Mason shook his head, not used to this lighthearted teasing she tossed at him. The banter he got from Shon was different, more brash and crude.

"You know, you keep it up, and you might be able to go out into Cadence soon."

Seria's statement jerked him from his thoughts. "Cadence?"

"Aye, get some fresh air and sunshine. The exercise will be good for you."

Mason stared at her. "How far is it?"

"It's across the bridge and up the hill a bit." She stopped to put her hands on her hips. "You mean you had no idea all this time where you've been?"

He rubbed his thumb across his fingertips, trying to calm his speeding heart rate. "Well, I didn't know where you dragged me to. I was not myself for a while."

"And I never told you?" She clicked her tongue. "I apologize."

What were the odds? Some good could come from his setback after all. He had a rare opportunity. He was practically *in* Cadence. And no one knew him. He could blend in with the rest of the civilians, study the layout of the place, and learn what he could about its guard. Maybe even get inside the fort. Then he could take it all back to Commander Bruin, as he had intended in the beginning. His time here did not have to be a complete waste after all.

"Are you still with me?"

Mason snapped his attention back to her. "That sounds like a good idea. You could give me a tour."

She frowned. "A tour? Aren't you based here?"

Blast. "Well... this was my first jaunt here. I still don't know the town well."

"Your first time in battle, and you get yourself nearly killed."

There was that look of sincerity again. The one that always made him want to squirm. "Aye. Just my luck."

She tossed him a victorious grin. "I thought you didn't believe in luck."

He rolled his eyes. One would think someone who talked so much would eventually run out of rejoinders.

"In any case, I'd be happy to show you around. As soon as you're up to it."

Mason worked to control his eagerness. He could last that long. And by the time he left, he would have enough information for Jader's army to break through the Gateway and into the Old Realm. "Perhaps in a few days. Thank you."

Her lips quirked into another smile. "Do you want some help getting back to bed?"

His initial response was to refuse. But his legs were beginning to quiver, so he gave a short nod. She tucked herself against his side and wrapped an arm around his waist. The smell of fresh air and soap assailed his senses as she guided him back to his corner of the room.

"How does it feel?" she asked as they approached the bed.

At this proximity, he saw her face clearly, but trying to read her thoughts was like trying to see through a wall and made his head hurt. Her eyes were every bit as bright and green as he remembered, but they offered no more answers than the freckles, and she didn't have many of those. Just a few over her nose.

That nose wrinkled, and he jerked his head away. Great. Now he was staring like an idiot. "Feels fine."

Relief swept through him like a chill breeze when she stepped away.

"Are you sure you didn't overdo it?"

He gave a single nod but refused to look at her. What was his problem? His boredom must be getting the better of him if he was getting caught up counting the freckles on his hostess' nose.

Seria kept a careful watch over her patient as the afternoon wore on, but Mason did not seem to be in any more discomfort than usual. He was in a strange mood, however, and rarely made eye contact.

A knock interrupted their supper, and a look of wariness crossed Mason's face. Seria checked that the breastplate was covered before opening the door, praying it was not Ira again.

"Lena!" Without thinking, she opened the door wider and stepped back.

Her friend gave her a wide smile and glanced over at Mason sitting on the bed. "I apologize for intruding."

Mason's bowl sat forgotten on his lap, and he stared back at Lena, his features strained.

"It's no intrusion," Seria hurried to say. "We were finishing up. This is my patient, Mason."

Lena gave him a nod, her expression open and friendly. "It's a pleasure. I'm sure Seria has been treating you well. She's quite the expert at tending to injuries and infirmities."

Mason's Adam's apple bobbed. "Aye. She's done well by me." His tone was cool, despite the compliment.

Lena turned back to Seria. "I won't stay long, but I wonder if I could speak to you for a moment?"

"Of course." Seria met Mason's look with a slight frown and stepped outside. Would it have killed him to be a little more polite with her friend?

"Is something wrong?" she asked when she caught up to where Lena stopped a few steps from the entrance.

"I do apologize again, but I assumed you haven't heard what is happening tonight."

"Nay, I suppose not."

Lena's face grew serious. "The Royal Army is riding out tonight."

"You mean, they're leaving?"

"Nay. The word is they're investigating a report of trouble, but they're preparing for another potential attack in the Gateway."

Seria put her hand on her chest. "Not again."

"I'm afraid so. They're leaving at sundown, so a lot of the civilians will be gathering to wave them off. I thought I'd let you know, in case you wanted to join us."

"Aye, thank you."

Lena's gaze flitted back to Seria's cabin. "I hope I didn't come across as rude to your patient, but I wasn't sure you'd want him to hear about it. At least not from a stranger."

"I appreciate your considering him. I'm sorry if he came across a bit unfriendly."

Lena shrugged. "I see all kinds in the fort." She squeezed Seria's hand. "I'll see you at sundown."

Seria thanked her and exhaled, her heart going out to the prince and all the Stewards potentially riding into another battle. *Lambient, be with them. Protect them.*

Her mind went to the man in her cabin. Mason would want to know what had transpired, even if he was still far too unable to do anything.

She entered the room to see him limping back to the bed from the direction of the window. Had he been watching them?

His expression was unreadable but tense as he sat on the cot and faced her again. "Problem?"

"Aye, I'm afraid there is." Mason would not appreciate her prolonging the news. "The Stewards received news of trouble, so they're riding out at sundown to investigate."

His face blanched, and his jaw clenched. He stood and cast a quick look all around the room.

"It's nowhere around here, Mason. To be honest, I don't know where they're going. Lena didn't say. And in truth, it may be nothing but a faulty report. In any case, there's nothing you can do to help right now."

"I don't want to sit here and do nothing." He growled the words past clenched teeth.

"The townspeople are going out to wave them off. It's too great a walk for you, but we could wave from here."

His brows crashed. "Wave?"

"Aye." Seria hurried to the trunk and pulled out one of her mother's scarves. "It's something that got started by civilians of the Gateway when the soldiers ride out. It's our simple way of showing our support and sending our prayers with them." She yanked a scrap of tan material out. "You can wave this if you want."

"I don't want to *wave,* Seria! I want to get out of here."

His sharp answer stopped her short. He stood like a stiff board, fists curled at his side, heat glittering in his eyes.

"I-I'm sorry. I suppose that does sound silly to you." Her apology did nothing to erase the terse lines on his reddened face. "I understand how you must feel not being able to help, Mason, but—"

"You don't know anything." He shook his head and gave a sharp gesture at the door. "Just go, Seria. Leave me be."

Unsure what to do, she stood rooted to the spot, clutching the scarf in trembling fingers. She had expected disappointment or frustration, but this was more than that. This was anger, anger at being left out.

There wasn't much time left, so she moved to the door, though the show of support had been soured for her. She took one more look at Mason before she left, but he was sitting on the bed, his face turned away.

With a sigh, she closed the door behind her and headed for the bridge. At the last minute, she decided not to join the townspeople. Lena was the only one who would miss her, and Seria no longer felt like socializing.

Not that this was a social gathering. She stopped on the far side of the bridge, her stomach twisting into a knot as visions from Rackson came back to her. Was Rackson's fate to be repeated in another town?

She could hear the buzzing up the hill as men, women, and children gathered in front of the cottages. It sounded like they were having a party. What was the matter with them? Did they not realize how serious this was? The Stewards could be locked in another battle. They could die tonight, and Cadence was treating it like a celebration.

They had not experienced what she had, huddled on the top of that hill in Rackson. Their vision had not been stained with the horrors of war and death, or their nostrils tainted with the repulsive mix of blood, sweat, and smoke.

Seria crossed her arms in front of her to ward off the chill beginning at her core. She was all too familiar with death. It arrived before one was ready, ripping families apart and taking young lives before they'd had a chance to begin.

Maybe it was a good thing Mason had not decided to come. She turned to look back at her little cabin. He stood in the doorway, bracing himself so he would not fall. A faint stirring of hope lit the dark edges of her soul. It was not the honorable way he wished to stand with the Stewards, but maybe he would feel gratified to see them off. Honor did not always happen on the battlefield but in small moments of shared support from those left behind.

Should she go back and stand with him? After a brief inner debate, she decided against it. This was something Mason had to deal with on his own.

Fighting the nerves that threatened to paralyze her, she faced the dirt road the Stewards would travel. As the sun lowered itself in a bed of reds, pinks, and purples in the deepening blue of the sky, she did the only thing she could for the Stewards heading out into the night.

She prayed.

22

The message had arrived a short while ago from one of their concealed Steward allies in the New Realm. Movement and rumors concerning another small town in the southern region of the Gateway did not point to a full-scale attack, but the source was a trusted one, and Eric had learned not to underestimate Jader.

He stood over the table and pored over the map with his captains, his shoulders taut. The lieutenants hung back from the senior officers but were present for the deliberations.

"We don't want to stir up a hornet's nest by riding in too strong," Dudley said. "But we want to be prepared."

Eric nodded and tapped the map. "If we ride out tonight and take the direct pass, we should get there by midnight."

Braylee nodded and relief filled Eric that he had the captains' support. He was already feeling unsteady enough in this leadership role.

"How many men do you wish to take?" Braylee asked.

Eric rubbed his jaw as anxiety mounted. In his mind, he could see the Shadowmen he faced in Rackson. "I think the militiamen should stay behind."

The shuffle of feet from the nearby lieutenants told him that not everyone agreed.

"You fear we'll face Shadowmen again?"

Dudley's question made Eric cringe, though he doubted Dudley meant anything disparaging by it. "We know Jader is utilizing them. And we don't know how many he has. The militia does not have the same advantage against them as the Stewards."

It was hard to read the older men's faces, but they did not seem turned off by his counsel. Eric turned to the other group. "If you have any concerns, feel free to declare them now."

Draven spoke up. "You have to travel past forest country to get into Cuthrel. What about the threat of grizlons if you take so few men?"

"They should be hibernating in the north by now," Dudley said. "Cuthrel is out of the way of their usual hunting grounds."

"There is no evidence that Cuthrel is in any danger of attack," Eric added. "We want to be prepared, so we will take one platoon and leave two behind on call."

Draven still did not look convinced, but he said nothing more.

"Then are we set?" Eric asked, resting his hand on Lavrynth.

"Aye, sir," Dudley answered for them.

"Then let's go."

Draven spoke again. "My men are already saddled and ready." A hint of pride leaked into his tone.

Eric caught a shared look between the captains before Braylee pushed away from the table. "Lt. Draven, your platoon will stay behind with Capt. Dudley."

Draven stiffened. "I beg your pardon, sir?"

"Half of my brigade will ride with us part of the way on standby, but I need you to remain here."

"But sir!"

Braylee stood. "Are you questioning me, Lieutenant?"

Draven halted his objection in the face of Braylee's scowl. "Nay, sir."

"Good. There's no need for the whole brigade. Someone has to remain behind."

From the way Draven squared his jaw, it was clear he was not appeased with this explanation.

"All right then, if there's nothing more, let's get your men ready to go," Dudley said.

Braylee's half-brigade was soon mounted and ready. Eric sat astride Oakley staring back at the men behind him. It had been a while since he had been in charge of an operation.

And the last one had not gone so well.

Curling his fingers around the handle of his Beacon, he pushed the thought away. This was not a battle they were riding to. At least he prayed it was not.

Braylee joined him at the front, sitting tall atop Uralis' prancing steed. At the reminder of his mentor, Eric ground his teeth. *Lambient, guide my way. Don't let me fail these men or the people of Cuthrel.*

By the time they headed out, many of the civilians of the fort had lined the street, waving flags, banners, headscarves, and kerchiefs. The mood was jubilant, like the people had no doubt the Stewards would be victorious. Or rather, they had no idea what the Stewards would face.

It was the same outside the gates. The town of Cadence waved them off in a grand show of support and cheer. Eric appreciated the gesture, done, for the most part, in sincerity, but he could not help but cringe.

How did these people know that some of the men behind him would not be killed before the night was out?

As he followed the standard-bearer through the narrow streets of Cadence, his attention was drawn to a lone figure down the hill outside of the town. A blonde woman, too far to make out clearly, stood apart from everyone else and waved her cloth like the rest.

But it was her stance that grabbed him. She stood hunched over, with one arm wrapped around her waist. Waving the Stewards off seemed to bring her sorrow, rather than the excitement of her fellow townspeople.

Eric lifted a hand to acknowledge her. She paused and responded with her free hand. Then Eric spurred Oakley to a trot and passed her by. The troops behind him followed suit until the hoofbeats vibrated across the bridge over the creek, and they left Cadence behind.

It was a small moment, one Eric doubted anyone else noticed. But the girl's actions brought a comforting truth to the forefront of his mind.

Not everyone considered war a cause for celebration.

Cuthrel, the Gateway

Eric kept at a steady but unhurried pace. Scouts rode on ahead to scope out the situation in Cuthrel. So far, reports had been reassuring. No sign of trouble.

The scenery around them changed as the night wore on. The trees fell away to rockier terrain as they swung south around the cluster of bluffs and escarpments that bunched around the opening of the Slate Mountains. They rode parallel to the Slates, with the woods and hills to the west, rising like a black wave under the full moon.

Eric took comfort that the stars were out, twinkling like jewels in an ocean of dark sky. Head tipped back, he soaked in the glow of the night lights.

"Harlon returns."

Braylee's statement pulled him back to the ground in time for Harlon to rein his horse to a stop in front of him.

"Cuthrel lies beyond the next slope," he said. "All looks peaceful."

Eric nodded. "Good. How long?"

"About an hour's ride more."

At Eric's nod, Harlon rode back toward Cuthrel. They would meet him again at the border.

Cuthrel soon lay before them, silent and sleeping, nestled in a shallow ravine. Beyond the gulley, boulders of all sizes and shapes lay scattered over the land, like someone had tossed a handful of pebbles on the ground and left them there.

Those stones could provide almost as much cover as a forest full of trees.

Eric chewed his cheek as they approached the town, watchful and tense. Many of the cabins were dark, the inhabitants asleep and oblivious to their arrival.

Harlon waited for them at the town's edge. "The report is the same all around. No sign of Darkmen or trouble in general."

That's what Eric wanted, but it opened the question as to why they were there. "Any sign of our source?"

"None, Sire."

Eric's fingers tingled, and trepidation snagged him. Something wasn't right. He rubbed Oakley's neck, still peering through the darkness. "Leave a squad here. Let's ride around Cuthrel."

Braylee looked behind him. "Sgt. Ollen, take your squad in the town and keep watch."

"Aye, sir."

Ollen led his twenty men out of formation at a trot down through the main street in the middle of Cuthrel. Eric could hear them taking positions at various spots in the town. Watching and waiting.

"Something feels off," he confided to Braylee as they took the rest of the Stewards around. "I did not expect an attack, based on the report, but this is too quiet."

"I agree." Braylee's broad face was drawn tight. "If I didn't know any better, I'd think it was an ambush."

The word alone sent alarm through Eric's veins. But as they ventured out into the surrounding area, spreading out as they went, there was no sign of an attack. There was no sign of anyone.

Braylee stopped beside him and scratched his beard. "Maybe the report was faulty."

It was possible, but if that was the case, why had they not heard anything more? "Let's stay close to Cuthrel tonight and stand guard. We'll talk to the town leaders in the morning and see if there have been any disturbances recently."

Braylee gave the call to the knights exploring the area. As they all turned their mounts back, Eric sat still in the saddle. His heartbeat throbbed in his ears. It was too quiet. The earth was poised, ready to shift beneath his feet and shake him to his core.

He breathed out through his nose. *Calm, Eric. You need to stay calm.* There was no sign of trouble for now. "Let's go, Oakley."

His horse blew and threw his head up, ears swiveling. Eric's unease accelerated, and he gripped the reins in sweaty hands. The ground vibrated beneath him. The Stewards looked all around them while their horses danced about nervously.

A deafening roar—high-pitched and grating—sounded through the night, shooting ice down Eric's spine. It was quickly followed by several other howls, then something large crashed through the night, barreling toward the Stewards.

Six monstrous beasts thundered into view under the moonlight. Long, rangy limbs with leathery elbows and two thick, short horns over bearlike heads instantly identified them to Eric. Tremors overtook his hands.

From beside him, Braylee gasped. "Dear skies above. Grizlons."

23

The horses lost their heads in their panic, bolting and fighting the bits. Eric spun Oakley in a tight circle in time to see the grizlon in the front slide to a stop and stand to a mammoth height of twelve feet. It roared, exposing yellow fangs as sharp and deadly as a lion's.

Harlon was the closest, his face blanching at the sight of the beast.

"Fall back!" The yell tore from Eric's throat. But it was too late. The biggest grizlon leaped for Harlon. The horse fell with a scream, and Harlon caught the grizlon's claws full in the abdomen.

There was no time to grieve the fallen man. The other five grizlons were already tearing through his men like cats with mice. Horses fled in terror, with or without their riders. Bloodcurdling screams pierced Eric's soul.

The grizlons shouldn't be here. This wasn't their territory, nor was it their hunting season. They should be migrating to the cool northern hills to sleep through the approaching summer.

One of the monsters broke away and veered for Cuthrel, its black lips twisted in a snarl.

"Don't let them in the town!" Eric shouted, struggling to hold Oakley in place. The citizens of Cuthrel would be helpless against the rage of such brutes. Several Stewards headed it off, turning its wrath on them.

Eric's jaw clenched as another man fell from his saddle. He grabbed his bow and threw an arrow against the nock, bracing Oakley between his thighs. The horse shuddered and squealed but held his position.

Eric steadied his shaking hands. *Please, Lambient, don't let me miss now.*

The arrow flew and buried itself in the grizlon's neck. It let out a furious shriek, but it did not let up in its onslaught.

The Stewards in the back surged forward, their weapons at the ready. Braylee broke away to lead a squad in an assault against one of the grizlons.

Eric started to follow when an arrow whizzed inches from his face. He jerked back, casting a look all around. There was no one in view who would be shooting at him. A misguided Steward shot?

A shadow fell over the land. Eric looked up. A cloud had drifted before the moon, dousing what little light they had.

A Steward nearby peeled off his horse, a dart embedded in his neck. Several others cried out as more arrows found their marks.

What was happening? Eric put another arrow in place but had no idea where to send it. Death and chaos by grizlon filled his sight wherever he looked. What new invisible threat did they face?

Invisible. His blood ran cold. Mercies. There were Shadowmen here.

Lights flashed as Beacons were drawn. Nearby, Braylee's men struggled against their grizlon. Blood poured from its wounds, but none of the men could get close enough to deal a deadly blow. It pounced and trapped a man under his paws.

Eric shot another arrow, catching the beast in the side. It released the man but braced itself for another fight.

Were these things incapable of being killed? They bore the size and strength of a bear, but the agility and speed of a cat, and arrows could not pierce their thick skin deep enough to make a difference.

A growl interrupted his thoughts, and Eric looked straight into the face of another. Cold terror snaked down his back. Oakley reared, and it charged at them. Eric grabbed for his Beacon, but the grizlon rammed them before he could release it from his belt. He flew off of Oakley's back and hit the ground hard, his lungs emptying. He jumped to his feet and spun in time to see the grizlon swipe at Oakley's shoulder with deadly claws. The horse fell under the force of the blow.

Eric finally jerked his light rod free and held it up. Light pierced the darkness around them. The beast turned his way and snarled but was blinded by the radiance. It shook its head and stumbled away.

The sound of approaching horses drew near from behind. Sgt. Ollen led his squad into the midst of the bedlam, all of them wielding their Beacons. The woods were flooded with light as other Stewards finally had a chance to pull their rods out. Braylee took advantage of the moment to drive his sword deep into his grizlon's neck. It let out a deafening scream and fell. The remaining grizlons turned and ran.

Ghostly figures took shape under the growing glow of the Beacons as the Shadowmen became known. They let off another volley of arrows that Eric tried to deflect. Some hit their targets; others dropped harmlessly to the ground. Then the Shadowmen were gone, lost again to the darkness.

A familiar chill settled over Eric, and he looked up to see a gray-headed Shadowman leering at him from behind a cluster of rocks, his fingers wrapped around his stone. The same one who had attacked him in

Rackson. Before Eric could react, Ollen's squad had reached him. The Shadowman stepped back and disappeared into the night.

Braylee had to refrain from dragging his feet as he walked with Eric back to Cuthrel. His body was beaten and weary from battling the grizlon, and his arm stung where a claw had caught it. But he was alive, so he could not complain.

The prince led his horse carefully, coaxing him in soothing tones. Oakley favored his injury but followed obediently.

The citizens of Cuthrel were gathering, all staring at the ragtag bunch of soldiers as they approached. Braylee raised his hand. "We have wounded. Is there a healer?"

The men and women exchanged looks before a white-headed man stepped forward. "I am sorry, but we have no healer here who can help you."

Eric handed the reins to Sgt. Lionel. "I am Prince Eric of Paladin. We encountered grizlons and a band of Shadowmen outside of your town. If there is anyone who can assist the wounded, we would be greatly indebted."

The man bowed his head, then shook it. "I am Modric, mayor of Cuthrel. Again, I'm sorry. There is no one here who can do as you ask."

"You have no healer in Cuthrel at all?"

Modric wiped his hands on his tunic. "This is a small town, Your Highness. We do not have the same advantages of so great a city as your Calla." He still did not answer straight out.

Braylee's attention moved across the faces of the crowd. Many of them stood back with strained features, and others stared back with raised chins. But none of them offered to help. None of them said anything.

Eric's expression reflected the same unease that spread over Braylee's mind. These people were scared. "Has the emperor sent any representatives here recently?" Eric asked.

Modric shook his head. "Nay, Your Highness. We're a peaceful town."

"You've had no trouble of late?"

"None, sir."

Braylee spoke up. "Mayor Modric, our men encountered several grizlons beyond your town. It's very unusual for one grizlon to be spotted so far south during this season, let alone six."

"That is strange, sir, but we've not seen any until now."

"So, you're saying they've only just arrived?" Eric asked.

"It appears that way, aye." Modric clasped and unclasped his hands before him.

He was clearly afraid, but the more they questioned him, the more he maintained his position. There were no healers who could help the Stewards, and they had had no troubles recently.

Eric tried one more time. "Good sir, if your town suffers anything at the hands of Jader's men, we are prepared to defend you or to evacuate you to a safe place. Please consider this if you have any need of it at all."

Modric's cheeks went white. "Nay, sir. I assure you, Cuthrel is well."

Eric looked at the people behind him. "Hear me. Jader is striking out against the Gateway towns. He will set his sights here if he hasn't already. I offer free passage back to the stronghold if anyone fears for their life."

No one moved.

"We appreciate your kind offer, Prince Eric, but we have no reason to leave," Modric said.

After a long moment, Eric gave a single nod. "May we fill our canteens at your well?"

There was a slight hesitation before Modric answered. "Of course, Your Highness. You are welcome to refill before you go."

His last statement made it clear that he did not wish them to stay any longer than they had to.

Eric walked away, his head bowed low. Braylee turned to Ollen. "See that the wounded are cleaned up and prepared for the trip back."

"Aye, sir."

Motioning Lionel to help Ollen, Braylee followed Eric to Oakley's side. Eric gripped the saddle with both hands and pressed his forehead against the seat. "They're scared to death, Braylee, and I can't do anything about it."

"We can't force our help on those who refuse it."

Eric leaned back and touched Oakley's quivering, bloody wound. "The cuts aren't too deep, fortunately. He should recover completely. If we can find someone to help him." Then his face contorted, and he pressed a fist against his mouth. "I should've never come out here,

Braylee. All I did was get our men killed and make things worse for Cuthrel. It was all for naught."

It was a hard blow for anyone, much less the man struggling to resume leadership he had once laid aside. Braylee started to leave him, but then recalled Uralis' last direction to him. Prince Eric had every reason to fold under such weight, but there was too much at stake. "Prince Eric, you did not make any decision without the full support and agreement of your captains, much like Uralis would have done in your place."

Eric's head jerked his way.

"You cannot take the blame for every action that goes awry, even if you are in the lead. This was clearly the work of Jader, and we know he is not one to act randomly. Think this through."

Eric's brow furrowed as he studied the ground. "What were the grizlons doing here? And so many of them?"

"My guess? Those Shadowmen had something to do with that."

"But how?" Eric clasped his hands behind his neck and paced a few steps. "They don't have control over animals, do they?"

"Not that I know of." Braylee chewed the inside of his cheek. "But something drove those beasts here."

Eric's eyes widened, and he clapped once. "They did it in the dark. They could drive them unseen and safe anywhere they wanted."

"It makes sense, but this is more than a day's journey from where they hibernate. How could they keep from being attacked when the sun rose and exposed them?"

"They had help." Eric pointed up. "Bruin Pralus."

"Of course." The dark commander's infamous weather Gift would provide the cloud coverage they needed to keep the Shadowmen concealed.

"So, they're using the grizlons to hold sway over Cuthrel and keep them quiet." Eric sighed as he looked out over the town. Most of the people had dispersed, not wishing to associate with the Stewards.

"But why?" Braylee crossed his arms. "Why Cuthrel? It's out of the way and would be insignificant to Jader."

"Mercies." Eric rubbed his hands over his face, then gave Braylee a grim look. "Our source."

24

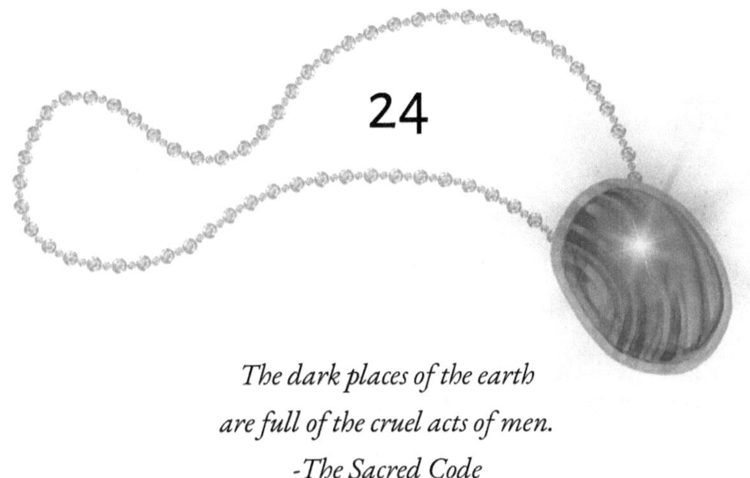

Ignadon, New Realm

Jader folded his hands on his lap as two of Bruin's men hauled a bedraggled man in civilian clothes into the throne room. Bruin led the way, his face set like granite, unmoved by the pleas of the man behind him.

In the back of the room, another Darkman stood, gripping a young boy by the elbow.

Bruin stopped before Jader and bowed his head. "Emperor Jader, I present to you the spy who alerted our enemies of our dealings in Cuthrel."

The Darkmen shoved the spy to the floor.

"What is your name, stranger?" Jader asked, coolly.

The man raised his bloodied face enough to look Jader straight in the face but said nothing.

Bruin looked to the Darkman in the back and nodded. The soldier wrenched the boy's arm behind him, provoking a yelp.

The answer came quickly then. "It's Statler, Nebb Statler."

"See, we can be civil, can we not, Nebb Statler?" Jader smiled down at him. "Tell me, friend. Why did you feel the need to inform the Stewards of our business?"

Nebb squinted. "I never claimed to be no spy." His accent rasped with the rough brogue of commoners.

Jader cocked a brow. "Are you denying it, then?"

"Your men broke into my house and dragged me here without giving me a chance to defend myself."

"He carries this, Emperor." Bruin produced a clear glassy rod of twelve inches or so and dropped it before Nebb's knees.

A sour taste filled Jader's mouth at the appearance of the rod. "That is quite a pretty trinket you have there, Nebb. Is it yours?"

Nebb lifted his chin. "You don't like it?" At another cry from the boy, he flinched.

Jader pinched his lips together, containing the heat that swelled within him. He stared at the fool before him until he could speak without revealing his disgust. "Did you, or did you not attempt to send information to the Stewards?"

At yet another silent response, Jader looked to Bruin. "Pray, how old is the boy?"

"About eleven years, sir."

Jader stroked the scar on his cheek, as wariness spread over Nebb's battered face. "Take him to Joshun."

Bruin dismissed the Darkman with a lazy wave. The boy began to holler and fight as the soldier carried him from the room. "Papa! *Papa!*"

"Nay!" Nebb jumped to his feet, only to be knocked back down by the Darkmen guarding him. "It's me you want. I'm the one who notified the Stewards. Let him go!"

His son's cries, mixed with grunts and scuffles, still echoed from the hall. "Your son looks to be a lively one, Nebb Statler," Jader said. "Fear not for him. He shall do well in Joshun."

"Not him!" Flushed with rage, Nebb drove his elbow into the gut of the Darkman closest to him and swung his fist at the other one as he rose from his crouched position on the floor.

Bruin stepped in and ducked another blow. Grabbing Nebb's neck, he stuck the tip of his sword into the man's side. Nebb sucked in air, sweat pouring from his face. Bruin forced him down to his knees again as the other two Darkmen regained their position, weapons out.

Nebb's anger rolled off of him like waves. "Do not punish an innocent boy because you hate all that is good and just. What monster sends children to a place of torture to—"

Jader stood to his feet. Shadows spread across the floor until they reached the man before him. Nebb froze, his features strained and twisted. Jader held him in his dark grip a moment longer, then released him. The shadows fled, and Nebb fell forward on his hands with a groan.

"I am curious, my friend." Jader stepped down from the throne and stood before the quaking man. "Why would you, a mere *common* man, risk everything to notify the Stewards, who have no legal jurisdiction in the Gateway, of our affairs on this side of the mountains?"

Nebb pushed himself back on his heels. Tears streamed down his ruddy cheeks, but his look was steady, his jaw firm. "The Stewards have every jurisdiction in the Gateway. It's by their presence alone that you are held at bay." His inflection strengthened as he spoke.

"Very strong words for a man who has just lost his son."

The man quivered. "The truth still stands, despite your evil deeds." His voice fell, but the words still carried easily.

"You never answered my other question, Nebb." He toed the rod. "Is this yours?"

A moment passed before Nebb looked up at him. "You shall fall to the light of the Lambient, Jader. Your powers of darkness will not hold up." In the fervor of his declaration, his civilian speech fell away, and he spoke in clear tones befitting a man of greater stature and position. Much like a knight of another order.

Jader sniffed and held Nebb's penetrating glare. "Again, you boast a strong speech as you face imprisonment."

Nebb let out a grim chuckle. "Do not toy with me, Jader. We both know I will see no earthly prison if you have any say in it. But come what may, you cannot hold me prisoner, whether you give me bars or death."

"And what of your son?"

The words hit their mark, and Nebb's head dropped. "The Lambient will see him through," he rasped out.

Jader let out a bark of laughter. "Your *Lambient* delivered your son to your enemy."

"His ways are not mine." Nebb exhaled heavily and sat up straight again. "But He knows all, and He knows best."

Jader sneered. "Pick it up."

Bruin stepped closer, his sword in hand. The guards already had their blades out, the tips but inches from Nebb's back.

Jader looked down his nose at the prisoner. Awareness stared right back at him. This man knew he was about to die. Inhaling deeply, Nebb lowered his eyes to the rod before him. Tenderness filled his expression as he reached out to grasp it. The Beacon responded to his touch, illuminating in his hand.

Jader gave a nod, and Bruin plunged the sword into Nebb's side, followed by the other two Darkmen. Nebb let out a low grunt, then slumped forward, his blood spilling to the floor. After a moment, the Beacon in his hand dimmed, then went out.

Turning his back on him, Jader took the steps to his throne. "Get the mess cleaned up."

A few servants jumped forward to carry out his bidding.

Bruin spoke. "The man's wife will be quite desolate without her breadwinner."

Jader frowned at him. "What is that to me?"

"I know our emperor wants nothing but the best for his people. The woman's chief concern will be for her young daughter."

"That so?" Jader leaned back and smoothed his robes over his knees. "How old is the girl?"

"I would say over eight years, sir."

"Well, we can't have children starving without the patronage of a father." Jader stared down at the dead Steward. "Send her to Joshun as well."

25

The early evening birdsong was muffled out by the sound of heavy footsteps. Seria paused on her way back to her cabin and stared.

The Stewards traipsed their way back over the big bridge, looking tired and beaten. Many of them had ripped clothes marked with blood. There was no missing the horses with bodies draped over their backs.

Their arrival was so far removed from the victorious send-off the crowd had given them the night before that Seria wanted to sit and cry for them. The crowds gathered again, this time much more subdued and somber.

What had happened? Had they run into the Dark Army again? They brought no refugees from Cuthrel, so she feared the situation must have gone awry. From her location, she could not gauge the level of injuries many of them would have come back with, but she wished she could do more than stand there and gawk. Even her prayers did not seem to be enough. How she wished she was in the position to help.

The Stewards wound their way away over the creek and out of view into the town. Seria shivered and looked down to where her hands gripped the wooden cane she held, reminding her what she was supposed to be doing.

Swiping at the moisture clinging to her eyelids, she finished the trek home.

Mason had already awakened and blinked at her. "Did you go some-where?"

She forced a smile and held out the stick. "I thought this might help, so you won't hobble around like such an old man."

He took it from her and gave it a tentative try. "Where'd you get it?" It was rough with a slight twist to it but solid enough to hold him.

Seria perched on the bed and watched him shuffle around the room. "Lena's grandfather used it before she got him a better one. I figured it'd be a lot easier than hopping around, especially outside."

"I'll be fortunate if it doesn't stick me with a splinter. But it does make a difference." He held it up. "Thank you. Very much. This was very kind."

"You're very welcome. Consider it a peace offering." She hated to spoil the moment, but she refused to live as she had before, tiptoeing around his feelings.

He flicked her a glance. "Peace offering for what?"

She shrugged. "You were pretty upset last night, so I wanted to make sure we could still be civil."

The cane *tap, tap, tapped* across the floor until he stood before her. A frown settled over him, but it did not seem to be directed at her. "I was upset, but not at you."

"I figured as much." She hesitated. "The Stewards came back this morning."

His jaw clenched, and his attention riveted on the floor at his feet. "And?"

"They look pretty rough, but most of them returned. I have no idea what happened."

He turned and limped away, attempting to put more weight on his bad leg for the first few steps. His shoulders hunched around his neck, and he flexed his fingers over the crook. "Well, at least that's over."

For now. Mason didn't say it, but Seria could sense it hovering between them. Last night's battle was but one of many that were to come.

The sound of pounding feet approached a moment before Byron burst through the door, searching the room until he found Seria. "Sanjo's sick!"

Seria jumped to her feet. "What? How do you know?"

"He can't get up."

"Oh, no, not again." Seria hustled out the door, Byron on her heels. They hurried around the house to the tiny, dilapidated shed next to the house. She could hear Sanjo's labored breathing before she reached the door.

The animal lay on the ground, his sweat-covered sides pitching up and down as he gulped in air. His nostrils flared, and he flipped his tail in discomfort. Large, brown eyes rolled in her direction, beseeching her to do something.

"Easy, Sanjo." She sank to her knees next to him. Byron crouched at Sanjo's back, stroking him.

There was a shuffle at the door, and Mason stepped in, leaning on his cane. "What's wrong with him?"

Seria shook her head. "I think he got a batch of bad hay."

Byron's thin face pinched. "Then it's my fault?"

She reached across the donkey and squeezed Byron's arm. "No, Byron, of course not. I'm afraid I can't always afford anything better." Her chest heated. When would she get to stop scrimping and scraping to feed herself and a single donkey?

Sanjo swung a front hoof, leaving a groove in the soft dirt in front of him. He rubbed his head up and down against the ground and snorted. Seria bit her lip as guilt squeezed her. "This isn't the first time this has happened, but he sounds pretty bad." First, Mason got sick, and now Sanjo. She clenched her fists and ground her teeth. "Gracious, can I not take care of anyone anymore?"

Mason drew closer. "Is there anything you can do?"

"There's a root I've used before, but I have to force it into him." The donkey's wheezing tore at her. "I don't have any with me right now."

"Then go get some." Mason lowered himself next to her with a soft grunt. "I'll stay with him."

Seria jerked her head toward him. "Really?" She cast a quick look at Byron. Was it a good idea to leave them alone?

Sanjo moved to get up, then sank back into his bed of straw.

Mason rubbed Sanjo's wide forehead. "We'll be fine until you get back."

Seria had never heard him sound so serene. His voice, low and even, wrapped around her nerves and soothed the jagged edges. "All right." She patted Sanjo as she stood. "You keep him calm."

Mason moved to take her spot, his hand still moving in slow circles on Sanjo's head. "We'll take care of him." He spoke in a soft rhythm, not looking at her. "Go."

She hurried to the door and glanced back. Mason stroked Sanjo's sweaty neck, while Byron rubbed his side. The urgency of the moment propelled her outside, where she gathered her skirts and ran for a nearby thicket. Once in the shadows of the trees, she dropped to her hands and knees, digging through the undergrowth and sending silent prayers to the Lambient for her hooved friend.

Please don't let Sanjo suffer because of my negligence. Hours seemed to stretch by while she searched. It was still early in the season. Maybe they had not started growing yet. Tears caught in the back of her throat. What could they do for him then? Sanjo had always been so faithful to her. She couldn't fail him now.

There! Her lungs exhaled at the large, pale green leaves. She pulled the plant up by its roots, cradling it in her hands as she made a dash for her cabin.

While her hands moved to wash the roots and add them to the pot already hanging over the hearth, her mind shot to the shed. What was happening? Was Mason keeping Sanjo calm? Would he acknowledge Byron at all?

Her heart knocked against her breastbone in her exertion. After an eternity, the root finally heated through. She poured the liquid into a pail and grabbed the leaves she had set aside. "Please, let this work."

The scene in the barn was far more tranquil than she had expected. Sanjo still heaved, but he lay relaxed, with Byron's head resting on his side. Mason stroked Sanjo, still murmuring. He looked up at Seria. "Did you find what you need?"

"Finally. How is he?"

Mason gave a nod. "He's holding his own."

Byron lifted his head and blinked at them.

Seria knelt next to Mason, at Sanjo's muzzle. She rolled one of the leaves into a funnel. "He's not going to take this well."

Mason raised the long head off the ground and cradled it in his elbow so she could pour the liquid into his muzzle. "Boy, hold the leaf for Seria."

Byron moved to Seria's side without question, and she showed him how to hold the leaf funnel at the gap in Sanjo's gums. She looked to

Mason, who gave a nod. He massaged a circle on Sanjo's forehead, while Seria tipped the pot, letting the brew spill into the leaf funnel.

Sanjo tried to jerk his head away.

"Hey, you ol' stubborn beast." Mason tightened his grip. "Hold still." He readjusted the head and kept on rubbing.

Seria braced her shoulder against Mason's—warm and supportive, as she struggled to pour more of the liquid, and then more again. "I think that's enough." Her voice shook as she set the pot aside and put some space between her and Mason. "It should settle his gut and hopefully flush out the toxins."

Mason laid the donkey's head back down with a pat and cast a quick look at Seria. "Now I know how you felt trying to get whatever that stuff was inside me."

Seria caught a rare grin creep up on his face, and a quick burst of laughter escaped her. Some of the tension left her neck as she wiped her damp face. She must look a sight.

"Byron, you should go home now," she said. "Your mother will be wondering where you are. There's nothing more we can do for him tonight."

Byron patted Sanjo's neck, his gaze darting to Mason's and then back down.

"You did good, kid."

The boy's head lifted, and he met Mason's look. Seria smiled at the expression on his young face. Wary, but pleased and trying to hide it.

Without a word, Byron gave Sanjo one last stroke and left.

Seria let out a long exhale that left her as drained as an empty mug. She glanced over at Mason, warmth overtaking the chill in her spirit. "Thank you so much, Mason. I don't know if I could've done it without you."

He shrugged and smoothed the hair in Sanjo's mane. "Sounds like you've managed before."

"But if you hadn't kept him so calm, I never would've gotten so much of the brew down him." She cocked her head at him. "I didn't know you had it in you. You must have a touch."

He sat back with a cringe. "I wouldn't call it a touch. My brother was the one who had a flair with the critters." His forehead creased, and he shot her a quick look.

Seria reigned back the surprise and curiosity his reveal had unleashed. If she overreacted, he may never confide in her again. "Well, in any case, thank you."

Mason shrugged. "Sure. Glad I could help."

Seeing his discomfort, Seria turned her attention away. A lump formed at Sanjo's easy breathing. Her animal friend would be fine. Because of Mason. She bit back a smile. There was a softer side to Mason after all.

"Looks like he's ready to get some rest," Mason said after a moment.

Seria smiled at the dozing donkey. "That's exactly what he needs."

"Well, then we should let him get to it." Mason used his cane to push himself back to his feet. To Seria's surprise, he stretched a hand out to help her.

Keeping his recent condition in mind, Seria prepared to push herself up without pulling on his hand. But he pulled her up with more vigor than she expected, and she narrowly avoided falling into his arms, bracing her free hand on his strong shoulder. How could it still be that solid after being bedridden for so long?

Mason's face was inches from hers, his amber eyes staring straight back at her. Heat rushed up Seria's arm and into her cheeks. She stumbled back out of his space with an awkward laugh. "Whoops. Sorry." *I guess his strength is coming back faster than I thought.*

One side of his mouth curled up, and he dropped her hand. "Don't be."

Seria swallowed, cleared her throat, and left the barn without another word. For once, she had no idea what to say.

26

For you were once in darkness,
but now for a little while, you walk in the light.
-The Sacred Code

"So, what's the story of that ol' donkey?" Mason sat with his sore leg stretched out in front of him. Sitting in the shed had left him achy and stiff.

Seria looked up from the pot she stirred on the hearth. "What do you mean?"

"Is he a longtime pet?"

She turned with a smile, spoon still in her hand. "Nay, nothing like that. Someone in Cadence was going to destroy him, so I worked out a deal. Free laundry for a month in exchange for the donkey."

"What was their reason?"

"They said he was dangerous."

"Dangerous?" He cocked a brow. "That bag of bones?"

She chuckled. "Don't be mean."

He put his hands up to placate her. "I'm not, but anyone who thinks that old beast is dangerous is looking for a reason to get rid of him."

"You're not wrong. They were tired of him. He couldn't pull his weight because of his age, and they wanted to be rid of him. So..." She shrugged.

"You took him." Of course, she did. This girl would take in every stray and beggar and let them eat her out of house and home.

"He's done right by me. And it's because of him that I was able to cart you back here."

Mason hid his amusement at how defensive she sounded.

"I know he doesn't have a lot of years left, but he's been good for me. Gave me someone else to think of besides myself."

"Well," he shifted his position, "I don't blame you."

She blinked at him. "You don't?"

For some reason, her surprise irritated him. It was the same look she gave him in the barn when he offered to help. As if he would be so cruel to a defenseless animal. "Sure." He pushed himself out of the chair. "There's no reason to put an animal down because you're tired of it. It's a waste."

"You know, for once, I think we agree on something." She watched him hobble back to his spot in the corner. "It must've hurt sitting on the ground so long, but you're getting around well. A few more days, and I think you'll be ready to get out and about for a while in Cadence."

Frustration gnawed at him as he swung his feet onto the bed. His body still ached, but he wasn't willing to wait another few days. The boredom alone was about to drive him mad. Sanjo's illness was the closest thing he'd had to excitement in weeks.

But Seria would not be pushed, not anymore. Not since their little spat. And if he pressed too hard, she was bound to get suspicious. Perhaps it was time to go a little deeper with his act. Get her a little more willing to yield.

He let his gaze wander to where she puttered about in her minuscule kitchen area. It might not be too bad. He certainly did not find her repulsive.

Long hair the color of corn silk framed her flushed face. Her fair complexion would be flawless if not for that scattering of faint freckles, which did not turn him off a bit. And with those vivid green eyes, she could be downright appealing. Especially when she wasn't talking like her life depended on it.

Though her infatuation with the Stewardship still turned him off, maybe he could work that to his advantage. He would have to be careful, but he could pull it off. He had not missed her reaction to his nearness in the shed earlier. What girl wouldn't be flattered at the favor of a knight? Especially a wounded one.

She was a far cry from the lusty companionship Dreeya offered. But still a woman, nonetheless. This was different than what Dreeya wanted. He needed Seria's compliance. What if this was the only way to get it?

His skin heated with the possibility while he watched her, ready to jump headfirst into this next phase, to sweep Seria off her feet, to win her worship.

Seria stepped away from the fireplace, scratching her head, and caught Mason looking at her. At her earnest expression, his pulse jumped. Maybe this would be easier than he thought.

Then she flashed him a preoccupied smile and turned her attention back to the pot over the fire. "So...I was thinking about changing up our stew. How about having it with no potatoes?"

All eagerness drained from him in an instant, and he ran a hand over his face.

Then again, maybe not.

Mason managed to sit at the table that night for their dinner of potatoless stew but was too distracted to eat much. So much time had already been lost.

"You feeling poorly?" Seria asked.

"Nay."

"You're scowling at your dinner."

He schooled his features. "I'm sorry. I was just...thinking."

"You miss the potatoes, don't you?"

"Not at all." At her skeptical look, he forced a smile. "Your cooking is quite satisfactory, no matter what you prepare. I appreciate it. I really do."

Seria regarded him for a long moment, her lower lip tucked between her teeth, muffling back a giggle.

Wait. Was she laughing at him?

She covered her mouth with her hand. "I'm sorry. I don't mean to laugh; it's so rude."

He flattened his lips and worked to keep his tone steady. "Could you tell me why? Please."

At that, Seria let out a loud guffaw.

Throwing his napkin on the table, Mason leaned back and frowned at her, trying not to let his temper flare. Maybe she was the one losing her mind.

She wiped tears away. "Oh, goodness. I must be tired." She caught his scowl and tried to stop laughing. "Again, I'm sorry, but you're trying too hard to be something you're not."

His irritation evaporated, to be replaced by a thick strand of wariness. Surely, she did not mean... His spine stiffened, and he straightened in his seat.

Seria winced. "That came out all wrong." She rested her arms on the table and leveled him with a knowing look. "I appreciate you trying to be polite, but I would rather you stop forcing it."

He scowled at her. "I don't know what you mean." What was she implying? Did she know more than he had believed? Already, his options flipped through his mind. He was far from whole, but he had no doubt he could overcome her if he had to.

She sat back, still smiling. "I think you must be a brave man with a lot of honor, but it's clear you could care less about proprieties."

It took a minute for her words to sink through. "Proprieties?"

"Aye!" She let out another chuckle. "You look like it causes you pain every time you have to say please or thank you. I certainly don't want to be any source of discomfort, so if it makes you feel better, let's forgo the show in manners."

Her twinkling eyes and teasing look finally got through. Relief washed over him like a wave. So, she had seen through his act, but not all the way through. He slumped back in his chair and shook his head at her, wanting to strangle her and laugh with her at the same time. "So, why didn't you tell me this a fortnight ago? Could've saved me a heap of trouble."

She threw back her head and laughed, the sound filling the room. Although not quite ready to join her, he was nonetheless surprised at the grin stretching across his face.

"Look at that, you are capable of smiling." Seria grinned and took her empty plate from the table.

Mason schooled his features and gave her a scowl, which she merely giggled at.

"Do you feel up to checking on Sanjo one last time?" she asked.

"Sure, why not?" What else was there to do?

"I know you must be bored to tears here. It won't be long before you're completely back on your feet."

He blinked at how close her words hit his thoughts. "I would think you'd be tired of my company." He reached for his cane and took a few careful steps to join her by the door.

She smiled at him. "I don't know. I've gotten accustomed to having you around." *I might actually miss him when he's gone.*

Mason stared. Her lips had not formed the last statement, yet it echoed in his head as clear as if she spoke it out loud.

"You all right?"

Stirring, Mason nodded and tried to get another glimpse into her thoughts.

He's got the loveliest eyes I've ever seen.

Triumph blossomed in Mason's chest. He, for certain, had not conjured that thought up. The fuzziness in his vision and his mind had cleared at last.

"Are you ready?"

Mason gave another quick nod and followed her. What did this mean? Were his faculties fully restored? Could he control someone yet? There was one way to know for sure, but was he ready for that? Controlling Seria too soon could create problems he was not ready for.

Walking didn't pain him like before, but was he able to stalk the distance to the fort, with the potential of meeting unfriendly faces? The slight throbbing in his side caught his attention, sending a tendril of disappointment and confirmation through him.

He wasn't ready yet. But he was getting close.

Seria observed Mason's shuttered face, and a coil of apprehension twisted inside her. She had released him from his show of manners so he could relax, not so he could withdraw and shut her out again.

The trip to the barn was made without incident or conversation. Sanjo was up and chomping on fresh green grass growing outside his door, but Mason did not express much relief in his recovery. He stood back and let Seria tend to the animal.

Seria clamped her lips together. Fine. If he didn't want to talk, she'd let him have his silence. She gave Sanjo one last pat and then turned for the short walk back to the house. Mason hobbled alongside her. Just when she thought they were becoming friends, his mind was miles away.

She looked down at the cane. He wouldn't need it for long. Then he would be back to his old life, with nary a thought to the girl who talked too much.

A fist-sized rock sat on the path before him, but he did not notice it with his head in the clouds. Before she could caution him, he stepped on it and tripped forward on his bad leg. Without thought, Seria jumped in front of him to catch him, throwing her hands around his waist.

His weight almost bowled her over, and she spread her feet out to brace herself, but it wasn't enough to hold him up. He stumbled forward, knocking her back. But his arms wrapped around her as he caught his footing, and somehow, managed to keep both of them from falling.

She gaped up into his face. "Are you hurt?"

"Just... hold still." The words were ground out through clenched teeth. He took a slow, deep breath, an unreadable expression crossing his face. His arms tightened.

Something warm spread through Seria's core. Those eyes of his were so close and mesmerizing. She cleared her throat. "Um, we're going to have to stop falling into each other like this."

He blinked and straightened with a grimace, taking her up with him.

"You didn't hurt yourself, did you?" She bit her lip at the way he held himself.

"I don't think so."

"I hope you didn't tear your side open again." She retrieved his cane and handed it to him.

Mason's jaw clenched.

"I'm sorry for being so clumsy." She took his arm. "I was trying to keep you from falling."

"I'm fine." The words were stilted and terse.

Seria held her tongue until they reached the cabin. With painstaking care, Mason lowered himself onto the bed. She wasted no time in checking the wound. The skin was red hot, but nothing had torn through.

"I don't think it's too bad. You may want to take care for a couple of days, though. You put some strain on the wound."

A flash of hesitance flitted across his face, and he looked her straight in the eye. "You can still take me to Cadence tomorrow."

"I'm sorry, but you almost ripped that hole open again, and then you would've been right back where you started."

His face fell, and he sat back against the headboard, shaking his head.

He's in a foul mood tonight. "Let's not pout about it." She teased and reached for clean dressing.

He glared at her. "I'm not pouting. I'm just—"

"Frustrated?"

"Nay, I'm—"

"Disappointed?" At the shake of his head, she tried again. "Angry?"

He threw his hands up. "I was going to say tired, but you won't stop talking for me long enough to let me speak for myself."

"Sorry." A smile broke through before she could stop it. "My mama used to say I spent more time trying to talk for other people than I did for myself."

"Not sure about that, either," he grumbled.

A brief silence fell as she worked.

"I must say, you are very good at this."

She raised her head. "At what?" Mason was not one to give away praises.

He motioned to what she was doing. "I know trained physicians who can't do this without making their patients miserable."

"Oh." An odd pleasure at his compliment swept over her. "I had a good teacher."

"Who was that?"

She kept her focus on the bandage as pain squeezed inside her. "My mother." Wiping her hands on a towel, she left him where he was to prepare their meal. True to form, he did not ask any more questions.

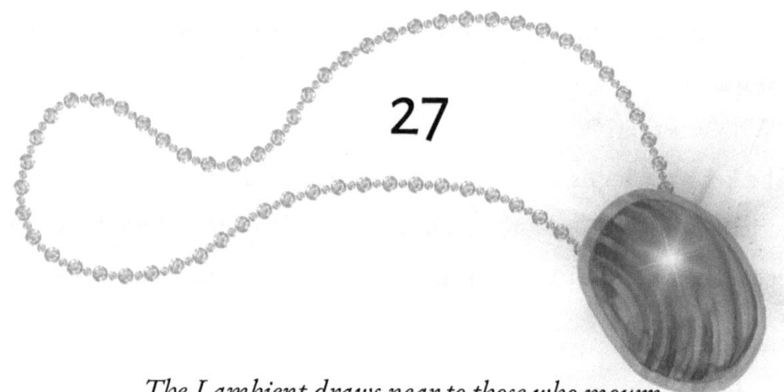

27

The Lambient draws near to those who mourn.
-The Sacred Code

Mason stirred, his mind already working to place what had awakened him. Soft moonlight streaming through the window told him it was not yet morning. He raised on an elbow and scanned the dark room, his skin prickling. Something had broken the stillness of the night. He glanced down at the bare floor and blinked. Seria was gone.

Wide awake now, he threw the blanket back and pushed himself upright. Upon spotting her sitting at the table, he relaxed. She was wrapped in her blanket, hunched over. Then, the sound he couldn't identify fell on his ears. Soft, muffled sobs.

Seria, crying? The idea was so foreign that he stood and crossed the small room. "Are you all right?"

Seria started at his approach and scrubbed at her cheeks. "I'm fine."

He moved in front of her and waited for her to look up, but she lowered her head and attempted a smile that came out crooked and forced.

What would drive her to sit in the dark and weep? "Really?" The word sounded inane as soon as he said it, but awkwardness had invaded him. It was clear she was not fine, but he wasn't good with this.

"A silly dream, that's all. Sorry if I woke you." Her gaze flitted up to meet his, then went back to the floor.

The brief moment of eye contact was all Mason needed. A cold jolt went through him, and his jaw slackened at the thoughts now playing in his mind.

He wasn't the only one plagued by nightmares.

"It's late." Her tone was flat. "We should get some sleep."

What could he say? For once, she didn't want to talk. And Mason knew better than anyone that empty words of comfort availed nothing. He nodded and backed off, swallowing sand. "Sure."

Seria lay down with her face turned away, and he sat on the side of the bed. As he stared at the back of her head, her memories descended over him.

A man and woman, Seria's parents, dead in the yard. Three young children, also dead. Her whole family. While a band of killers rode away without a thought to the lives they had taken. It was stamped in Mason's mind now, clear as day. He had witnessed the same scene before. Or at least one similar.

His hand strayed to the scar under his collarbone. The twelve-year-old wound had healed on the outside but left a sharp pain inside him that could be appeased with nothing but the execution of justice.

With a sharp inhale, he squeezed his eyes shut to dispel his own images of cruel riders and fallen victims. Goosebumps settled over his arms. It seemed he and Seria shared more than a house. He shook his head to dismiss the thoughts and stretched out on the bed. *Don't get soft on her, Mason.* She was, after all, loyal to his enemies.

She'll be fine. By morning, she would be rested and back to her chatty self. And he could put what he had seen behind him and focus on what was ahead.

But it took no time the next morning for Mason to realize how wrong he could be. For the first time since he awakened in her cabin, Seria did not greet him with a mouthful of words and her usual smile. Instead, she remained quiet and withdrawn. She fixed his usual oats, then stepped outside to busy herself with laundry. Mason did not hear so much as three words from her.

The atmosphere in the cabin grew more strained as the hours crawled by. This was worse than the tension after their first confrontation. How strange. He could not count the times he wished she would lose her voice or that he could control her into quiet. But now that silence reigned, he found it heavy and stifling.

The pictures of her memories swirled in his head. Every member of her family was murdered and left for dead, leaving Seria to find them. The question of why burned within him.

He bent his neck side-to-side, trying to ease his taut muscles, and rubbed his face. Her sorrow stirred memories of his own, and that was the last thing he needed. He had finally shed them from his dreams since being stuck here.

Small talk didn't work, not that he had ever been very good at it. Seria answered in monosyllables and never looked at him, so he could not get any more answers. By the time midday rolled around, Mason was wound as tight as the string of a bow.

He would much rather have an annoying Seria than a silent one.

Rain started to fall that afternoon, but Seria was not about to be deterred from her work and lugged the washtub inside. Mason could imagine her soreness from scrubbing numerous piles of laundry, but that pain paled in comparison to the one that had descended over her heart. So, she kept busy.

"Want some help?" he asked.

Her head snapped up from where she crouched over the small washtub. "With this?"

He shrugged. "Why not?"

She squinted at him. He hid a smirk at the skepticism in her mind. He had not exactly tried to be helpful. "Don't look at me like that. I did help with your donkey."

Seria pushed herself off the floor and waved toward the tub. "Have at it."

He lowered himself to his knees, grunting as he did, then rolled his sleeves up and pulled a garment from the water to give it a brisk rub against the washboard. He could feel her gawking at him, but he ignored her and scrubbed dutifully for several minutes. After a moment, he heard a muffled chuckle.

"I usually try not to scrub a hole in one spot."

"I'm not." He frowned up at her.

"I'm sure you're not, but you'd better let me finish."

He read her concern. "Stop fretting. I'm not going to tear it. This isn't the first time I've done laundry." Mason dropped the clean shirt into the water and reached for another. "I'm not as incompetent as you think."

"I didn't say that."

"But you were thinking it." He continued working as he talked. "How 'bout that tour you promised?"

"It's raining. Besides, you shouldn't push yourself today after pulling your side yesterday."

"What do you call bending over a washtub?"

"You offered."

He pointed his finger at her. "You're right. Remind me not to do that next time."

Seria shook her head, a small smile lifting her lips. The sight lightened his mood for the first time since the night before. He waited to see how long it would take her to ask the question bouncing around in her head, demanding to be released.

"What are you doing?"

There it is. "Laundry."

"That's not what I mean." She shook her head. "I mean offering to help, carrying on a conversation like this is normal. Why?"

"Are you telling me I'm usually a bore?"

She crossed her arms and leveled a hard look on him, not about to let him off.

He leaned back on his heels, searching for words that wouldn't let on what he knew. "It's been a little too quiet today, even for my taste. I'm already bored out of my mind, so I had to do something drastic to get some noise in this place."

"I thought my carrying on annoyed you."

So, he hadn't done a good job of hiding his feelings. "Well, it does usually." He lightened his tone with teasing. "But at least it gave me something to listen to."

Her cheeks suddenly flamed, and her thoughts blazed across her mind, remembering how he found her crying in the night. *He's feeling sorry for me.*

"I'm not feeling sorry for you. It's like I said. I'm sick of the quiet. The silence is driving me mad." He stopped and stared into the water; he'd already said too much.

Seria gave a breathless laugh. "If I didn't know any better, I'd think you were reading my mind. You keep saying what I'm thinking."

He raised his head and stared at her. Her exhaustion and swirling emotions pulled at him. For the first time, he sympathized with her. He knew what it was like to lose everything. "How do you know I can't?"

She laughed. "A few lucky guesses, and now you're a mind reader."

A small, crooked smirk stretched across his face. "I've had a *lot* of lucky guesses."

"Is that so?"

Resting his knuckles on his thighs, he looked her straight on. "You don't believe me?"

She scoffed. "That you can read my mind? Nay, but I'll give you a chance to prove it." She put her hands on her hips and tilted her head, her thoughts playing out clearly to him.

"You think I'm stringing you along, but you're humoring me because I'm doing your laundry for you."

Seria's jaw unhinged.

He couldn't stop his grin. "And I do have lovely eyes." He gave her a wink and went back to his work.

She collapsed into a chair. "What—*how*?"

"It's a Gift." He shrugged.

"A gift? You mean a Gift of the Moon?" At his nod, her mouth dropped, and she glared at him. "Have you been reading my mind the whole time?"

He chuckled and put a hand up. "Nay, ma'am. It's only been a short while since my vision cleared up. I guess that knock on the head put it out of commission for a little while."

"Oh. Good. That would've been irksome to find out."

"Irksome? You mean like someone finishing all your sentences for you?"

She waved his statement away. "That's nothing in light of this. I've heard of those who have special Gifts, but I've never actually met anyone with one. So, how does it work? I mean, can you read everybody's thoughts?"

Mason wrung out a garment. "When I get a brief look into their eyes, I can see what's foremost on their mind."

"So, every time you look at someone, you're reading their thoughts?"

"Not exactly. If I don't want to, I can keep myself from doing it."

"How do you do that?"

He rested his wet hands on the edge of the tub, entertained by her interest. At least she wasn't thinking about her dream anymore. "It's like when you're in a crowded area with a friend, and everyone's talking. It doesn't take a whole lot of effort, but you have to intentionally block out everything around you so you can hear your friend, right?"

She gave him a nod. "Sounds like a normal day at the farmer's market."

"It's the same for me. If I don't want to know what you're thinking, I intentionally block it to keep from reading your thoughts."

"I declare. My father used to talk about the Gifts, and it's always intrigued me, but this is a bit unsettling. So, why didn't you tell me before? It might've been nice to know my guest can read my mind."

Her question gave him pause. Why had he told her anything at all? It wasn't wise to feed her too much information, and now she knew what he was capable of. Well, not completely. "Guess it never came up."

Her face twisted. "So, does that mean...?"

"Aye." He shifted his scrutiny to the tub before him.

She inhaled. "You know about my family." It was more a statement than a question.

A brief silence fell. Her face clouded over again; the light gone out. "Do you have them a lot?" he asked. "The nightmares, I mean?"

"I used to." She pulled at a loose thread on her ratty apron. "Not for a while, though. I guess Rackson's attack stirred up some of those old memories."

Mason gripped the edge of the washbasin. He could attest to that.

Her eyes took on a faraway look. "My father was still alive for a few moments after I found them. But there was nothing I could do, despite everything my mother taught me about the healing ways."

Her pain shouted from the depths of her expression and the rawness in her words.

"What happened?" He could have pulled his tongue out. Why would he ask her that?

But the question did not upset her. If anything, she appreciated of his attention and was ready to talk about it. She drew in a long, shaky breath, but when she answered, her tone was steady. "There was a powerful landlord who wanted my father's acreage. After a while, I guess he got tired of making offers, so he took matters into his own hands."

"He had them killed over the land?" At her short nod, he asked, "Was he ever caught?"

Her shoulders hunched. "I didn't stick around to find out. I was scared to death they would come back for me, so I threw everything I owned in the back of our wagon and never looked back. I never had a chance to bury them." Her voice hitched at the last.

The image seared itself to his mind. A young girl, scared and grieving, leaving everything behind. "And you ended up here."

"That's right." She let out a hollow chuckle. "Almost starved to death my first year. Cadence is a nice place but not too kind to those with nothing to offer. One day, I happened to overhear someone complaining they never had enough time for their laundry. Without thinking, I offered my services. Before long, I had a whole list of customers. It never pays much, but it keeps me fed and pays the rent for this little shack. Guess I can't complain." A small smile lifted her features, and a dim glow radiated from her green depths.

Mason shifted his jaw as he turned his attention back to the sudsy water. Even after losing everything, Seria did not have one ounce of bitterness in her. And she still had enough generosity to reach out to others, like the beggar kid and that ancient donkey. *And me.*

"My brother...he was murdered, too." The words were out before he could stop them, and his chest clenched. But something about her openness had pulled it from him. For some reason, he wanted her to know he had suffered, too.

"Liam?"

No surprise she had made the connection to the name he had cried out in his illness. His neck tightened, and he nodded.

"I'm so sorry."

How had this happened? All he had meant to do was distract her from her bad dream, to get her back to her lively self so that her memories would not bring his own to the surface. Instead, he had slipped and let her get close enough to glimpse the old scars he had kept hidden for years. But their sense of loss linked them, bringing with it a strange relief.

"Did you lose any friends in Rackson?"

The soft question caught him off guard, and his mind jumped to the men and women in his camp. To Shon and Dreeya, the closest he had to friends at all. Were they still alive? "I have no idea."

She crossed her arms in front of herself and shivered. "So much fighting. So much death. Such a shame to see so many Stewards die. And Darkmen, too."

He jerked his head up toward her. "Darkmen?"

She blanched. "I'm sorry, I don't mean to upset you, and it may be foolish, but I can't help but think of those young men and women fighting. It doesn't matter where they came from or what they're standing against. Inside, they're all people with feelings and dreams." Her voice dropped. "And all of that is cut short by a senseless fight in the woods between two armies."

Her contemplation fell on him, and he held it. She didn't flinch, even knowing he could read her every thought and her genuine sorrow for the lives lost. All of them.

"But at least we're making them proud, right?"

He blinked. "How's that?"

"Well, think about it." She leaned forward. "Despite our losses, we didn't let the tragedy define us. We could be eaten up with bitterness and hatred, but we're not. My life is nothing grand, but I'm making do. And I try to live out the principles my parents passed on to me. And you." She gave him a wide smile. "You fought against the Dark Army to protect an innocent town. You turned something terrible into something good."

The words hit him like blows from a hammer, breaking the connection from moments before. Something unfamiliar squirmed inside him at the way she beamed at him. How could she do it? How could she find anything good in the loss she faced? The questions swelled inside of him until he couldn't hold back any longer.

"But what about justice?" At her quick look, he tempered his tone. "I mean, don't you want that killer to pay for what he did to you?"

She started to speak, then hesitated, weighing her words. He kept himself from reading her answer, wanting to hear it spoken out loud.

"Aye," she finally said. "I do want him to pay for what he's done. To suffer the way he made me suffer." Wrinkles marred the smooth skin of her forehead. "I want him to hang from a tree or be burned at the stake. Or at the very least, get what he gave my family."

The brutal honesty with which she spoke wrenched at him. Her face reddened, and he got a glimpse of the same burning rage he lived with, lurking beneath the surface, belying her vision of innocence and charm. Just a hint, but it was there. Anger at the wrong that had befallen her. The desire for vengeance.

His lungs emptied at the sudden, crazy urge to tell her everything. Surely, she would understand why he was there, what he had to do. She may be the only person who could.

Then she sat back in her seat, her expression softening, and shook her head. "But, then again, what would it change? My family will still be gone. And if I stoop to that level of desiring blood for blood, am I any better than the man who killed them?"

Throwing ice water in his face could not have stung more. He gritted his teeth, wanting to argue or lash out. But reason withheld him. This was not the time.

Seria was wrong. There was always a place for justice. There had to be. He had spent the last twelve years of his life holding out for it.

28

The rain continued to fall the next day, closing Seria and Mason up in the cabin much like their first few days together. As she folded another client's laundry, she marveled at how much had happened since then and how different things were now.

They never returned to the topic of their lost loved ones, nor did they touch on anything else that could be described as deep. Seria knew next to nothing about Mason's brother, but she was still beyond amazed at what he had revealed. The last thing she wanted was to make him regret opening up to her by pressing him for more.

However, something else had changed. She couldn't put her finger on what it was, exactly. Mason was still restless and distracted much of the time, but the impatience she had sensed before was missing. The atmosphere was not thick with tension, as if that one conversation brought with it a common bond that overlooked their differences.

Seria smiled to herself as she stuffed the clean clothes into a bag. Could they be any more different? She was naïve to anything beyond her four walls; he came across as experienced and worldly. While she talked about anything and everything that popped into her head, Mason preferred to stew over his thoughts.

And he could read people's thoughts.

His Gift should intimidate her, but instead, it fascinated her. She had nothing to hide. *Except that I thought he had lovely eyes.* Her cheeks warmed a bit at the reminder. At least he was kind enough not to tease her about that. Too much.

A light mist fell, carrying with it the smell of fresh grass and clean air. Seria opened the door to freshen the muggy cabin and glanced over to where Mason napped on the cot. His wounds were all but mended by now, but he would have to refrain from strenuous exercise for a while yet.

After his first offer, he continued to help her with the wash and some of the household chores, though he still tired easily. It seemed to embarrass him that he couldn't keep up with her. It was rather endearing.

Glancing out the door, Seria saw a client's daughter approaching with quick, sharp steps, her shawl held over her head. *Oh no.* She grabbed a bag from the corner, hoping to make the transaction outside to keep from waking Mason.

The skinny teen wasted no time in making the intent of her arrival known. She crossed her arms and jutted her chin. "Mama says she's not paying you the full amount, since it's late, *and* I had to come get it."

Seria nodded without argument and traded the bag for the coins offered her. The clothes should have been delivered days ago. "I'm sorry."

The girl took the bag and walked a few steps, then stopped. "Oh, and Mama says if it happens again, we *won't* be using your services any longer."

Seria sighed as the girl left. Her third unhappy customer this week. The last two deliveries had resulted in similar conversations.

When she stepped back inside, Mason was sitting up in bed, stretching.

"What was that about?"

"Oh, nothing important." She waved it off with a little laugh, then caught herself. "Well, I've had a few clients upset with the timing of my deliveries."

He considered the bags scattered through the room. Clean clothes in one corner, dirty clothes in another. "Guess I've made it hard on you?"

"It wasn't your fault." She moved to finish bagging another bunch.

"Well, why don't we try to deliver the ones you've got done today?"

She stopped and looked at him. "Really?" At his shrug, she squinted through the door at the gray sky. "Not sure the rain's gonna hold off long enough."

"So, we'll do what we can."

They took off at a brisk pace, each lugging two bags apiece. Mason left his cane behind and took the heavier bags from Seria's stubborn grasp. He was through being coddled. As they walked the short distance to her nearest neighbors, he could see Seria was right. The rain would not hold off for long.

At each house, he stood back and observed the interaction. Seria was given her meager pay, and sometimes another bag of laundry. No one said thank you. One snippety lady made it known that she was not satisfied with the speed of her work. Seria merely apologized and promised to do better, whereas Mason considered dumping the woman's clean clothes in the mud.

"Why do you put up with it?" he asked after they had delivered the last bag.

She glanced over at him. "Put up with what?"

He waved back at the cabin behind them. "That broad called you a servant." The mere idea of someone degrading him like that sent heat up his neck.

"Oh, that." She shrugged. "I am a servant of sorts. A servant of the people."

"A servant doesn't get paid. You shouldn't put up with that kind of treatment."

"Sometimes you have to put up with unfair treatment. I need the work."

"That doesn't mean you have to allow people to disrespect you." Where was the spirit she used against Ira?

She cocked her head. "I know some of them can be a bit hateful, but underneath that hatefulness is a person who has loved and lived and lost. I don't know what they're dealing with. Mayhap that woman was down to the last of the clean clothes and her last coin. That wouldn't make anyone happy to see the washerwoman show up at the door, and late at that."

Mason shook his head at her logic. "And sometimes there's plain rudeness."

A small smile appeared on her face as she glanced up at the sullen sky. "Trust me. I've seen enough rudeness to know it for what it is."

The way she said it jolted him back to when he had degraded her status as a washerwoman. He rubbed the back of his neck. *Blades.* Was that only a week ago?

They were mere feet from the door when the skies opened up, and the downpour started. Seria laughed as they scampered inside the dark cabin. "In any case, I never pictured Stewards for doing laundry." She twisted her damp hair. "Seems a little below a knight's capabilities."

"Don't put the Stewards on a pedestal, Seria." He gritted his teeth and tried to keep the annoyance from bleeding into his words.

"What do you mean?" She put her hands on her hips and cocked her head.

Not for the first time, Mason realized she still looked him in the eye after finding out about his Gift. She didn't shy from it, choosing instead to trust him with her thoughts. There weren't many willing to take that risk with him.

He pulled his thoughts back to the topic at hand. "No one should be put up that high. Everyone's human. Stewards are no different." He had to bite back the words he wanted to use to describe them. Scum. Bigots. Butchers. A familiar flame burned inside at the thought.

"You're probably right." She crossed to the dark lamp on the table. "I'll put some supper on, then I better get to the rest of these clothes if I want to keep my customers happy."

Something moved in the house behind Mason, cutting his reply short. He spun around, peering into the shadows. Footsteps.

Someone was in the house.

"What is that?" Seria whispered.

He put his hand up to hush her, his windpipe tightening. The noise rose and fell, sending his pulse racing. Who was here?

I've been discovered! The thought screamed at him. Someone had finally reported him to the Stewards, and they had come to take him away.

But where was the intruder? There was no place to hide in Seria's little cabin. And not enough shadows to conceal a grown man.

Unless...was it a Shadowman? No one else could stay so hidden.

There was a sudden thump, and something crashed to the floor behind them. Mason jerked around as Seria let out a little squeal.

What Mason wouldn't give at that moment for a Shadowstone of his own. He heard more movement in the dark room. Anticipation vibrated his limbs. If it was a Shadowman, they could get him out of this. They would help him get into the fort. They would—

His attention shot to where Seria stood beside the table. He reached for her old, rusty sword braced in the corner, and stepped in front of her.

"Hello?" He called out.

Nothing.

By this time, Seria had a wooden spoon gripped in her hands. "Stay behind me," he directed lest she go swinging a utensil at a master swordsman. Apprehension tried to clog his mouth, but he gulped it back. He had to stay sharp. "I know you're here."

Light footsteps approached, close. He gripped the sword, unwilling to swing at a Shadowman ally. He stepped forward, blade up. No one. At the sound of more scurrying, he moved again with a growl. Once again, there was nothing.

What was going on?

Seria stood flat against a wall, almost lost in the darkness. Mason stood in the middle of the room, gripping the sword and straining to see.

There was more movement, and Seria gasped. Mason blinked when he caught a glimpse of a small, shadowy shape darting away.

"He's over there!" Seria followed the noise farther in the shadows.

"Seria, don't—where?"

"There!" The shape moved again. "To my left!"

"I can't see your left!"

The prowler moved again, and Mason raised his sword over his head, ready to bring it down in one, quick sweep. Two small, glowing orbs darted close to the ground. Lightning flickered outside, and Mason gaped at the small, gray creature standing before him. It gave a loud squeal and covered its dark face with its paws.

Mason's head bobbed. "What?"

It scampered away.

Seria dashed to stand in front of Mason. "It's a raccoon! Don't kill it!"

Mason lowered the sword and exhaled. "Why shouldn't I kill it?"

She was already looking around for the animal. "Because it's just a young raccoon. It's not trying to hurt us."

"Seria—"

At that moment, the animal darted out from under the bed, climbed up a leg of the table, and took a flying leap at Mason. Seria yelped as Mason jumped back. The raccoon landed on the floor and ran for the far side of the room.

"Not trying to hurt us, huh?" Mason scowled. The animal scurried past again.

"He's scared."

Before Mason could respond, it jumped out from its hiding spot and slid into the back of his legs. Knocked off balance, Mason's arms waved wildly as he fell backward over it, flat on his back. The raccoon screeched and ran out the open door.

Seria covered her mouth. "Are you all right?"

He groaned and propped himself up on one elbow. "Oh, I'm great! That's the thanks I get for sparing a lousy rodent."

Her eyes brimmed over with amusement, though she hid her smile behind her hands.

Mason glared at her. "I'm glad you find this so amusing."

"I'm sorry." She clasped her hands in front of her. "I don't mean to laugh." Her voice came out strained and tight.

He stared at her, his elbows on his knees. "I can tell."

A giggle escaped, and she bit her lips, her face reddening with the effort.

The absurdity of the moment hit Mason then, and he felt the faint beginnings of mirth tickling his windpipe. Before he knew it, chuckles built and escaped the rigid lines of his mouth.

The sound must have entertained Seria further because she held her sides and doubled over. In between chortles, she gasped out, "The great soldier...bested by...a little raccoon."

The image ran through his mind, and he threw his head back and laughed out loud, long and unrestrained. Their laughter echoed in the small cabin, weaving together in a sound akin to rivers gurgling and birds twittering. It loosened something inside him, something that had been tight and coiled for a long time.

"I've never seen anything funnier in my life." Seria wiped the tears on her cheeks.

He groaned as he tried to stand. "I have a feeling it won't be so funny in the morning."

"Oh, no." Her face dropped, and she hurried to help him up. "Are you hurt?"

He winced. "Well, it might hurt to sit down for a while."

She was off in another fit of giggles, which made getting up off the floor more difficult. By the time he was back on his feet, both were worn out and drained, but Mason did not mind.

He had not laughed like that since Liam's death.

29

Seria watched Mason pace from the window to the door like a caged animal from where she sat mending a worn stocking. He had certainly recovered enough from the raccoon attack the night before and now looked ready to claw his way from the confines of her small cabin. If it wasn't so dark and rainy, he probably would have.

She sympathized with him. He must have thought it would be easier when he was up and about, but having the mobility and nowhere to go had to be maddening.

She shook her head as he made another round in her tiny kitchen back to her door. "Pacing isn't going to make the rain go away."

He threw his hands up. "Does it ever stop?"

"We always get a lot of spring rain here."

When silence fell outside, he jerked around. "It stopped." He opened the door and stared up. After a moment, he turned back to her. "Let's go out."

Seria's head popped up from the stocking. "Now?"

"Aye. Didn't you say it's always better to fish after dark?"

"More like right before sunset." She made another stitch.

"What difference does it make? You're still out there after dark, right?"

She stared up at him. "Are you seriously wanting to fish?"

He shrugged. "Why not? You can show me your favorite fishing spot."

"It's so late, Mason."

"Surely, you're not afraid of a little darkness."

She narrowed her eyes at the challenge. "I didn't say I was afraid of the dark. But it is too late to go all the way out there. And I'm not sure I want to." She didn't know when she would ever be ready to go back to the site of so many unpleasant memories.

His posture slumped. "Well, surely, you have other places you fish."

"Of course, but they're not as productive."

He shrugged again, looking almost desperate. "I need to get out of the house before I go mad."

Seria pursed her lips in thought. It might be good for him to get out before he drove them both crazy. A bit of a walk would also help her gauge the level of his recovery. "All right. We'll go." When a gush of air left him in a rush, she laughed out loud. "Let's get to it then, before you lose your sanity. But you better take your cane, just in case it gets to be a bit much."

He retrieved the walking stick and stood in the middle of the room as she gathered her gear from a trunk under the window. "I don't think Sanjo's up to another trip, so we'll have to walk." She handed him her father's sword from the corner and lit her oil lantern.

"Where on earth did you get such a broken-down blade?"

She chuckled as she wrapped herself in a ratty shawl. "It's pretty rough, isn't it?" They stepped out into the night. Already a few brave stars peeked out from behind the disintegrating clouds. "My father came across it somehow. Always thought it was a good idea to have a weapon in the house."

"Did he know how to use it?"

She led the way to the footbridge and turned right alongside the swiftly flowing creek. "Oh, he played around with it and showed me a few moves, but he was no swordsman. It was more like a game to us." She let out a laugh and turned to better see Mason. "We used to play a game he made up called Get Me Loose, where we would literally tie each other up and try to free ourselves. I got pretty good at it, too." Memories of nights spent in laughter and challenges warmed her from the inside, creating an almost sweet pain.

"Sounds like an interesting way to pass the time. Maybe we should try it." He sent a grin her way.

"I don't think I want to try getting out of a knot tied by a Steward."

He lifted a lazy shoulder and looked away. "So, where are you taking me?"

"There's a spot a little ways from the cabin that I like to go to if I can't make it out to the good spot."

The soft, muted sounds of night surrounded them, enveloping Seria like a familiar cloak. Mason relaxed as he walked alongside Seria with not much of a limp. A night owl sent out a haunting call, followed by the song of crickets.

"How does it feel?" she asked.

"Not too bad." He didn't sound too winded, so that was a good sign. "How far from Rackson are we?" he asked.

"About three miles."

He gaped at her. "You walked three miles after dark to fish?"

"Technically, it's not usually dark yet when I head out, but it is when I come back."

Mason shook his head. "No one can ever accuse you of being lazy."

She gave a grunt. "Thank you, I think."

"How often do you make that trip?"

"Not very often. Though Sanjo helps. But I'll let you in on a little secret." At his open expression, she pointed to a cluster of bluffs around the mountain gap. "There's a passage through there that cuts my journey in half. I cut straight through the rocks instead of all the way around."

"A shortcut?" Mason perked up and peered at the shadowy bluffs under the star-speckled sky. The sliver of moon offered little light.

"That's right. It's not wide, but plenty big enough for me and Sanjo. I wish I'd found it sooner. I made that trip a dozen times before I came across it while berry hunting one day. You wouldn't believe the mess of berry bushes down there."

"Hmm. That's interesting. You might have to show me sometime."

A ribbon of pleasure ran through her. He'd said "sometime". Maybe they would stay in touch after he left.

They continued the hike to the creek in silence. Seria stopped at a gently sloping bank where the creek widened into a little pool. "Here we are. Isn't it charming?"

"Nice." He breathed in the cool, damp night air. There was no denying the satisfaction on his face, and she was glad she let him convince her to come out here. He did enjoy being outdoors after dark.

She set her lines down, grabbed a broken stick from the ground, and started tearing into the ground. In short time, she had several wriggling worms in her hand and held them up for Mason to see.

He put his hands on his hips. "I don't know too many girls who would dig their own bait."

The words were meant as a compliment, she was sure. But something about them stung, and she glanced down at her hand, filled with worms and fingernails encrusted with mud. Maybe it was improper for young women to dig in the dirt or go fishing. What must he think of her?

Are you going to let that stop you from ever fishing again? She lifted her chin and looked him straight in the eye, as well as she could in the moonlight. "Do you know a better way to fish?"

"I do not." His jaw twitched. Was he trying not to laugh at her?

Annoyed now, she turned her back on him and baited a hook. "Here." She handed it over. "I wasn't sure you could bait your own."

He took the pole and lowered himself to the bank not far from where she sat. "I wasn't trying to insult you." Amusement colored his voice.

"Why would I be insulted?" She tended to her pole and tossed the line into the water. "Let's just see who gets the first fish, shall we?"

He gave a short nod and turned to the pole he held in his hand.

A hush fell over them, stretching on until Seria felt foolish. She let her line droop. "I'm sorry."

Mason turned to her. "What for this time?"

"For getting so touchy about what you said. You didn't mean anything by it, but I guess I'm a little too sensitive about how people see me. I'm already not looked on in the highest regard by most of Cadence." The admission alone made her fingers tighten over the handle of her fishing pole.

Mason plucked at some of the grass by his knee. "I'm not very good with words." He tossed the blades up. "So...what's your plan?"

She frowned. "My plan? I'm hoping to get enough fish for breakfast."

"Nay." He shook his head and shifted to face her. "I mean your plan for your life."

"My life?" She cocked her head at him. "Mason, are you asking me about my dreams?"

His face flinched, and he recoiled. "That's not—"

She laughed and put a hand on his arm to stop him. "I know. I'm teasing."

He replied with a frown. "Funny. But surely, you don't want to clean other people's laundry for the rest of your life."

The very idea made her ill. "Not at all." She bit her lip. Dare she trust him with her long-held dream? No one else had ever cared to know, except for Lena, and she was so busy much of the time they rarely had an opportunity to talk. "I would love to be a healer someday."

"A healer?" His brows rose. "Why haven't you done it before now? You certainly have the skills for it."

Now there was a compliment that did not leave her second-guessing. "Well, it takes time and resources. Connections that I don't have." She bumped him with her elbow. "To be honest, I was hoping you'd help me."

He blinked. "How's that?"

"Well," she fidgeted to mask her eagerness. "When you go back, you could maybe spread the word. Let them know that I'm...available."

"Oh." His tone fell a little flat, and he turned back toward the water.

His reaction disheartened her. "That's not why I took you in. I would've helped you regardless. I'm not expecting any favors."

He held up a hand and gave a little smile. "I know that by now." He pulled a few more bits of grass up, his face intent and distant at the same time. Finally, he let out an exhale. "If there's anything I can do, I will."

It was a strange and vague answer, but Mason himself had admitted he wasn't good with words. "Thank you. I appreciate that." Seria shrugged off her disappointment and sent him a smile.

He did not offer one in return, but he nodded and gave his line a little wriggle.

"So, what about you?" Time to dig a little deeper.

"What about me?"

"What's your dream for your life?"

His expression went blank. "Justice."

She cocked her head. "Hmm. That's not a dream. That's a cause, albeit a noble one. But what if you see it done, and the world is full of justice? What do you want then?"

The peeping of tree frogs and crickets filled the space between them. Maybe she had pushed too hard. But he looked more thoughtful than upset. "I suppose, a home." The words were soft, truth dawning in them. "I've never had one that I can remember. We moved around a lot." A shadow crossed his face.

Seria's heart broke at the admission. "That's a good dream. Do you have anything special in mind?"

He shook his head, spinning a stick between his fingers. "Just a place that's mine."

"With a doting wife and family?" She nudged him again.

"I never thought about it. But maybe, someday?" A weak smile crossed his face, then swiftly disappeared. "But dreams have a tendency of not coming true. My brother thought he wanted to be a Steward." The stick broke between his hands.

"That doesn't mean we can't hold on to some dreams."

He lifted a shoulder, but his face shuttered, and she knew the conversation was done. But it was a bit of a breakthrough, so it was enough.

Another period of silence fell over them, and Seria started to wonder if the trip would be a waste when her line gave a dip. She gave two quick yanks and pulled out a silver-bellied fish. "Ha! Look who got the first one."

Mason's face eased out of the tense lines as he watched her unhook it. "I had no doubt you would."

Seria eyed the fish. "I'm not sure it's worth keeping though. It's too small for a meal if we don't catch any more, and I'd hate for its life to go to waste."

He chuckled and waved out at the water. "Then, by all means, give him a new chance at life."

She stepped closer to the water and released the fish. Watching it dart back to freedom after its short captivity stirred a yearning. How long would it take for her to free herself of her current status? Especially if Mason was hesitant to help.

"Seria, don't move."

Mason's sharp command startled her but cut through her awareness before she moved. "What's wrong?"

He pointed to the left of her feet. "Viper."

A coiled gray snake inches from where she crouched. Horror slid down her back like a cold rain. "What do I do?"

"Stay still." His stare was fixed on the serpent as he positioned his feet beneath him in a smooth move. "I'll get it."

She whimpered. "Don't scare it!"

"Shh. You don't want it to bite you."

"You're right. I don't," she hissed. "So, what are you doing?"

"I'm going to move it."

Her mouth went dry. "Nay! I'll stay put until it leaves."

He moved closer. "That could take all night, and I don't know the way back."

She gritted her teeth as he took another step. "Mason. Stop."

"Don't worry." He soothed, as if he was talking to Sanjo. "I got it."

Her heart fluttered and flopped when the snake lifted its scaly head, tongue slipping in and out. Visions of poison shooting through her body filled her mind.

Mason crouched down beside her and reached around her. The slight brush of his arm sent chills down her back. He put his other hand on her arm, steadying her. "Almost there."

His hand shot out, and Seria nearly jumped out of her skin. The snake writhed in Mason's firm grasp. "See, I told you I'd get it."

Seria put her hand over her throat. "Oh goodness. I thought I was going to die."

He shook his head with a sad look. "Such little faith." He walked away a few paces and tossed it in the brush. "I don't think it'll bother us again."

"What, can you read its mind, too?" Seria checked the ground before dropping in a heap on the bank. "I hope you've had your fill of fishing for the night."

"We haven't caught anything."

She held up a finger. "Correction. I did catch something. But I'm too rattled to keep a line still in the water." She picked his line up and shoved it at him.

A slow grin spread over his face. "One little snake, and you fall apart."

"That's easy for you to say." She stood with her arms full of her pole, shawl, and lantern, her skin still crawling with how close she had come to being bitten. "You weren't the one inches from a poisonous viper."

"Oh, it wasn't poisonous."

The statement stopped her in her tracks. "What?"

He gave a lazy wave behind him where he had released the snake. "That was a harmless creeper."

She dropped the bundle at her feet and dug her fists in her hips. "Then why in the world did you let me think it was poisonous?"

He matched her pose. "Because you act fearless about everything else, I wondered if anything scared you."

Seria stomped her foot. "Why, you..." She reached down for a handful of mud and slung it at him.

He swung around so the shot hit him in the back. "Noble knight who rescued you from a snake?"

"I was thinking scalawag!" Her annoyance bled into humor as she watched him duck another onslaught of dirt and grass. "And here I thought Stewards were honest and upright."

Mason scoffed. "Shows what little you know about Stewards. But then again, you're nothing but a *washerwoman*." His eyes widened in exaggeration.

"Oh, that's it." She filled both hands and advanced.

Mason put a finger up and glanced all around them. "Easy now. You don't want to stir up the night wolves."

She wrinkled her nose. "I don't know if I should believe anything you say anymore."

His grin slipped a little, and he let out a hollow chuckle. He reached down to retrieve her old sword, turning it over in his hands. "Maybe you shouldn't."

"Aw." She dropped the mud and rubbed her dirty hands together. "It was all in jest." It was encouraging to see him come out of his shell in a lighthearted attempt at play. He was so serious most of the time.

Mason did not reply as he retrieved his pole. Seria observed the tense lines that settled again over his features. Maybe he had some regrets in his past, something that caused him to doubt his trustworthiness. To assure him she thought nothing more of his stunt, she busied herself gathering the supplies she had dropped. "If I can't handle a trick done in harmless fun, then the fault lies in me, not you."

When he still did not answer, Seria stood and grinned at him until he looked her way. He snorted at her goofy stance, but his face relaxed a bit.

Good. There was no reason for him to feel guilty over a simple little ruse. Sure, he was moody and a bit self-seeking at times, but underneath that hard exterior was a good man.

Even if he did not believe it himself.

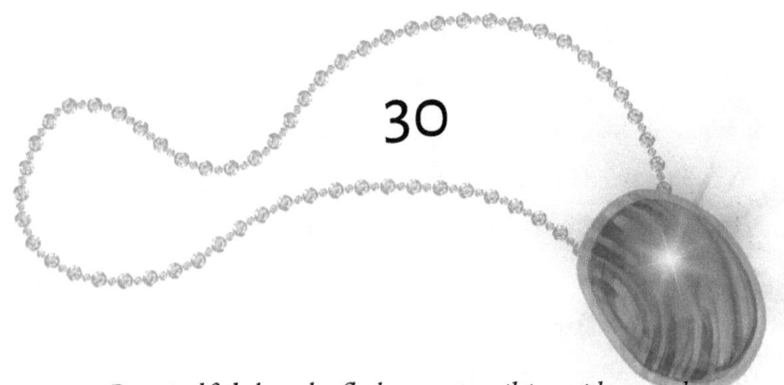

30

Eric scowled as the arrow hit the outer board. Not his, thank the Lambient. Though his bow and quiver hung on his back, this time he was an observer, monitoring the training taking place. But the man firing the bow had already missed several shots. Same as the man before him. The sad fact was that Eric had yet to see a clean round from this group. He asked the attendant to see the marks and frowned at the parchment as if it was to blame for the poor performance.

The field was dotted with men garbed in green leather, sparring, wrestling, or exercising. Grunts of exertion and clashes of steel against steel punctuated the space around him.

Both Captains Dudley and Braylee were present, as well as most of the lieutenants, observing and taking notes. It was the most intense day of training since Eric took command, but he felt it was necessary. The battle at Rackson, as well as what had happened in Cuthrel, still haunted him. They needed to be sharper, faster, ready for anything.

Three platoons had already run through the archery and swordsman-ship tests with flying colors. But Lt. Draven's platoon was lacking. They had let the offense break through their position during the mock attack and had lagged noticeably behind the rest in the other tests.

Eric squared his jaw and braced himself for what he must do. "Lt. Draven." He stalked forward to where the lieutenant stood watching the archery test.

Draven glanced over his shoulder at Eric's approach, his casual stance coated with nonchalance. He nodded once in respect, but Eric did not miss the obstinate jut of the chin. "Your Highness?"

"Your men's performance is inadequate today."

The lieutenant shrugged and turned to survey the archery field. "'Tis only a training day."

Irritation sprung. "No training day should be treated lightly. It prepares them for the real thing." Eric held up the parchment. "Your men took the lowest marks in all the tests today, Lieutenant."

"They have it when it counts, Sire, I assure you. The day's almost over anyhow."

Eric clenched his fists, aware of the attention their conversation was getting from the men around them. "Do they? It was your platoon that fell apart during the siege at Rackson, correct?"

Draven bristled. "We don't know how that happened."

"Aye, I think we do." Eric held his gaze. "Your men were not prepared. When they met resistance, they fell apart, as they are doing now."

"Are you implying—?"

"I'm implying nothing." It sickened Eric that he had to have these words with one of his officers, especially with others watching. But this was too vital to sweep under a rug. "I'm stating it outright. Your platoon needs work. And you will stay out here with them until their marks improve."

A heavy silence fell. The stares of the onlookers felt like needles on Eric's skin. No one was shooting anymore, and the sounds of sparring had let up.

Draven's eyes narrowed. "No disrespect, Sire, but I have difficulty answering to a marshal who chose to spend the last decade in his comfortable chambers while we Stewards defended the land."

Eric ground his teeth. "Nonetheless, you still answer to me."

"I answer to Captains Dudley and Braylee."

The shock of his impudence mixed with hot anger. "You're veering on insubordination, Lieutenant."

A muscle twitched in Draven's jaw. "I appreciate your concern over my men, *Your Highness,* but I'm in charge of them. They've trained enough today." He turned away.

"Lieutenant." Eric steeled his voice. "You will do as I directed."

Draven smirked. "I'm sorry, sir, but I don't see how my platoon will improve under the command of someone who cannot shoot a straight arrow."

Heat surged down Eric's spine. *If you let him walk away, you lose the respect of every man on this field.* He whipped his bow around and grabbed an arrow from his quiver. The arrow flew past Draven, and he jerked back, his face reddening.

"What are you doing?"

Eric drilled his hot stare into the man. "Lt. Draven, you are called to the Council Hall. Immediately."

The shock of the crowd rumbled over him. A call to the Council was the highest form of reprimand. It sometimes meant a hearing before the Councilmen, which could lead to severe consequences. Rarely had a Steward ever had to face a call.

Draven's brows slashed down, and his lips stretched over his teeth. "Aye, *sir*."

Eric nudged with his chin to move the angry man on. As they passed the target, someone whistled and muttered. "Would you look at that?"

Draven glanced over at the target and faltered.

Eric's arrow was dead center.

"Prince Eric, I didn't expect to see you here," Councilman Gayner greeted as Eric and Draven entered the coolness of the main building.

"I have some business I need to conduct."

Gayner's look skittered to Draven and back. "I see. Should the Council convene?"

Draven stiffened beside him.

"Nay, Gayner, not at this time," Eric said. If at all possible, he would avoid a formal hearing.

"Very well. We're in our chambers if you need us."

"Thank you, sir." Eric led Draven down a short hall and into the meeting room at the side of the Great Hall where Eric had been given command of the Steward Army. A command that was now being challenged. He stepped inside the room and held a hand out to the table in the center. "Please take a seat."

Draven sat on the edge of the bench, his back straight. Anger exuded from him, mixed with a good measure of apprehension.

Eric sat across from him and clasped his hands on the table in front of him. He clenched his jaw for a long moment, letting the silence sit. How was he to handle this? His men needed to see him as their commander if he had any hope of leading them to victory against Jader's army. But Draven was well-liked and respected among the Stewards and militiamen alike. Handing out a reprimand to a Steward officer could create more distance. Yet, he could not let the insubordination go unchecked. *Lambient, give me wisdom in this.*

He straightened and looked across the table to where Draven sat staring at him, his mouth clamped tight. "Lt. Draven, here in this room, you are free to speak your mind. Nothing you say will go beyond these walls. Is that understood?"

Draven narrowed his eyes, clearly not expecting that. "Aye."

"Good. Now, Captains Dudley or Braylee would have you demoted and transported back to Calla for your actions."

It was slight, but Eric caught the flinch that flashed across the other man's face in trepidation of being sent back home disgraced. Behind the disrespect and laziness, a good man resided who believed in this cause, had vowed to serve the Lambient. But it was so easy to let the flesh overtake the intentions of the spirit.

Eric exhaled to release the tautness in his spine. "But as much as I respect and rely on my captains, I must operate by my own convictions. And I am a man who believes in second chances."

Draven avoided eye contact, his shoulders still set in a rigid line.

"I have read your records. You have a pristine reputation for leading your men and conducting yourself in a manner befitting a Steward officer. Yet you have not shown me that man."

"Mayhap because you've not been here long enough to see it."

The remark stung, but at least he was talking. "Fair point. But I am here now. And despite your misgivings, I am your commanding officer."

"A commander who does not want to do anything but hide behind walls."

Eric sat back in his seat and wrestled his pride. He had given Draven the floor. "Do you care to elaborate?"

"It's a known fact that you once led the Stewards, but you gave up the leadership and fled back to Calla. All without an explanation from the Royal family or anyone else."

Eric rubbed his palms together. The silence had been his father's instruction, but Eric had embraced it at the time. It was plain to see how wrong they had been.

Draven was not done. "Now, we are supposed to accept you as our leader, yet with Shadowmen on our very doorstep, you still do nothing to search for their source of power. There is no chance of defeating Jader as long as that pit remains. Even after the threat they brought to Cuthrel, nothing is done."

Agitation squirmed in Eric's belly. The Shadowpit again. How long would he have to be reminded of his failure in finding it? "I understand you feeling that way."

Draven let out a little scoff. "But you don't plan to do anything about it?"

"Not at this time."

"Then why wasn't Marshal Uralis allowed to search for it when he was in command? Maybe we would not be facing war with Jader had he located it and destroyed it."

Maybe. Or Uralis could have failed as Eric had and caused more people to die. A cord wrapped itself around Eric's neck, making it hard to speak. His mind was pulled back to those years in the army when his confidence had verged on arrogance, which had led to a mistake he would never get past. He blinked the memories away and gulped past the cord. "Marshal Uralis never insisted on going out on an expedition for the Shadowpit. He offered, but the king and I both felt it best to turn our focus on protecting our people."

"Like those in Rackson?"

Mercy. Why had Eric opened the door for Draven to speak freely? He looked down at the table.

"Did I take my freedom too far?" There was a hint of accusation in the question.

"Nay. I gave it to you. You ask good questions, but I'm afraid I don't have the freedom to answer them the way you wish." Eric cleared his throat. "Unfortunately, my decision stands, as well as my title as Marshal. My word is the final one, and I will not have my officers question me openly in front of the others."

Draven crossed burly arms over a thick chest, irritation simmering in his icy blue gaze.

Eric met it straight on. "Speaking of Rackson, why did your men fail to hold the reserve line?"

Now Draven stared at the table, a muscle in his jaw twitching. "They were taken by surprise by an attack at the rear, and there was a lot of confusion. It's still unclear."

"In the past few weeks, your men have consistently performed poorly in the training fields, as noted by both the captains, as well as what I've observed today. It's been recorded that Captain Braylee has already addressed this with you. That, along with the breakdown in Rackson, speaks of your lack of leadership. I will not have officers I cannot depend on."

Draven's hard expression twitched with uncertainty again. "So, what does that mean for me?"

Eric considered the man before him. With war on the brink, he could not afford to lose any of his officers, especially one so capable as Draven. "What would you do in such a situation with one of your men?"

The lieutenant blinked at the question. "I don't know, sir. I've never faced it." Because no one else would dare to speak in such a way to an officer.

Eric nodded. After a moment, he stood. Draven went to his feet as well. "You are to return to your men, Lt. Draven, and I want you to double the time you and your platoon are in the training fields. Perhaps you will see better results on the next training day."

Draven's nostrils flared, but he said nothing.

"And one more thing." Eric hardened himself against the regret clawing at him and met Draven's glare. "If you choose to openly defy my orders, you will be removed of your title and returned to Calla under Jervis's authority. Understood?"

"Aye, sir." Draven's cheek twitched as he managed a tight nod.

"Good. You are dismissed."

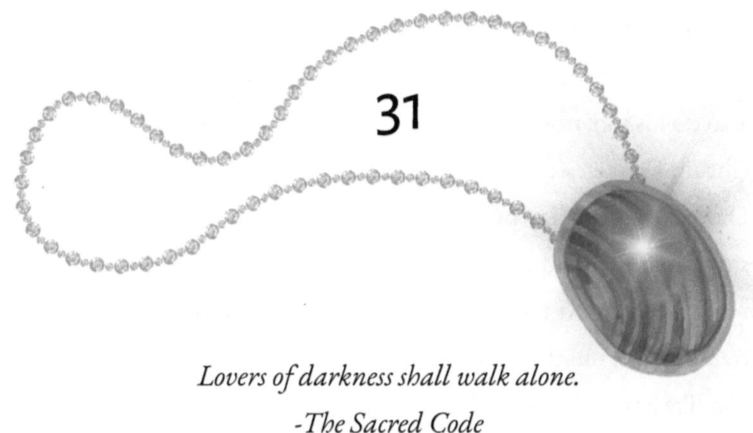

31

Nothing more was said about going into Cadence, though the weather was mild and sunny. Instead, Mason watched Seria work in a feverish pitch, as if trying to outrun a fire right at her heels. A quick insight into her thoughts revealed her concern over losing any more clients, so he was loath to show his irritation. She had already sacrificed a lot of time, and some paying customers, because of him.

All this ran through his mind as he dumped another load into the washbasin outside and started washing. He scrubbed soap over a tunic with a little more force than needed. Shon and Dreeya would poke fun if they saw him now. Mason Grey, respected scout and Darkman and future Shadowman of the emperor's army, reduced to a washerman.

Why had he ever offered to help her in the first place?

Because it's the least I can do before leaving. She had, after all, saved his life.

An uncomfortable feeling slid around his gut at the thought of leaving her to this mundane, degrading lifestyle. Her skills were being wasted on soapy water and canvas bags. By her own admission, she wanted to be a healer and had the makings of a fine one. And she hoped he would help her.

But that would never be.

And that's not my fault. He clenched his fists and his resolve. He was here to do his job, not to worry about a Steward loyalist. Helping her get caught up was a gesture of appreciation. That was all.

They worked all day on the never-ending piles of clothes—washing, rinsing, draining, and hanging—stopping for a few minutes to eat. Byron had been by to take care of Sanjo, so Seria was spared that extra distraction. Garments hung over every spare space in the cabin, closing him in like a trap. How did Seria stand it?

Maybe he should go now, head out after she was asleep and get into the stronghold. His breath quickened at the thought, but then rejected the idea. He needed a way in, one that would draw little-to-no attention. Traipsing about in a military fortress he did not belong in after dark was not the way to do it. He had left his cloaking wrap behind in Rackson. Besides, he couldn't see his way around in the dark.

Not without the Shadowstone.

Mason ground his teeth together and stretched the tired muscles in his back. Noticing how quiet it had gotten, he glanced over and found Seria dozing off in her chair, a folded robe in her lap. He called her name before she toppled to the floor. "Why don't you go to bed?"

She roused and began folding again. "I can't. I still have more to fold, then I'll be ready for my deliveries. And on time, for a change."

He shook his head at her tenacity. "You've been going nonstop all day."

"You go ahead. I can finish this."

Mason stood. "Nay. You're practically asleep on your feet. It's time to quit."

She looked up at him, fatigue shadowing her clear complexion. "I'm fine."

His heart pricked. "You're not." He took the robe from her and pulled her to her feet. "You take the bed."

"I can't do that."

Her weariness bled into each slow step. "No arguments." He helped her into the bed and covered her with the blanket, much like she had done for him many times. A few strands of her hair fell over her smooth skin, framing her young face. The picture of innocence.

She stirred and blinked up at him. "This is where you sleep."

It sounded like an invitation, though Mason knew it was the furthest thing from Seria's mind. Still, something about the way she looked up at him with those big green eyes pulled at him. It would be so easy to crawl in bed beside her, and she was drowsy enough to be sweet.

No attachments. He clenched his fists and shook his head. "It won't hurt me to sleep on the floor tonight."

A huge yawn split her face. "I'm tired."

The obvious statement made him smile, and something stirred in him again. He brushed a blonde strand off her face. "You work hard."

"I have to." She would not be awake much longer. "I can't lose any more business."

The weariness and anxiety weighing on her smacked him. Her work had suffered because of him. She had put her business aside to care for him. She had sacrificed a lot...for him. He was not used to anyone putting his well-being ahead of their own. And the guilt creeping up on him was new as well.

She forced her eyelids up again. "Thank you."

"For what?" He pushed the words out.

"For helping me. Being my friend."

A friend? The word knocked him off guard. He was a Darkman, ready to use her however he must. To dispose of her when he left, so as not to leave any witnesses. *Then why all the help to get her caught up in her work?*

A friend.

His fingernails dug into his palms as he stared down at her, sleeping now against his pillow. She had been faithful in tending to his needs, unaware of his true identity, of the lies he fed her.

Turning away from the serene picture, he lowered himself to the floor. Irritated by the direction of his thoughts, he dismissed the conflicting feelings—a sure sign that he had let himself get too soft. But not for long.

He still limped a little, and his side pulled on him at times if he pushed himself too hard, but there was no reason to stay. It was time. He would slip out as soon he had accomplished one last job. The one Jader had appointed him.

Getting inside the Cadence Stronghold.

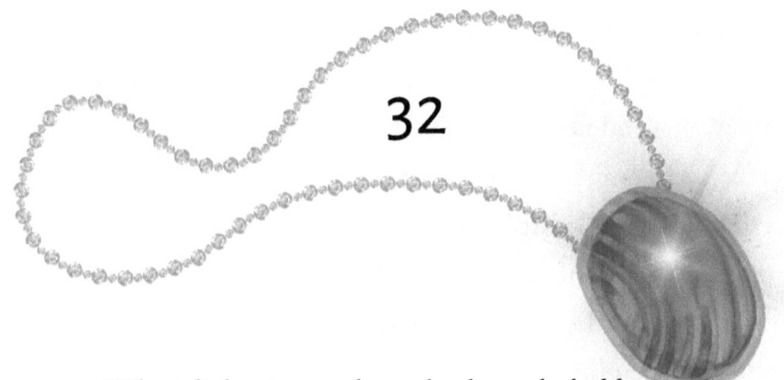

32

Why is light given to those who choose the hidden way?
-The Sacred Code

A loud knock cut through the morning, interrupting Seria's attempt to break her fast. Her limbs felt weighted down by exhaustion, despite sleeping like the dead in her own bed. She had risen with the sun to deliver a few bags on this side of the bridge.

Mason had helped, though he seemed distracted and reserved, most likely growing weary of the never-ending work of washing and drying. Appreciation for his help budded inside her. Giving up the bed was such a kind gesture—though quite unlike him—that she wanted to repay him in some way. She still had more bags to deliver, but they could wait until she had given him the tour of Cadence she had promised.

The visitor pounded again, jerking her back to the present. She hurried to the door, but not before another knock sounded. Goodness, this visitor was impatient.

Ira's slurred, angry speech greeted her.

"I want my money back! And I'm not leaving until you hand it over, hussy! You know you owe me."

Seria deflated, weary with his constant tirade. "Ira, how many times are we going to go over this? I told you. I'm not paying you a pence more. I've already taken care of—"

"Then I'm going straight to the authorities, you little wench!" Spittle flew, and she jerked back out of reach. Ira pushed his way in and stood between Seria and her whip. "They'll have you shut down in no time. And then what's an ignorant girl like you going to do? Huh?"

Seria's insides boiled at his gall. "Get out of my house, Ira." She eyed the distance to the whip, but if she took a step, Ira would clamp his meaty hands on her. Maybe she should grab a spoon. She would not let him manhandle her again.

"You're no good for nothing else!" Ira waved his flabby arms around. "You lose your laundry, you've got nothing!"

Seria squelched her temper back as her body tensed. He had not been this upset since the first day he overwhelmed her. *Stay calm.* "You're intoxicated, Ira. Get out, or I'll—"

"I'll own you, girl!" Ira stuck his face near hers. "I'll own you, and then we'll see what good you are as a woman!"

Wood scraped against the floor, and they both swiveled to see Mason approaching, his expression black. Seria had completely forgotten he was in the room.

Mason squared his shoulders and moved to stand behind Seria. "Is there a problem?" he asked, hard and cold as ice in the dead of winter. But his presence sent assurance over her, warm and strong like a blanket.

Ira blinked at him. "Who are you?" He took a small step back.

"A guest. A patient, actually, and this is the second time you've disrupted my recovery with your little temper tantrum."

"Now, listen here, fella—"

"Nay, you listen." Mason grasped Seria's arms and moved her aside. "From what I hear, she's already recompensed you for the tear. You're not getting another thing from her."

Ira's face turned a shade darker. "What do you have to do with this?"

Mason's hand shot out and grabbed the side of Ira's stout neck. The man huffed in surprise but did not budge.

"Mason!" Seria gasped, but she made no move to stop him. When was the last time anyone had stepped in to defend her?

A cocky grin broke through the chill on Mason's face and lit a fire in his eyes so that they glittered. "As a matter of fact, I have nothing to do with this matter. But I would certainly enjoy rearranging that fat face of yours. And right now, you can't lift a finger to stop me."

Ira gaped at him without a sound.

Mason let go and drilled that hot gaze into Ira's. "Now get out of here. And run, don't walk."

A strange daze slid over Ira's expression. "At once." He quivered with his double chins as he nodded. Then he spun around and trotted away with short, unsteady steps.

Mason's face lit in a victorious smile. Seria's jaw hung as he stepped back and closed the door. He frowned when he looked her way. "What?"

She shook her head, taken aback at his fervor. "Um. That was nice of you. If not a bit harsh."

He shrugged. "Maybe he'll leave you alone for a while."

Seria crossed her arms and leaned against the wall by the door. "I would hate to be the one to face off with you on the battlefield. You had him running for his life."

Another grin spread over his face. "It didn't take much."

"What did you do to him? He looked paralyzed with that hold you had on him."

He shook his head. "A little trick I learned somewhere."

Seria put a hand up to her neck. "You had a nerve, didn't you?"

"More or less."

"Which one?" She felt around. "This one?"

He rolled his eyes. "I can't tell which one you're referring to."

"This one." She reached out and touched the side of his neck. "Right here?"

"Would you—would you quit that?" He grabbed her hand.

She smiled up at him. "Sorry."

He jabbed a finger at her. "I go showing you something like that, and you'd use it on me the first chance you got."

"I would not."

"Aye, you would."

"Nay, I wouldn't."

"Aye, you—" Mason growled. "If anyone else pestered me the way you did, I'd lay them on the ground."

She beamed up at him. "So, what are you going to do to me?" Mercy, was she flirting with him? It was improper to be so bold with a man, but she found herself willing to cross the lines of propriety to see those eyes spark with life, rather than glaze over with disinterest.

He took a step closer. "Maybe I'll hogtie you and leave you here."

"My, someone got out of bed in a mood."

"I didn't sleep in a bed, remember?"

Aye, she did remember. Which was why his harsh words had no effect. Despite his hard and distant exterior, she was starting to believe that inside he was nothing but a big softy.

"Softy?" he growled.

She laughed out loud. "I'm sure that's not what a knight wants to hear but serves you right for peeking into my thoughts." Her heart swelled that he cared to know what she was thinking.

His features tensed, and his scrutiny sharpened. A squeeze of her hand told her he still held it in his larger one. "Don't think too much of me, Seria," he said, low and heavy. Then, he let go and turned away. A chill squeezed its way between them, but Seria refused to let it dampen her mood.

This man had been buffeted by life. It would take time for him to let down his defenses, but she had seen glimpses past that mask he held tightly in place. He was afraid to let anyone close. But whether he liked it or not, he was her friend, and she would not give up on him.

They left for Mason's tour of Cadence soon after. Mason wore his own boots again and refused to take the walking stick. The bridge was passable, despite the recent rain. She cast a quick look back as Mason crossed the wooden planks in silence, tracing the path of the creek, where it snaked toward the Slate Mountains. Where they had gone fishing a mere couple of nights ago.

They topped a small hill, and the town of Cadence spread before them, nestled in the crags of the Slates. Beyond it, in the narrow gap between the mountains, the fort stood like a stone wall—the same wall that separated Cadence from the Old Realm.

Cadence was small but teeming with activity as Seria and Mason merged with the foot traffic in the streets. Merchants and hawkers shouted out their wares, while shoppers strolled from cart to cart.

"How many people live here?" Mason asked, stepping aside to miss a goat herder.

"Between three to four hundred people, I'd say. Most of them are refugees."

"From where?"

"The New Realm. Folks who fled Jader's realm."

A brief scowl darkened Mason's face, but he said nothing as he stood and took in the hustle around him.

Seria waved at a familiar face amid the crowd. "Oh, there's Lena!"

Lena returned the wave from behind her barrow, surrounded by several patrons.

Seria moved on. "I was hoping we could visit, but it looks like she's busy. But that's good, I suppose, since she's earning money to start her own bakery. She's the one who sent those delicious tarts we ate a while back. She and her mother live in the fort."

Mason turned his head back to Seria. "The fort?"

"Mm-hmm. Her mother runs a little bakery there. Does pretty well, from what Lena says."

He glanced back at Lena. "Interesting."

The larger-than-usual number of booths and carts clicked in her mind. "Oh, no wonder it's so crowded today. The farmer's market is in town." She heard an uninterested little grunt beside her in reply.

She drew near to a cart of flowers and tried to picture how the little bright splashes of colors would brighten up her dreary little shack. The gray-brown walls and floors surrounding her every day were quite depressing but other than a few little wildflowers, there was little she could do about it. It must feel so miserable to Mason. She kept her face averted, lest he pick up on her thoughts.

Someone jostled her, and she stumbled to the side, expecting to bump into Mason. Instead, empty space threw her off balance, and she almost lost her footing. "Mason?" She searched the dozens of faces around her, but there was no sight of him. Where was he? She called his name again, turning in a slow circle trying to spot him and checking the ground to make sure he had not taken a spill.

Confusion nestled in her breast and on her brow. Why would Mason leave her?

33

"That was easier than I thought it would be," Mason said with a tight chuckle to the compliant woman beside him.

Lena gave a nonchalant shrug.

Mason shook off his uneasiness and looked around. They were in a quiet part of the lower courtyard, in a small open space to the left of the gate and behind a cluster of civilian homes. "Let's walk like all is normal."

Lena nodded and continued on, her will firmly under his control. His fingers tingled as they passed a garden and a well, inching closer to the courtyard.

"Lena?"

Mason jerked to see a militiaman approaching.

"Good day, Hiram," Lena greeted, her tone normal.

"I thought you were working in the farmer's market." Hiram cast Mason a suspicious look. "What are you doing back here already?"

Mason stepped in his path. "Stay quiet."

Hiram's face relaxed. "At once."

This could not be more perfect. Hiram could get him to the areas he needed to see, and Lena would help get him out again. He looked to the young woman. "Wait here for me."

"At once." She sat on a barrel and folded her hands, as if she had all the time in the world.

As soon as he was given the order, Hiram led the way at a brisk pace. Mason held his breath as they walked through the keep gates beneath the gate tower into the lower bailey. No one stopped them. He took in the wide-open inner courtyard they would have to cross.

To their left stood another group of civilian homes. Straight ahead stood the Great Hall, where the officers lived and met. A bell tower stood a few yards from the hall.

Militia reservists moved about, their dark clothing mixing in with the colorful tunics of the Stewards. Bitterness churned upon seeing the red capes, but he reined it in and fought for control. He tightened the laces on his bracers, savoring the feel of familiar leather wrapped around his forearms.

There were at least a hundred knights in the courtyard alone. Many more would be positioned throughout, and who knew how many civilians lived and worked on this side of the curtain wall. Mason's trained sense of vigilance rose to the forefront. His nerves prickled with awareness.

He turned to his guide. "Who's the commander here?"

"The prince of Paladin."

Mason halted and stared at him. His head spun, dizzying him. "Eric Passion?" The name came out forced, hoarse.

"Aye, sir."

Clenching his teeth, Mason stood stock still for a few seconds as a barrage of memories washed over him, stirring up the familiar rage he had lived with for half his life. "Where?" He growled the question.

The guard pointed to the two-story hall.

Mason took special notice of the structure. It stood on the far side of the courtyard, an impressive, white-stone building, complete with tall, green stained-glass windows and a large balcony on the second floor. His fists knotted the front of his shirt as he pictured the prince inside, retiring in lavish quarters. Mason turned away for now, but he tucked the information into his memory. The day would come when he would bring it to good use.

They moved farther into the fort, Mason ever watchful. He kept Hiram at his side, squeezing as much information out of him as he could. His spirit stirred to leave some mark behind, some kind of destruction. Something to hurt the Stewards in some way, albeit small. But now was not the time. He was not in the physical condition to fight his way out. So, for now, every little bit of information he gathered would have to suffice.

"What's the current state of the Stewards?" he asked his accomplice as they rounded the hall.

"There's been some division."

Division? Among the united ranks of the faultless Stewards? "Why's that?"

"Some are not happy with the prince taking over the Stewardship."

Now, this was a valuable piece of information. How could Eric lead a disputing army to victory? Mason smiled at the thought.

The fort was nothing if not efficient, boasting of several barns and two large buildings to house the hundreds of Stewards and reservists. The large mess hall with an attached kitchen stood across from the main building. Behind them were the small buttery, granary, and bakehouse sheds and farther still were the huts that housed the keep staff.

With every step, Mason's muscles grew tighter and tighter. Though they had not aroused any suspicion as of yet, his ears hummed in expectancy of confrontation. Sweat dripped down the sides of his face. Just a little longer.

They were crossing back over the courtyard, making their way back from the weapons keep, when the hairs on the back of his neck lifted. He jerked toward the balcony, and the world spun to a stop. The prince stood there. Staring right at him.

Blood rushed to his head and cold hatred sprang. There he was, mere yards away. Mason's tight fingers itched for a sword, a bow, *something*.

The door beneath the balcony opened, and a dark-headed Steward headed his way. Ice ran down Mason's back. He spoke to the obedient guard, motioning with his chin at the big man approaching. "Keep your friend from following me. At any cost."

"At once." Hiram drew his sword.

Blades. There was no way he would make it back to Lena now, so he headed for the gate.

"Ho, there!" The Steward called out but was cut off by a jab from Hiram's sword.

Mason found two more men by the gate. They watched him suspiciously, but neither were Stewards, so he caught them both in a straight-on look. "Close the gate behind me. And don't let anyone else through."

They jumped to comply. "At once."

Mason stopped and sent the prince one more dark glare. Time had run out, but he would be back.

Eric's scalp crawled at the pure hatred exuding from the man's countenance. The stranger touched his forehead in a cocky salute and headed out the open gate. Two reservists hurried to close the portal behind him. Then he was gone.

Shock and outrage poured over Eric as the scene played out like a bad dream. Braylee was forced to draw his weapon against Hiram, and the two reservists charged anyone who approached the gate. His own men were turning on each other.

It can't be. Eric's lungs turned inside out. This was it. This was the source of dread clinging to him the last few weeks. He spun from the balcony and grabbed his sword. *Please don't let them hurt one another,* he begged the Lambient as he rushed for the courtyard. The steps stretched on unending as he pounded his way down, fearing what he would find when he got outside.

Braylee stood before Hiram like an enraged warrior, his face as dark as a thundercloud, ready to deliver the final blow to the less-experienced militiaman still coming at him.

"Braylee, wait!" Eric raised his hand, and the sword flew from Hiram's hands, landing out of reach in the dirt.

Braylee took that chance to step in and swing his fist, knocking the man off his feet. Then he put the tip of his sword to Hiram's chest.

"Don't hurt him." Eric reached out toward the two gatekeepers, and they promptly lost their weapons as well. He aimed his next directive at a pair of young Stewards nearby. "Bind their hands, and take them to the barracks but see that no harm comes to them." When they stared back at him, dumbfounded, he barked. "Do it now!"

They jumped to oblige. Others joined the melee as all three men wrestled and fought against the ropes and their comrades. It took several men to restrain each of them.

"What's going on?" Braylee asked. "Do we have traitors among us?"

"Nay. I fear that stranger was none other than a Reader."

Braylee's jaw slackened. "A Reader? Is that even possible?"

"I'm afraid so." He let out a groan. "What rotten timing. There have been but three known cases in history. None in the last hundred years. Why now?" Was it too coincidental? Could this Reader be working with Jader? A cold dread filled him.

"That would explain what happened here." Braylee exhaled and sheathed his sword, still steady and calm, despite the worry lingering. "What now?" He tossed the decision back to Eric.

Weakness overtook his limbs. How could he do this? How could he take on Jader, his Dark Army, Shadowmen, and a hostile Reader? It was impossible.

But the task was his so he would do what was required. He ground his teeth. "Search the town. We can't afford to let him out of Cadence."

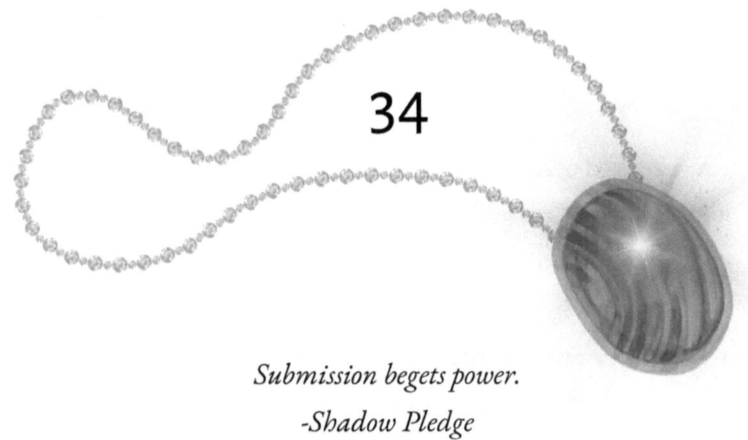

34

Submission begets power.
-Shadow Pledge

The wretched prince would soon have his men on Mason's tail, so everywhere Mason turned, he gave orders, creating bedlam in the streets. Vendor carts were knocked over, spilling their wares in the dirt. Fighting broke out in the street. All the while, adrenaline pumped through him as he charged through the crowds, his objective set on the woods beyond the town.

His stay in Cadence was over. And so was his time with Seria.

A knot behind his sternum made it difficult to breathe. This was what he wanted. A clean break.

"Mason!"

He swiveled to see her hurrying to his side.

Blades.

"Where have you been?" she asked with a furrowed brow. "I was sure you had gotten lost or hurt again."

Oxygen lodged in his craw like a pebble, and his mind spun for a plan. With his limp, those Stewards could catch up with him in no time. Seria could provide him leverage. Besides, she was a witness. She knew too much about him. He couldn't leave her behind.

She peeked at the bedlam behind him. "What happened back there?"

Mason stepped close. His veins throbbed, and he clenched his teeth against the drum in his head as she looked up at him in surprise. "Come with me."

Her eyes glazed over. "At once."

For a brief moment, guilt lifted its head at how easily she followed him. Then he stomped it down where it belonged. He had used his Gift dozens of times. Why should it be any different with Seria?

It took them a few minutes to leave the dust of Cadence behind and cross the border into the thick woods. Even then, Mason could not relax. What distraction he had caused in the town would not hold the knights for long.

Seria stood beside him, casting a curious look around them, but much too quiet for her. The silence unnerved him.

He turned in a circle. What was he going to do now? Run all the way to Bruin's camp with Seria in tow? Hold her hostage and demand a mount from the Stewards? Both ideas left him with a bad taste.

Movement farther ahead in the distant woods arrested his attention. He tensed and strained to make it out. It was in the opposite direction of Cadence, so it could not be the Stewards. Not yet.

Mason focused on the apparition as it took shape, revealing a group of men coming over the distant hill. Hope sprang when he made out the dark clothes. They were small and almost indistinguishable, but there was no mistaking the red-headed leader: Shon, his closest cohort in the Dark Army. Most likely, the scouting party had been assigned to keep an eye on the Gateway without being spotted.

Relief poured through Mason's limbs. This was it, his best chance to break away and rejoin his allies. They were right there! There was but one problem.

A faint snap in the woods behind him brought his head around. A group of Steward knights trudged their way up the hill. Following his trail. He ducked down—pulling Seria with him—bells of warning jangling in his ears.

This was all happening so fast. Darkmen on one side, Stewards coming up on the other. And he was in the middle. Again. Perfect for another crossfire. What were the odds?

Not how he planned his exit.

Neither group was within sight or earshot of each other yet, but it wouldn't take long. Seria crouched beside him, still not uttering a word. Tension pressed against his temples, and blood pounded in his ears like a drum. Sweat poured down his back.

With the Darkmen so close, he no longer needed the collateral she offered him. Shon's band could get Mason out safely.

Logic screamed not to leave any witnesses that could incriminate him. It's what Bruin would expect of him. What any Shadowman would do—remove any obstacles standing in the way of their cause.

She looked up at him, her expression devoid of the usual spunk and curiosity he had come to know. Acid filled his gut. He clenched his jaw, every possible scenario racing through his head. It would look like an accident. A tumble from the hill. Or a misstep right in the middle of the coming brawl. He never had to lay a finger on her.

His glare drilled into her; the words poised on his lips. Instead, a low growl escaped him. "Get in the bushes. Now." He ground the words past a rigid throat. "Don't make a sound and stay there until *everyone's* gone. No. Matter. What."

Without her usual dozen questions, Seria turned and crawled into the thick brush. The branches and thorns caught on her skin and clothes, but she did not hesitate. When she was in position, she turned to peer back at him through the brambles. A sharp pain pierced him. "This is not...I never—" He snapped his mouth shut. One never apologized to the enemy.

Another crack drew him around. The Stewards were getting closer. He glanced back at her one more time. After weeks of wanting nothing more than to leave Cadence, why the rock in his gut?

Because this girl had done more for him than anyone else, with the exception of Emperor Graulik Jader.

The reminder drew him up straight, and he spoke one last time. "Thanks for getting me back on my feet." And then he turned away, leaving her concealed in the bushes. He trod down the hill with leaden limbs, opposite where the Stewards were coming from, and stalked through the trees to get to Shon, but he had to be careful. Showing up without warning would get an arrow through him. Shon acted first and asked questions later.

Catching another quick glimpse of his friend, Mason let out a soft, coded whistle. Shon halted, raising his hand to stop the others. Mason sent out the call again, and Shon responded in kind. Mason stepped out of hiding, and the men gawked.

Shon shook his head. "Mason, where have you—?"

"Shh!" Mason glanced behind him. "I've got a band of Stewards on my trail on the other side of this hill. We gotta shake 'em."

Shon's face sobered. "Got it." He grabbed an extra sword from his pack and tossed it to Mason. "Can you still handle one of these?"

The weapon felt good in his grip. "You have any doubts?" Anticipation washed over him as he twisted his hand around the hilt.

Shon's teeth flashed white in the shadows. "About you? Never."

They spread out and hunched down in hiding, waiting for the Stewards to approach. Mason let Shon take the lead. A strange hush fell as they peered through the forest.

The band of Stewards drew nearer, their murmurs barely detectable as they discussed their next steps. Mason held his breath and waited.

Shon jumped up with a shout, and the dozen or so Darkmen burst from hiding and attacked. The Stewards reacted with lifted swords.

Mason ran to meet a Steward and raised his weapon in challenge. He moved with confidence and ease, throwing himself into the fighting. It felt good to be out here again, fighting for a cause he still believed in. He had feared the weeks with Seria had softened him.

Images of Liam falling before a Steward filled him with hot rage, and his movements accelerated. The Steward went down, and Mason turned to block a blow from another one. His side burned with every gulp of air. A swift kick knocked his opponent flat on his back, but Mason's bad leg buckled, and he dropped to one knee. Sucking in a sharp wheeze, he braced himself with his sword. Fire streaked through his side.

Both sides fell back at that point, and Shon called for a retreat.

Mason's gaze shot to the bushes on the hill, and his breathing quickened.

"Come on!" Shon hooked his arm and pulled him up. "We gotta go before they send reinforcements."

Mason dismissed his hesitation and followed Shon. There was no reason to go back anyway. Now that Seria knew the truth, she would despise him.

As they sprinted through the woods, Shon glanced over, his red hair bouncing with the brisk pace. "Do you mind telling me what happened? We all thought you were dead."

Favoring his aching leg, Mason gave a quick shake of his head. "Glad to prove you wrong."

They were moving too fast to carry on a decent conversation, so Mason promised to tell it in full when they reached their destination. He didn't allow himself to dwell on what was behind him. There was too much ahead. He was free!

So why did he feel like he was dragging an anchor with his feet?

Almost an hour later, Shon raised his arm to point. "Right over the next rise."

"Good." Mason panted. The trek through the uneven woodland was doing a number on his weakened body.

They caused quite a stir when they broke through the tree line and into the camp. Upon seeing him, Feegan broke into a run.

"By the moon, what's happened to you, son?"

The tan tents scattered throughout the small clearing in semi-organized groups filled Mason with an overwhelming sense of relief. He bent over to brace himself against his knees and raised a hand, unable to speak. His side and leg throbbed madly. That incessant drum pounded in his head.

Feegan called for some water. "Take your time."

Shon held the mug so Mason could drink. "You all right, mate?"

Mason struggled to stay on his feet. Blackness pressed in on him, sucking the oxygen from his lungs. He tried to shake the shadow falling over him. Whether it was coming from the gathering dusk or somewhere within, he could not tell.

"Easy, there." Shon sounded miles away.

Dots danced before his vision, and the ground rushed to meet him. There was faint shouting, but he could make nothing out. The clear green of Seria's huge eyes filled his mind before he plunged into complete darkness.

The room grew darker as the sun descended outside, but Seria did not light the lantern. She sat motionless at the table, as she had done since crawling from her hiding place hours after the fight. Her hands lay limp on her lap.

Something was wrong. Deathly wrong. Her mind scrambled to fit the pieces together. But no matter how she arranged them, they did not make sense. A haze convoluted the memories that knocked about in her achy head, almost like a bad dream she could not remember.

Mason had fought the Stewards—had *killed* one, from what she could see from her hiding spot. Seria shook her head. There had to be a reason. Maybe the Darkmen had caught him and forced him to fight for them. Maybe his head injury caused him to forget what side was good and right. Something had to be amiss for him to use his sword against the Stewards.

But Mason had opposed them without hesitation, steel against steel, blood for blood. He meant every move he made. The truth began to sink in, seizing her oxygen and leaving her head pounding.

Mason was a Darkman.

Rushing filled her ears, and a chill seeped into her bones, numbing her. *Nay.* He couldn't be. He wouldn't deceive her so completely. But even as the silent, feeble cry echoed in her head, Seria knew it was true.

How could she have been so blind? Her need for importance had overridden all the signs. Looking back, there had been plenty. His stiff civility and short temper, the memory lapses, the odd excuses—the list went on. But she let it all go unheeded. And now, she was left to pay the price.

If anyone found out, her reputation would be ruined, what little good standing she had, shredded. Her cheeks scorched at the possibility.

She clenched her fists and swiped at the table, knocking dishes and laundry to the floor. A strangled cry ripped from her as she pounded her fists against the wood. How could he? After all she had done for him. After all they had shared.

The moment passed, and she slumped against the table, tears streaming down her face. Her heart shriveled, and the hurt swelled, consuming her. And she was afraid it was there to stay. In the midst of her turmoil, one question reverberated in her mind, shattering her further.

What have I done?

35

"Welcome back."

Mason turned his head toward the speaker. Shon sat on a short stool beside the cot, his elbows on his knees. The block of silver moonlight on the ground through the tent opening told him it was after sunset. He was back in his tent, back home.

Something sharp poked at his relief. This was no home. This was a cover that could be packed up and moved in a matter of minutes. But it was the only home he had known for the last dozen years.

He shook the depressing thoughts away. "How long have I been out?" It felt like he had been eating gravel.

"Hours. Bruin wants to see you as soon as you're able."

Mason palmed his gritty eyes. "Let him know I'll be ready shortly." He was more than ready to make his report and get back to a sense of normalcy.

Shon didn't move. "You all right?"

"I'm fine."

"You sure?"

Mason squinted up at him. "Why the questions, Shon?"

Shrugging, Shon hesitated. "You were gone for a fortnight and a half. And then you come back all busted up, with Stewards after you. You seem different."

Mason looked away, biting back the urge to snort. "I'm fine."

Shon stared at him.

"Give me some time, and I'll take you out on the dueling fields again." Mason shot him a cocky grin.

"Aw, now I don't know about that. You know I can best you any day."

Now Mason snorted. "Why don't you make yourself useful, and tell Bruin I'll be in soon?"

He lay on the cot for a moment after Shon left. Unbidden, his mind drifted to Seria. His time with her was over. He was free, what he had wanted all this time.

So, why was there a stone lodged between his ribs?

Mason threw his blanket off and reached for his shirt. It was time to get back to his way of life. And Seria was free to return to hers.

"So, the prince is still in in the Gateway?"

Mason answered Bruin's question. "Aye, sir. He's assumed the role of leader in the event of their last commander's death."

"And you say there is division among the troops." Bruin paced the ground in his personal, spacious tent, stroking his whiskers.

Mason stood with his hands clasped behind his back, looking straight ahead. Feegan listened in from a chair nearby.

"And where were you these twenty-one days?"

Everything inside him jumped at the question, and he had to work to keep his expression indifferent. The question was to be expected. The commander was a stickler for details, but the answer died on Mason's lips.

"Mason?" A trace of impatience colored Bruin's voice. "Who were you with?"

"A mere peasant." He forced his jaw to unclench to release the stilted words.

"What became of them?"

Blades. He had left a witness. There was no way he could rationalize that, not to Bruin. A Shadowman would not have hesitated to kill her. "I took care of him." The shock of his own words hit him in the gut.

Bruin paused and stepped closer, studying Mason's face. "You mean, you eliminated him?"

Mason hesitated before meeting Bruin's look. "That's right." There was no going back now.

Bruin exchanged smiles with Feegan. "Another job nicely done."

"Thank you, sir." It was a desperate hope the officers could not hear how hoarse he had become.

The meeting went on a few minutes longer before Mason was finally able to escape the confines of the tent.

What had he done? He'd looked his commander in the face and lied. Why? For Seria? She was of no importance to him.

He chewed the inside of his cheek as he walked. Seria had saved his life. Twice. His lies would ensure she would not be bothered. A small debt he could pay. That was all. He owed her nothing else. She lived under the overpowering influence of the legalistic Stewards, and her feelings of awe and admiration were more than clear. That was something he would not tolerate. Ever.

His fists clenched at his sides. Baris had always said Stewards were not to be trusted. Had warned Mason over and over not to take them lightly, that they were not the heroes the people of the Gateway believed them to be.

Stalking through Bruin's camp, cluttered with squeaky wheels, coarse laughter, and horse snuffles, Mason could hear Baris' caution in that long-ago memory. *"You mark my words, Mason. Those Stewards are dangerous."*

Mason had always laughed him off. Until the day of the hunt.

The encampment crowded in on him, stifling him. Mason stepped through the perimeter of the campsite, into the darkening woods, and leaned against a thick oak.

He could almost hear the excited chatter of the boys. It echoed in his head, though he had never gotten close enough to hear anything but screams. The attack happened before Mason could reach them.

The chatter morphed, just like in his dreams, and soon the cries shrieked through his ears. Mason bent and braced himself against his knees, gritting his teeth against the torrent of fury he kept locked inside. Fought against the tears biting at him. Tears were for the weak.

He spun and slapped his palm against the rough bark. Again and again. Relished the sharp pain it sent through his hand and up his arm. He pressed his forehead against the tree and let the same rush of rage and vindication sweep over him as it had at that moment when he lifted his bow and launched an arrow.

And killed his first Steward.

But he remembered little more beyond pain and darkness. All he knew now was that the Stewards rode away triumphant, leaving the bloody scene behind. Fifteen teenage boys had been killed, as well as Baris. Mason was the lone survivor, left for dead at the edge of the woods with an arrow sticking out of him.

Almost of its own will, his hand rubbed the scar under his collarbone. If it had not been for Jader's men finding Mason, he would have been one of the casualties, and no one would have known what the Stewards had done. But Jader had taken him in, treated him like one of his own. Mason owed his life to the emperor.

The calm of the sunset seeped into his bones, chilling the fire licking at his spirit. A gray sky cast distorted shadows over the woods, and the chattering of birds stilled.

Mason ground his teeth, his resolve strengthening. If it took the rest of his life, he would see the Stewards dismantled and their leader brought down. For Liam. For Baris. For the other Handan boys. This was why he was here, why he had spent weeks pretending to be the very thing he despised. So that he could get back here and resume his pursuit of justice.

He shook his head, sending the haunting images back into the abyss of his mind where they belonged. As a boy, Mason would have never believed what the Stewards were capable of. Until he saw for himself.

Baris had been right.

The image of the prince, looking down from his high perch, danced before Mason now. He tightened his fists against the raw scrapes on his hands and stretched his rigid neck. Someday, Mason would fulfill his promise and kill Eric Passion.

The man responsible for the Handan massacre.

Jader was in his quarters when word came that Bruin had arrived. His commander must have important news to make the long trip to Ignadon at such a late hour instead of using the Shadowstone to send a message. Jader granted Bruin immediate entry to meet him at the throne room.

Bruin stopped at the base of the throne and bowed his dark head. "Emperor Jader, Mason Grey has returned to the camp."

Jader straightened and gripped the arms of the throne. "When?"

"Late this morning."

"And I am only now being informed?"

"I apologize, but he was dead on his feet and still recovering from injuries he received. I wanted to get his report first."

"And that is?" Anxious anticipation spiraled through him. With the untapped potential of Mason's Gift, he had become a crucial component of Jader's quest for the Old Realm.

Bruin went on to tell all he had learned from the scout, finishing with his news about Prince Eric leading a divided Steward Army.

Jader's mind moved quickly as he pulled himself from the throne and moved to a tall table where a pitcher sat. Filling two goblets with wine, he handed one to Bruin. "A divided army would be most difficult to lead, would it not?"

Bruin's face lightened in humor. "Most difficult."

"I believe a trip to your camp is in order, Commander Bruin, so that I may check on my brave young scout myself."

"As you wish, Emperor Jader."

The commander left to rest before the journey back to the camp in the morning, and Jader gave his servants orders to make his own preparations. Once left alone, he sat for a long time on the throne, staring into the shadowed corners of his room. He stroked the long scar on the side of his face.

It had taken much perseverance and work to get to where he was now, in complete power of the New Realm, and the Old within his grasp. But he had to admit luck had been on his side. Luck that the people had grown weary of the rigors of the Sacred Code and yearned for freedom of choice. Luck that he had mastered the ancient powers that allowed him to control and create darkness. And luck that he had learned of a teenage orphan with a Gift far beyond Jader's wildest hopes.

Jader looked past the dark walls and rooms of the castle, back to his early days with Mason, earning his trust and, in time, winning his loyalty. Now, Mason was one of his finest Darkmen, and his most powerful. If the scout were to take on Jader's Shadowstone, he would be virtually unstoppable.

The Shadowstone. Jader still thrilled at the power those stones bestowed upon the men and women of his Dark Army. It was pure ingenuity that had driven him to channel his power into the stones, allowing some of his dark strength to be passed onto his protégés. His army was growing stronger. Soon, it would overcome the Passions' weak, pathetic Stewards, and Jader would rule both the New and Old Realms.

Aden Passion had once called him a fool for the path he had chosen. Now, his son stood poised to fight against Jader's power. Jader clenched his fist and watched the shadows in the room grow, reaching into every inch of wall and floor until the room was pitched into black. A smile stretched across his face, pulling the scar tight.

Both father and son underestimated him, but they would soon realize the gravity of their mistake.

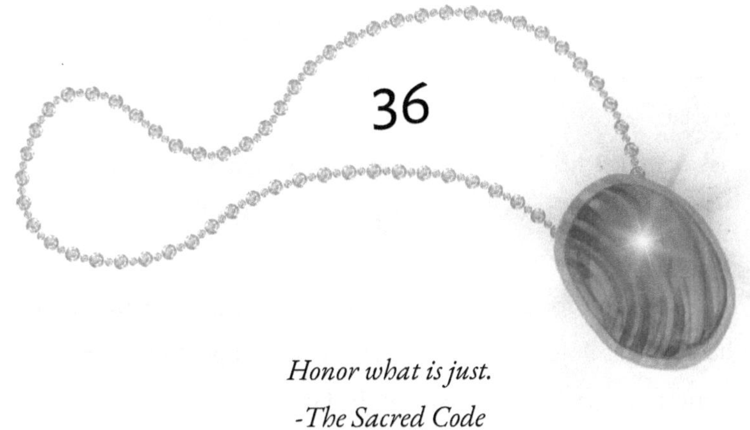

36

Honor what is just.
-The Sacred Code

A loud, single knock resounded through the room before the door burst open. Seria jumped from her chair, knocking it backward. She gaped at the serious-looking Steward filling the doorway. He held a restraining hand up.

"Stay where you are, miss," he said, stern but calm. "We have reason to believe someone could be hiding here."

Ice tingled in her fingertips, and all hopes of secrecy dashed to pieces.

The man stepped aside so his three companions could enter. They walked in, already scrutinizing the small space.

The leader spoke again. "Has anyone been here?"

Her heart threatened to pound its way out of her body. Before she could answer, one of the men called out.

"Sir Abel!"

Stark fear gripped her upon seeing the Steward armor in the man's hands. The armor she had believed to be Mason's.

"Parish's suit." Abel's face flushed as he glowered over her. "Where is the Darkman?" He ground the words out; gone was the composed demeanor he had carried with him moments before. In his place stood an enraged defender of the Gateway.

Panic squeezed her, and she lost all ability to speak.

Another man stepped into the house. "Nothing in the shed but a donkey, sir."

Abel clenched his jaw. "He's gone." He stared Seria down, his face livid. "And I'm willing to bet she helped him escape."

"No!" The word squeaked out. "I didn't—"

"You can save it for the Council, miss." He stepped forward, and she flinched. But his hold on her arm was firm, not rough. "You'll stand trial for aiding and abetting the enemy of the Gateway and the Old Realm."

Another man stepped to her other side. Did they believe her capable of escaping with her legs shaking as they were?

Fear and shame lanced at her as she was led from the house and taken through the streets of Cadence. The stares of her fellow townspeople burned against her skin. She bit back a sob before it could escape. Her weeping would do nothing to move the Stewards. She had committed a serious offense, and they would see justice served. The penalty for Darkmen was harsh; hers wouldn't be much better.

A short time later, Seria stood before the tall podium, trying not to let the Council see her shaking. She was finally inside the famed stronghold but could not recall one thing she had seen on the way.

Stewards stood guard on either side, their expressions unreadable. She buried her trembling fingers in the folds of her tattered brown frock.

Don't get sick. She had woken with a pounding headache, disoriented and faint. Now, her stomach rolled and twisted, while her heart raced, making her light-headed. The three gray-headed men seated in front of her did not appear sympathetic.

The head of the Council gave her a firm look. "I demand an answer, young lady. Where is the Darkman?"

"I-I don't kn-know."

Another spoke up. "Surely, you know the penalty for treason. What reason do you have for harboring the enemy?"

She had already tried to explain this once. "I didn't know. I mean, I thought he was a—"

The first man cut her off. "Is it true he was under your roof for *weeks*?"

She gave a quick, jerky nod.

"That Darkman walked right into this garrison," the third added. This one looked a little softer, but still resolute about doing his job. "The town of Cadence was left in chaos. Two Stewards were killed in the wake of his departure. What have you to say about that?"

Anger flickered and flared without warning. Anger at Mason for putting her in this position and herself for allowing it. And at these councilmen and Stewards who treated her like a criminal. She had done nothing wrong. "I told you how it happened." She stared back at the head Councilor.

He scowled back at her. "Jader wants nothing more than to breach the Gateway. Thanks to you, he very nearly reached his goal!"

What little bravado she had presented dissipated. Her body swayed, and her empty stomach twisted and churned.

What more could she say? These men wouldn't believe her, wouldn't even listen to her. She could already hear the door of the dungeon closing.

"I remember someone calling out to me. I turned, and there was this young man." Eric listened to Hiram's account with a heavy sense of foreboding.

Hiram shook his head in disbelief. "I'd never seen him before. He told me to attack Braylee, and I just…did it." He slouched. "I can't explain it. It was so easy for me to succumb. I'm so sorry, Your Highness."

Eric spoke up. "It's not your fault, Hiram. Readers are powerful."

He had come to the infirmary to find Hiram and the other two men in their right minds, but with throbbing headaches. Their perplexed reaction to the Reader's control called to mind the young soldier he met right after the battle of Rackson. These men were not his first victims.

He looked up to see Braylee approaching.

"Excuse me, Prince Eric, but do you have a minute?"

After assuring the three men there would be no repercussions, Eric followed Braylee outside.

"There's been some new developments on the Reader, sir. The Council is meeting at this moment."

Eric's heart sank at Braylee's look. "How bad is it?"

"A young woman from Cadence was arrested this morning for being an accomplice. She's standing trial now before the Council."

He was in Cadence all this time? Eric moved in the direction of the hall with Braylee beside him. It took several minutes to reach the building, and then the two men slipped inside unnoticed and took a seat on a wooden side bench to watch the proceedings.

Gayner was listing the girl's crimes. Hiding and assisting the enemy. Withholding information from the executives of the law in the Gateway. Treason.

The girl in question stood like a statue, staring at the men before her. At the accusation, she lifted her chin, though the confusion and vulnerability etched on her young face belied the picture of strength she tried to exhibit. *This* was the woman accused of being the Darkman's accomplice?

Maybe she had been controlled by the Reader the whole time. He dismissed the possibility. There was no way she could have physically withstood the control for that long without collapsing. Nay, she had tended to the man of her own autonomy.

Something gnawed at him. Why did she seem familiar to him?

She was given one last chance to defend her actions. "I already told you." Her tone, though soft and halting, was resolute. "I didn't know he was a Darkman."

Eric rested his chin on the tips of his fingers as the trial drew to a close, and not in the girl's favor.

"Your actions have caused great distress here," Gayner said. "And the consequences could have been dire. There can be no leniency. People have died; more may yet die because of what he's done."

Not much more than a girl, yet she stood, gnawing her lip at whatever fate was about to be handed to her. Was she lying about her role?

She crossed her arms, bracing herself for the verdict. Her shoulders curved forward in defeat. And then it hit Eric where he had seen her. This was the girl waving the Stewards off as they left for Cuthrel the week before.

Gayner picked up his mallet. "Thereby, you will be transported to Paladin for sentencing by King Aden."

Eric shot to his feet before the man could bring the mallet down. "Councilmen!"

The white-robed men all stood to their feet. "Your Majesty." The Stewards straightened as he strode down the aisle.

"Please, take your seats." Eric sent a glance to the girl, moved with compassion by her white, pinched features. Despite the stubborn set to her chin, she was terrified.

He stood before the desk and hesitated. Now what? Something compelled him to act on the girl's behalf, too strong to let him sit back and do nothing. "I'm here to propose clemency for this young woman."

There was a sharp intake from the girl, barely heard over the protests of the council.

"Prince Eric, this girl harbored a Darkman in her house for weeks. And of her own free will."

"Yes, she did, Councilman Gayner." Eric nodded. "Nursed him back to health, I understand."

"That's right."

"All the while, believing he was one of us." He approached the high desk, tilting his head back to see them. "It could've been one of our own."

"But it wasn't." One of the others spoke up.

Eric brought his hands up to the edge of the desk. "We all know the cunning of Jader's subordinates. Especially one with a Reader's Gift."

"You know the Code, Prince Eric." Gayner raised his head high. "We can't afford to show tolerance for those who've fraternized with the likes of Jader and his Darkmen."

"You're right. But if we've come to the place where we can't allow a person room for forgiveness for honest mistakes, then we've already failed the Code."

Gayner frowned and exchanged looks with his fellow councilmen. Eric caught a dark look flash across the face of a Steward standing guard a few feet away. He ground his teeth. This would do nothing to help bridge the gap between him and his knights.

But he forged on. "You have proven to be more than just and fair. I am but requesting clemency." He did not wish to override their decision. But he would if he had to.

The third man spoke. "How do we know she's telling the truth? We have witnesses who saw her with this man."

"I suppose we can't know for certain," Eric admitted. "But we also have no proof that she knew he was a Darkman at the time. And we cannot pass judgment unless we have hard evidence that she willingly worked with him."

"You could be opening the door for our enemies."

Eric stepped back. "Look at her, gentlemen." He directed their attention to her. "Is this how you see our enemy?"

The girl's long, blonde hair hung in a riot about her stark white face, marked by angry red scratches and a few freckles that stood out against her pale skin. Her hands, also scratched, were clasped so hard her knuckles lost all color. Dressed in worn, homespun clothing, she appeared small and helpless. But also strong, somehow. At their scowls, she tucked a strand behind her ear, another hand smoothing the front of her dress. Eric's sympathy mounted yet again.

Gayner's movements faltered, and Eric saw past the men's stern expressions. These leaders carried compassion alongside their devotion to the Code.

"Sirs, you know me." Eric's words were soft as he met the men's collective gaze. "I am painfully aware of the catastrophic consequences that come about as a result of rash decisions."

He paused, letting the words sink in. The men on either side of Gayner cast furtive glances at the Head Councilman.

"I do not take this decision lightly." Though the admission cost him, Eric was determined to have his way. "I will take custody of the girl, give her a chance to make things right. With your consent."

There was a long, heavy silence for several heartbeats. Then, with a slow nod, Gayner said, "Clemency granted, Prince Eric. She's in your charge."

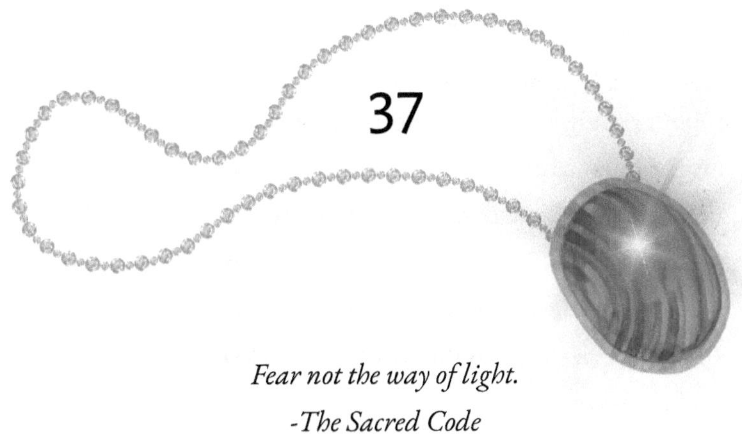

37

Fear not the way of light.
-The Sacred Code

Trembling overtook Seria's limbs as the tall, blond man took her arm and led her from the hall. It seemed she was forever being led around by strange men now.

What had happened?

The man stepped outside and turned to her. "Are you all right, miss?" He stood several inches over her, so she had to tilt her head back to see him. Her head swam, and she took a faltering step back, bumping into a big man with dark features. Both stared at her intently, expectant.

Of course. He had asked her a question. Seria scrambled for the answer through the sludge in her brain.

"Miss?" The blond man spoke again.

"She may be in a state of shock, Sire." The man behind her startled her. His deep voice echoed in her head.

"I think you're right." The tall man looked upset. Had she done something wrong? Of course. She was on trial for taking care of Mason. Because he was a Darkman, not the good man she thought he was.

"Miss?"

Seria stared up at him. "Wait. Are you the prince?"

"That I am."

Seria put her hand to her aching temples. "I don't understand."

The prince spoke again, and Seria tried desperately to keep up. Something about resting and talking more tomorrow.

Prince Eric looked over her head. "Captain Braylee, please escort her to the guest chambers, and see that Ruth tends to her needs." His blue gaze met hers once more. "We can talk later when you feel more like yourself."

Seria turned to the Steward behind her. The gentleness in his expression defied the size that could crush her. Still yet, she flinched as he reached for her arm.

"Don't worry, miss. You're safe now."

She was again led away, this time to a tall, important-looking building and up a flight of stone steps. Still trying to make sense of what had happened, she was surprised when she found herself in a spacious room with thick, red drapes. Where was she?

"Ruth will be here shortly."

Seria must have responded because the big man—was his name Braylee?—nodded his head and began to leave.

"Wait!"

He halted. "Miss?"

She turned her palms up. "What happened?"

Captain Braylee's face softened, and he turned to face her. "The prince requested your clemency, and the council granted it. You are in his custody now, and there is no sentence."

Seria clasped her hands together. "But why would he do that? Mason—the Darkman—was in my house. I mean..." She gave a slight shrug.

He gave her a small smile. "Our prince believes in your innocence." He gave her a nod, then left her alone with her thoughts.

Standing in the middle of the room, she blinked and attempted to rein in her swimming senses. Her breathing accelerated, dizzying her.

Questions flew through her mind with such speed she was unable to pick any out and make logic of them.

She had fully expected a guilty verdict. Had braced herself for the idea of spending her days and nights in a dungeon. And now she stood in a spacious room because the prince—the *prince* had believed her innocent and granted her clemency.

Her legs quivering, she crossed the room with leaden steps to the huge bed against one wall. The coverings looked soft and inviting, but for all she cared, it could have been burlap.

Sobs broke through. An eternity had passed since morning, everything lost in a strange muddle of pain, shock, and anguish, and meshing into a blur in her head. The arrest. The trial. The clemency. It was too much for her exhausted spirit to grasp.

She wrapped herself in one of the thick blankets on the bed and curled up in a tight ball, trying to shut out the world, tears dampening her pillow. Sleep was impossible.

Heat bubbled in her, boiling and churning, ready to explode in an eruption of red, hot fury. Not only was Mason not a Steward, but he was a Darkman, an agent of the emperor. Oh, to see him face to face again. Her fingers itched to give him a good thrashing with Ira's whip. If she could but go back and redo the last few weeks!

As soon as the thought materialized, she grew still. Her whole life was a wreck, all because she had taken a wounded stranger in, a stranger she had come to think of as a friend. A friend who turned out to be an enemy of the Stewards. Her reputation was ruined, and she was now a prisoner of the prince. Nothing good had come from her knowing Mason.

But still, she couldn't imagine doing anything different. Had she known from the beginning who Mason was, she would not have left him to die when she could have saved him. Her conscience wouldn't allow it.

She could not sit by and watch a man perish, Darkman or not, even if it meant standing against the Stewards and Prince Eric.

And that knowledge frightened her more than anything else.

38

The wicked shall be ensnared by his own
lies he speaks in the dark.
-The Sacred Code

Shon burst into Mason's tent, huffing. "Emperor Jader's coming."

Mason's head shot up from where he examined the wound in his side. "What? When?"

"Now."

"*Now?*" Mason searched for his blue shirt. It was the last clean one he had left decent enough for a visitor like the emperor. "I'm not fit to see him like this!"

"Let us forgo formalities, shall we?" Jader spoke as he ducked through the open flaps and stepped inside. "I believe we are past that."

"Emperor Jader." Both men came to attention, saluting with their fists crossed and heads bowed.

"At ease, gentlemen."

"I apologize for my appearance, Emperor," Mason said. "I didn't know you were coming."

"You look well," Jader said. "After your ordeal, I half-expected to find you abed."

"Nay, sir."

Jader turned to Shon. "Could you give us a moment, young man?"

"Of course, Emperor Jader." Shon gave a half-bow and left.

Mason had finally located his shirt when Jader turned back to him. The older man looked down at the nearly-healed hole in his side. He shook his head. "I shudder to see how close you came to death, Mason."

Mason shrugged and slipped the shirt over his head.

"It must have been difficult." Jader turned at the entrance to look outside. "Being surrounded by the enemy. So close to the one responsible for your brother's death."

Mason's hands slowed in tying the strings. "Aye. It was." There was no use denying it. Jader knew him better than most.

"Did you see the prince?"

"Once. From across the courtyard." He ground his teeth and pulled a thick leather vest on over the shirt. "I wanted to kill him on the spot."

"I understand." Jader faced him again. "But we must not let our anger cloud our good reasoning." He raised his head and narrowed his dark eyes. "I am going to request a negotiation with Prince Eric."

Mason blinked. "Emperor?"

"This bloodshed has got to stop. I will make my request to Eric, peaceably. Let him know what it is I want. Give him a chance to compromise, especially concerning the Gateway villages he has claimed for his own."

Mason frowned around a deep inhale. "What do you think will come of it?"

"Absolutely nothing, to be honest. But I do not want to be accused of being a monster. If there is to be a war, it will be his wish, not mine."

It sounded reasonable, but Mason recoiled at the idea of giving the prince any chance at all for reconciliation.

"I know you want to see justice served for your brother," Jader said. "Let me assure you, Mason. It has a way of coming about. And you shall play a strong hand in seeing it done. But patience is of the essence right now."

Mason dropped his head and nodded.

"I want you to be with me when I go into Cadence."

The comment drew Mason's head up again. A sharp blade cut through his lungs. Was he ready to go back so soon?

Jader continued. "Let the prince see you face to face, unashamed and unafraid."

The idea dizzied him. Would he be able to control himself if he saw Eric again? He set his chin. "I'll do what I must." The words came out in a growl.

Jader smiled. "Wonderful."

Shortly after Jader ended his visit, Mason joined Shon to break the fast. The camp was humming with activity. Horses and mules stomped and snorted. Tent flaps rustled in the slight wind. Men and women hurried about on their prospective tasks; many of them stopped to greet Mason.

Shon talked nonstop as they made their way to the meal tent.

"We all thought you were dead, you know. You've set the whole camp to buzzing since you showed up. Everyone's making up stories."

Mason shrugged. "I got shot and was laid up."

Shon's arched brows challenged him. "Aye, but where were you all this time? Someone kept you alive. How'd you keep 'em from exposing you?"

"I managed."

Shon tilted his head back, his red hair flipping back off his face. "You kept him under your control thing the whole time."

Mason scrambled for a reasonable explanation.

Shon chuckled. "I'd hate to see what kind of shape he was in by the time you were done with him!"

"Right."

"What'd you do with him at night to keep him from running off?"

Mason hesitated. "Well, sh-uh, *he* was so worn out by the end of the day, all he did was sleep." This was getting ridiculous.

"Kept him pretty busy, huh?" A grin lit up Shon's tanned face.

Mason gave a short nod. "Aye." He thought of all the trouble he put Seria through. "Pretty busy."

Shon was not done yet. "Well, tell me—"

A feminine voice cut in. "Come on, Shon. Let the man catch his breath."

Both men turned to see a tall, willowy brunette approaching. Pleasure and dismay merged at Dreeya's appearance.

She stepped to Mason's side and put her hand on the back of his neck. Without hesitation, she pulled his head down and pressed a kiss to his cheek. She traced his jaw with a long finger. "I missed you."

Mason cleared his throat. "Good to see you, too."

She scrutinized him. "You still look a bit pale to my thinking."

"I'm fine." Gah. Was he incapable of speaking more than a few words at a time?

Her hands tugged on his vest. "Why not let me bring some color back to those cheeks?"

Mason stiffened and took a step back from her proximity. "Ah, maybe another time."

"Now who needs to let the man catch his breath?" Shon quipped.

Dreeya shot him a frown before turning her hunger back to Mason. "You take care of yourself. And remember, there's always room in my tent."

"Trust me, I remember."

Shon waited until Dreeya sashayed away, then eyed Mason.

Mason frowned at the scrutiny. "What?"

"I don't know." Shon squinted at him. "Something's different about you."

"Because I didn't take her up on her invitation?" Mason shook his head. "I've never been one of her puppets."

"Maybe not. But you were gone so long, who knows what's going on in that head of yours now."

Mason gritted his teeth to hide his frown as Shon launched into a description of all that had happened in the camp since his disappearance. He wanted things to go back to normal, to forget where he had been. How was he going to do that if Shon and everyone else kept reminding him of his absence?

"Are you listening?"

Mason's head snapped up. "Aye...I'm listening."

Shon huffed. "Sure, you are." He gave Mason one more searching look before he entered the meal tent. Mason stood still for a moment, rubbing one of his bracers before he ducked to follow Shon into the tent.

What's wrong with me?

39

Late morning sunlight shone on Seria's face when she blinked back to wakefulness. Her mind was surprisingly clear after the trauma of the day before. She sat up in bed and took her first good look at her surroundings.

A dark, wooden table sat at the head of the bed. Across the room stood a polished wardrobe with intricate carvings. A davenport with silk pillows rested on another wall. Deep maroon banners hung on the white stone walls, adding a splash of color to the elegance.

It was all so grand. And she was completely out of place here. Her drafty little shack called to her. And Sanjo! A pang hit her. What would become of the poor creature? Would Sanjo pay for her ignorance?

This was the first time in years she did not have never-ending bags of laundry waiting for her, and she would give anything to have them back. Not that her clients would allow her to touch their things now. Her face heated at what they must think of her. The town launderer, arrested by Stewards.

She shuffled across the floor to the window overlooking the street below and pushed the heavy, red drapes aside. People and knights meandered about without a care in the world. Flashes of red capes and gray tunics mixed in with the blue and green fabrics of the civilians. Dogs barked, horses nickered, and men shouted. A few children darted in and around the adults.

The Gateway Stronghold. After stopping to stare in awe from a distance so many times, she was finally here. But it was nothing like she had imagined her first visit would ever be.

She clenched her teeth against the humiliation that tried to overtake her again. The shame of her arrest was not how she would last be remembered. This was her chance for a fresh start.

What chance? You lost that when you invited a Darkman into your house!

The doubts took hold, and she bit her lip. How could she be seen as anyone important now? She recalled the way the Council had stared down at her. The arresting Steward officers were no better. The prince, of all people, was the only one who had thought to give her a chance.

Seria reined in the doubts, pushed them back into a bottomless well, and sealed it up. How many times had she wished for an opportunity to get out of Cadence? This was it. Though it had come about in less than desirable means, she would not miss it.

Ruth arrived a little later to escort her down the flight of steps to meet the prince. Seria eyed Ruth's dove gray dress and black tunic. Next to Seria's tattered clothes, Ruth looked like royalty in her servant attire.

How could she meet the prince looking like this?

Because this is all you have. Seria inhaled and held her head high, though it killed her. Her freedom belonged to the prince, and she would do all she could to earn it back.

Seria spotted him as soon as she stepped outside. He stood from his perch on a simple wooden bench and sent her an inviting smile. "Did you sleep well?"

Ruth slipped away and with her went all of Seria's courage. "Um, fine, thank you, Your Majesty." Was that what she should call him? Or was Your Highness the correct term?

"It occurred to me after we parted last night, I never thought to ask your name."

"Seria Gayle."

Eric gave her a searching look. Remembering how Mason could read her thoughts, she dropped her gaze and fiddled with the broken laces of her tunic. A mere few days ago, she would have loved to meet the celebrated prince of Paladin. But not like this.

"You must be famished. Shall we break the fast in the mess hall?" The smooth timbre of his speech made her feel like a country mouse.

Dine with the prince? "Thank you." Her voice scraped through her teeth.

"Good. I'm sure Nola has a fine menu for the day." He offered his arm, and she took it, trying not to dwell on the strange picture they made. The tall, dashing prince with his finely tailored tunic and trousers, walking alongside the disheveled peasant in rags.

He pointed out several items of interest as they walked to the mess hall. The fort was two miles wide at its broadest and tapered in, walled in on the north and south by the Slates. It was well-run and organized, much like its own small city. Roads, homes, and businesses stood at every turn. Prince Eric told her it took nearly an hour to walk a straight line from one side of the garrison to the other.

The mess hall was a massive, sprawling structure with double doors. A long, open room stretched out from the entrance, with a large fireplace on the opposite end. Rectangular wooden tables stood in rows, but to her relief, there were not many diners. Her late morning start had saved her from the probing curiosity of strangers. For now.

They were soon seated at a table, plates of hot, steaming food before them. Seria stared at her plate. Roasted chicken. A savory mix of carrots, cabbage, and onions. White bread. A chunk of cheese. And ale. Her mouth watered at the spicy smells wafting upwards.

"Is everything to your liking?"

The prince's concerned question brought her head up. "Oh. It looks lovely."

He smiled and nodded for her to begin before picking up his utensils. The first bite was heaven, melting and swirling in a collision of flavors and seasonings she had not tasted in ages.

They ate in silence at first, for which Seria was grateful. When was the last time she had eaten like this? No wonder Mason turned up his nose at her oats and stew.

Prince Eric waited until her plate was empty, and she had drained her cup. "Last night, you seemed overwhelmed."

She sat up straight and gave a quick nod. "I was. Please excuse my behavior." Funny how much more ready she felt after eating a full meal.

"No apology needed. It was a lot to take in. I do have a few questions if you're up to it."

Her hands fidgeted in her lap. "Aye, Your Majesty." No matter how she felt, that would be the expected answer.

"I understand you cared for the Darkman for several weeks. Is that correct?"

She coughed. "Aye, three to be exact."

"Can you tell me how that came to be?"

"I was in the woods the night of the battle." It felt like such a long time ago now. A whole lifetime.

He sat back. "You were in Rackson? Why?"

"Well, not exactly in Rackson, I was outside the border, on a little hill, actually. But I was close enough to see everything." *Slow down, Seria. Answer the question.* "I was fishing."

"Fishing?" His eyes lit up. "Is this a pastime of yours?"

She squirmed, then shrugged. What if it was not proper for maidens to fish? "My father taught me, but I only go when I need to or have the time."

"I see." He nodded. "And your parents? Are they still living?"

Pain gripped her. Now the questions were probing, stirring more painful memories. "Nay, sir."

"So, you live alone?"

Alone. Aye, that described her condition. More alone than she had ever been in her life.

"How badly was the Darkman wounded?"

"He had an arrow wound in his side and one leg. And he had been kicked in the head by a horse."

Eric rubbed his chin. "And you cared for him yourself?"

She started to nod, then answered out loud. "Aye, sir."

"And he thanked you by leaving you to pay for his crimes." He shook his head. "Typical Darkman, with no thought for anyone but themselves."

Seria rejected the idea. Mason did care. She had seen too many signs, albeit subtle ones. Inside the hard shell he wrapped around himself beat a good heart.

Her silent defense startled her. Did she still believe that after the way he left her?

Eric straightened and clasped his hands together. "Miss Seria, I'd like for us to come to an understanding."

Seria froze in her seat. What kind of service would the prince expect from her? Her imagination ran in some directions she wished it hadn't.

"I stepped in at your trial because I believe you were innocent of the wrongs he committed while under your care. And I want you to have a chance to prove your innocence."

A thin glimmer of hope stirred.

"The particulars of your clemency state that you are under probation. You are free to do and move about here as you please, within reason, of course. You are not indebted to me or obligated to serve me in any way, but you will be expected to see to your own needs. I will assist you in any way I can. Does this suit you?"

Her scrutiny drifted from his sober face. He expected nothing from her but to live in the fort as an upright, working citizen. Reprieve broke free from the knot in her air pipe, and she let out a sigh. She could do that, had been doing it for years, before Mason's arrival had wrecked her life.

Maybe she was being presumptuous to trust him too soon. It sounded too good to be true.

But he was the prince, she argued with herself. A Steward. True, she had assumed Mason a Steward, but it had not taken long for her to learn he was nothing like what she had believed Stewards to be.

"Miss Seria?"

Seria jerked. She had let her mind wander while he was waiting for an answer. "Aye, it suits me, Your Highness. I mean, Your Majesty."

He gave her a smile, one that chased away the somber lines around the corners of his eyes. "Let's reserve the majesty for my father, shall we?"

He spoke with such casual kindness that she felt no embarrassment, just relief at knowing which title to use.

"This is a great opportunity, an opportunity for a new start, to make a new life for yourself," he said. "You need that, in light of all you've been through."

The prospect held her in a wonderful spell. It was as if he had read her desires with the same ease as Mason. The thought dampened her spirits. Mason had had dreams, too, and she doubted he shared them with many people. But he had shared them with her. Would he ever see them fulfilled? Or would his decision to serve the Dark Army destroy any chance of that?

Eric went on. "If I might make a couple of suggestions, there is an elderly lady down the street who takes in boarders. She might have room for you."

She licked her dry lips. "That sounds wonderful."

"And Nola is about to lose some of her kitchen help here at the hall. I think they're moving back to the Old Realm. Ayna Carwright recommended you for the job. Since Ayna has been a longstanding citizen and employee of the fort's bakehouse, Nola is willing to offer the job to you, if you don't mind hard work."

Ayna Carwright, Lena's mother! Thankfulness bloomed that the kind lady had spoken for her, so much so that her answer burst from her. "I don't mind. I used to wash five loads of laundry a day. Sometimes more." She caught herself. "Your Maj-Highness."

He smiled. "I somehow didn't think you would."

Seria gave him a hesitant smile in return. Working in the mess hall had to be a step up from doing everyone's laundry for a few pence.

Another thought hit her, and she bit her lower lip.

"Something else?" he asked.

How could she ask for anything now? He had given her the very thing she had hoped for, especially after she believed she had ruined any chance of a better future.

But Eric waited, his face patient. So, Seria took a deep breath. She had to say something. "Well, I don't mean to cause any more trouble. But...I have a donkey."

40

"Can you believe this slop?" Dreeya plopped down next to Mason, facing Shon. Voices hummed around them as the large meal tent filled for the midday meal. She made a face at the plate before her. "You'd think they'd have better fare by now."

Shon nodded around a bite. "I'm so sick of rabbit, I'll probably run the next time I see a coney."

Mason stared at the roast rabbit, cheese, and fresh white bread on his plate. "You should've seen what I lived on for weeks."

Dreeya pouted in a show of sympathy. "Was it awful?"

"What'd you eat?" Shon asked. "Locust legs?"

"Nothing that bad. But I got pretty tired of pottage stew. With no meat. Nothing but mushy vegetables. And oats for breakfast. Every day." Because that was all Seria had. And she shared it with him. His hand tightened around the mug he held.

"Ugh!"

Dreeya's exclamation startled him back to the present.

"Pottage?" She snarled a lip. "I'm glad it was you and not me. No wonder you haven't been yourself."

Mason shrugged, stirring his food. "It could've been worse. After a while, I didn't notice anymore. It was pretty filling."

He stopped short and looked up to see his friends staring at him. "But it was worse than this slop."

Dreeya cast him a smile. "How 'bout we skip this slop and head back to my tent? We have a little time before we have to get back to work."

Mason bit back his irritation. Would she ever let up? He was still forming his answer when Dreeya called out to a teenage boy passing by.

"You there, Crue!"

The boy stopped and spun around, his face draining of color.

"Did you think you could hide the damage to my saddle?" Her face hardened, sharpening her stunning features.

"I-I'm sorry, Lady Dreeya. I dropped the brush into the bucket of oil and forgot to clean it before I used it again. I fixed it as best as I could."

"Fixed it?" she snapped. "You call that fixing it? It's ruined. I'm reporting this to your supervisor."

"Lady Dreeya, please! I'll repair it as best as I can. I can't lose this job."

Dreeya put her hand up. "That's not my problem."

The boy's stance slumped as he turned and left in silence.

"What was that all about?" Shon asked.

Dreeya sniffed. "The bum left a stain on my saddle."

"How bad?"

"Bad enough to see."

Mason took a sip of his wine. "All that for a stain?"

Dreeya stared at him. "Mason, he's incompetent. I'm not worried about hurting his feelings. He's got to do his job right or get out."

"Aye, but he's just a boy."

She scoffed. "I have no patience with children, and I won't have my belongings destroyed by brats with no business touching it."

"Since when did you have a soft spot for kids, Mason?" Shon asked.

Drawing up short at the question, Mason let out a harsh laugh. "Soft spot?" First Seria thought him a softy, and now this?

"Why are you defending this boy?"

"I'm not. Help's hard to come by. That's all."

"Well, you can let him clean your saddle." Dreeya scraped her plate. "I'm not putting up with him."

Of its own accord, Mason's mind went to Seria's willingness to help young Byron and his family. He stood to his feet. "I've had enough of this garbage. I'm heading out to the field."

Not giving them time to reply, he dumped his plate in the basin waiting at the large tent's opening. He pushed the heavy flaps out of his way and stepped outside, fully conscious of the strange looks his companions sent his way.

"But, Captain, he's not helping his own case! She let a Darkman through the gates. No one's going to trust her."

Braylee held on to what was left of his patience while the younger man ranted. He appreciated the Stewards' commitment to free speech, but how had he become a sounding board for all those who disagreed with the prince's actions? "Maybe not upfront, Sgt. Lionel, but he's become responsible for her."

Lionel's frustration rolled off him. "I don't understand. It's bad enough that so many of the Stewards don't think *he* should be here. But now he's hurting himself."

"We can't expect him to throw her to the lions, can we?"

The younger man squeezed the bridge of his nose. "Captain Braylee, I have been defending the prince to my comrades. Trying to convince them he has the wisdom to command us. And then he goes and takes in a girl who not only sheltered a Darkman but—"

"Sir Lionel."

Braylee lifted his head to see Eric approaching, his face set in stone.

Lionel straightened and gave a bow of acknowledgment. "Prince Eric."

Eric faced the younger knight. "I understand my recent decision does not settle well with you."

"Nay, sir, I mean, that's not—"

Braylee chewed on his cheek at Lionel's fluster. Lionel did not have as much to say now. Braylee understood Lionel's doubts—he himself questioned the prince's move in openly pardoning the girl, but it was time the prince took a stand against his scoffers and asserted himself as their leader.

Eric's stance relaxed. "I respect your opinion, Sir Lionel, and I appreciate your concern. However, my decision stands. I believe the girl is innocent, and I aim to give her a chance to rectify her mistake. I would do the same for anyone in her position, and I expect my Stewards to accept that my decision still stands."

Lionel's Adam's apple bobbed. "Of course, Sire." He lowered his head. "If you'll excuse me."

After his swift exit, Braylee rubbed his upper lip and looked to Eric, who frowned.

"I'm sorry, Captain, but I'm weary of being questioned for every move I make."

Braylee put his hands up. "You'll get no argument from me. It needed to be said."

Eric sighed and looked where Lionel disappeared to. "I may have asserted myself on the wrong one, though."

"Nay." Braylee shook his head. "It's time the Stewards start respecting you, no matter how they feel. What you did was necessary and right."

"How would Uralis have handled such a situation?"

"Oh, he had his fair share of disputes, yet he handled them like a stern but caring father would his children." Braylee nudged his chin in Lionel's direction. "He would've handled that much as you did now."

Eric's face pinched. "'Tis a shame the marshal did not survive Rackson."

Braylee hesitated but a moment. "You are the true leader, Prince Eric, same as every Passion prince before you. Uralis paid his dues and led the army well. But this is your army." He watched for Eric's reaction.

It was slow in coming, but Eric finally nodded, and the wrinkle in his brow smoothed. "You are correct, Captain Braylee. I thank you once again."

Tired now, Braylee bid the prince good night and headed to his quarters. Too many conflicting dilemmas rolled about in his head.

Eric's compassion was applaudable, and Braylee was glad to see him put Lionel in his place. But Lionel was right in that Eric's request for clemency did nothing to improve confidence in the new marshal, and the last thing they needed was more division among the ranks. The Stewards would not soon forget that the girl harbored a Darkman, especially in light of their recent losses. For Eric to be so swift to forgive would be as hard for some to swallow as bitter tea.

An uncomfortable band stretched across Braylee's stomach. Would the girl's presence undo all the good Eric was attempting to accomplish in protecting the Gateway?

The large throne room was dark, much to Jader's liking. He stood at a window, looking out at the gathering dusk, his favorite time of day. Someone stepped in behind him.

"How is he?"

"Doing well, my lord," Bruin answered. "He's about returned to his former strength and has been spending his spare time in the archery fields or training grounds. He is most anxious to get back to work. I had to insist he take a few days off to recover."

Jader frowned as he turned. "Something feels off."

"Why do you say that, Master?"

Shaking his head, Jader made his way up the stone steps to his elaborate throne. "I cannot say exactly." He thought back to his visit with Mason at the camp. "His zeal seems to have lessened some. I see it in your reports, without seeing it for myself. I can feel it."

"He's been through a lot. If anything, he is angrier."

Jader stroked the dark beard on his chin. "What do we know about his benefactor?"

"Not much. He didn't talk much of him."

"Why?"

Bruin crossed his arms. "Not sure. But Mason said he eliminated him."

"I want to know who he was. We know nothing about the influence Mason was under for those weeks." Jader steepled his fingers and rested the tips against his chin. "I will not have anything get in the way of his being solely committed to our cause. He is much too valuable an asset."

Bruin scratched at his whiskers. "Are you having doubts?"

"Not particularly. But I am not willing to accept anything at face value. Especially where he is concerned," Jader said. "Mason is a powerful being, more than he realizes. When the time comes that his Gift is fully developed, I want to ensure it is used for our benefit. Especially now with Eric Passion in the forefront."

Bruin had no reply. Jader sat in silence for a long moment. Few of his knights had as much reason to hate the Stewards and the Code as Mason. And few had the capabilities the young man possessed. Jader had great plans for the Reader and, until Mason's recent holdup in Cadence, nothing but confidence they would be carried out without a hitch.

"See what you can learn. I want to know who he was with."

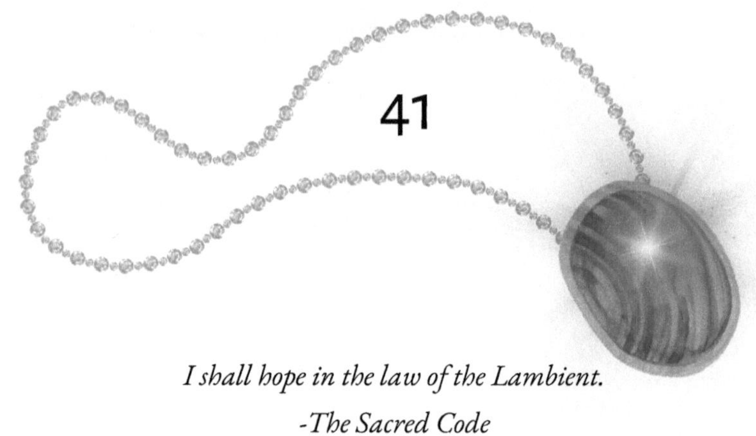

41

Seria patted Sanjo's rough hide as she led him down a side road of the Gateway Stronghold, heading for nowhere in particular. She was more than happy to have her old friend back and snatched the opportunity to see more of the citadel.

Sunrise had not yet broken through the pink and purple sky. A cool breeze descended from the Slate Mountains and chilled her skin. The roads were almost empty, so she maintained a leisurely stroll.

A thrill swirled inside her, along with a swarm of butterflies. The last two days had been spent settling into her new room and getting to know Mallie, the kind landlady the prince had introduced her to. The rest of the time had been spent familiarizing herself with the fort. Her job in the kitchen started that morning.

As of yet, she had not met anyone beyond Mallie, but that could be attributed to the fact that she kept to herself. Her recent trial was still fresh on her mind, and she was unsure how she would be received. But she was fascinated by what she saw during her early morning rambles. Each day brought about a new place of interest.

As she strolled down the quiet street, she noticed a simple, squat structure of wood to her left. The position of it drew her attention more than the appearance, for it was dreadfully plain with not so much as a single flower growing along the walls.

A sign hung on a post outside the door, and Seria drew closer to read it. *Luron Furvor, Infirmary.*

A gasp escaped her, and she stopped in her tracks. The infirmary! Instant interest pulled her to the entrance. Now, this was a place she could do some good. This was what she had dreamed of.

Seria wrapped Sanjo's rope around the hitching post and scratched his ear. "Wish me good luck, old friend."

The entrance opened right into the main room. Rows of cots stretched out before her to the other end of the room. There were two doors on the opposite wall, the physician's living quarters and office, most likely.

A few of the cots held sleeping patients. The scents of hemlock and lavender permeated the space and tickled her nostrils. But it was a soothing smell, recalling to mind the many times her mother used the herbs in her ministrations.

She moved farther in, searching for the physician. All she had to do was inform him of what she knew about the healing arts. She could do so much to assist him here. Her palms dampened the closer she got to his door.

As she passed one man, he shifted and moaned. He coughed, so hard and deep the cot shook. Her ribs ached in sympathy.

"Do you need anything, sir?"

The gray-headed man blinked up at her. "Well, miss, you're a sight for sore eyes."

Seria smiled down into a weathered face. "That's very kind. That cough sounds tough."

He waved a hand. "I'm tougher."

"Is the physician here yet?" She poured him a cup of water from the pitcher sitting beside his bed.

The man pushed himself up to a sitting position and accepted it with a grateful nod. "Luron will be out soon, I'm sure. He likes to poke and prod his patients before he breaks his fast."

The warmth in his tone spoke of genuine respect for the man, which eased Seria's anxiety. "Has he treated your cough already?"

"Gave me some sage last night, and it seemed to help some."

Which was probably his nice way of saying he still coughed throughout the night. "Has he tried the waterstar flower?"

The man scratched his head. "Can't say as I've heard him mention it."

Seria sat on the edge of the cot next to his. "It's a large pink flower, very decorative. But most people are unaware that its petals are also good for clearing the lungs of infection. They can be soaked right in water like a tea. Doesn't taste as good as they look in the wild, but it works. I'm Seria Gayle, by the way."

"You can call me Gus." He stretched his hand out to take hers. "I've never seen you around here, but I must say you've already brightened my morning."

She beamed at him. This was why she had come. Visions of working in this room alongside the doctor, bringing some cheer and comfort to the bedridden, danced in her imagination. "Waterstars grow in abundance in early summer, but I'm sure there's some already growing around here. I can talk to the physician about getting some for you."

"Can I help you, miss?"

The crusty voice behind her pushed her to her feet, and she swiveled to face the stern, probing glower of a gray-headed man with deep lines on his face. "Oh, are you Luron? I mean, the physician?"

"That's right, and I don't usually allow visitors this early in the morning."

His cool statement penetrated her confidence, and she wavered. Then she heard Gus smother another cough and lifted her chin. "I'm not a visitor. I came to offer my assistance. I know quite a bit—"

Luron put his hand up. "I don't take unsolicited help from the streets, young lady."

The streets! Heat flooded her cheeks, but she went on like he had not cut her off. "I know quite a bit about healing herbs and plants. I was telling Sir Gus, here, that the waterstar flower does wonders for clearing lungs. I can get some for you, if you'd like."

"Now listen, miss." Luron narrowed his eyes. "I'm the physician around here, and I'm not in the habit of taking medicinal advice from young women. Especially young women who do not know their place."

"Now, Luron, there's no call to be unfriendly. She's merely trying to help."

Seria stared back at Luron, her teeth clenched. He faced her head on, his stubborn jaw jutted. Disappointment raked over her, tearing into wounds that had only begun to heal. Tears stung, but she was not about to let him see her break.

She turned to Gus, who gave her a pained shrug. "Sir Gus, it was lovely to meet you." She stressed the last word in one last jab at the physician. Not that it would faze him. She held her head up high and fumed all the way to the door.

Sanjo gave her a little nicker as she jerked the rope from the post. She led him back down the street, the mess hall looming behind them. Her job awaited her where she would wash dishes and cook food and serve diners.

But she would not be practicing her healing arts with the calloused Luron Furvor.

A knot formed, and she blinked through the moisture forming behind her eyelids. What did she expect? She had arrived at this fort a mere two days ago, and that was because of a crime against the law. Did she really believe she could waltz around and become someone important with a friendly smile and her knack for talking too much?

"Where are you off to in such a hurry so early in the morning?"

Lena's greeting snapped her head around. "Oh, it's you!" She threw her arms around the smaller woman.

Lena laughed and accepted her hug. "It's good to see you, too!"

"I'm sorry." Seria drew back, fighting tears again. "It's just...I don't know very many people here yet."

Lena gave her a long look. "You look upset."

"Oh, I'm fine." She swiped at her face. "I had a run-in with the physician, that's all."

"Luron?" Lena frowned. "What happened?"

"He was not impressed with me, but come to think of it, I was not awestricken, either. I pray he's a better doctor than what he led me to believe."

"He's well-liked around here, but I think he's pretty set in his ways."

Seria shrugged it off. "I wish I had more time to talk, but I'm on my way to put Sanjo up so I can start working with Nola. Tell your mother thank you for the recommendation, by the way, though I'm sure you had something to do with it."

"Happy to help. Can I walk with you a while?"

"Aye, I'd love to have your company." Seria took Lena's arm, her spirits lifting.

"I was worried about you when I heard about the trial," Lena said.

Seria fought the embarrassment that threatened to stain her face. "I was worried about myself for a while."

"I can't imagine how it must have felt to discover your patient was a Darkman and had infiltrated this fort."

Unsure what to say, Seria gave a little nod. She was still trying to process the truth herself.

Lena cocked her head. "Funny thing. The day it happened, Mason came to pay me a little visit at my booth."

A trickle of dismay went down her spine. Why would Mason go see Lena?

Lena looked straight ahead. "He demanded I take him to the fort." Looking around them, she spoke quieter. "And apparently, I didn't feel I had a choice because I did what he asked."

Seria stopped in her tracks. "Oh, Lena!" Shame and horror clawed at her that Mason had threatened and used her friend. "I'm so sorry!"

Lena arched a brow. "Why? Were you the one behind it?"

"Nay, but..." She dropped her head. "Did you get into much trouble?"

"Oddly enough, no. The Stewards came the next morning and asked me a few questions. Then they left. Nothing more was said." She shrugged. "Then again, I was under the weather that morning, so maybe they took mercy on me." She squeezed Seria's hands. "But I didn't tell them I had met him before at your cabin. I'm not sure what happened that day, but I know you, my friend. Whatever got you pulled into the mess with that Darkman, it wasn't your fault."

If only that were true. "I don't know what to say. But I'm glad there were no repercussions."

"Like there were for you?" Lena's expression was full of sympathy.

Seria let out a sigh. "It's no one's fault but my own."

"I'm not sure I agree, but something tells me I'm not going to convince you of that."

"I must say, I did not expect such animosity from Stewards, though. Not after all I had heard them to be."

"That's because you're too trusting."

"What?" Seria drew back, hurt by the statement.

Lena reached for her hand. "I'm sorry how that came out. I love the way you believe the best in people. Stewards are certainly a breed set apart from the rest. But living amongst them so long in the fort has opened my eyes to how human they can be. They're not infallible."

Mason had said something similar, though he had spoken from an entirely different point of view. She forced a smile. "That's a good reminder. And I'm sure things will work out. Especially now that I've run into you!"

"Good." Lena gave her another quick hug. "I'll let you get back on your way. Mother is waiting for me. We'll talk more?"

"Definitely." Relief and regret blanketed themselves around her as Seria watched her friend walk away. She was due at the mess hall in a few minutes, so she pushed back the tears that wanted to come and went on her way. She would cry later.

She led Sanjo back to the stables where the prince had arranged for boarding. She could not help but chuckle every time she led Sanjo past the stalls where the officers' horses were housed. Big, beautiful stallions and geldings watched her make her way down the center aisle, trying to figure out the little gray animal and its owner. But she was starting to make friends with them. They nickered now when they saw her.

Seria released Sanjo into the large open area at the end of the building, where a few other donkeys were kept—all robust and stout working animals. Again, Sanjo stood out with his sagging back and droopy lips.

Much like she stood out in this fort, the girl with the ratty clothes amongst respectable civilians and knights.

"No matter, Sanjo." She rubbed the wrinkles around his nose. "I love you just the way you are."

The sun had risen by the time she arrived in the kitchen, ready to do anything Nola asked. A big-boned woman with plump arms, Nola regarded Seria with a shrewd look, as if unsure of her new hired help. Regardless of her feelings, she made it clear she needed Seria's help and did not hesitate to put her to work.

The kitchen was large, spanning the width of the mess hall. In the middle of the wall shared by the two buildings was the massive hearth, where a crackling fire roared and large pots hung. The smell of dough and spices infused the warm air.

Though hard put to keep up with the older woman, Seria threw herself into the task of cooking for the hundreds of knights who would arrive looking for their breakfast. Fortunately, Nola was always close by, coaching her on where the supplies were kept and how much of each ingredient to put in what dish.

"You're doing good, missy." Nola rewarded her at one point with an approving nod. "You get in there and do what needs to be done, and you catch on quick. I like that."

Relieved at the woman's patience, Seria peeled potatoes with numb, shriveled fingers. She could hear the mess hall beginning to fill with knights ready to begin the day. Nola still had her hands full getting the last of the food cooked.

"Go ahead and offer them some cider. That'll hold 'em over for a while."

Seria lifted a tray laden with cider and mugs, steadying it before she took it out to the hall. She felt the stares of the inhabitants as soon as she walked into the mammoth room and faltered. Lifting her chin, she approached a table with two knights.

"Would you like some cider?"

One of them, a young man with dark hair looked up at her in surprised disgust. "From you? Thank you, but nay. I don't trust friends of Dark-men."

Seria's face flooded with heat as he stood and brushed by her.

The other man sat quietly through his friend's outburst. "I'll take some." He sounded amicable enough.

"Aye. Of c-course." In her flustered state, she nearly tipped the whole tray. She finally set everything down on the table to pour him a cup.

"Thank you." He gave her a genuine smile. "Don't let Lionel upset you. He's always been a bit opinionated. I've had a few run-ins with him myself."

"I'm afraid he's not alone in his opinion, though." She clamped her mouth shut. *Don't whine, Seria.*

He shrugged. "Let them think what they want." He stood and put his hand out to her. "I'm Ollen Knavis."

She clasped his hand. "Seria Gayle." Her name came out hesitant and shaky.

"Thanks for the cider, Miss Gayle." Ollen sat again and lifted the mug for a drink. "Nothing hits the spot in the morning quite like it."

"That's what my father used to say, too." Desperate to talk of something else, she went on. "He never made a move until he had a cup to refreshen him."

"Sounds like my kind of man."

His soft brown eyes shone with kindness, and his smile came easily. That he spoke to her at all was a balm to the ache in her soul.

"I'm sure things are a little strained around here right now. But they'll get better. The Stewards are a stubborn bunch, but they'll come around."

"Thank you, Sir Ollen." At least she remembered how to address him.

"Call me Ollen. Friends don't have to be so formal."

"Then you can call me Seria, friend."

He nodded and didn't hold back a genuine grin.

It was difficult to move on to the rest of the men after Lionel's reaction. Not all were friendly; some followed Lionel's lead and left before she could even approach. Others accepted her offer of cider warily. But a few spoke to her in genuine friendliness. It made for some awkward moments, but at least she could survive the morning.

Her spirits drooped, however, as she headed back to the kitchen. Maybe Lena was right. Maybe she had been naïve about the Stewards.

42

After taking a few days to recuperate at Bruin's order, Mason threw himself back into his work. While careful not to overdo it, he gave himself little time to think on anything but getting back into form and readying himself for the future.

The days were filled with conditioning, training in the fields, and instructing the newest recruits. He had been assigned the latter task not long before his assignment in Rackson and was eager to get back to it. The fervor of the new soldiers-in-training and their awe of his skills with the sword and crossbow always gratified him. He usually left these sessions pleased with what was accomplished for the day.

He especially enjoyed working with his star student, Areem. The young man had become a part of Feegan's company when he was nine, a hard-headed boy with a quick temper. Now seventeen, Areem sported dark features and a fiery disposition. He worked longer and harder than the rest of the class and looked forward to the day he would be instated as a full-fledged Darkman. Mason saw a lot of himself in Areem; the boy would go beyond his expectations.

Since resuming his duties, however, Mason found his enthusiasm lacking and ended each day drained and dissatisfied. Nothing went right.

The weather had turned cool as spring dragged its feet to summer, especially out in the open field where there was no wind block. Staying warm took more energy than dueling.

And he grew impatient with the slow progress of his trainees. Most of the young men and women spent so much time complaining about the work or the weather that they did not improve their skills. Even Areem had lost his edge. Mason scolded and lectured as much as he instructed.

After one such disappointing session, Mason retreated to his tent and threw himself on his cot. What was wrong with everyone? Where was the motivation, the drive he had witnessed before? With this kind of half-hearted performance, they would never be ready for an all-out offense against Eric's Stewards.

One of the company servants interrupted his doldrums from outside the open tent door. "Sir Mason?"

"What?"

"Shall I collect your laundry, sir?" The diminutive man inclined his head humbly.

An image of Seria bent over a tub of soapy water materialized before his mind's eye, sunshine hair framing her flushed cheeks, and a carefree smile lighting her face.

"Sir?"

Mason jerked back to the present and sat up. "Take it and get out."

The man jumped to attention, snatched the bag of dirty clothes, and made a hasty exit.

Resting his elbows on his knees, Mason rubbed the back of his neck and groaned. It was still happening, no matter how busy he stayed. Thoughts of Seria still cut in at the strangest times, like now.

I can't let a little stray disrupt my focus. He forced himself to his feet, took his cape, and wrapped it around himself. In an attempt to clear his mind, he stepped out into the cool evening. A brisk wind brought up goosebumps on his arms. He met Shon a few yards from his lodging.

"I thought you were in for the night, Mason."

"Got restless." Mason shrugged. "How's your training going?"

"Great!" Shon launched into a description of how his novices were flourishing. "This weather pushes them. Keeps them moving to stay warm. How're yours?"

More disgruntled than ever, Mason sat on a stump and sulked. "Going slow. All they do is complain and argue."

"Then you use that to motivate them. You're not their governess."

"I know that." His words came out curt.

Shon put his hands up. "If I *had* to admit it under threat of death, I'd say you're the best instructor Bruin's got. You always found a way to use the negative to bring out the best in the kids, especially that kid, Areem. You've made them work their little fingers to the bone until they turned out the way you expected Darkmen to be."

Mason blew out between clenched teeth. He knew very well how he had done it in the past.

"So, why isn't it working for you now?"

"It's this group. They're not like the other groups I've had."

Shon put his hands on his hips. "Mason, this is your second group! Every set is going to be different. Don't blame them if things aren't going well. You're the one who's got to get through to them."

Mason glared up at him.

"You can sit there and scowl, or you can take it upon yourself to do something about it."

"All I wanted was a little support, *friend*." His statement drew him up short. Since when had he called anyone friend? He who always preferred to be alone.

Shon winked. "I don't have a spare shoulder for crying on. That's what mamas are for!"

Mason gave a light shrug. "You're the closest thing I've got."

"Wh-I'm what? I'm no mama! I'm the one that's gotta keep you in line when you start feeling sorry for yourself."

Mason gave him a shove. "Right."

They both looked up at the sound of someone stomping toward them. Mason took notice of the massive man's stormy face.

"Hey, Lyoth, what's got you so heated?" Shon's question stopped the man before he passed.

Lyoth scowled, pushing his stringy hair back. "Sitting around, doing nothing, that's what." His voice was full of gravel. "Bruin insists we can't make a move."

Mason stood so as not to strain his neck looking up at him. "What would you suggest?"

"Get in before they can stop us. You've already gotten in once. Imagine what the two of us could do if we were together."

"Aye, but I couldn't do it like that again, Lyoth. Nor would I want to."

Lyoth slanted him a look. "You know I can get in."

"And you're 'bout the only one who can at this point," Shon added. "What then?"

"You sound like Bruin." Lyoth brushed past them.

Mason called his name and waited until the big man turned. "We'll get our chance."

Lyoth stared at him for a long moment before he moved on.

"What was he thinking?" Shon asked.

Mason pulled a face. "I don't know, Shon, not with that Shadowstone on his neck."

"Oh." Shon chuckled shortly. "Right."

"But I understand what he's feeling," Mason said as they resumed walking. "It's..." He searched for the words.

Shon tilted his head, his disheveled hair flopping forward. "It's what, mate?"

Seria would've already had my sentence finished two or three times by now. Mason shook the unbidden thought off with a scowl. "Nothing."

Shon squinted at him. "What's wrong with you?"

"Nothing, just tired of this conversation."

"Me, too, especially since it's not going anywhere."

"Neither are we." Mason motioned to the path in front of them. "Can't you walk any faster?"

"Me? You're the one hobbling like an old man."

"Sure." Mason scoffed, glad to have the subject changed.

He ended up spending the rest of the evening with Shon, enjoying the other man's quick wit and brutal honesty. Funny, Mason never noticed that about him before. Maybe the time with Seria had made him more aware of people's good points, made him more willing to laugh.

Or maybe it made me too soft where other people are concerned. The last thing he needed or wanted was any kind of relationship to distract him from his goal.

Bruin was waiting at his tent when Mason returned more than an hour later. "Commander." The greeting sounded shrill to his ears. "I'm sorry I kept you waiting. Did you need something?"

"To speak with you, Mason, if you have a moment."

"Certainly. Let's go inside."

Mason stepped aside and let Bruin enter ahead of him, his mind spinning with questions.

The officer did not keep him waiting. "Jader has been concerned, Mason."

"About?"

"You."

Mason blinked at him. "Me, sir? Why?"

Bruin moved about in the small space, not looking at Mason as he spoke. "He seems to think you've lost some of your fervor for our mission."

"That's not true." Mason's assurance was swift. "It's taken me longer than I thought to get back into the normal routine, that's all."

Bruin nodded. "My thoughts exactly." He smoothed the dark goatee on his chin. "I told him there was no cause for concern." His glittering eyes turned on Mason. "Mason Grey would no more harm our cause than cut off his own arm."

"You're right."

Bruin stood motionless for the space of several heartbeats, his face unreadable. "I know you've been through a lot. But we're on the brink of change such as the Aged Realms have never known. Jader is making preparations to attempt a negotiation. Between you and me, I don't think anything will come of it."

Mason agreed.

"But he wants to at least make the offer." Bruin's brows dropped. "Once that happens, and Eric Passion refuses to comply, we will need every man to be completely focused, ready to do what it takes to see Jader's objective carried out."

"Aye, sir." Mason nodded.

Bruin gave him a small, calculating smile. "I know that when the time comes, you'll be ready to do your part, Mason."

"I will, Commander. Please, let Master Jader know there is nothing to worry about. I'll be fine."

"I'll do that." Bruin hooked his thumbs on his belt and tilted his head back, as if he had more to say. After a short, heavy silence, however, he bid him good night and left the tent.

Mason dropped down on his cot and clamped his hands behind his neck. Great. If Jader was expressing concern, all the way from Ignadon, then it was too obvious Mason was not himself. The events of the last few weeks had set him off until he could no longer do his job.

"No more." He straightened his back and tightened his resolve. Shon was right. It was time to stop putting the blame on others and take responsibility for his actions.

Seria's face pushed its way into his mind. He allowed himself one moment to recall everything she had done for him, then gritted his teeth. All of that was behind him, and it did no good to dwell on it now. His mission was laid out before him. He had no time for sentimentality, especially for someone who stood on the wrong side of the line.

43

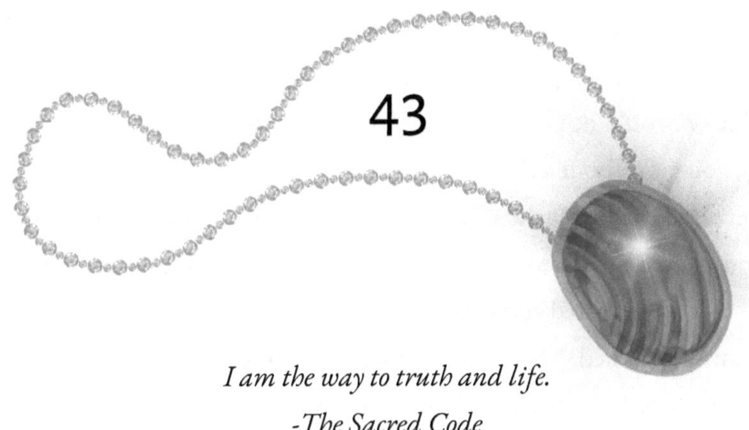

Eric stood beside the cot, heartsick for the man lying on the cot before him. An urgent call from the infirmary had pulled him from his dinner. The man, a longtime Steward, writhed in agony as cough after cough ripped through him. Eric's ribs hurt to watch him.

"Easy there, Gus." The physician put a gentle hand on Gus's head.

Falling back against the pillow, Gus wheezed. "I'm about out of options, aren't I, Doc?"

The gray-headed doctor's eyebrows bunched together. "Now, Gus. You hang in there."

Eric shook his head as Gus began coughing again. "How long has it been this bad, Luron?"

Luron spoke low. "It got worse this morning. Now, he can barely breathe. I fear it's going to be a long night for him."

If he lasts that long. The unspoken words hung between the two.

"Isn't there anything more you can do for him?"

At that, Gus brought a hand to his face and took a shallow breath. He lay so still for a moment that Eric began to worry they were losing him. Then he spoke, easing Eric's mind for the time being.

"There's one thing we haven't tried yet."

"Gus." Luron scolded. "We can't do that."

"What's he talking about?" Eric asked.

Luron would not look at him. "Your young friend was here the other day, going on about a flower."

Eric hid a wince at the reception Seria must have gotten. Luron was a good man, a dedicated doctor who genuinely cared about his patients, but also opinionated and quick in his judgments. "I see."

Luron frowned. "Now, Your Highness, you can't expect me to take the girl's word. There's no telling what it would do to him."

Gus lowered his hand and looked to Luron. "We both know my time's about spent, Doc. Seems to me it won't matter if it poisons me at this point. I can't hold up much longer like this."

His words were punctuated with more hacking. Eric watched the indecision play across the doctor's face. He held his tongue, letting physician and patient talk this out. After a long moment, Luron put his hands up. "It's your choice, Gus."

Gus gave a weak nod. "Go ahead."

Luron straightened and looked at Eric. "I'll send someone to fetch it, and we'll give it a try."

There was nothing more he could do, so Eric left Gus to Luron's capable hands. But his insides churned. The thought of losing Gus killed him. The man was a seasoned Steward, well-liked by young and old, who spent most of his time reaching out and helping those around him. He was too good a man to suffer from something like this.

What if the flower did not work? The loss of a good man would be a huge blow. But Gus was right. He wouldn't last much longer in his condition. What other chance did he have?

"You didn't tell me you went by the infirmary."

At the statement, Seria turned to see Eric had joined her on her morning walk to the mess hall. "Was I not supposed to?" Maybe there were restrictions to her pardon after all.

"You're free to go anywhere you want. But I hope you were not taken aback by Luron's, shall we say, *brusqueness.*"

Seria squinted against the early morning sunlight, thinking back to her first impression of the doctor. Curt. Bristly. "He didn't want my help."

Eric nodded. "I could not ask for a finer doctor or a more devoted man. But he's a proud, stubborn man."

Like many of the Stewards she had come across in this fort. "I do hope he treats his patients with more tact." Instantly, she regretted the words. "I apologize, Prince Eric. That was out of line. He has every reason not to trust me." Even in her newfound freedom, there were constant reminders of her mistake.

Eric took a moment to reply. "It may take a while to earn their trust, Miss Seria. But it will be worth it. All things worth fighting for usually do."

It sounded like he spoke from personal knowledge. He looked down at her and gave her a sad smile. "But know you're not alone in this."

"I know. You've been so supportive from the beginning. I may not have shown it then, but it does mean a lot to me."

"Well, I appreciate your kind words, but that's not exactly what I meant." A shadow fell over his face, his attention drawn across the street. Seria followed his focus to where Ollen Knavis walked with stiff posture. "You're not the only one outside the Stewards' good graces recently," Eric said.

"What do you mean?" She shook her head at herself. When would she learn to stop talking so much?

But the prince was not put out by her question. "I'm afraid some of the knights in the Gateway also have doubts about *me* being their marshal."

Seria frowned up at him. "Why wouldn't they trust you, of all people?"

He cocked his head. "I don't think it's a matter of trust. They know where I stand, what I'm willing to fight for." He shrugged. "But they don't quite believe in my ability to lead them."

"But you're the prince." Seria turned her palms up. "Wouldn't that make you the obvious choice to lead them?"

"Not necessarily. Mistakes were made in the past, and I'm afraid I've spent the last few years rather silent." His face shuttered. "Their last commandant was a capable warrior before his recent death. His is a difficult role to fill. But I didn't tell you this so you would pity me." His tone lightened. "Or to cast a negative light on my Stewards. I wanted you to know I understand how hard this all is right now. And it may take some time, but I believe you'll be able to win these proud men over. Then they'll wonder why they ever doubted you."

She was about to reply when Eric looked over her head to someone approaching.

"Luron, how's Gus this morning?" he greeted the physician.

Gus. The kind man Seria had met. The intensity on Luron's face filled her with dread. "You're not going to believe this." Luron positioned himself so that he could see Seria.

"Believe what?" Eric's voice hitched.

Luron rubbed his jaw. "Gus went the whole night without coughing."

Eric exhaled. "He did?"

"I kept going back to check on him, afraid he was slipping away. But he slept like a child."

Seria froze when Luron's consideration fixed on her.

"Your tea worked, young lady. And I owe you an apology."

"Oh, well, there's no need—"

For the second time since they met, Luron put his hand up to stop her. "Aye, there is. I've been a man of medicine and healing for many years. I've learned to consider the knowledge and experience of others, no matter what their background, and absorb it into my own, learn from it. It was a code I adopted when I first began. I wasn't going to allow my pride to get in the way of making people better." He paused, his gaze unwavering. "I'm afraid I broke that code with you the other day, and I pray you will accept my apology."

She smiled. "I do. Thank you."

"How is Gus this morning?" Eric asked.

"Alert and hungry. He still has a few spells, but nothing like before. We gave him another dose before breakfast. Then he ate like a starving bear."

Eric let out a loud exhale. "I couldn't have hoped for better news, Doc."

Luron agreed, and Seria was pleased to see the relief evident on his face. The man genuinely cared about his patients. He looked to Seria again. "I don't know how you knew of that tea, missy, but you certainly knew what you were talking about."

"It was something my mother taught me."

He smiled. "Well, I'll know next time to take your suggestions a little more seriously."

Warmth surged through her. *Next time.* As if he expected to see her again in the clinic.

The doctor left them to return to his patients. Seria blinked up at Eric. Had she dreamed the whole scene?

He grinned down at her. "At this rate, it won't take you long to win the Stewards over. Gus happens to be a favorite around here."

"I'm happy I could help." It was the truth. But the promise of what this could mean for her future filled her with absolute giddy delight.

44

Light shines in darkness, yet,
those who dwell there see it not.
-The Sacred Code

"You must be willing to do whatever it takes to get your job done." Mason looked into the faces of the young people seated before him. "When the time comes, you've got to know that you will not let anything—or anyone—stand between you and your mission."

A skinny teen in the back of the group spoke up. "Does that mean women and children, too?"

Areem snorted at the question.

Mason didn't give himself time to consider the weight of the question before answering the boy. "If someone is standing between you and the greater good for which you are fighting, then aye, that means women and children, too. What we're fighting for is too big to allow for weakness. And if you're unsure you can go through with that, then now is the time to get out."

Then why did you leave Seria alive? The hypocrisy of his own statement sat like a bitter herb on his palate. *That was then. This is now.*

He shifted back to the present to study his students, reading every one of their thoughts, their doubts and hesitations or eagerness and confidence. This was a crucial part of the training, the time for the recruits to realize what was expected of them. No life was worth endangering their cause.

What is our cause exactly? The question had been uttered earlier that morning. He could hear his answer like it was being repeated back to him.

To keep the lies and the rigidity of the Code from overpowering the people's freedom of choice. To take the tyrannical king and his prince down so that Jader may have a chance to offer something better to the people of the Old Realm. And to completely destroy the Stewards who have assumed the right of taking the law into their own hands.

He believed all that, had devoted his life to becoming a Shadowman so he could further that very cause he was teaching his students.

Yet when it came down to it, he could not remove the threat of a single witness, one who had probably already run to the prince with all she knew about Mason.

He ground his teeth and shut his reflections down. "Think about this for the rest of the night. Then, if you're ready to continue, meet me at sunup on the jousting field."

The students began to disperse, quieter than usual. Mason was gathering his sword and supplies when he looked over to find Areem in front of him.

"Master Mason."

Mason crossed his arms in front of him and waited.

Areem halted. "Oh." He lowered his head in a quick, glib bow of respect.

"What do you want, Areem?" Mason's tone was dry.

"When are we going to be done with the pretend drills and get to the real thing?"

"Pretend?"

Areem nodded. "I'm tired of having to hold everything back. I'm ready to slash some Stewards."

Mason stuck his tongue in the side of his cheek to hide a smile. "In time, Areem, when you're ready."

"I'm ready now. There's nothing you've tossed at us that I haven't been able to do. I could have passed the finals a week ago. You know I'm the best fighter in this group."

And modest, too. "You're ready when I say you are. The trials are given at the same time. No exceptions. If you're as ready as you think you are, then use this time to hone your skills and help your peers."

A frown turned Areem's features down. "It's a waste of time."

"And by thinking that, you show you're not as ready as you thought."

Areem's shoulders slumped. "Aye, sir."

Mason shook his head as he watched Areem walk away. Then he turned to see Bruin approaching.

"Problem?" Bruin asked.

"Not really."

The commander pointed his whiskered chin toward the young recruit. "That one there shows a lot of promise."

"You're right about that."

"Much like you as a young man."

Thinking of the impatience Areem had displayed, Mason had to agree. He could not count the times he had wanted to forgo the "pretend" and get to what he considered important.

"You have certainly turned your group around this past week, Mason."

"I was getting a little sloppy in my work." He slid his sword into its sheath. "Once I got myself in hand, they shaped up as well."

"Good, I'm glad to hear it." Bruin hooked his thumbs on his belt and eyed him. "Jader is coming into camp tomorrow."

Mason raised his head. "Is he still planning on going to the fort?"

Bruin nodded. "He's being cautious of how we approach the Gateway. We have no intentions of walking into an ambush. Jader will handpick those he wants to go with him. I'm sure you already know you'll be one of them."

"He's mentioned it."

"That won't be a problem for you, will it?"

"Nay, sir. Why would it be?"

"Oh, I don't know." Bruin stared at him, his face unreadable. "Wanted to make sure you hadn't formed any attachments to the place. Or its people."

"I assure you, Commander, I have no attachments," Mason said. "I was ecstatic to leave Cadence behind." *Sure. That's why Shon had to almost drag you from the woods.*

Bruin smiled, though it didn't reach his eyes. "You're a good man, Mason. It's no wonder Jader holds you in such high regard."

"I take that as the highest compliment, sir."

Bruin took his leave, and Mason made his way to the stables. He had a little extra time before supper would be served. Not willing to sit around with nothing to do but think, he decided to take his horse for a run.

His days had been filled to the brim lately, mostly by his own doing. At sunrise, he met with his students for training. Then he took to the fields after the noon meal for a long, strenuous practice. Then there was another session with his trainees. If there was time, he would go out for a ride, maybe do a little hunting. The cooks were always in need of fresh meat. By the time he cleaned up and had something to eat, he was more than ready for bed.

He liked it that way and pushed himself hard, staying busy and productive. This was how to ensure his readiness to face the Stewards when the time came. And by keeping his body busy, his mind was occupied as well, making it easier to focus on the task at hand. Unlike a week ago, he would not be held back or distracted by anything.

Or anyone.

At the stables, he led his horse to the hitching post and slid the blanket over its broad back. He could have asked one of the boys to do it, but he didn't mind handling his own horse. It gave him the chance to check the animal over.

He liked the big roan that had been presented to him the year before. The horse was independent and surly but did what was asked of him. They made a good pair. As Mason settled the saddle in place, he glanced over to see Crue sitting on a stump, his head down.

"Don't you have something better to do than sit around?"

Crue started and jumped to his feet. "I'm sorry, sir." Then he continued to stand there.

Mason tightened the cinch. "You gonna answer me, boy?"

"Oh, um, nay, sir. I mean, I don't have anything else to do, sir. Not really."

Patting the horse's neck, he led it to where Crue stood. "Nothing at all?"

"Well, sir, after I tainted Lady Dreeya's saddle, I'm not to touch her things."

"Can you show me Dreeya's saddle?"

His cheeks flooding with color, Crue led Mason to the side of the tent where the saddles were kept. Being careful to keep his hands off the saddle, he pointed to the stained spot.

Mason almost shook his head. The oil stain was no bigger than a bean and barely noticeable behind the stirrup. To think this was what Dreeya had made such a fuss over was almost laughable.

Outwardly, all he said was, "That's a stain, all right."

"Aye, sir." Crue was unable to lift his face.

Mason turned his lips down. Why was he wasting his time on the boy? He had better things to do. But the shame Crue wore tugged on him. "How much work you getting?"

"Since Lady Dreeya reported me? None, sir. After others heard, they don't want me working for them either."

Good grief. Putting a boy out of work because of an oil stain? Mason was all for the servants knowing their place and doing their job efficiently, but there was such a thing as fairness, too. "Makes it pretty hard to get paid, doesn't it?"

"Aye, sir." Crue's expression was lanced with worry. "Bruin will have me relocated back to the village."

Mason knew the routine. If a servant did not perform his duty, he or she was expelled from the camp and expected to make their way.

"Do you think you can manage to care for my things without messing them up?" He intentionally kept his manner gruff.

Crue's head came up. "Are you serious, sir?"

He waved at Dreeya's saddle. "Only if you can keep something like this from happening again."

"Aye, sir, absolutely, sir!" Crue nodded rapidly in his fervor.

"Fine, then." Mason inhaled through his nostrils. "You do a good job for me, and you'll have more work again."

Crue beamed. "Aye, sir! Thank you, sir!"

With nothing more to say, Mason gave him a curt nod and turned away to mount his horse. He looked back as he trotted away to see the boy staring after him.

Like many of the servants, Crue was probably an orphan, working in Bruin's camp to feed and clothe himself. If he could not support himself, he would resort to thievery. All Mason had done was give him a job to keep him from becoming a nuisance.

It was nothing more than that.

45

Eric knocked on the door a second time. "Braylee? Are you awake?"

The door was yanked open, and a disheveled Braylee frowned at him from the entry to his chambers. His black curls stood out all over his head, and his whiskers were in need of a trim. "I am now."

Eric blinked at the growl in his tone. "I...ah...would you like to break the fast?"

"Now, sir?" Braylee's eyes narrowed. A red crease lined one side of his face.

Though tempted to laugh, Eric dared not, feeling much like a precocious youngster getting scolded by an impatient older brother. "I'm sorry. I didn't mean to disturb your rest."

Braylee sent him a fierce scowl and rubbed his hands through his tangles. "Well, I might as well. Since I'm not sleeping. *Your Highness.*" He was still mumbling when he closed the door.

Eric's jaw dropped as the big man slammed things around in his irritation. So, this is what Braylee was like in the mornings. He had tried to warn him. Eric covered his mouth to muffle a chuckle at what sounded like a chair being shoved out of the way. What a contrast to the mild-mannered knight he had come to know!

After a while, the noise from the other side of the door began to die down. Loath to hurry him along, Eric rocked back and forth on the balls of his feet while he waited. When Braylee finally made his appearance, he looked every bit as calm and unruffled as he ever did.

"Ready to go?"

"Aye, Your Grace."

They left the main building together and walked silently side by side across the street to the mess hall. Eric cleared his throat. Was it safe to speak?

Braylee beat him to it. "I must apologize for my behavior, Sire."

Unable to help himself any longer, Eric doubled over and laughed, long and hard. At Braylee's confused face, he roared louder.

"You certainly weren't exaggerating when you warned me about your morning moods, were you, my friend?" He slapped Braylee on the back.

A begrudging smile worked its way onto Braylee's noble face, and a subtle blush spread over his broad cheeks. "I'm afraid not. It's had me nearly tossed out of my own house by the wife a few times." He squinted at him. "You're not upset?"

Eric chuckled again. "Not at all. But I will certainly remember this in the future. Unless I require another good laugh."

Braylee's face was wry. "I thank you."

Seria was clearing off a table when they entered the noisy room. The knights began to rise in obligatory respect, but Eric raised a hand.

"Enjoy your breakfast, men."

Eric settled at a table and looked around. Ollen's sullen face came into view. The young knight stood and made for the door, his footsteps quick and brusque. But right before he left, his expression softened, and he raised a hand to someone in the room. Eric glanced over in time to see Seria smile and wave in reply. Despite the burn of Ollen's rejection, a trace of amusement cooled it. It appeared as though Seria had made a friend.

He smiled up at her as she approached with a pitcher of steaming, hot brew. "I can see you're already hard at work."

"I never knew what all went into feeding you Stewards," she said as she poured two cups. "Nola is running her feet off trying to keep up with everything. Sire."

He hid a smile at how she tacked on his title at the end.

"Did you do the cooking, too?" Braylee asked.

"A little."

"Good. Maybe it'll be edible."

Seria laughed. "I'm not too sure about that. The most I can manage is oats and stew. But I thank you, all the same."

Braylee gave her a fatherly wink. Seria left them to get their breakfast, her steps light and quick, with a smile that dashed away the anxiety that had before marked her face.

Eric watched the young woman as she went about her work. Her presence elicited mixed reactions from the men. She always offered an easy smile, though it was not always returned. Still, she maintained a gracious attitude, even with the snubs. Eric would not have been so cordial.

Uneasiness grew inside him. Had he made a mistake in stepping in for her? It certainly had not done any favors with his relations with the Stewards.

Ollen's friendly wave as he made his hasty departure came back to Eric's mind. A tendril of relief loosed his tension. Maybe there was still a chance that she would be accepted, despite her innocent mistake.

Maybe he had not ruined things for the both of them.

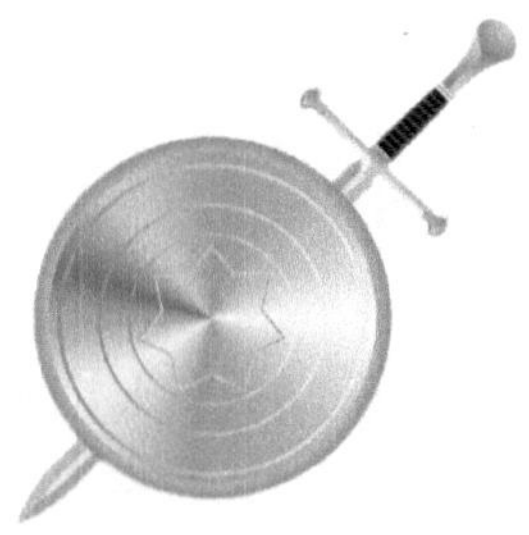

"Prince Eric?"

At the feminine voice behind him, Eric turned to see a petite brunette approaching. He was due to the training field for an early evening session, but her face was so full of purpose that he stopped.

"Might I have a moment of your time?" she asked.

"Of course, miss...?"

"Lena Carwright. My mother runs the bakehouse."

Eric tilted his head back. "Ah. She also runs a small bakery from her house, correct?"

She nodded. "We both work together, aye. I also take a booth to Cadence occasionally."

Recognition hit him. "I had a pastry from your cart once. It was delightful. My soldiers can't get enough of your treats."

A small smile lifted the corners of her trim lips. Then she sobered. "Sir, is it your intention that Seria Gayle looks like a prisoner during her probation here?"

He blinked at her forthrightness. "I beg your pardon?"

Lena raised her chin slightly. "I understand that she is under your custody, correct?"

"How would you know that?"

She smirked. "Soldiers like to talk while stuffing themselves with sweets. But if it is true, you do a poor job of caring for your charges."

Eric slumped as he massaged the back of his stiff neck. Now the civilians were challenging him?

Lena's face softened, and she took a step back. "I apologize, Your Highness. I do not mean to overstep."

Her apology eased the cord between his shoulders. "None needed, Miss Lena. I can see you are a good friend to Miss Seria."

"I try to be." Her smooth brow puckered. "I commend your stepping in for her, but I fear she will always be looked on as an outcast."

And the poor state of her clothing did nothing to build her standing in the judgment of the people. Why hadn't he thought of that? "This time I really do beg your pardon. I'm afraid I overlooked this need."

A smile set her eyes to dancing. "Not surprising. Most men don't consider the state of one's clothing to be a priority, merely that their charges are clothed at all."

Eric chuckled and put his hands up. "Guilty."

"I would have seen to this myself, but I cannot offer her anything from my wardrobe."

Nay indeed. Seria was not a tall woman, but Eric guessed she stood several inches taller than her diminutive friend. "Have no fear, Miss Lena. I will see to it."

She bit her lip as another wrinkle creased her forehead.

"And I will be most subtle about it," he added. In the short time he had come to know Seria, he knew her to be proud and capable. He would not want to insult her independence.

Lena nodded and smiled. "I thank you, Your Highness. Seria is a gem, and I pray it's but a matter of time before the rest of the fort sees that."

"Sir!" Lionel ran up to them, breathless and hair disheveled.

Eric tensed. "What is it, Sergeant?"

"There's a fire, sir. In the Fourth Square."

One of the civilian blocks.

Lena cried out. Without a word, she gathered her skirts and dashed in that direction.

"Wait!" Eric ran after her, Lionel at his side. They quickly overtook her and rounded the corner of the kitchen, where a crowd had gathered. Smoke billowed from the room of a small hut. Flames licked the edge of a window.

"Mama!" Lena screamed and bolted for the house.

Eric caught her around the waist before she could go any farther. "Nay, Lena!"

"My mother's still in there!" She fought him, tears streaming.

He gripped her upper arms and looked into her distraught face. "We'll get her out."

Crackling and snapping filled his ears. Ash and sparks floated up from the roof. His heart clenched at the thought of Lena's mother trapped inside.

Seria burst through the crowd, her mouth agape. She spotted Eric holding Lena back and hurried over. "Oh, Lena."

Eric pushed the distraught woman back a safe distance. "Stay here." He caught Seria's eye, and she moved forward to grasp her friend's trembling arm.

"It'll be all right, Lena." Seria's voice hitched.

Eric left the young women and sprinted for the house.

"Captain Braylee's inside!" someone shouted, and the clench around his chest tightened.

Men—Stewards, militiamen, and civilians alike—rushed around with buckets and canvas. The efforts were valiant, but there was no order, no plan. Nothing but panicked chaos.

"Make a line to the well!" he shouted. With a few words, the men formed a line from the well to the house. Every few seconds, a bucketful of water was thrown on the flames. A few others stood at the edge of the house and battled it with wet canvas bags. Another group replaced them, and the men ran back to resoak their bags.

Ollen ran into the chaos. "How many are in there?"

"Two," Eric answered, already heading for the door. But a beam groaned and slipped. Simmering timbers fell from the roof, inches from where he stood. There was a great scraping sound, and everything over his head shifted down. Then part of the roof collapsed and slid right for him.

46

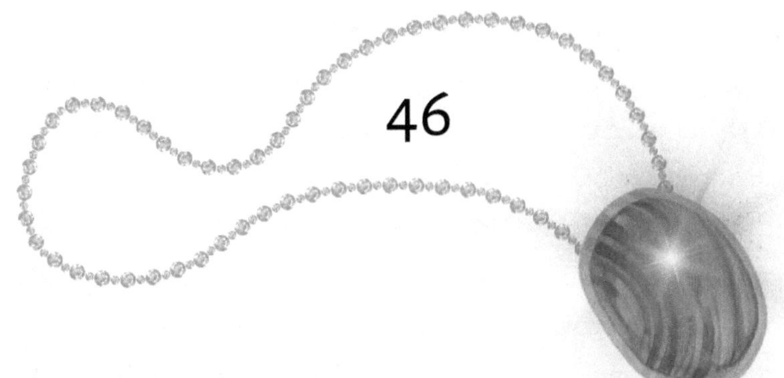

"The Lambient is the power behind the Gifts of the Moon—this mysterious distribution of diverse abilities. The individual possesses but a minute taste of His goodness and might. May those who are graced with these gifts choose to use their abilities for the good of mankind."
-Commencement speech given by Steward Grand Marshal Uralis Faunt

Seria smothered a scream as the roof came down, but the prince's hands up shot up, and the burning ridge hung suspended in midair.

Ollen jumped back, glanced up at the rubble above him, and then dashed inside the smoldering house. A few boards slipped, blocking the door. Seria's breath lodged in her windpipe, already burning from the smoke and ash.

Eric's face strained red with the effort of holding such weight. "Clear the entry!"

Civilians and soldiers appeared from all sides. Some continued tossing water onto the flames, while others soaked the surrounding structures to keep it from spreading. Others dragged smoldering planks away from the doorway to open the exit. A few grabbed poles, slats, whatever they could get their hands on, to assist Eric in bracing the building to keep it from crashing down.

The heat was intense, even where Seria stood a safe distance away. What must Lena be going through, watching all this? She reached for Lena's hand and got nothing but air. Lena was nowhere to be seen.

Oh no, surely not.

She turned back to the building being consumed by fire. Her friend was inside that oven. The wild inclination to run for the building rushed through her. There was still no sign of Braylee or Ollen. The thought of losing Lena and her dear mother pulled a strangled sob from her. She wanted to flee the scene, but she stood rooted to the spot, peering through trembling fingers. *Oh, Lambient, save them!*

"Move, move!" Eric's order was sharp, and the men instantly fell back. Eric stepped forward and gave a shove with his hands. The roof slid backward, away from the door. Another beam skidded down, but he stopped it before it crashed down.

And then through the fire-edged portal they came, Braylee carrying Lena's mother, and Ollen supporting Lena. As soon as they were through, Eric dropped his hands, and the house fell in. He leaned forward and braced himself against his legs, panting.

The relief gushed through Seria's lungs. "Thank you, Lambient." Her shaking knees nearly gave out, but her concern for her friends drove her forward to where Braylee gently laid Lena's mother on the ground.

"Mama?" Lena coughed and crawled to her mother, who lay unconscious. "Oh, Mama, please!"

Seria laid her head on the older woman's breast. "She's alive, but she sounds seriously congested. Someone better take her to the infirmary."

Braylee moved to scoop Ayna up again. Lena burst into tears and covered her face with her hands. "It's my fault!"

Seria gathered her in a hug. "Don't blame yourself, Lena. You don't know what happened."

Lena lifted her tear-stained face. "Nay, I left a towel by the fire. I was in such a hurry to talk to—"

Eric stepped in and took Lena by the arm to help her stand. "Let's get you to the infirmary with your mother, Miss Lena."

She clutched at his arm. "But I'll never forgive myself if—"

He stopped her again. "How about we go see how she's doing before we borrow trouble?"

The play of emotions walking across Lena's face broke Seria's heart. She took Lena's other arm and led her to the infirmary, praying Luron would have good news.

As they left, she glanced back at the site. While some still worked to ensure the fire didn't spread, others watched their marshal leave, respect emanating from their gazes.

A faint trace of optimism bloomed, despite the sorrow of the situation. This had been a small crisis for the Stewards in the face of the threat they still faced, but maybe this would be a turning point for many of them. The prince had stepped in without hesitation and taken charge, and as a result, no lives had been lost.

Her attention was drawn to Ollen, who did not look Prince Eric's way as he passed. He stood to himself, his soot-covered head lowered and hands on his hips.

Seria bit her lip. What would it take for the rest of them?

A short while later, Seria stepped out of the infirmary to find Eric still waiting.

"How are they?" he asked, lines creasing his forehead.

"Ayna has a lot of smoke in her lungs, but she's awake and talking" Seria answered, touched by his concern. "Both are tired and hoarse, but nothing rest and fresh air won't cure."

His face sagged. "I'm sorry they've lost their home, but at least they're safe."

"My feelings, exactly." A pang hit her at how close she came to losing them. Lena was her one longtime friend, and Ayna was the sweetest lady, always offering Seria some new treats.

"Your friend is a brave woman to go into the fire after her mother."

Seria scowled. "Brave and foolish, you mean."

Eric smiled. "We often do foolish things to save those we love."

The sun dipped low in the sky, and Seria quickened her steps. "Oh my, I'm late."

"I spoke with Nola to let her know what happened. She understands."

"Thank you." She slowed a little but still did not wish to keep the kind woman waiting too long. She glanced over at Eric as he fell into step beside her. His face was screwed up in thought. "That was wonderful," she said.

"Hmm?"

"I didn't know you could move things like that."

He smiled. "For a few minutes, I wasn't sure I could hold it any longer."

"But you held it. Long enough for Braylee and Ollen to find them." Seria shook her head, her feelings of shock and fear rushing back over her. "My, your men certainly showed themselves today. Not one of them stood back. I think all of them were ready to go in if they had to."

Eric nodded. "I believe that. The Stewards are nothing if not courageous. The reservists, too, for that matter."

Seria cocked her head. "Now, see, that's something I've been wondering about. What's the difference? I've noticed that some wear gray and some wear red."

"Not every knight who serves under my father is a Steward," Eric answered. "The Militia Reserves—they have the gray tunics—are an essential part of his army, the biggest part, in fact. Brave and faithful to the core, they serve wherever they are needed."

"Like guarding the Gateway."

"That's right. We've always had a few Stewards based here, but for the most part, the militia was all we needed. Until now."

"So, how does one become a Steward?"

"The Stewards are a special force formed by my family many years ago. They lead the militia." He shifted to face her. "They take the title of Steward when they are willing to sacrifice all to follow the Code and serve the Lambient with their whole heart."

Seria started to say more, then her face heated. Her questions had annoyed Mason. She turned away and picked up her pace.

"Don't be afraid to ask. I always enjoy sharing."

She hesitated, but the subject was a nice diversion from the traumatic turn of the evening. "I've heard a lot about the Stewards and the Code all my life, but I'm afraid I don't know much about either." That was pretty obvious when she thought Mason was a Steward. "My parents tried to teach me, but I was a child and didn't take it very seriously then."

"What do you want to know?" Eric tucked his hands behind his back and slowed down, as if he had all the time in the world.

"The Code. What is it exactly?"

"The standard which we strive to live by." He tilted his head back and quoted, "'Defend the helpless, uphold what is right, preserve what is good, protect the innocent, regard the pure, honor what is just, maintain what is true.'"

The words rang like poetry. "My. That sounds so profound."

Eric smiled. "I've always thought so. Of course, that is but a surface idea of what makes up the Code. The complete writings of the Code are kept in the Steward Halls at the capital of every kingdom."

"How do you know if someone has accepted the Code and is ready to be a Steward?"

"The Beacon lets us know." He pulled his light rod from his belt. Seria watched in awe as it lit up. "It lights up when the person bearing it has truly accepted the call to serve. There are a lot of good knights willing to fight and die for the king, but if they are not truly surrendered, then they are not true Stewards."

"Where does the light come from?"

Eric pointed up. "From the Lambient. The very source of all light that resides far above what our mortal eyes can see. His light is so pure and so powerful that the sun draws from him."

"And do the Gifts come from the Lambient, as well?"

"That's right." Eric paused to bow his head to a passing lady. "It occurs when the moon passes over the Lambient and reflects off His light. Infants born at that moment are blessed with a Gift."

"That's amazing." She had never met anyone with a Gift. Not until Mason. "Darkmen don't believe in the Lambient, do they?"

"Not like you and I do."

"Then how could he—*they* have Gifts of the Moon?"

"A good question. One I've thought about often." He took his time with his answer. "First of all, one's faith in the Lambient does not negate or prove His existence."

"True."

"Remember, the Gifts are bestowed on whoever happens to be born in that instant. Unfortunately, many choose to use their Gifts for their own gain, or to serve the Dark Army."

"That's sad."

"Aye, it is."

Her last moment with Mason came rushing back to her. Him walking away, her hiding in the bushes like a coward. Something sharp pinched at her emotions.

"You're thinking of him."

She nodded. "Feeling ashamed. When it became clear what Mason was, I didn't do anything but hide in the bushes." She shook her head, unable to forget how she felt, watching the fight break out before her. The fight Mason led. Weights attached to her heart. No wonder the knights of the Gateway resented her.

"You were frightened, Seria. That's understandable."

"But I knew I should do something. Instead I sat in a fog." She frowned. "Too much of a coward, I guess, to make myself do anything more than hide."

Eric's face lit up. "Did he tell you to hide?"

"Aye, but that shouldn't have mattered." She frowned. "Not by then, anyway."

"Seria, 'tis not your fault you could not react."

"Sure, it was. I—"

He put his hand up. "Mason's Gift consists of more than reading thoughts."

"What do you mean?"

"He can also gain temporary control over someone's will, get them to do his bidding. It's very dangerous and very powerful, virtually impossible to resist."

She stared at him. Would she ever cease to be surprised by the man she had taken in? "That's what he did to me?"

"More than likely," he said, his words tinged with regret. "Control typically lasts a little while past the initial moment of contact. The victim is left exhausted and weak, with a severe headache."

Her hand came up to her lips; he had described exactly how she had felt the following morning. The now-familiar feeling of betrayal multiplied. "He controlled me. That's why I couldn't do anything to help."

Eric's mouth sagged. "I'm sorry, Seria, that you had to find out in such a way what Darkmen are made of."

Seria rubbed her arms against a sudden chill. On one hand, it eased her mind to know she had had no control over her actions. On the other hand, it made her feel used and vulnerable. How else had Mason manipulated her? Had she taken care of him all that time by Mason's will, rather than her own?

Nay, that couldn't be. Mason had resented her help in the beginning, had hated being there. That was more than clear. And she had not felt the effects of his control until after he told her to hide. The rest of the time, she had been in her right mind. Which meant that every moment they had shared up to that point had been real.

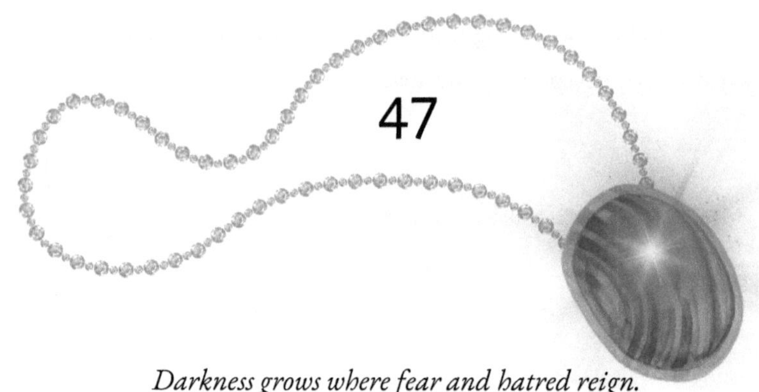

47

Darkness grows where fear and hatred reign.
-The Sacred Code

Jader arrived at Bruin's camp right after the last meal. The Darkmen stood at attention on either side when his company rode in. Jader acknowledged their formal greeting with a nod, then released them back to their regular activities.

He dismounted and made a circular sweep with his arm. "Everything looks well, Bruin."

"Thank you, my emperor," Bruin responded with a bow. Jader saw past his meek façade to the arrogant mien he possessed. The trait had carried him far, thus Jader tolerated it, so long as it never became a problem.

They made their way toward the large, elaborate tent set up for Jader's brief stays. "What is the status of Cadence?"

"They're holed up in the town. I think Mason's recent escapade has left them a bit skittish."

"Good." Jader let a small smile slip. "And the prince?"

"From what I can tell, he keeps inside the garrison."

"So, he has not changed much."

"His men patrol the town daily, and he's increased his numbers since our skirmish in Rackson. He has men stationed at other Gateway villages, especially since the incident at Cuthrel."

"And what of your latest assignment?"

Bruin's jaw tightened. "I found her."

Jader cocked a brow. "*Her?*"

"That's right. My contact came across a fat drunk more than willing to tell all for a few coins. It wasn't a common man Mason stayed with, but a girl. A poor girl, the town's laundry washer. What's more, he left her alive."

Though surprise swirled through him, Jader refused to give place to anger. He had to be rational, in full control of his thoughts. Bruin, on the other hand, had no such qualms. His features had grown dangerously sharp.

"Can you tell me more?"

"She lives alone," Bruin growled. "Or at least she did before she was arrested."

"Arrested?" They had arrived at Jader's tent, and Bruin held the flap open for him.

"Shortly after Mason left, she was taken into Steward custody. Apparently, they didn't take kindly to her assisting a Darkman."

Jader sniffed. "Of course not." He rubbed his scar. "So, Mason chose not to tell us of this girl. Interesting."

"Interesting?" Bruin's nostrils flared. "He lied to us, sir, *and* left a witness behind. And you say it's *interesting?*"

"Calm yourself, my friend."

"I don't understand, my lord. Aren't you angry at his deceit?"

Jader smirked. "Am I happy about it? Nay, Bruin, I am not. It is obvious Mason feels some kind of attachment, or at the very least, an obligation to this girl."

"Aye, so—"

"You know as well as I do of Mason's hatred for the Stewards. And with good reason. One little peasant girl is not going to change that. If anything, she could eventually prove useful to us."

Bruin still looked doubtful. "And what of Mason?"

"What of him? You told me yourself he's in rare form now, more driven than he's ever been." He put his thumb to his lips. Careful, thoughtful planning had gotten him here. He would not let impulsive decisions rule him now. Mason's allegiance was too valuable. "He is the reason I put off this meeting with Eric. I want him clear-headed and unshakeable."

"And you still trust him, despite his deceit?"

"I trust no one, Bruin. But I am confident Mason will play his part tomorrow."

"Why is it so important he go with you at all? He could stay behind with the others."

Jader shook his head. "Nay. I want Mason to see Eric, face-to-face. Keeps his hatred fresh, his thirst for revenge sharp."

"And thus, his allegiance clear."

"Exactly." Sitting down in the lush chair provided for him, Jader folded his hands across his lap. "We'll leave for the fort first thing in the morning. I want Mason Grey by my side."

Mason climbed on the back of his horse with heavy limbs, consumed with the endeavor ahead of him. Jader had already spoken in private with the Darkmen accompanying him to Cadence. He stressed that he wanted no trouble. His ultimate goal was a peaceful talk with Eric. Nothing more.

But the underlying warning was there. There was no guarantee how the Stewards would react at their arrival, despite the peace banner flying over their heads. So self-righteous were they, Mason half-expected to be ambushed as soon as they reached the town.

As he sat astride the saddle, his posture unyielding, he stared straight ahead, not seeing the camp, the tents, or the Darkmen readying for the trip. His vision went back to the last time he had seen his brother alive, before he was slain by a bloodthirsty Steward. He would soon see the one responsible for the death of Liam, Baris, and the other Handan boys. When the moment came, would he be able to keep his hatred reined in? The last thing he wanted was to let his emotions get the better of him.

There was movement at his side, and Bruin halted his horse. "You ready, Sir Mason?"

"I am, Commander." Something about Bruin's expression unnerved him. For the last few days, there had been a hardness in the commander, as if Mason had done something to offend him, but he had no idea what.

Bruin studied him. "I can see you're already boiling under the surface."

He took a deep, cleansing breath. "I won't lose control, Commander."

"That wasn't a reprimand, Mason." Bruin's stern expression eased some. "Our anger and hatred can be a powerful weapon against our enemies. It keeps us strong and focused."

"I can see why." Mason shifted in the saddle. "All I can think of is what I'd like to see happen today."

Bruin smirked. "I'm guessing it has nothing to do with a peaceful negotiation?"

He clenched his jaw. "Far from it."

"I know how you feel. But we'll abide by Emperor Jader's wishes today. Then, when the time comes for action, we'll know we did everything we could."

Jader was at the front now, looking over his men. He motioned Bruin and Mason to join him at the front. Mason was honored beyond words to be asked to ride at Jader's left side. Bruin, of course, rode on Jader's right, with Shon and Dreeya positioned behind Mason.

Mason sat tensely, his ears straining to hear the order to move. When it came, a rush of anticipation surged through his veins, though he tried to mask it. He did not want to give Jader or Bruin any reason to doubt his focus. But he couldn't squelch the hope that things would take a turn for the worse. Mason would not miss a chance to kill Eric Passion.

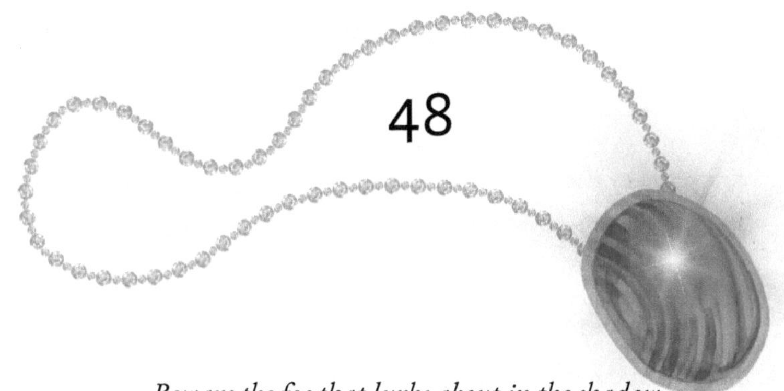

48

"What will you do?" Seria asked the two women across the table. She was due soon for her shift at the mess hall soon, but she stopped to check on them first.

"Oh, Seria, dear, don't you worry about us." Ayna reached over and patted Seria's hand. She still rasped from the smoke when she spoke. "This isn't the first time we've had to start over. We're fortunate to have friends who offered us a place to stay for a while. We'll be fine."

Seria shook her head at her friend. "I still don't know what you were thinking, going into that house. Or how you got away from me!"

Lena shrugged. "I thought I could be quicker getting her out the back way. And I would've, too, if she hadn't been unconscious."

"My brave, foolish girl." Ayna patted her daughter's cheek, then left the two younger women to visit while she rested.

"How are you?" Seria asked.

Lena shrugged, sadness lurking in her expression. "I'm all right but so relieved Grandfather isn't living with us yet. I guess his independent streak served him well this time." She clasped her hands on the table. "I learned when we lost Papa that life doesn't always go the way we planned."

"No, it doesn't." Images of Seria's own family flitted through her memory. And of Mason, but she shoved his face away. "What of your business?"

"My cart was by the house, so it's gone. Lucky for us, I had the money I'd saved in my pocket. That'll give us something to put toward another house."

"But that will mean waiting longer for your bakery!"

"Can't be helped. It'll come in time." She let out a small laugh. "I may be a bit older than you, Seria, but I've still got plenty of years left in me."

"Of course, you do; that's not what I meant."

"I know. You're being a good friend."

The words caused pain deep inside her. What would Lena think of her after she shared what she had learned? "There's something I think you need to know. The day Mason ordered you to take him to the fort, he...controlled you into it. It's part of his Gift."

Lena nodded. "I know that, too."

Seria's jaw slacked. "How?"

"You forget, I'm the one he controlled. I knew I wasn't in my own will. Besides that, I live in the fort. I hear things."

"Please know I had nothing to do with it."

Lena squeezed Seria's arm. "Of course, I know that. You would never do anything to intentionally harm anyone."

Relief was an almost tangible gift as Seria took her leave a while later. She had so few friends in this fort that Lena's graciousness was a balm to her wounded spirit.

"Good morning."

Seria smiled up at the prince who had joined her without her noticing. "Good morning to you, Prince Eric."

"You seemed a little down yesterday."

"I'm better." It was true. Learning the scale of Mason's Gift had left her bereft at how little she had known him. But Lena's positive attitude and graciousness were enough to lift her spirits. Seria had a new life now. It did no good to keep dwelling on the past, no matter how her soul ached.

She was about to speak further when a flash of light at Eric's side caught her eye. "Um, your Beacon is blinking."

Eric reached for the rod and grinned. "Come along, Miss Gayle. I'd like you to meet my father."

"How can I do that?"

"Follow me and find out," was all he would say. She followed him through the courtyard until he reached a small pool of water, surrounded by stones. He wriggled his eyebrows at her, then lowered his Beacon until the tip of it touched the water. The surface of the pool began to swirl and bubble. When it cleared, a white-headed man looked up at them from the water. He bore a strong resemblance to Eric.

"Good morning, Father," Eric greeted. "How goes it in Calla?"

"Fair and quiet for the time being." Much to Seria's amazement, the older man sounded as clear and distinguishable as Eric. "How are things in the Gateway?"

"Not much has changed since the last report." He waved Seria closer. "I'd like you to meet our newest resident. Seria Gayle, this is Aden Passion, King of Paladin."

As soon as she fell under the scrutiny of the ruler of Paladin, Seria became completely tongue-tied. King Aden gave her a wide smile, his blue eyes twinkling. "Good morning, Lady Seria."

"Thank you. I mean, good morning to you." Catching herself, she tacked on, "Your Majesty."

Eric looked ready to burst into laughter, for which she gave him a light glare. What was he thinking introducing her to the king without warning?

The king's face lit up. "I do hope my Stewards are not too distracted by her charm to do their duty."

"That's certainly not a problem." Seria blushed at her bluntness. "Sire."

Eric spoke up. "I'll try to keep them focused."

"Good." Aden grew serious. "Have you any more news of Jader's movements?"

Seria stepped back, glad to have the attention turned away from her. Getting to know the prince was overwhelming enough, but to meet the king—even if it was through a pool of water—was too much.

"We've not heard anything for a while," Eric told his father. "I don't think he's going to—" He stopped and stood up straight. His fierce expression wrapped a cord of tension around Seria's stomach.

"What's wrong, son?" Aden asked.

"I don't know." He shook his head. "Something's wrong, though."

"I understand, son. If you must go, don't hesitate," Aden said. "We'll speak another time."

Eric nodded, rather preoccupied. "Aye, I need to go." He took the Beacon from the water and hung it back on his belt. The pool returned to its usual form.

Never had Seria seen someone's mood change so drastically. "What's wrong?"

"I wish I knew," he whispered, looking around. "You go on to the mess hall. I must find Braylee. If you see him, let him know I need him. Immediately."

49

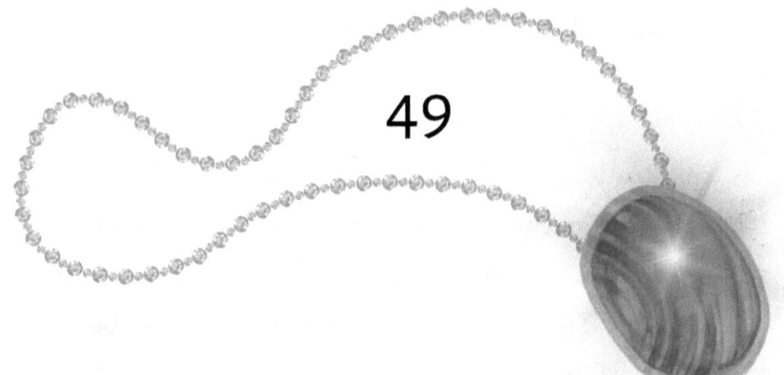

"Send a second squad to the town." Eric's order was brisk and clear. "Have all streets covered, and if possible, keep the civilians inside. I want scouts in the woods. I'm to be informed immediately of anything out of the ordinary."

Lt. Draven nodded, his expression impassive, but he left without hesitation to carry out the order.

Eric looked at Braylee, his skin tingling. "I have no idea what I'm preparing for. But I can't shake this feeling."

"I understand, Sire. We'll do what we can until something happens."

Unable to stay still for long, Eric headed for the wooden steps that took him to the top of the wall and scanned the outer bailey below. He could not see Cadence beyond the outer wall, but there was nothing that hinted at any kind of danger. The gates opened beneath him as the patrol rode through the bailey and out the second pair of gates into Cadence. He got a brief glimpse of Sergeant Ollen's serious face before the younger knight disappeared amid the town.

Eric braced himself against the stone wall. Questions swirled around in his head like a whirlpool. Something was brewing. He was positive about that. Something which could mark a turning point in this standoff. The fear that had planted itself deep inside now struggled to take root and grow.

I will not let his will be carried out in the Old Realm. He gripped his Beacon. The New Realm had already been taken over by Jader's brand of law and order. It would not be done in the Old Realm. The Old Realm had the Code which it lived under. The Stewards would protect it until the last knight fell. The Beacons would have to be darkened before Eric would ever stop fighting.

He reined in his thoughts. It would not come to that. As long as the power of the Lambient resonated from their Beacons, Jader and his Dark Army would fall.

We'll take it day by day. And we'll start by taking on the challenges this one holds.

"How often do you get these premonitions?"

Eric greeted Seria with a weak smile when she joined him at the wall, appreciating the brief respite she offered. "More often lately than I used to."

"Can you see the future?"

"Nay. It's an intuition when something isn't right."

She crossed her arms in front of her. "Sort of like a gut feeling."

"Aye, a gut feeling."

"Is this part of your Gift?"

He angled his head. "It's more of a family trait. My strong instincts have been passed down through the Passion bloodline for generations, as far back as my great, great, great grandmother at least. Like Lavrynth."

Seria frowned. "Lavrynth?"

He drew his sword from his side, rubbing his fingers over the intricate diamonds and stars carved into the golden hilt. "The family sword. It's been passed from father to son and used in more battles than any other sword known to man." Memories of his father teaching him how to hold it came to the forefront of his mind, teasing a small smile. "It's been told that the Lambient himself forged this blade in the Slates and handed it to my ancestor."

"It's beautiful." She chewed her lower lip. "So, what's your gut telling you right now?"

He grimaced and slid his sword back in the sheath. "That something's about to change."

There was a shout from the top of the wall, and the gate opened. Lionel galloped his horse through. Eric rushed down the steps to meet him. He could hear Seria hurrying to keep up.

The young man's face was flushed. "Prince Eric, Jader is coming."

Eric exhaled sharply, and a soft gasp escaped Seria. "How many does he have?" he asked, as Braylee and Dudley rode up to them.

"Two dozen is all, sir. Sgt. Ollen is watching them now. They're riding under the peace banner."

Eric froze. "The peace banner?"

"Aye, sir."

Dudley frowned. "It could be a trap."

"More like a scheme." Eric scowled. "Jader has no interest in peaceful correlations. There's something he's hoping to accomplish with this ruse." He rubbed his hands up and down his thighs, his mind moving faster than he could keep up with.

"What will we do, prince?" Braylee asked.

Eric clenched his jaw. "Someone bring me my horse. We'll let him in and see what he wants." He looked up at Dudley. "Get everyone behind closed doors. I don't want any man out here, save the Stewards. They are to be on horseback and in formation when he gets here."

"Aye, sir." Dudley was already on his way to see it done.

"Lionel, put all the reservists on standby in their quarters and replace them with Stewards. Have Ollen's squad meet Jader's company and escort them here. *Peacefully.*"

Lionel nodded and spurred his horse back out.

Eric gave a few more orders, then took Seria's arm and led her to the main building. "Seria, I want you to wait inside my chambers."

She nodded without a sound. Her cheeks had washed out, and her eyes nearly swallowed her face. Eric forced himself to slow down and look at her. "I have a feeling Mason is riding with Jader."

Seria stumbled. "Oh, Eric." Her distress was obvious by the casual use of his name. "Surely not."

"I don't know for sure, but for my own peace of mind, please go to my room and stay there until he's gone. After what he's already done to you, I won't risk him trying anything more."

She grasped his arm with bruising strength. "But how do you know he won't try something on you or one of your men?"

"He can't harm us. The Beacons protect us from his power."

Her mouth came open. "That's why you want only the Stewards out here with you."

"Aye, now please, take yourself to my room and stay there. Don't let yourself be seen."

She drew in a shaky breath, gave his arm another squeeze, and then moved through the doors of the keep. Eric waited at the bottom of the steps until he knew she was safe in his chambers. Then he spun on his heel and stalked back to where Braylee had his horse saddled and ready for him.

Jader would soon be at the border of Cadence.

Mason sat tall in the saddle as they approached Cadence. The mountains rose on both sides of the gap, casting their lofty shadows. He curled his lips at the dozen Stewards waiting for them at the edge of town. His insides churned. There were sure to be more knights, watching them unseen.

Riding ahead, Bruin brought his steed to a sideways halt, calling out once they were in earshot. "Sirs! Emperor Jader of the New Realm wishes an audience with the Prince of Paladin."

One of the Stewards replied stiffly. "The prince requests we escort you to the keep."

Bruin bowed his head. "We are most grateful." His manner was smooth.

Mason gritted his teeth as they came abreast with Bruin again. Of their own will, his eyes drifted to the side, where he spotted Seria's cabin down the hill from Cadence. All looked quiet and still. Too still. The washtub was on its side, as it had been the last time he was there. No laundry hung on the lines. The window was barred. And there was no sign of Sanjo grazing outside the shed. It looked like no one was home. But where would she be? She had no other place to go. No family.

Stiffening at the course of his thinking, he jerked back to the front.

They were within the town boundaries now. A few bold spectators stood at their doors, watching the procession. Mason guessed Jader's peace banner gave them the nerve to come out into the open. He skimmed over a heavyset man standing off to himself, and then looked again. Ira's double chin sagged at the sight of him.

Mason gave him a hard glare. *Aye, I remember you, scum.* As he got closer, he allowed himself a peek into what the man was thinking. Alarm streaked through him.

Seria had been taken by the Stewards. Mason tightened his hold on the reins and read the whole truth. She was arrested the morning after Mason left her, accused of aiding and abetting the enemy. And Ira was the one to turn her in.

The snake. Heat rushed to Mason's head, and he drilled his hot glare into Ira's. The fat man blanched in the face of Mason's rage.

What had they done to her? A sick feeling came over him at the position he had forced her in. He knew what the Stewards were capable of. Whatever had happened to her, he was responsible for it.

"Mason?"

With a start, Mason shook his thoughts away and glanced back at Shon, who gestured to the front of the caravan. Giving a quick nod, Mason turned forward and urged his horse to catch up. He tried to shake the fog that had fallen over him; he had to stay focused on the garrison up ahead. But the discovery of Seria's arrest would not be put off.

Where is she now? The penalty for aiding a Darkman would be harsh. Especially coming from the likes of Aden and his son. There was no telling what they had done to her. Mason clenched his jaw, sending streaks of pain through his face. At that moment, he could have killed Eric Passion with his bare hands.

To think they would carry out a sentence of death or imprisonment on an impoverished peasant girl was despicable. Seria was innocent. He could testify to that. She had thought him a Steward the whole time. But of course, the lordly prince of Paladin would not consider anything but his own judgment.

He's worse than a snake. The sick feeling intensified. He could feel Shon looking at him again, but he ignored him.

"Open the gates!"

The command yanked Mason back to the present. They had passed the outer wall without his awareness. He had to pay attention. The gatekeeper gave him a cold look from his post above. Mason sneered up at him, then squared his shoulders and fixed his stare on the gates as they swung inward.

50

Where darkness and light shall meet,
confusion and sorrow shall prevail.
-The Sacred Code

Eric felt ready to snap like a whip. His man had let him know the moment Jader and his Darkmen arrived at Cadence's border. Now he waited. Not a word was spoken among his Stewards, every eye trained on the gateman.

Never had Eric felt so responsible for the Gateway and his kingdom of Paladin. He wondered at the wisdom in allowing Jader entry into Cadence at all, but if he rode under the peace banner, Eric could not refuse this assembly. Not until he knew what Jader wanted to say.

Gripping the Beacon at his side, Eric exhaled long and slow through his nostrils. The pressure he was under became a physical force thumping against his sternum.

Braylee leaned toward him. "This is but a meeting, Sire."

Eric nodded. "So he says."

"He brings no more than two dozen with him. You've got your Stewards at your back. There's nothing he can accomplish here today."

Eric chewed the inside of his cheek and absently stroked Oakley's mane. How he wished the Stewards behind him were more unified. "I can't help thinking he's planned more than a meeting."

"If he does, we'll deal with it when the time comes."

The call came then, startling Eric so that Oakley snorted. He met the faithful Steward's eye before turning to give the order to the gateman.

Then he waited for his first glimpse of the man who swore enmity against his father. The emperor who had claimed all of the New Realm. The dark lord who had disavowed the pure light of the Lambient for shadows.

Jader held his head high as his procession made its way through the gates. His sharply angled cheeks twisted into a cordial smile as he approached.

Two men rode with him, one on either side. The man on Jader's right must be the infamous Bruin Pralus. His size and intensity gave him away. The commander was imposing in his height and build, taller than Braylee and almost as broad. The cold eyes that stared out from a stone face glittered much like the gray storm clouds he could summon with his Gift.

Eric identified the man on Jader's left with a passing glance. This was the man who had infiltrated the fort and controlled Eric's men into turning on each other. The man Seria had tended to for three weeks before he revealed his true loyalties.

This was the Reader.

Instead of encouraging eye contact, Eric maintained his focus on Jader. The older man walked his horse until he stood before Eric. His attention drifted to the mounted Stewards on either side, and a leer quirked on his face.

"Greetings, Prince Eric." Jader gave a humble bow. "I am deeply honored and grateful you agreed to meet with me. May we go somewhere to discuss the matters at hand?"

There was no way Eric was allowing this man and his two accomplices to step foot any further in his fort. "I feel this is as good a place as any... Emperor." He tacked the title on flatly.

"Very well." Jader crossed his wrists over the saddle horn. "Our mutual friend, Nebb Statler, sends his regrets at being unable to join us."

Eric's insides jerked, though he fought to keep the emotion on his face. Nebb Statler. His contact in Cuthrel.

Jader continued. "He has been relocated since last I spoke with him, but from what I hear, his children are thriving in their new setting."

The message was clear. Nebb was dead, and Jader had taken his offspring. There were rumors of a place in Joshun where children were taken to be raised as Jader's soldiers. But there was never any proof of it.

Eric's fingers curled into a fist, gripping the leather reins like a lifeline. Silence reigned over the men behind him, though he could sense the tension tightening in anger. Bile rose in his esophagus, and he clamped his teeth against it. Now was not the time to show his weakness. Grief would have to come later.

Before he could gather himself enough to speak, Jader tilted his head back, looking down his long nose. "I trust your father is well?"

"You are not here to speak of my father, sir," Eric finally ground out. "What brings you to the Gateway Stronghold?"

"Of course. I appreciate your forthrightness. No sense in wasting time, eh?"

Eric did not reply.

Jader settled into a more comfortable position. "First of all, I would like to express my deepest appreciation to one of your civilians. I understand if not for the young lady's charitable actions, my scout, Mason Grey, would surely have died."

The Reader's head jerked toward his emperor, and his face blanched at the mention of Seria. Eric's apprehension mounted yet again. "She was misled."

That drew Mason's attention back to Eric with a scathing look.

"Is that what she's telling you?" Jader clicked his tongue. "What a pity. I had hoped she felt the same way I did."

Mason shifted in his saddle, his expression as hard as flint, and fingered the hilt of his sword

"And that is?" Eric asked. What was Jader trying to do?

"That this senseless dispute has gone on long enough, leading to nothing but hurt and death on either side."

"I don't find this dispute, as you call it, as senseless as you claim, Emperor."

Jader tilted his head back. "I feared you might think as much, which is why I have come with a proposition."

"And that would be?"

"We both know you and your father have no lawful jurisdiction over the Gateway, Prince Eric. And while I do not blame you for establishing a community here, I do resent the fact that you have the final say on who comes and goes through."

Eric held his tongue and let Jader continue.

"I have no interest in taking over the Gateway or the Old Realm, as so many of you seem to think." Jader went on, his tone as smooth as polished wood. "All I wish for is the same chance so many others have. To be able to pass through this community and make a place for myself in the Old Realm."

"I am aware of what you aim for, Jader." Eric forced the words around a tight jaw. "To spread your brand of lies and deceit. To tarnish the validity of the Code and dim the light of the Beacons."

Jader chuckled at this. "Why, Prince Eric, you make it sound as though your *Lambient* can be overthrown by mere unbelief. Surely you have more faith than that in your supreme being."

Eric drew up tall as Braylee's quiet "Easy" fell on his ears.

He's trying to rattle you. After a quick prayer to the Lambient Jader had mocked, Eric faced the man head-on. "What do you want, Jader?"

51

Heat bubbled in Mason's torso, the tension so thick, it suffocated him. The Stewards had to feel it, despite their cool demeanor. How could Jader be so calm? And how dare the prince sit so nonchalantly through it all, like he was blameless when Mason knew well what kind of man he was.

"I am not here to cause trouble," Jader continued. "All I want is to end the bloodshed. I think enough mothers' sons have died."

Eric leaned forward. "Then why don't you content yourself with the power you've gained in the New Realm? Why bother yourself with what's on the other side of the Gateway?"

"Because I cannot abide with anyone living in bondage to an ancient Code that strips them of their freedom." Jader's voice rose in his fervor. "I believe your people deserve what my people have, freedom and security, if they so choose. Surely, you don't deny them freedom of choice."

"My people and the people of the Old Realm do have a choice. To live by the standards of the Sacred Code, or to leave. Our kingdoms were founded on those principles, and we'll not turn from that."

"To enforce your Code upon a people is no different than the tyranny you accuse me of."

"Then why are there so many refugees from your *free* New Realm?"

Jader gave him a patronizing smile. "You should know as well as I do, Prince Eric, that it's impossible to please everyone. And we both know you've lost people to my side as well."

In an effort to cool his seething emotions, Mason scanned the area around them without moving his head. The Stewards flanking the prince sat tall and stiff in their saddles. No other living creature was around, save a small line of donkeys tied in front of the building's entrance behind Eric. In the middle stood a skinny, sway-backed animal with a worn gray hide.

The world lurched to a stop, and he gripped the horn to keep from swaying. *Sanjo.* What was Seria's donkey doing here? Unless...

His skin crawled, and he jerked back to Eric, who stared back at him with his jaw jutted. In an instant, every ounce of rage came boiling to the surface.

Eric's unwavering regard dared him to do something—a dare Mason was more than happy to meet. His teeth ground together as images of Liam's death flooded his mind. This was the man who had same as killed his brother. And now he had taken Seria for himself.

The prince's glare sharpened. Mason's fingers tensed around the hilt of his sword. Every muscle tightened, ready to move.

Jader said nothing during the silent exchange between the two younger men.

One knight at the front of the line to Eric's left lowered his hand to his weapon. "Watch yourself, Darkman."

"Or what?" Shon spoke up, lifting his sword and pointing it at him.

"Draven, nay," Eric charged as the Steward drew his sword. Mason whipped his out, followed by the rest of the Darkmen. The Stewards instantly responded in kind. The horses danced under their tense riders.

"Stop!" Eric shouted to his knights, raising his hands. He turned blazing eyes on Jader. "Call your men down, Jader!"

For the first time, Mason spoke to the prince, frigid and hard. "Emperor Jader will be addressed appropriately."

Eric glowered at him. "He's not my emperor."

Something snapped, and rationale fell by the wayside. Unable to hold his fury any longer, Mason raised his sword, visions of vindication flashing through his mind. Enough waiting.

But before he could make a move, his weapon was wrenched from his grasp and flew through the air. It landed several feet away, sticking straight up with the point wedged in the dirt. Mason gritted his teeth at Eric's stretched-out hand. "You best hope you don't ever lose that Beacon on your belt, Steward."

"I'll be careful." Eric gave a careless wave, and the sword fell over.

Jader raised his hands. "Stand down, men. We did not come here for trouble." He faced Eric once more. "All I wanted to do was come here and have you understand the wisdom of my words, but I see Aden raised as big a fool as he. I pray your people do not suffer at the hands of your own stubborn pride."

"Is that a threat?" The question came from the dark Steward at Eric's right.

Jader's lips thinned. "It's a warning. We will see your tyrannical Code stamped out and freedom given back to the people."

"This meeting is finished." Eric's face reddened. "Take your men, and leave Cadence. The next time we see your Darkmen within the Gateway, we'll assume it's an act of war and treat it as such."

Jader gave a subtle nod. "If that's the way it is to be, so be it."

Eric addressed one of his men, never taking his regard from Jader. "Sir Ollen, have your squad see these men to the woods."

"Aye, sir."

Mason's nostrils flared as he shot one more visual dagger at Eric. Then, right before he turned his horse's head, something drew his attention up to the open window above them. A breeze rustled the curtains. Or was it something else?

"You should go, Reader."

Mason sniggered at the title. So, Eric knew what he was. Good, let him worry about that for a while. But he held his tongue and kicked his horse's flanks. Before leaving, he wrapped his legs around the saddle, gripped the horn with one hand, and leaned over to grab his sword from the ground with the other. He slid it back into its sheath in one smooth motion without the horse slowing a step.

Not bothering to resume his position at Jader's side, he followed his company back through the town, his thoughts anchored to what was behind him. Anger churned in that black hole inside him but for Seria's sake this time. What had his actions cost her? For the first time, he wished things had been different.

In an effort to distract himself from the guilt piling in his gut, he ground his teeth and glanced around at the Cadence onlookers. A familiar blond-headed boy with ragged clothes watched the soldiers file through the middle of the town, a frown on his face. The boy reached down to pick up a small rock. Looking toward Bruin, he leaned back, ready to fling it.

Mason hollered out. "Drop it, kid!"

Byron complied at once, though still of his own free will, and fixed his stare on Mason. Up ahead, Bruin slowed his horse to look back. Mason caught a look of irritation cross the older man's face.

He didn't have a lot of time, but Mason drew near enough to read the boy's thoughts, desperate to know something, *anything*, about Seria's outcome.

All Byron knew was that someone had come to her cabin the day after her arrest and taken possession of the donkey. So, Seria had lost all titles to what little freedom and possessions she had claimed.

The depth of Byron's confusion about Seria's sudden disappearance from his world set Mason aback. A rush of emotion pulsed through Mason's body, and for the first time, he felt a trace of sympathy for the boy.

As though aware that Mason was reading him, Byron lifted his chin and ran off.

"What was that about?" Bruin asked.

"Nothing but a street waif, trying to be tough."

Bruin gave him a searching look. Mason returned it, hoping Bruin could not see the turmoil rumbling inside him. To Mason's relief, Bruin turned ahead again. "Never did like kids."

Mason caught one last glimpse of Byron disappearing amongst the buildings of the town. The Stewards had not noticed the brief encounter.

"Let this be a reminder that you are not welcome in the Gateway." The Steward called Ollen sat tall on his horse when they reached the town border.

"Don't break my heart," Mason snapped.

Ollen's face flushed. "You talk tough now, Darkman. You weren't so brave when you were alone, were you?"

Bruin cut in. "We'll be on our way, boy. But don't be deceived. This isn't over." Bruin paused in expectation of Ollen's reaction.

Ollen set his chin. "We'll be ready."

Mason scowled when Ollen looked his way, his expression unreadable. But there was a challenge there, one Mason wished he had the time to accept.

"Let's go, Mason." Bruin sounded bored with the entire exchange. Mason followed him, ready to put as much distance from this place as he needed to gain control of his emotions again.

The band of Darkmen kept a swift pace to their campsite. Feegan and the others came out to greet them, eager to hear how the meeting had gone.

Jader made the announcement. "We must prepare ourselves for war, ladies and gentlemen. The Prince of Paladin will not listen to reason. We have no choice but to take the offensive. The Passions will fall, and the Old Realm will be ours, as with the New!"

A cheer rose, and the Darkmen lifted their swords in a show of support. Mason held his high over his head, but the image of Seria, alone and a prisoner of the prince, filled his mind until he could see nothing else.

The sun had disappeared long ago, but the night held no sleep for Seria. She stared up at the ceiling, her emotions pulled in a hundred different directions.

She doubted Eric had considered the balcony in his chambers. If he had, he never would have sent her there to wait. She had not intended on eavesdropping on the tense exchange between the prince of Paladin and the emperor of the New Realm.

But she had.

From that balcony, she heard every word. And from behind the drapes, she got her first glimpse of Emperor Graulik Jader. A shiver passed over her now at the chill he emitted.

She had known of him her whole life, as he held control of much of the New Realm by the time she was a young girl. Her parents had played their parts as docile citizens under his rule, but their children had been reared to respect the Sacred Code, albeit subtly. Seria remembered overhearing them discussing the growing unrest of the land. They had talked of moving their family to the Old Realm, but something always held them back. And in the end, they never had the chance.

A great sadness overcame her, and the ceiling blurred into a haze of grays and blacks. If her mother and father had gone ahead with their plans to leave the New Realm, her whole family would still be alive. They would all be together, making a life for themselves somewhere in the Old Realm.

And she never would have met Mason Grey.

A tear broke free and made its way down her cheek until it met its end on her pillow. Seeing Mason again, positioned at Jader's side like he belonged there, had rocked her more than she had expected. A part of her had wanted to hide and never see him again. Not after the way he betrayed her. And not now, when she had a tentative handle on her life again.

But another part of her had yearned to see him one more time. For what reason, she could not comprehend. To convince herself that he was a part of the Dark Army? Did she still doubt what had happened in the woods?

Maybe it was more than that; maybe she longed to heal the cracks he had inflicted. Instead, something in her shriveled and died upon seeing his stone-cold face, so unlike the one she had come to know. Gone was the smile she had discovered during those trying weeks. This man looked so resolute and dark. So empty.

I miss him. The realization, once admitted, took root and grew. She missed the Mason she had come to care for, despite their turbulent start. He knew more about her than anyone alive. And she had gotten a glimpse into his soul at the pain he carried about his slain brother.

She squeezed her eyes shut as that terrible meeting played out in her mind again. The threats. The raised swords. The anger.

The moment Mason had looked up at Eric's balcony had frozen her, so sure was she that her foolish actions had gotten her spotted. But something in his expression, distorted as it was through the curtains, had grabbed her. He looked lost, desperate. And that look splintered the already fragile pieces of her heart.

Because despite her best intentions, Seria's heart was more involved than it should be. The man was angry and bitter, true. But he was wounded, too.

"My brother...he was murdered." His voice, reluctant and heavy with grief, echoed in her mind. The charade had faded in that laden statement. She still hurt by his pretense and the betrayal, but one thing was clear. When Mason lost his brother, he lost a part of himself, as well.

What if there was more to him than he had displayed that afternoon? Seria's breath hitched. It was possible, wasn't it? She had seen glimpses of it through the cracks of his hard persona. There was a good man in there. Was there still a chance that man could come back?

52

The moon hung low and pale, held by invisible cords in the velvet black sky. Stars spilled over the dark sky, sparkling like diamonds. The mountains and forest all around had turned black in the night. A few night creatures made their appearance known, cutting through the stillness with their calls and cries.

Mason sat on top of a boulder a short distance from the camp, worn out from the strenuous workout he had put himself through. But nothing loosened the mountain-sized knot tightening around his abdomen.

He stared out into the night scene, not seeing anything. He was supposed to be reveling in the potential of war. Jader's forces would soon do what they must to defeat the Passions and their Stewards. Victory and retribution were on the horizon.

Jader had requested he meet with him after tomorrow's morning meal. Mason had yet to address his lies. But his apprehension failed to distract him from the affairs of the day.

Seria's arrest had knocked him off balance. More than it should. She had fulfilled her purpose, getting him well so he could get back where he belonged—serving Jader in his quest to rid the world of the archaic Code. That was where their relationship—if he could go so far as to call it a relationship—ended. Her views and faith in the Stewards and the Lambient made it impossible to continue any further association, if he had a desire to do so. He did not have time to look after a foolish young girl, no matter how naïve and guileless, and no matter how much he owed her.

So, why the knot in his gut? Why did it feel like the hole in his spirit had been ripped open farther?

He dropped his head, elbows on his knees. She had witnessed the meeting, watching from behind the curtain. Somehow, he knew it. She was there, a captive of the prince of Paladin.

Mason clenched his fingers together, insides roiling. *Eric Passion.* The man was responsible for taking everything away from him. What kind of man sends his army to take down a band of teenage hunters? What possible motive could he have had? Power? The pure thrill? And now, he had taken a poor girl and punished her for being the kind, generous person she was. Yet he had the gall to accuse Jader of cruelty?

Mason's hands began to tremble, and an ache formed between his temples. He pinched the bridge of his nose and breathed in deeply. The chasm in his spirit vibrated and thrashed. How long did he have before he lost himself in the depths? Fear rose up, cold and rank.

For a while, that ever-present hole had disappeared, so much that he had almost forgotten about it. The realization hit him like a mallet, chilling him. He had not felt it once during his time with Seria.

Not ready to deal with what that was supposed to mean, he pitched to his feet. It was late, too late. He was tired and thinking like a fool. Losing a night of sleep would not accomplish anything. Tomorrow was a new day, along with an expected meeting with Jader, and he wanted to be ready for them both.

After a restless night, Mason skipped breakfast and waited for the summons to Jader's tent. Once it came, he stood outside the emperor's tent, palms slick with sweat. How was he to answer for his deceit?

At long last, Jader called him to enter and greeted him. "You look tired, my friend."

"I'm fine, Emperor Jader," Mason replied, unwilling to reveal his difficulty in sleeping. Every time he tried, he was haunted by a pair of green eyes.

Jader gave a sad shake of his head. "Our meeting yesterday was quite upsetting, but do not let it worry you, son. We shall take care of our enemies soon enough. In the meantime, we have business to discuss. Please, sit."

Mason took a seat at the small table across from him. His insides hardened at what disciplinary action would be handed to him. It was his good fortune that Commander Bruin was absent from this meeting. It was awkward enough with the emperor.

"You have been through a lot, Mason, especially recently. Not many men would have made it back to us in one piece."

"Barely."

Jader chuckled. "Aye, but you still made it back. And your capabilities and dedication surpass many with greater seniority and rank. You have long evaded an officer's title, but it is high time you receive one. I am appointing you to First Sergeant. Bruin is assembling your squad as we speak."

Shock washed over him. The honor was great, but that wasn't what he wanted. A sergeant had to work with the people. Mason preferred to work alone, to *be* alone. "But I don't have the Shadowstone." What a ridiculous statement. Most of the leaders in the Dark Army did not have a Shadowstone. An elite few had earned that right.

Jader gave a small smile. "Nay, but now that you have brought it up, I believe you are ready for the final test for the Shadowstone."

His lungs emptied. "You do?"

"Absolutely. You are younger than most, but I have no doubt you will wield it efficiently."

He had expected a demotion or punishment. But this! "I'm honored by your vote of confidence. What will my test be?"

Folding his hands on the table, Jader leaned forward. "Eric most likely assumes I will lead a charge against the fortress, which is ridiculous. I have a more subtle plan of action. I intend on getting some of my best Shadowmen through the Gateway fortress and into the Old Realm. Once there, they will begin to infiltrate the kingdom of Paladin and others. Therefore, by the time we do get through the Gateway, the people will be, how shall I say it? More *receptive* to my message."

"Sounds like a good plan. How will they get there?"

"I want *you* to get them through."

Mason blinked twice. "Me, sir?"

"You have been inside the fort; you can find your way around. If you accomplish this mission, you will have obtained the right to wear the Shadowstone."

"How do you want me to see it done?"

Jader waved a hand. "The details I leave to you. I plan to send three squads—all Shadowmen. Feegan will lead them once they are through. When you return, we shall hold the ceremony."

Mason's mind spun. He wanted nothing more than to take on the Shadowstone, but how was he supposed to get thirty men in and out of the fort, and survive in the process?

Jader folded his hands on the table in front of him. "In doing this, you will have to make your way inside. While there, feel free to do whatever is necessary to see this thing through."

Mason frowned. Why wouldn't he do what he had to? Did Jader doubt he could?

"What I am saying, son, is that you will no doubt meet Eric, face to face."

His gut jumped. This could be his chance to see Eric pay for his brother's death.

"Do you understand what I am saying, Mason?"

Letting a long breath out through his nostrils, Mason gave a slow nod. "I do, sir."

"I knew you would."

Mason shook his head, overwhelmed at the opportunities Jader was opening up for him, but he had more to say. "I want to say, Emperor Jader..." He hesitated a brief moment. "I apologize for not being upfront about..."

"The girl?"

"Yes." He cringed. "It was wrong of me to deceive you."

"Mason, I understand you would feel strongly toward your hostess. She did save your life, after all. What I do not understand is your need to hide that from me. It is not like I would wish to harm the girl. I am not a monster, despite what some on the far side of the Gateway believe." A hint of injury rang, and Mason was quick to reply.

"I know, sir. And I should've realized it then. I do regret it now."

Jader smiled. "Give it no more thought. You have other, more important issues to concern yourself with now."

Mason nodded, his back lightened from its load. He should have known better. Seria was not a threat, and Jader had no reason to go after innocent civilians. Like he said himself: he was not a monster.

It took all day of wrestling and plotting, but Mason soon had a plan to get Jader's men through the fort. He met with Bruin and Feegan for the final details. They decided the infiltration needed to happen immediately, but to do that, he needed a solid strategy. His men could not simply sneak over the wall. Well, except for Lyoth, but it would take too much time for the rest to climb over.

The men Jader selected for their task in the Old Realm were all veterans, seasoned and hardened by their years of service. The troop was large enough to be formidable but small enough to move freely once they were inside. It was the getting inside part that Mason wrestled with. He would be the only one without a Shadowstone.

Bruin cautioned him one last time. "The others will have the Shadowstone to help them see and to cloak their movements. You won't have either advantage."

"I understand, sir. I'll be careful."

"Bruin and I will help as much as we can with your cover of darkness," Jader added. "But you will be on your own."

Mason nodded, the gravity of the situation pressing down on him. So much was at stake. Jader's plans. Mason's ambitions.

The moon was already high in the sky, but they would not make their move for another few hours, which gave him ample time to go over his course of action again and make sure there were no flaws.

"Good luck, sir."

"Best wishes, Sir Mason!"

Mason gave the well-wishers a wave. Everyone was pulling for him, which but added to the pressure.

Shon caught him before supper. "You'll get them through," he said with a single nod.

"Thanks." Mason hesitated. "And about the lies—"

Shon put his hand up. "You have your reasons." His olive face sobered for a moment, as if trying to read Mason. Then he brightened. "I trust you. Just don't forget me when you're a high and mighty Shadowman."

Mason sent him a light punch. "Forget you? Believe me, it's impossible."

A little later, Dreeya appeared at his side. "I'm so excited for you, Mason." She slipped her fingers through his. "The Shadowstone!"

"I don't have it yet." He gave her a small smile.

"Nay, but you will." She tugged at his hand. "There's not a Darkman here with your talent."

"Thanks."

"I can't help but feel a little jealous, though." She winked. "I mean, here you are going to bigger and better things, and I'm stuck with a bunch of no-goods."

"I'm sure you'll get by." He teased her, though he continued his pace.

"That's easy for you to say. I don't know where Commander Bruin gets his servants, but they're the most incompetent bunch of people I've ever met. You know how my saddle was ruined by that stable boy."

Mason gave her a shrug. "It wasn't that bad, Dree. He's working out fine for me."

"Of course, he is! I knocked some fear into him, so he straightened up. Now, I need to get a hold of the cook, if that's what you want to call him." She gave a hard laugh. "His potatoes were undercooked, and he tried to serve them to me like that! And the wine was absolutely flat. I almost gagged trying to get it down. I threw the whole tray back at him and told him to start getting things right, or I was going to have his hide and serve it for dinner!"

She went on about someone else who did not complete his job to her standards, but Mason was too busy mulling over a revelation to listen.

Dreeya complained a lot. Nothing was done right, nobody knew what they were doing, nothing was good enough for Dreeya Campton.

Seria has practically nothing, and I still never heard her complain.

He grunted and shook his head to rid his mind of her image once again. *Blades.*

"Are you listening?"

"Come here." He stopped and pulled Dreeya to him. She instantly responded in kind, throwing her arms around his neck. He kissed her long and hard, disregarding anyone standing around. He was not exactly gentle, but Dreeya clung to him like a hungry animal, running her fingers through his hair. When he broke away, her eyes gleamed.

"Now, that's the Mason I've been wanting to know," she said, low and husky.

He stared at her, speechless. How long had he been tempted by her charms? And in one moment of frustration, he let her in. The kiss was passionate and untamed, but it left him empty. Like sharing it with a stranger.

"How 'bout we finish what we started?" She leaned in close. "My tent or yours?"

Mason pulled back. "I don't have much time."

"We don't need a lot of time."

But Mason still held back. "I'd better stay focused."

Dreeya pouted. "When you get back?"

"Um, sure." He stepped away from her tight embrace. "When I get back."

She dropped her arms. "I'm holding you to that."

Mason watched her strut away. *Get a hold of yourself.*

His task lay before him. Getting Feegan and his men through the stronghold. Once he did that, the Shadowstone he had worked for all this time would be his. Then things would be set aright. He would no longer be unsettled, but focused, driven. And whatever doubts and uncertainties had taken hold of him would be quenched by the stone.

He gave a slight nod as he entered his tent. That was all he needed. The Shadowstone.

53

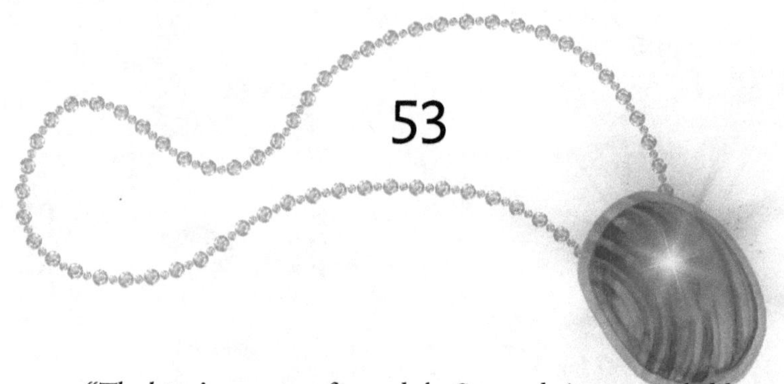

*"The king's ancestors formed the Steward Army to uphold
the values of the Code and to guard the cause of the Lambient."*
-Commencement speech given by Steward Grand Marshal Uralis Faunt

The Gateway Stronghold hummed with commotion. The prince had issued orders for the citizens of Cadence to be brought into the safety of the keep. Seria could still hear his words to his men echoing in her ears: *"If Jader were to attack the fort, they would be the first ones hurt, and I will not have innocent civilians slaughtered."*

The Stewards were kept busy, assisting wherever they could. Fear and apprehension marked the face of every man and woman who entered the keep. Many of the children treated it like an adventure. She could feel their excitement. They were going in the keep! A few of the older ones seemed to understand the gravity of the situation.

Seria found plenty to keep her mind occupied as well, which she needed. She helped get Byron's family settled in and managed to sneak a visit with Lena and her mother. Then she moved on to offer her assistance to the other families. For the most part, no one acted like they remembered why she had been arrested and they welcomed her help. She spotted Ira at one point, but the man took pains to avoid her, which suited her fine.

As she moved about, always at the back of her mind was the possibility of an incoming attack. Eric believed it was imminent. When would it happen? And would Mason play a part in it? Of course, he would. He was loyal to Jader, after all.

The sky was beginning to darken when she wrapped herself in her shawl and made her way to the mess hall. Halfway there, she spotted Ollen up ahead and smiled. They had crossed paths several times in the hectic day, and each time Ollen made a point of speaking to her, giving her assistance if she needed it. Now, hours later, he was still busy, repairing a worn door.

"So, Stewards fix doors now?"

He looked up with his easy smile. "Our job is never done." He straightened and gave the door a final check. "That should do it."

"Looks good."

"You heading back to your place?"

"Actually, I was going to see if Nola needed help at the mess hall."

He offered to walk her there, and she accepted, glad for his company. They talked easily, discussing the people of Cadence who now lived behind the fortress walls.

"Is it getting easier for you?" Ollen asked at one point.

Seria considered the question. The last few days had not been as strained, aside from this threat by Jader. While she couldn't say the knights had fully accepted her presence, they at least tolerated her now. Though it could be that they were distracted. "Maybe."

"I heard what you did for Gus. That certainly made a difference. Give it more time, and they won't remember what they had against you."

She clung to the assurance. "Prince Eric said something similar."

Ollen nodded but did not reply.

Seria glanced over to see him staring at the ground. Should she ask? It was none of her business. She snorted softly. Since when did that ever stop her? "What do you have against the prince?"

His head snapped up, and he gave a hollow chuckle. "What makes you think I have something against him?"

She slanted him a look. "I see your face every time he comes around or when his name is mentioned. You don't care for him."

"I like him fine as a person or prince." There was no missing the tense lines that formed on his cheeks.

"But not as the Grand Marshal."

He rubbed his jaw. "I guess I'm not very good at hiding my feelings."

"But why? What can you possibly have against him?"

Ollen hesitated. "My mother was widowed when I was young, but she never wavered in her resolve to see her son raised up right. Before I could even talk, she told me stories of the noble Stewards, how they defended the weak and stood up for what's right." He tossed her a grin. "I guess she did a good job because as I grew, all I wanted to be was a Steward. So, as soon as I was able, I joined the king's militia army. Uralis was already commander, but for some reason, he took a liking to me and sort of took me under his wing. It was under his guidance that I became a Steward."

His features darkened. "I was in Uralis' company when we rode to Rackson. A family had gotten trapped in a burning house, but I managed to get them out before it caved in. I sent the parents running with their girls, and I was coming behind with the boy. I had almost gotten him to safety when a group of Darkmen appeared out of nowhere in front of me and the boy. I figured that was it for both of us."

He exhaled again, taking on a faraway look. His words came slow and careful, heavy with feeling. Seria almost reached out to touch his arm in sympathy, and then thought better of it.

"Then there was a shout, and there stood Uralis." He gave a short, humorless laugh. "He took three of them down before they could turn their weapons on him. But there were too many of them for him to have a chance."

Seria closed her eyes. How awful for Ollen, watching his mentor die. "And that's why you can't accept Eric as your leader."

He ran a thumb over his knuckles. "Wrong or right, Seria, I can't see him in Uralis' place. That man gave his life for me. The prince is courageous, but he spent years in the castle while the marshal did his job. Not a word of explanation."

For a moment, Seria didn't know what to say. Who was she to give this man any kind of advice at all? She had not known the prince long. How could she be sure Ollen was wrong? Then she got a glimpse of Ollen's face, the lines in his brow and tautness in his jaw. "You know what I think?"

"What's that?"

She cocked her head. "I think you need to forgive yourself."

Ollen shot her a startled look. "What?

She raised her hands. "Pardon me if that sounded bold, but could there be a part of you that's blaming yourself for not saving your marshal?"

"I don't—"

Now she did put a hand on his arm. "Don't answer that. And forgive me if I spoke out of turn. But will you at least think about what I said?"

Ollen looked her way, though she sensed he was not really seeing her. Finally, he nodded. "Aye, I'll think on it."

They parted ways at the doors of the mess hall. Already Seria could hear the murmurs of the larger-than-usual dinner crowd. But she hesitated a moment and watched Ollen disappear into the shadows of the night, aching for the sorrow he carried with him.

Death had a way of leaving its mark on those behind, be they Steward or Darkman. In the absence of the loved ones it took, there was room for bitterness and regret to grow that, if left unchecked, could bloom into anger, even hatred.

Seria clasped her cold hands in front of her. And sometimes that hatred could turn a good man into a killer.

54

The day is far spent. Night has fallen.
-The Sacred Code

Underneath a clear midnight sky, Mason led three squads of Shadowmen through the still woods outside Cadence. They all wore black leather tunics and breeches under their chain mail, covered with dark cloaks, and carried crossbows and swords. All but he wore thin, silver chains around their necks; at the end hung a smooth, purple stone—so dark it was almost black. An almost physical ache to hold his own pulsated through him.

Mason took them around the eastern border of the town, hugging the shadows of the forest. He swathed his cloak tighter around him. The wrap would help him blend in with the shadows, but its function would be limited. Without the cover of the Shadowstone, he would still be visible to the naked eye.

When a shade fell over the valley, he glanced up where, minutes before, stars had sparkled. Now clouds formed, snuffing out the little glow they had offered. Bruin was already at work.

The closer he got to Cadence, the harder his heart thumped. Of its own will, his observation swung to the right, where Seria's cabin stood down the hill, hidden from his view by the night. That the Shadowmen had no trouble seeing what was beyond his field of vision gnawed at him. He absently rubbed one of his bracers.

Your time's coming. Besides, this mission wasn't about Seria. It was about smuggling the task force into the Old Realm so they could strengthen Jader's efforts there. And getting the Shadowstone.

The clouds thickened as they hustled around the empty town. Eric must have pulled the people into the fort. Almost like he knew something was happening. Mason's insides squeezed. He had heard rumors of the Passions' unnatural acuity, but Eric would expect an army attack, an invasion, not an infiltration of Shadowmen. Wouldn't he?

They approached the first gate on swift, silent feet. Mason's boots made soft thuds with every step, but the Shadowmen made not a sound. Another benefit of wearing the stone.

A Steward stood watch from his perch in the tower. Mason plastered himself against the wall, beneath the guard and out of view.

Lyoth utilized his Gift to scale the wall with the uncanny grace and speed of a lizard, then eased his way to the top and positioned himself to strike the oblivious guard. The big man pounced, and Mason cringed at the sounds of a brief, muted scuffle. If at all possible, Lyoth was to keep the man alive.

After a long, nerve-wracking wait, the heavy gate gave a soft creak as one side slowly worked its way inward. Mason slipped through as soon as it cracked enough. Feegan and the rest followed and fanned out on both sides of the gate, hidden against the stone wall. Mason ascended the steps to where Lyoth held the guard.

Lyoth nodded to the unconscious man on the floor. "He's coming around," he whispered, his craggy face lit up with a victorious smile. The Steward's Beacon sat dark and useless in his hold. "This thing won't bother you now."

Mason knelt over the guard and waited for him to awaken. "Stand up."

"At once." The reply was groggy but instant.

"Stand watch and don't let anyone know we're here. Leave the gate open until I come back and close it after me. Don't let anyone else through, and *don't* sound the alarm."

Mason asked a few more questions about the night guard then stepped back so the man could resume his position.

"Are you sure he'll last?" Lyoth asked.

"Without that thing," Mason gestured to the lightless rod, "he's ours for the rest of the night."

Lyoth tossed it over the wall.

They made their way down to where the others waited, and Mason took the lead again, careful to avoid the watchpoints. They eased their way forward through the outer bailey, the most open space in the fort. Huts and tents lined the wide courtyard, most likely housing the citizens of Cadence. A few windows shone with soft lantern light. Not everyone was asleep at this late hour.

His senses on high alert, he crept past the central well and approached the inner wall—the "killing field," as this area was sometimes called. Not a good time to think of that.

One more gate.

Feegan, barely seen through the dark, tapped Mason's back and pointed up at the larger gate tower. Two men. A Steward in the right tower and a militia reservist on the left. Mason caught Lyoth's attention and nodded at the militiaman.

Once again, they positioned themselves by the wall, and Lyoth went up the left side. Feegan moved a few feet from the wall, crossbow in hand, and waited. As soon as Lyoth leaped over the top, Feegan aimed at the Steward on the other side of the gate.

The man let out a grunt and disappeared behind the wall. The sound of his fall seemed to echo in the night.

The gate opened, and they all poured inside. Mason's mouth went dry. They were in!

"Hey, Frakes, why'd you open the gate?" Someone called out from the darkness, jerking Mason around as footsteps neared. One of Feegan's men fired, and the body was dragged to the shadows.

Footsteps sounded above as other guards approached the gate from either side. Feegan gestured, and the Shadowmen ventured into the open and turned back to the gate. One by one, arrows were fired, and the night guards were silenced.

Attacking from within had made the knights easy targets.

Mason's pulse skittered as he darted up the steps to take care of the gateman. After leaving the same orders with the now-obedient Frakes, he and Lyoth met up with the rest.

They were in, but it was too easy. Something was bound to go wrong.

Mason looked at Feegan and nodded once. This was where they separated. Feegan turned left, and a third of the men followed him into the darkness. They would circle the civilian square, past the infirmary, and approach the back gate from the north.

Lyoth circled to the right with his group. Just before disappearing into the shadows, he looked at Mason over his shoulder. His lips twisted in an eager sneer, and he was gone.

A chill went down Mason's spine, and he glanced back at his group. He could not fail this. Too much rode on it. Jader's victory. The Shadowstone. Mason's promise to Liam. And finally filling the hole in his innermost being.

He braced himself and stepped away from the shelter of the gate tower and into the inner bailey, wide open and dangerous. Any movement, however subtle and camouflaged, would be instantly spotted.

His band would go straight through the middle, between the Great Hall and the Mess Hall. If all went well, they would arrive at the gate first and remove the night guard before the next two waves arrived. Then they would ensure the rest got through.

Mason kept his head low, mind racing as he neared the halls. A few more strides, and he leaned back against the stone wall of the refectory, near the front corner. His men passed before him, disappearing in the night as they continued their path onward.

Mason kept the rear, his crossbow up and ready, and peered through the dark for any signs of trouble. He leaned to the left to check in front of the hall. Movement on the other side of the building brought his weapon up and aimed. A figure carrying a lantern. A woman.

Seria.

He sucked in a rough breath and jerked the bow down. Time froze, as did Mason himself. His insides folded in half as he watched her stroll through the darkness.

What was she doing out here so late? And moving about freely, outside of the prince's grasp.

He pressed flat against the wall, scanning the darkness frantically. His legs tensed, ready to bolt after her. What if she was seen by his allies? They would not take any chances, not tonight. But would *he*?

Jader's words of caution came back to him. *"If you want to succeed in this mission, Mason, you must make sure that nothing or no one will intervene. Stay focused on your task, nothing else."*

He ground his teeth together. Most likely, she was headed for the barn to see that confounded donkey.

Good. She would be out of the way. Besides, she wasn't the enemy here. The Shadowmen were not targeting civilians. They were after a bigger prize. And so was he.

Yet he stayed a moment longer, drinking in the sight of her as the space between them lengthened. A lifetime passed in a few heartbeats. He had to go before she saw him. Yet, with every step she took away from him, Mason's will was torn. Another few steps, and she was lost in the night. Safe away from where his Shadowmen were working.

A faint roll of thunder grumbled in the distance, reminding him of how little time he had. He compressed his trembling hands into tight fists. The mission. That was all that mattered. Justice for his brother. Death to the prince. The downfall of the Stewards. That would satisfy the vast emptiness inside.

Braylee stood in the inner courtyard, fists on his hips. Draven had his men spread too thin. Annoyance plucked at him. Despite the prince's warning, Lt. Draven's performance was still less than desirable. His childish apathy was a defiant ploy against the new marshal. Braylee had allowed Eric to handle the insubordination last time, but Draven was still a part of his brigade. There was no room for unreliable officers in Braylee's company, no matter how many chances Eric wished to give.

The sky grumbled, and Braylee moaned. Not the best time for a spring storm. The hour was late, and his bed called to him.

The gates loomed ahead, shrouded in darkness. Braylee headed that way to check in with the gateman. As he neared, the back of his neck heated.

The gate was open. Surely Draven's men weren't that reckless.

Picking up speed, Braylee tried to recall who would be on duty. Frakes Henries, if he was correct. Frakes had always proven to be a dependable gateman and a good reservist, so there must be a reason.

It better be a good one.

Frakes met him at the top of the steps. "Good evening, sir."

Braylee returned the greeting as he joined him in the tower. "How is everything up here?"

"All is well, sir."

"Then why is the gate open?"

"Sir?" Frakes gave him a blank stare. The sky flickered, exposing a dark bruise coating the side of his temple.

Braylee's scalp crawled. "Has anyone been through here tonight?"

"Nay, sir. Nobody." Frakes stood stiff as wood.

"Then how'd you get that bruise?"

Frakes' mouth opened and closed twice. "I fell."

Braylee's fingers twitched. Frakes stared back at him without restraint, but something was off. "What's going on, Frakes?"

There was a slight hesitation, then Frakes grabbed Braylee by the throat and gave him a hard shove back. Caught off guard, Braylee went tumbling headlong down the stone steps, landing in a heap at the bottom. Pain scattered through his head and spine. Then all went black.

55

Eric jolted upright in bed, blood pounding and ears ringing. He waited for the warning bell, a call, a knock—anything to explain why he awoke in such a start. But there was nothing but his own unease.

He swung his feet to the floor and trudged to the window. How long had he slept? It was late when Braylee insisted he finally make his way to bed. There was always something else he needed to check to be sure of the security of the keep.

The mood was tense, at best. Jader had all but threatened war. The night watchmen of both reservists and Stewards were put in place at key locations on the wall and throughout the fort. Civilian men offered their services, if ever needed. Plans were laid out for women and children to be kept safe, should an attack come. No one was allowed in or out of the gates unless granted permission.

Yet nothing moved beyond the borders of Cadence, not so much as a breeze.

Eric moved the drapes aside, still unable to shake the feeling that Jader would not wait long to act. He had informed his father of all that had transpired, from the meeting with Jader to the decision to move their people into the garrison. Aden had given his approval. It did Eric's spirit good to know his father supported him. Especially with so many of the Stewards doubting him.

The tension among the Stewards was a topic he had not shared. Though things had improved some after the fire, they were not on stable ground yet, and he did not want his father to worry any more than necessary. Winning the Stewards' trust and respect was something Eric had to do on his own.

All was black outside, except for a faint flicker of lightning, followed a few moments later by a dim echo of thunder. Surely, this fledgling storm had not awakened him in such a panic.

The sky had been clear earlier, the moon hanging low and bright in the sky and the stars sparkling like bits of glass flung across dark cloth by an unseen hand. But all were hidden now by thick clouds.

Back home in Calla, Eric relished the occasional thunderstorm. There was something so awe-inspiring about watching nature flaunt its power. But there was no wonder in this storm. He crossed his arms against the chill spreading throughout his body.

Something wasn't right. A familiar sensation twisted in his abdomen, setting his nerves to buzzing. A warning. Where once it had been cloudless, now a storm brewed. *This is Bruin's doing.* Jader's right-hand man with the uncanny Gift over the weather.

Eric spun around and threw his clothes on. As he tightened his belt, he made certain his Beacon was securely clipped. Then he took Lavrynth and rushed from the room.

At the double doors, he took his Beacon and wrapped his fingers around it, then hesitated. What if he was wrong? If he summoned the Stewards from their warm beds for a mere spring storm, it would do nothing to improve his status. The last thing he needed to do was overreact and give him men more reason to doubt his ability. Maybe this storm was not Bruin's doing.

But the pinch in his belly convinced him otherwise. And in the end, what carried more weight for him: improving his reputation or doing what was necessary to protect this fort?

Eric clenched his jaw and gripped the Beacon. It pulsed in strength, one long glimmer followed by two short ones. Not the call to arms, but an alert. If he was wrong, he would deal with it then. But for now, he would make sure his men were ready.

Seria stepped inside the barn and hung the lantern on the hook beside the double doors. Already the quietness was broken by eager nickers and snuffles. She laughed. "Have patience, I'm coming."

It was late to be visiting the animals, but she had stayed well into the night to help Nola catch up on the increase in work since the civilians of Cadence had moved into the fort. Then she had worked with Lena and her mother in baking extra bread for the morrow. She had not had a chance to visit Sanjo all day and wanted to share the bounty of carrot scraps she had confiscated from the kitchen.

Eric's big gray stallion pulled on his rope, his nostrils quivering as she approached. She laughed softly as she set a carrot tip on her flat palm. "To be so big and brave, you certainly don't mind begging for treats."

Oakley lapped up the snack with a sigh of contentment. The nasty cut on his shoulder was healing nicely.

Braylee and Dudley's horses both huffed in protest.

"You know I wouldn't forget you." She gave them both their bites and moved to the left end of the barn where the six donkeys all watched her. "I have enough for everyone if you all share."

They stood lined up at the bar gate, waiting their turn. One by one she gave them each a chunk, scolding a pair for nipping at each before she could get to them. Sanjo stood all the way to the right, watching with an almost amused expression on his long face, as though sure she would have extra for him. And she did.

"Good thing the lieutenants' horses are all in the dry lot." She chuckled as she scratched Sanjo's head. "I've got you all spoiled."

Something shifted in the corner outside of the donkey stall, and she jumped. A small figure sat on a large pile of hay out of reach of the horses.

"Byron! What on earth are you doing here?"

The boy shrugged and glanced at Sanjo, who stood with his nose over the bar. "Came to check on him."

It should have come as no surprise. Byron had not seen Sanjo since her arrest. Of course, he would take the first chance he got to visit his furry friend. "Isn't it late for you to be out wandering around?"

"My folks are used to it."

Sanjo stretched his thin neck out until he could nibble at Byron's ear. A rare grin—small but sincere—lit the boy's face.

"I think Sanjo missed you, too." Her smile completely undid whatever scolding she had thought to attempt. "But in any case, we should probably get you home now." Thunder echoed outside. "Preferably before it storms."

Byron nodded without argument and stood, scratching Sanjo's white muzzle one last time.

The barn doors creaked open, and Seria paused, expecting to see the stocky blacksmith coming by to check on why a lantern was burning. Instead, two unfamiliar men stepped in. The dim light reflected off the purple-black stones they wore around their necks.

Seria's skin prickled, and she grabbed Byron's arm, pushing him in the stall behind Oakley's large form.

Her movements caught the attention of one of the men. His thin face lit up with a sardonic smile. "Looks like you were right, Lyoth. Wonder why our buddy let her go a-wandering around so late at night."

Seria froze as the massive man called Lyoth raked his cold gaze over her from behind long, greasy hair. "My guess is that he's too soft to kill her." At his words, and the casual way he spoke them, her limbs began to shake.

As Lyoth stepped farther from the light of the lantern, he blended in with the shadows of the barn. Like a Shadowman. Seria's stomach dropped, and she looked around for an escape. The doors hung open behind the two men. The other exits opened up into dry lots at either end of the barn, but she would never reach them before the men caught her.

Scream!

She had no sooner opened her mouth when Lyoth lunged from the darkness and clamped his meaty hand over her face. Her fight instinct came out in full force. She wriggled and writhed, swinging at him with her fists and feet, but his grip was ironclad.

The donkeys shied from the fence, bunching up on the far end. Oakley snorted and tossed his head, pulling against his rope.

Lyoth shoved her against the bar so that it dug into her back. "Dantus, get a rag." He moved his hand enough so Dantus could push a nasty cloth inside. The rancid smell hit her senses before the taste did, sending her head swimming.

Pain grabbed her shoulder blades as Lyoth wrenched her arms behind her back. She bit down on the rag, then gagged. At the burn of rough rope on her skin, she clenched her fists and stiffened her wrists. After wrapping the binding tight, Lyoth pushed her to the ground where Dantus bound her feet.

Lyoth doused the lantern and headed for the door. "You take care of things here." His cold glance fell on Seria briefly. "I'll be back. I've got something to take care of."

Byron's peaked little face peeked out from the shadows of the middle stall. Seria shook her head, hoping he would understand. There was nothing the little boy could do except get killed. The thought shot terror through her. He ducked back farther.

Dantus untied a cloth bag he carried and poured something along the walls, ignoring her as he stepped around. The sharp smell of black powder swarmed her nostrils, burning with every inhale.

Her blood chilled. This man was going to blow up the stable. The long building and outside lot housed dozens of horses. A loss like this was not only a blatant and cold slap in the face to the Stewards but would seriously impede the army in their transportation.

But worse, Byron was still in the barn.

The sounds of snorts and whinnies met her ears. The horses stomped their feet and moved about in their stall, pulling against the restraints that held them. The stranger and strong odor had unnerved them.

Panic clawed at her, and she pulled against her binds. Dantus was alone. There was no better time than now. She had to get Byron out of there.

Dantus moved down the aisle, his back to Seria as he poured.

BOOM! The sky echoed and flashed menacingly. Rain began to pour outside, filling the barn with its roar. Seria's heart skipped a beat at the cover the storm could provide. She met Byron's gaze and tilted her head toward the open doors. He blinked and withdrew a bit, shaking his head. She hardened her features and motioned again. He licked his lips and slipped to the front of the stall. Then he waited, his trusting scrutiny on her face.

Seria held her breath, waiting for another rumble. As soon as it hit, she nodded, and he ran, the storm masking his frantic footsteps. He slid in the mud outside the door, caught his footing, and plunged on. Her lungs emptied, and her eyes stung. Byron was safe.

Mason circled the Steward before him in a clash of metal against metal. The Steward was bigger and threw his weight around, but Mason was faster. Seeing an unguarded chance, Mason spun his sword, flipping the other man's weapon out of his hand.

When the knight lay dead at his feet, Mason exhaled and stared down at the body. The hole deep inside him swirled and roiled, never satisfied. His sword felt weighted, as did his spirit. How many more would he have to kill before the night was done?

He shook the thought away and moved forward, always watchful. His band was already in position at the back gate, ready to help the next two groups through. Mason had finished that part of his mission.

The sky exploded in a booming crescendo of light, revealing someone dashing across the inner courtyard in his direction. Mason ducked back into the shadow of the wall, gripping his sword with both hands. As the person neared, it became clear that he was small. Small and childlike.

Blades. Mason darted out and grabbed Byron around the waist, carrying him to the safety of the wall next to the doors of the Mess Hall. Byron let out a cry and fought against him until Mason gave him a rough shake.

"What are you doing out here, kid?" The answer flew across the boy's mind and into Mason's. A rock slammed against his ribcage. *Seria!*

"He's gonna kill her!" Byron cried, his stare wild and panicked.

Blood roared in Mason's ears, and his fingers tightened over Byron's trembling arms. *Stay on the mission. Focus on the mission.*

Seria's in danger!

Mason jerked the door open, pushed the boy inside, and looked him in the eye. "Stay in here." He barely caught Byron's compliant response before he slammed the door and raced for the barn.

56

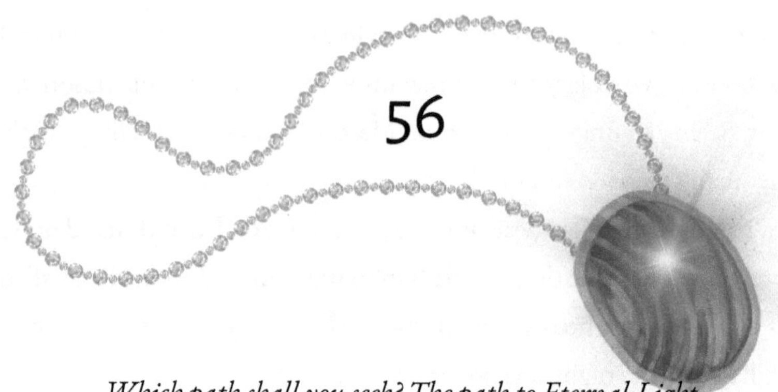

The games. Think of the games you played when you were young. Seria clamped her teeth over the foul rag, fighting the heaves that waved over her. Everything her father taught her whirled through her mind, too fast to latch onto one useful tidbit. She slowed her thoughts and breathing, relaxed the tension in her arms. Then she maneuvered her bound hands beneath her backside, then her legs, and finally out from underneath her feet. Once they were in front, she wriggled her wrists and nearly cried at the way the ropes loosened. Just a bit, but it was enough. Back and forth, she worked her hands through the rope, ignoring the way they tore into her skin. She could do this—had won in countless timed games before. But this was no game.

One hand slipped through. She squelched a sob and jerked the rag out of her mouth, swiping her tongue over her dry lips. She picked at the ties around her ankles, biting back tears at the needles that stung her clumsy fingers when the blood rushed back. The door beckoned to her, but she could not make herself go. Not yet. She couldn't leave Sanjo behind. And the Stewards needed their horses.

Keeping Dantus in view, Seria pulled her feet underneath her and stood, stepping to Oakley's rope. A couple of tugs later, the horse was free. He tossed his head with a nicker and Seria froze. Dantus never looked up. She repeated the process for the other two horses.

Not daring to make a sound, Seria patted Oakley's face and beseeched him to find help. Then she slapped his hindquarters. The big gray squealed and aimed for freedom, the other two horses following at his heels.

"Hey, what're you doing?"

Seria dashed to the box stall and threw the bar out of its release. The donkeys all scampered after the bigger horses. She bolted for the door after them, but Dantus stepped in the lantern light, blocking her flight. Sliding to a stop, she grabbed an empty water pail and flung it at him. *Lambient, help me!*

Dantus's arm shot out and knocked the pail to the side, then he pounced, grabbing her by the throat. A dagger flashed in his hand. "I can make you comply, girl, whether you want to or not. You can go with us whole or in pieces, makes no difference to me."

Screaming was impossible with the vice grip on her neck. But before she could fight back, Dantus jerked, and his hold loosened. Seria pushed him back, coughing and panting for oxygen. He slumped to the floor. She stared at the dart sticking out of a red-stained hole in his back. Blood spilled from the wound and dripped onto the floor beneath him.

She looked up. The sky flashed, highlighting Mason at the door, crossbow in his hands, and eyes wide in his white face. The world tilted to a stop. "Mason, what are you—?"

He threw a hand up to stop her. Seria froze where she stood, afraid to move.

Mason stared at the dead man and shook his head, backing away. He gave her a wild look. "Just... stay here!" Then he jerked the door shut between them, disappearing back into the night.

Seria broke with the closing of the door. Trembling overtook her, and tears flooded down her face. The dead man sickened her, and she edged away. Her dry throat ached with every gulp.

She was safe. Byron was safe. The horses were safe. The assurances throbbed through her panic in time with her erratic heartbeat, little by little bringing back calm. But in the midst of the trauma and shock, another small ray of hope beamed, casting light on the shadows that threatened to close her in. Mason had rescued her.

From one of his own fellow Darkmen.

Mason braced himself against the wall of the Great Hall and wheezed. What had he done? He gripped the sides of his face and bent over, fighting nausea. What would Bruin do to him if he found out? What would Jader think? He had killed one of his own men.

The very idea of Dantus manhandling Seria had filled him with such rage, that he could not stop himself. But this was not supposed to be about Seria. This was about his mission for the Shadowstone. So, why would he risk everything for a peasant girl?

Images of Seria teasing a laugh out of him flashed through his mind. Before he met her, he had not laughed in years.

He growled low and deep. He didn't need to laugh. Laughter was too close to happiness, and happiness had died with Liam. Because of Eric Passion.

The sky lit up. Someone stood on the roof of the Mess Hall, and Mason's fingers tensed on his sword. Lyoth stepped to the edge of the building, looking up and down the street, searching for something. A jolt shot through Mason's spine.

What was Lyoth doing out here? He should have had his team to the back gate by now. Had he seen what Mason had done?

Lyoth dropped back out of view, and Mason waited, lungs frozen. After a few minutes, he forced himself to relax. Lyoth was gone, doing what he was supposed to do. And it was time for Mason to do the same.

Then a resounding blast rocked the night, separate from the rolling thunder. Mason flinched and ducked, looking around wildly for the source of the noise. A yellow glow appeared in the direction Lyoth had gone.

He gritted his teeth and cursed. Apparently, Lyoth had come with his own agenda. Mason's posture went rigid at the thought. Was Lyoth trying to sabotage Mason's mission?

Frustration, confusion, anger, and fear all wound around together, tangling into a tumultuous ball that threatened to choke him. Beneath his wet clothes, cold sweat broke out, chilling his heated skin. His lungs siezed, and his head pounded. He was losing control of his mission and his emotions.

Once again, he heard Jader's whisper in his ear. *"All those conflicting emotions that war within you will be mollified when you see justice. Everything will be clear when you receive the Shadowstone."*

Mason closed his eyes, willing his body to calm. His mind went over the strategy he had put together for the night. His group was already in place. Lyoth had gone off course, so Mason was no longer responsible for what happened to him. His best bet was to make sure Feegan's men had gotten through.

Gripping his sword and steeling his resolve, Mason turned his back on the hall and strode forward. The mission Jader had given him was almost done. Then it would be time to fulfill his vow.

Rain beat at the top of Eric's head, streaming down his neck as he passed through the midst of civilian huts. His Beacon shone before him, enough for him to see where he was going. All was still around him, save for the storm. Not a sign of trouble yet. But his rigid shoulders hunched up at his neck, and he could not shake the agitation coiling through his body, stiffening his fingers.

A groan sounded in the dark, and he halted, raising his rod. Alarm slammed through him at the prone body of a Steward lying on the muddy ground. Eric ran to his side, rolling him back gently.

"Draven!"

The lieutenant's head lolled, and he struggled to focus on Eric. Blood seeped through his shirt and washed away in the rain. "Shadowmen," he rasped.

Eric swayed. *Shadowmen in the fort?* It couldn't be. He shook his head against the shock and focused on Draven. "Let's get you to Luron." The futility of his statement pierced him. The man's life was ebbing out before him.

Draven waved a weak hand. "Too late."

"Nay." Eric gritted his teeth and cradled the man's head on his lap. "I'll summon help."

"Sir." It took more strength than the Steward had to whisper. "You...were right...My men...weren't ready. They came...I'm...sorry."

Eric raised his head. A few feet away another dead knight lay. *Dear Lambient!* He pressed his fist against his mouth. "This is my fault."

Draven laid a bloody hand over Eric's. "Don't." His upper body heaved, and his eyelids drooped over his intense gaze—the same one that had challenged him so many times. "Just...go." The anger was gone, replaced with resignation.

Eric placed his hand over Draven's chest. "Go in peace, Lt. Draven Kilton." His voice faltered, and his vision dimmed. "Into the light of the Lambient."

The dying man attempted a nod, then breathed his last. Grief became a rock in Eric's soul, and he held Draven against him for a moment. Tears mingled with the rain on his cheeks.

Then he lay the dead Steward down and stood. It rankled to leave him lying there in the mud, but there was no time. There were Shadowmen in the fort, *his* fort. Grabbing his Beacon, he plunged ahead, in the direction Draven had indicated, back toward the Great Hall. Questions pounded at him in time with every stride. Where were they? How many were there? *How did they get in?*

His failure screamed at him with every step. Draven had been right from the beginning. Eric should have focused on the Shadowpit all this time. Maybe they wouldn't be in this fix now. Maybe Draven would still be alive.

A loud explosion split the air behind him. Eric skidded to a stop and jerked around. In the darkness, a flame lit the western end of the fort before the rain beat it back. He clasped his hands over his head and stepped back.

An attack. From within the fort. By Shadowmen.

How many people were going to die tonight?

Adrenaline coursed through his veins, and he tightened his hold on the Beacon. Instinct urged him back on the path he had been on, despite the pull to go back to the site of the blast.

The main building loomed to his right, and he approached the corner opposite the armory, his nerves crackling with premonition. He let the air locked in his windpipe leak out, then peered around the corner. At first, there was nothing but blackness. But under the flickers of lightning, he saw them. A dozen or so men in dark attire. All wearing stones around their neck.

One man headed for the armory, sheltering a flickering clay-colored sphere from the rain with his hand. Eric's heart ricocheted in his chest. *Explosives!* One of those incendiary devices, combined with the black powder in the armory, could take out half of the fort.

He ducked back and clipped his Beacon to his belt. Then he whipped his bow in front of him, slinging an arrow in place and dropping to one knee. Angling out away from the protection of the wall, he waited for another flash, then released the string. The arrow shot forward, and the man fell with a yell. The sphere rolled away, instantly soaked by the rain.

Eric had another arrow against the nock when someone pummeled him from behind. His bow went flying, and he rolled over the muddy ground with his unseen attacker. They broke apart, and Eric spun on one knee to face the seething eyes of Mason Grey.

57

Mason grasped his sword in front of him, trying to steady his wildly racing pulse. The moment was almost surreal. After all these years, he stood face to face with Eric Passion. "We meet again."

"So it would seem." Eric's hand dropped to his Beacon.

Mason smirked. "Don't want to lose your lantern?"

Eric glared back at him. "I'm in no mood for small talk." He pulled his sword from its sheath.

"Good. Neither am I." Mason charged.

The prince met him head-on, his skill with a sword not to be taken lightly. Mason did not rush, thought through every step. This was his chance. He could not lose this moment.

Their swords met again and again, the sounds of metal against metal lost in the mayhem around them. They moved around in a circle, locked in a dance of rage and death. He ducked one of Eric's blows, slashed at the prince's torso. Eric jumped out of the way, missing the blade by an inch. A bolt of lightning struck a nearby tree; it splintered and fell toward them. Mason dove out of the way as it crashed behind him. The prince rolled away, coming to a stop on the doorstep of a small cabin. Mason lunged again.

The force of Mason's attack sent them tumbling through the door. There was a scream from a corner of the room. Mason crouched down, giving the place a quick glance. A small fire burned in the hearth. One single candle sat on the table. A man and woman huddled on a cot in a corner, gaping and clinging to each other.

Eric stood to his feet on the other side of the room, his glare hot and steady. Resentment twisted at the way the prince stared straight at him. Mason had to get rid of that Beacon.

They met in the middle of the room, their swords crossed between them.

"Get out of here!" Eric shouted to the couple between clenched teeth. They scurried off the cot, staying close to the wall as they fled.

Mason ignored them and sent a barrage of blows that sent Eric backward. The storm continued to rage on outside, intensifying in the face of the hate-driven duel. Lightning flashed every few seconds, illuminating the fierce contours of his opponent's face.

Furniture was shoved out of the way. Dishes crashed to the floor. Their swords cut gashes into the wall, the table, and anything else that got in their way. They worked their way to the fireplace, where a large knife rested. Their swords locked, and Mason grabbed the knife, thrusting it at Eric. The Beacon appeared in Eric's other hand and deflected the blow, sparking and hissing. Mason squinted against the white light's potency.

"What's wrong? Can't take a little light?"

Mason glowered. "Too much light tends to blind a man."

"Only if he's used to hiding in the dark."

Mason shoved away, and the combat resumed. They darted in and out, ducked and jumped—swords, Beacon, and knife all flashing in the mottled shadows. They reached the door again. Mason parried Eric's blade and slammed it down, trapping it against the floor. Eric rammed into him, and they both tumbled back outside.

A heavy limb swung up and slammed into Mason's stomach when he stood. He hissed through his teeth and glared at Eric's outstretched hand. "You would resort to cheating."

"Cheating? You sneak in this fort in the dead of night, under the cover of Bruin's storm, and you accuse *me* of cheating?" Eric's words laced with tension. "Spoken like a true Darkman with no honor."

"Don't speak to me of honor, Steward!" His words lashed out like a whip. "You who would give the order to slaughter my brother like a dog."

Eric deflected another blow. "I don't give orders to attack lightly. If your brother stood against me, that was his choice."

Fire streaked through him, and he readjusted his hold on his weapon. "He had no choice in the matter."

"Everyone has a choice." The answer came calm and cool.

"Like you gave the casualties of Handan?" In the sputtering light, he saw Eric's head jerk up. "I don't call that a choice. I call it a massacre." Mason advanced again, but the prince blocked his move and returned with a counterstrike. Mason diverted it, his feet spread apart to brace himself. They circled each other before the cabin, swords and eyes locked. Eric drove his elbow into Mason's arm, and he lost the knife.

Mason moved closer and struck again. This time he made contact.

Eric let out a strangled yell as the blade sank into his side and stumbled back. Adrenaline pumped through Mason's veins, and he kicked at the hand that held the Beacon. The rod went flying, its light fading and disappearing into the night.

Eric's startled eyes flew to Mason's.

"Don't move!"

The prince froze.

Mason drank relief into his starving lungs and straightened. A wild sense of victory swirled over him, mixing with his exhaustion until it left him dizzy. He had done it. He was in control. "I've waited a long time for this, Steward."

Eric's jaw shifted.

Mason took two steps forward, his hands trembling. So much darted through his mind at that moment. "I lost everything that day. My home. Friends. My brother. And I made a promise." He croaked the words out.

Eric stared back at him, holding his side with one hand. Blood seeped between his fingers.

Red-hot emotion churned, and Mason wet his lips. How long had he waited for this moment? Now that it had arrived, would he cut Eric down, defenseless, as the boys in Handan had been?

Liam's face hovered in his memory, and he flexed his fingers. The promise. He had to fulfill the promise. Even now, with the fulfillment of his vow mere moments away, the hole writhed in him, gaping and growing. "You Stewards take it upon yourselves to end the lives of those who oppose you."

Raw apprehension lit Eric's face. Mason weighed his next words. It was time to end this.

"Take your own life."

Jader stood on a high cliff outside the mountain passage, his keen eyesight piercing through the distance and darkness and into the storm-ridden town of Cadence. What he would not give to see through walls. He tightened his fists, drew air in through his nostrils.

Bruin spoke. "Do you think he's had enough time?"

Irritation coiled through him. Bruin's lack of faith in Mason was tiring. Nonetheless, Jader humored him. "We must give Feegan and his men the edge. Your storm will have to guide his way now."

Bruin nodded.

Closing his eyes, Jader stretched his hands out and summoned that well of darkness that had served him for so many years. The same darkness that dwelled in each and every Shadowman under him. The same darkness Mason sought in completing this task. But for tonight, Jader willed it to fall over the town, flooding every inch and corner, dousing every light. He smiled as the complete and impenetrable shadow began enshrouding the valley. Like a growing tidal wave, it inched over the town and spread. Soon, it would reach the fort.

This was a small step in his stratagem, but an important one. Especially where Mason was concerned. Jader had waited for this moment when

Mason was ready to bend everything in his mind to fulfill Jader's bidding. By his own strength of will and desire for vengeance, Mason would get his Shadowmen through the gates, no doubt. And maybe kill the future king of Paladin while doing so.

Victory was near.

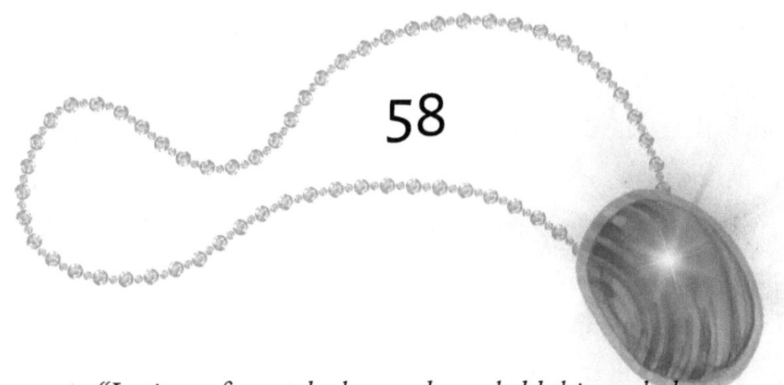

58

Seria huddled in Oakley's stall, her arms wrapped around her middle in an effort to stay warm. But her hands trembled from underneath her arms, and her toes grew numb. Her neck still throbbed from Dantus' grip.

The lantern hanging by the door flickered pitifully against the bleakness of the storm. Never had she faced such a monstrous squall. The walls shuddered and groaned, and she feared they would be torn away in the wind.

And then, without warning, the light went out. A whimper escaped her. No matter how much she blinked, she couldn't see a thing, save when the lightning flashed through the cracks of the barn. Pitch black pressed in from all sides, chilling her from the inside out. She was stuck in an empty, dark barn in the middle of a thunderstorm. Alone with the dead body of a Shadowman.

She blocked the blackness out with her hands. Stay calm. The storm would end. The darkness would lift.

But what would she find when it was all over? What was happening outside of these walls?

The door of the barn bumped open, and she cowered below the wall, clamping a hand over her mouth to quell the sob that formed. What if Lyoth had returned? The memory of his cold stare chilled her. He would not be pleased to see his friend slain on the ground. *Please, not again.*

Two sets of footsteps approached: a man and a horse. She crouched back farther in her corner as light filled the entrance before the door.

Her spine straightened. Light! The Shadowmen would not be using light. She rose on her tiptoes and peeked over Oakley's stall. "Captain Braylee!"

The big man's head jerked in her direction. "Miss Seria, what are you doing here?"

She rushed into the security of his warm embrace and burst into tears. His burly arms surrounded her, so much like her father's, and for the first time that night, she felt safe.

He patted her back. "Are you hurt?"

Pulling away, she shook her head and swiped at the dampness on her cheeks. This was not the time to fall apart. "There were Shadowmen."

His arms tensed. "Shadowmen? Here?"

She swallowed and gestured to where Dantus lay a few feet away. Braylee released her to inspect the corpse, his fingers lifting the chain that held the Shadowstone. A scowl darkened his face, despite the light of the Beacon. "What happened to him? Did you kill him?"

"Nay." She hugged herself again and backed away a step. What could she say? Would anyone believe that Mason had killed his comrade to save her? The Stewards despised him.

Braylee stood. "Don't trouble yourself over it now." He moved to gather the tack for his horse, still waiting for him by the door. "I suppose you're the one who released the horses?" he asked as he swung the saddle over his horse's broad back.

She nodded before realizing he was not looking at her. "Aye. They were going to blow the barn up."

Braylee paused and looked back at her. "And you got them out?" He let out a grunt. "That was good thinking on your part. I lost one mount already. I would've hated to lose another one so soon." His calm, deep timbre soothed her like a salve. But as she watched him tighten the girth and slip the bridle in place, her muscles tightened. He was heading back out into the storm, back into danger, and the idea of him taking the Beacon with him made her want to selfishly beg him not to leave.

Once finished, he turned back to her. "We need to get you to the infirmary."

She shook her head and tried to straighten against the cold. "You needn't worry about me." Her words came out shaky, despite her resolve. "I'm fine here. You go."

"Miss Seria." He settled a hand on her shoulder. "There's been an explosion."

"An explosion?" Understanding hit her then. They needed her help. Luron needed her. Her fear bled away into purpose. This was what she wanted but never had she pictured it like this. There was no joy in seeing her dream fulfilled. This was a nightmare. An infiltration of Shadowmen. A storm raging above. And somewhere, a man she had once thought a friend was a part of it.

Pain and anger competed for a place in her mind, but she dismissed it all and raised her chin. She still had a job to do.

She looked back at Braylee. "Of course. Let's go."

"Take your own life."

Eric inhaled sharply as everything went black. All around him, he could see nothing but yawning darkness. Jader's darkness—frigid and dreadful.

A cloud settled over his mind, and he struggled to think clearly. His limbs shook, and his fingers curled around Lavrynth. The urge to turn it on himself overwhelmed him. Streaks of red-hot pain shot through his side.

As if incensed by the darkness, the storm intensified. The wind became a constant roar and whipped his hair. Something—a door maybe—ripped away from one of the nearby buildings and slammed into him, knocking him back against the cottage.

The fallen shadow swirled around him, threatening to drown him in hopelessness. Despair. Failure. He slumped to his knees on the ground.

This is my fault. His men's resentment. The Shadowpit. Draven's death. His past met with the present to beat him over the head. He should've stayed in Calla. He should've died in Rackson. All he'd ever brought to the Gateway was tragedy.

Maybe this was for the best. Sweat broke out on his forehead, and he gripped the hilt with both hands. Fear and guilt throbbed through him. The darkness in him rose to meet the darkness without, ready to crush him between. There was no escaping the Reader's hate-filled control. There was no fighting Jader's power.

The light within you is stronger than the darkness without.

Uralis' words cut through the fog wrapped around him and echoed in his head. He saw his mentor on the ground, faith and confidence beaming from his wise gaze as he passed leadership onto Eric.

Warmth radiated from Lavrynth's hilt, enveloping Eric's clenched hands and shooting up his cold limbs. The storm's rage faded into the background.

At once. The submissive words sat poised on his tongue, but he bit down until he tasted blood. He could not do this on his own. But he didn't have to. The light within him was stronger than the darkness without.

His hands shook in their effort to pierce the sword through his torso. *Lambient, help me!*

A flicker lit in his spirit, blossoming into a flame. In a desperate move, Eric spun his sword and slammed the point into the ground before him with a grunt. As soon as he did, the pull was broken, and the fog over his mind lifted. Darkness still blanketed the fort, but it no longer gripped his spirit. He exhaled and fought to get his bearings. What had he done? Had he overcome a Reader's command? It was impossible without a Beacon.

The wind and din of the storm escalated, and the smell of mud invaded his nostrils. He caught glimpses of his surroundings every time the lightning flashed, but then was plunged back into blackness. Footsteps sounded nearby, and he shifted off his knees, raised his sword, and diverted Mason's sword to hit the wall behind him.

Don't look at him! He half-ran, half-stumbled out of reach from another blow, keeping his face turned away. No matter what he did, he could make nothing out except the sound of Mason stumbling and staggering behind him.

So, Mason couldn't see either. The Shadowstone allowed Jader's Darkmen to see through the thickest, gloomiest pitch-black known to man, which gave Eric a faint measure of hope. Mason was not a Shadowman, and for the moment, was as vulnerable as Eric.

Almost.

As long as I don't look at him.

"What's the matter, prince?" Mason taunted him. "Can't look me in the eye?"

Passion rushed through him, heating his body. He made himself straighten against the agony in his side. *You're stronger than this!*

Mason approached from the front; Eric sidestepped and hooked his foot around Mason's ankle. The sky lit up as Mason tripped and tumbled headfirst into the mud.

Go by what you feel, not what you see. His mind flashed back to the day he watched Braylee train. The knight's words repeated in his ears. *"It helps me focus better when I shut out what I can see."*

Except, in this case, Eric had to shut out what he could *not* see. While Mason scrambled to his feet, Eric closed his eyes and willed himself to forget the pain. Focus and feel. His instinct and perception rose to the forefront of his subconscious, and he gripped Lavrynth's hilt.

"Come on, Steward, surely, you don't think you can fight with your eyes closed."

Eric breathed calm into his body. "Does it matter at the moment?"

"We'll see."

Eric braced himself. Reached out with his senses. Then deflected a jab aimed at his abdomen. The jolt of steel on steel shot up his arms. He swiped another strike, then stepped forward and swung. Mason ducked his blow and rolled, ending up behind him. Eric brought his sword up over his head and behind him, sweeping Mason's blade away from his back.

Loud shouts sounded from a short distance away, and Eric's optimism surged. His Stewards were nearby. But he could not afford to let himself slip, so he fought to keep his eyes closed, his mental focus zeroed in on the other man. His senses and his acuity guided every movement.

Mason's strikes became harder, faster. Almost desperate. He was running out of time. Eric's lungs burned, and his wound blazed. Sticky warmth coated the inside of his shirt. Mason sidestepped in an attempt to slice his sword into Eric's torso. Eric gave a twist of his weapon, redirecting Mason's and taking the offense. Mason lunged, and Eric dropped to one knee, letting him fly head over heels across him. His sword ripped through the left sleeve of Mason's shirt, slicing through the flesh of his upper arm. Mason let out a loud yelp of pain.

"Prince Eric!" someone called.

Eric's eyes flew open. Beneath the flickering sky, Ollen Knavis hurled a light rod at him. The Beacon stayed lit in the air long enough for Eric to pull the airborne rod into his outstretched hand. Mason stumbled up behind him. Spinning around, Eric held the rod up, letting white light spill into the space between them.

Mason drew up short, one hand clamped over his wound. Eric stared back at him, unflinching, and forced himself to his feet. "It's over, Mason. Lay your weapon down."

Mason's face contorted in a mix of despair and rage. He glanced over Eric's shoulder at the approaching young Steward. "I won't be outnumbered by you butchers again. But I won't stop until you're dead." Mason spat the words out. "Just know that." Then he turned and bolted for the shadows.

Eric fell to his knees, holding his bleeding side. The sound of footsteps advanced, and then Ollen appeared at his side.

"Sir, you're hurt."

"I'm all right." He blinked water out of his vision and motioned behind them, where shouts mixed in with the storm. "What's happening, Ollen?"

"Shadowmen are trying to get through the back gate. They've got sharpshooters in position somewhere and have us pinned down. The Stewards are holding them back but can't get to the gate to stop them."

So, that's what this whole night was about. "Let's go." Eric pushed himself to his feet. His side screamed in protest, and he hissed. "How did you know I was here?"

Ollen looked away. "I went looking for you." He cleared his throat. "What about the Reader?"

Eric looked out into the darkness where Mason had gone. Someone should go after him, make sure he could never return to wreak havoc.

Let him go. At the silent edict, Eric shook his head. "Leave him be. We can't let Shadowmen into Paladin."

Ollen's brow creased. "It's too late, sir. Some have already made it through."

59

Mason's lungs burned as he ran. His left arm throbbed and stung like fire, the blood flowing and washing away with the water dripping off his hand. It hung limp and useless as he forced himself to keep going.

Disappointment beat at him. Eric Passion still lived. There was no sense of victory at accomplishing his Shadowstone mission because his personal mission had fallen short. He had let his brother down again.

A figure darted out in front of him, and he was forced to lift his sword with his good arm. He clumsily slashed the Steward's leg and staggered on. But there would be others, and he would have to meet each one head-on. What chance did he have of getting out alive?

Strange that the possibility did not conjure up his failure again. Instead, his numb mind centered on Seria at the barn—so fearful yet relieved to see him. He had killed a Shadowman, one of his own, for her.

And he would do it again if he had to.

The realization stunned his already dazed emotions. What did that mean for him now? He had worked half his life to become a Shadowman.

Another knight crossed his path, missing the scarlet colors of the Steward. A fragile thread of optimism streaked through Mason's weary spirit. He caught the man's eye under the constant flicker of the lightning above them. "Stop!"

The knight froze with his sword raised high. Mason stepped closer to him, determined not to lose the man's will.

"Keep anyone from following me."

"At once."

Mason brushed by him, leaving him to take care of anyone on his tail. What little strength he had left was fading.

But the gate was so near. And it was shut.

Panic ricocheted through him. It was supposed to be open. "Frakes!" Mason bellowed to be heard over the storm. "Open the gate!"

Nothing happened, and he quickened his stride. He heard a shout behind him. Despite evading them so far in the thick darkness, the Stewards would find him. They would know the gate would be his destination. If they reached it first, it was over.

"Frakes!" He ran headlong for the portal. No time to wait. Throwing the brace off the gate, he grabbed the handle and pulled with all his might. His feet slid in the mud underneath him, and his hands strained not to slip from the wet handle. A groan grew as he threw every muscle and fiber of his being into getting it open. White-hot pain tore up and down his wounded arm. A creak and a little give, then the gate worked its way inward.

Mason squeezed through the narrow opening. In the distance, Beacon light bounced in rhythm with someone's approach. Gripping the outside handle, he pulled again. His arm screamed at him to stop, but somehow, despite the hurt and exhaustion, he lugged the heavy gate shut, hoping to buy as much time as possible. Someone yelled from the other side, but it was too late. With one last mighty heave, it was done.

He was through the gate. The first gate. Which meant he still had to cross the lower bailey to get home.

Not home. The camp. He had no home. And nobody to share one with.

The killing field was surprisingly still, oblivious to the chaos left in his wake. He ran for the second set of gates, bracing himself for an arrow to shoot him down or a squad of soldiers to surround him. But the way was clear, and the gate was still open.

His mind spinning, he stumbled through the gate and down the empty streets of Cadence, leaving the fort, the prince, and Seria all behind. There was no satisfaction in the escape. Nothing but that infernal hole.

He made for the woods, letting the cover of the trees shield him. He ran and ran until he could run no more and tumbled to his knees, wheezing. Then he tipped forward and fell face-first onto the wet forest floor.

Eric followed Ollen around the wall of the barracks, both of them keeping low. Other Stewards crouched behind nearby sheds and other structures. Nothing could be seen beyond the circle of their Beacon lights. Sadness squeezed him at the bodies strewn out on the ground. When lightning flashed, Eric caught a glimpse of the tall gates in the back wall. Wide open.

Dudley stood perched at the corner of the barracks, keeping watch over the portal.

"Captain Dudley, what's the situation?"

Dudley pulled back and shook his head, waiting for another crash to finish echoing before answering over the wind and rain. "We're at a standstill. As far as I can tell, there's a cluster of Shadowmen holed up over there." He pointed across the way to the chapel at the back of the Great Hall. "We've got enough light to keep them from sneaking across, but there's a couple of men hidden on the back wall up there taking shots at us. They've been using all their dark tricks to keep the men uneasy."

Eric pursed his lips, considering all the options. The first and foremost concern was the gate. It had to be closed. He angled around Dudley to get a better view. Glancing down, he realized he still held Ollen's light rod in his fist. "Let's light up the Beacons. I'll get the gate closed."

"From here?"

"Nay." The task before him was clear. "I'll have to get closer."

Dudley scowled and looked out at the yard. "That's a big risk. Mayhap we should wait for reinforcements."

They could, but there was no telling how many Shadowmen were in the fort. Or how many had escaped it. "We can't wait."

The captain let out a heavy exhale. "None of the rest of us can get it closed, that's for certain."

Eric positioned himself to move, then felt a cold prickle go down his back. "Get down!"

A volley of arrows shot through the darkness behind them. One knight fell, and the rest took cover. Ollen pulled the wounded man closer to the wall and tore a piece from his tunic to press to the wound. Eric plastered himself to the corner. Trapped. One step one way would get him shot by the Shadowmen behind them. Another way would make him a target of the rest.

Light shifted in the distance, and the sound of pounding hoofbeats joined in with the cacophony of noise. Eric squinted through the downpour. A big bay galloped their way, following a light path thrown by the brawny Steward who rode him. Eric could not stop the smile that stretched across his face.

Braylee led a squad of Stewards, all on horseback. Their light exposed the Shadowmen trying to pin Eric's men down. Arrows flew, swords were drawn, and knights ran for the men in black.

Eric glanced back at the gate and ground his teeth. "Stewards!" he yelled. "Raise your Beacons!"

From all around him, the rods shone. The combined light grew until it filled the space. Eric stalked out into the open, his focus on the gate. He stood still, stretched his hands out—the Beacon still clasped in one fist—and energy flowed through him. The gates shook and began inching their way closed.

An arrow whizzed by his ear, and he faltered, losing his connection. Part of his Gift had to focus on deflecting the barbs shot at him, which weakened his concentration on the gate. Then the darkness swirled before him, wrapping around him like the choking hold of a constrictor. Tendrils of fear shot through him.

For a moment, he was paralyzed, locked in the darkness and doom of a Shadowstone's grip. Just like that night in Rackson, and then tonight when Jader's darkness fell, and Mason had him in his control.

Eric gritted his teeth. *Not. This. Time.* He clamped his jaw and lifted Ollen's Beacon. The light shot out, shattering the grip the blackness had over him. Then he set his chin and reached out with his mind for the gate again. Everything around him blended into a mess of cold rain, steel against steel, and the swish of arrows. With a loud creak and a jerk, the gates moved forward.

Braylee clenched his fist in victory as Eric withstood the powerful hold of an unseen Shadowman. The prince no longer needed Braylee to shield him. But no one could hold up to the strain of resistance while working the gate for long.

So where was that Shadowman?

Shouts rose from all around Braylee as he dismounted. Multiple shapes separated from the shadows and bolted for the closing gate.

"Don't let them through the gate!"

At Eric's call, Stewards rushed forward with swords and bows. The two sides met before the portal. Light spilled from the Beacons, exposing the hidden enemy. Swords clashed, and men fell on both sides. Eric flinched, and the gates wobbled.

Braylee stood his ground—sword in one hand and Beacon in the other—and waited, searching. Ollen fought nearby, his weapon moving in and out with speed and accuracy until his opponent fell. A man in black rushed at Braylee, and he ducked, flipping the man over his back to face Ollen's sword. He still sought the Shadowman who threatened Eric.

When a dark shape formed at the edge of the light, Braylee swung his rod over. There. A large man with stringy hair and empty eyes glowered at him from his hidden place in the shadows. Braylee tightened his grip on his sword as the Shadowman released his hold on the stone around his neck and met him head-on.

The Shadowman matched Braylee in height and weight, darting in and out with speed and swinging his blade freely. Braylee met him move for move, pushing past the pain in his bruised body.

They circled each other, their swords crisscrossing in rapid motion. Braylee felt himself being forced back against the building. The Shadowman's blade nicked his knee. Braylee grunted and sidestepped out of reach of the sword.

The other man grinned and stalked him. Braylee tensed and repelled another hard blow. He was evenly matched, but the Shadowman's arrogance would be his undoing.

Pulling on all his training and experience, Braylee favored his injured leg, enough to give his opponent confidence about moving in close. Then Braylee shifted his weight, gave a quick spin of his sword, and turned the point of the other man's away from him. Not missing a beat, Braylee took a step, driving his blade into the Darkman's torso.

The man froze, his pale eyes brimming with cold rage. Braylee pulled his sword back and watched him fall, feeling little regret.

A loud creak rent the air as the gates pulled shut, trapping the last of the Shadowmen inside the fort to surrender or die fighting. The din around Braylee began to die down. The storm itself lost its intensity. And then Jader's thick darkness lifted, leaving the soft, natural shade of night behind.

Silence fell. Beautiful, blessed silence without the echoes of thunder or shouts or steel. Braylee breathed it in, wincing at the pull on his sore muscles.

"Are you hurt, Captain?" Ollen asked as he drew near, wiping his sword against his wet trousers. "You look a little battered."

Braylee pressed his hand over the cut on his knee. It wasn't deep. "Had a tumble down the steps is all." Someone would have to go back and see to Frakes where Braylee had left him tied in the tower.

He made his way to where Eric stood, surrounded by Dudley, Lionel, and a small crowd of Stewards. The prince's tired, mud-streaked face lit upon seeing him, and he offered a hand. "I was worried about you, my friend."

Braylee grasped it with his own. "And I, you. But it looks like you survived the storm."

A cloud fell across his features. "Aye. But not without a price. We lost Lt. Draven tonight, amongst others."

A sharp pang went through Braylee. One of his lieutenants. "He should've been more prepared." Grief roughened his voice.

"Maybe, but the Shadowmen were aided by the Reader and took us all by surprise."

Lionel glared at the dead Shadowmen around them. "We should burn the bodies," he said.

"Burning's too good for them," another said. "They should be dragged out in the fields for the birds and beasts."

Braylee wrestled with his own conflicting emotions. He wanted nothing more than to let the younger Stewards carry out their intentions, but his conscience wouldn't let him. The Sacred Code had plenty to say about vengeance, even against the dead.

Eric spoke up. "Nay."

"Sire, they deserve no memoriam, no ceremony," Lionel said.

"There'll be no ceremony," Eric said. "But they'll be buried."

Lionel's face flushed. "Prince Eric, they're *Shadowmen*."

"Aye." Eric looked to Braylee, who urged him on with a nod. "They're men. Men who've let the shadows of doubt deceive them and corrupt them until they lost their souls. But they were still men."

"But—"

"Can you say you've never felt darkness rise in your spirit?" Eric turned his scrutiny to the small group of men around him. "Have you never fought the shadows of anger? Resentment? Unforgiveness?" His brows pinched. "Vengeance."

With every word, heads dropped. Lionel clenched his jaw, but his stance slumped a bit.

Eric continued softly. "I know I have. I've done battle with arrogance and pride. With fear. The difference is, I chose to surrender my weaknesses to the Lambient, to let His light fill those dark spots." He waved his hand at the bodies. "These men allowed themselves to be consumed by darkness and became enemies of the light. They made their choices, and I make no excuses for them. But I will not revert to the shadows that would hold me in their grasp because of their choices. They will be buried."

Ollen shifted and nodded. "He's right." He never lifted his stare from the dead men, but his complexion glowed with resolve. "We're all guilty of letting darkness in at times."

Eric cleared his throat. "Lt. Draven was right. I neglected in seeking out the Shadowpit and allowed fear to dictate what needed to be done, but no more. As soon as I am able, I will resume that undertaking." He paused to look out at the men around him. "I do beg your pardon for not considering the ramifications of my own mistakes."

Braylee could not be prouder of Eric if he was his own son. He was humble enough to admit his mistakes, but now he stood resolved and ready to move forward and be the leader Uralis had known he could be.

Ollen rubbed his jaw. "You're not the only one at fault, Prince Eric. We Stewards have our share." He glanced Braylee's way. "We should've been more united when you stepped into the leadership role."

"To be a leader, one must show himself a leader," Eric said. "I'm afraid I haven't done a good job at that."

"But you knew something was wrong tonight," Ollen continued. "You sent a call out to alert us before anything ever happened. We might've been taken completely unaware otherwise. And not only that, but I watched you face the Reader single-handedly. Everyone here knows how dangerous that is. One mistake could lead to loss of life or control, yet you stood your ground with nothing more than your sword and your Gift." Ollen gave a small laugh of awe and amazement. "You fought him with your eyes closed!"

Braylee fought a grin as Eric stood speechless. But Ollen wasn't done.

"Your Highness, the fervor you have displayed for our kingdom and our mission is unmatched. And you possess wisdom and intuition such as I have never before witnessed. Not even in a warrior as fine as our own Uralis. Those are the traits needed in a Grand Marshal. The traits that can lead us to victory."

There were murmurs of agreement all around, and Braylee's pride swelled again. These were the Stewards that Uralis had led and believed so strongly in.

The prince nodded, his mouth twisted in a weak smile, and held the Beacon out. "Thank you, Sgt. Ollen, for the use of your light rod. And your words." Then he winced and grabbed his side, his face turning white.

"Prince Eric, are you all right?" Braylee caught his elbow.

Ollen's eyes widened. "He was injured by the Reader."

Eric shook his head and teetered again. "I'm fine." Then he fell in a heap on the ground.

60

I have been placed in dark places.
-The Sacred Code

"I think you should rest."

Seria looked up at Ollen and wiped her damp forehead. "In a bit." How could she explain that her work at the infirmary was the only thing keeping her from falling apart?

"Miss Seria—"

"I told you to call me Seria."

A smile lit his tired face for the first time in hours. "Well then, *Seria.* You've been at this all night."

"So have you."

"Aye, but—"

"And you're not planning on going to bed anytime soon, are you?"

"Nay, but—"

"But, but, but." She grinned at him. "You're real quick with words, aren't you?"

One corner of his mouth twitched. "Not as quick as you are. You've been chatting a league a minute all night."

She gave a sheepish shrug. "I talk a lot when I'm stressed or tired. Keeps me focused."

"Speaking of which..." He slanted her a look.

"I'll rest soon. After I finish this row of beds."

"I'm holding you to that."

They worked side by side, as they had done for the past several hours. Luron had had his hands full with the wounded the night before and welcomed Seria's assistance. The good doctor was across the large room now, dozing on a bench.

The explosion, fortunately, had cost the fort a storage shed but no lives. But many civilians and Stewards had been injured throughout the night thanks to the blast, the storm, and the fighting.

Ollen had been more than helpful, and they made a good team. He always seemed to know what she needed before she asked. And he kept her mind off of Mason and the ache in her spirit.

It was nearing high noon when they finished. Seria barely had time to wash up before Ollen was ushering her out the door.

"Do you mind?" She rushed to keep up with him. "Some of us aren't so long-legged."

"Oh, sorry." He adjusted his pace to hers. "Better?"

"Much."

They walked in companionable silence for the next few minutes. Seria was the one to break it. "I heard about what you did, standing with the prince."

"Oh, that." He gave a weak grin. "It was long overdue. I let my loyalty to Uralis blind me to what Prince Eric has to offer. It's what Uralis would've wanted in the end." A frown darkened his face. "I realized you were right. I was blaming myself for Uralis' death. But even more than that, I was afraid of losing another leader. Rather than admit my fear out loud, I hid it behind a wall of disapproval."

"Everyone struggles with fears. It takes a lot of strength to acknowledge it out loud." She reached out and squeezed his arm. "Uralis would be proud."

Their steps dragged, both wrapped in their thoughts. Seria stepped around a limb. A fallen tree lay in the front yard of a small house. Was this the house Eric and Mason had fought in? She had heard the rumors, had seen Eric moments after he was taken to the infirmary. Heard him admit the Reader had slipped away from him.

But she had hidden her relief. Every time she tried to picture the two men trying to kill one another, something inside of her shriveled up. Mason had rescued her from one of his comrades and then went straight to kill the prince.

"I don't understand."

"What's that?"

She brought her head up, unaware she had spoken out loud. "Oh, um, this." She waved her hand at the disorder. "How can anyone justify this?"

Ollen did not answer right away. "They don't think as we do. Their sense of morality has been darkened and warped so that right is wrong and wrong is right."

Seria pictured Mason's stricken face in her mind again. "But how do they get to that point?"

"One step at a time. They let bitterness and rebellion take root until everything honorable has become something to be abhorred."

"Sad, isn't it?"

"Aye, but we can't waste our time pitying those who want nothing more than to destroy the Code and plunge the Beacons into darkness." His features shadowed. "Especially when people get hurt."

She licked dry lips at his stern words. "I know."

"I'm sorry, Seria." Ollen touched her arm, and his face softened. "I didn't mean to imply…"

"Of course you didn't." She forced a smile. "I appreciate your honesty."

He relaxed. "Good."

They fell into another silence that lasted until they were at her doorstep.

"Will you be all right?" The question was spoken gently.

She smiled up at him. Bruises covered his jaw, a deep scratch marred one cheek, and weariness clung to his eyes. Yet, he asked about her. "I'll be fine. Thank you so much for your help."

"Let me know if you need anything else."

"I will." She retreated to her room and sat on the chair, staring at the wall. Her body ached with exhaustion, her spirit sore and bruised.

For years, she had longed to use her skills to help people, to be a healer. She had that now, the chance of a lifetime. And she got to work alongside the Stewards she had so long admired. A dream come true.

So why did she still feel so empty inside?

Bruin Pralus sat in his tent with his elbows anchored on the table before him. He stared at the canvas wall on the other side of the small room, reflecting on how Jader's infiltration had gone.

Mason had been dragged into camp the night before, his arm dripping with blood, soaked to the skin, and half-dead with exhaustion. The scout had managed to stay alive in the Gateway Stronghold, after getting some of Feegan's men through and facing off with Eric Passion himself. He had fulfilled his mission, confirmed by Feegan himself in a late-night message to Jader. As soon as he recovered, he would receive the Shadowstone, the highest honor possible given by Emperor Graulik Jader.

But Bruin did not trust him.

It hadn't always been the case. Years ago, when Jader had taken the young man under his wing, mentoring him in the ways of the dark powers he possessed, Bruin had also had the pleasure of training Mason, shaping and molding him into the best scout in his army. In time, Mason had become their most reliable subject, ready and willing to do what was needed to secure their rule. And he was good, always accomplishing what he had set out to do.

But something had changed. Bruin could not put his finger on it. Ever since Mason's first return from Cadence, something was off. He had lied about those weeks of his absence. Why had he felt the need to cover up his time with the peasant girl?

The possibilities played themselves out in Bruin's mind, and he didn't care for any of them. He leaned back in his seat. Anger at the scout's deception and insubordination stirred. Never would he tolerate such actions from his men, but Jader seemed unconcerned, a fact that baffled Bruin. He was aware of the potential power Mason would bring to their side, but what about trust?

Bruin scratched his whiskered chin. Jader knew Mason better than anyone, knew the hatred he had for Prince Eric. Bruin still believed Mason wanted nothing more than to see the Dark Army overcome the Stewards, but something was missing in the scout, a light of resolve that had been there since the day he had first learned of Eric's part in the Handan Massacre. And despite Jader's confidence in the young man, Bruin could not rest easy. Maybe his concerns were unfounded, but he had observed Mason stumbling through his daily duties the last two weeks like a man lost.

It was that lack of passion that had moved Bruin to send Lyoth with another task: to watch Mason. Bruin clenched his jaw. There had been no word of him, so it had to be assumed the Shadowman had ended up dead, taking all he might have learned about Mason to the grave.

Jader would be expecting Bruin soon, so he stood and stretched the tension from his neck. Even if Jader had no such qualms about Mason's future, Bruin would be careful. He had stood by Jader as kingdom after kingdom fell before them in the New Realm. They had been unstoppable. Bruin would not allow one questionable Dark Scout to bring harm to their quest now.

Setting his chin, Bruin prepared to leave his tent and face his army going about their regular tasks. He would do as Jader wished; he would work with Mason as he had always done. But he would also keep a cautious eye on him. And the moment Mason proved he could not be trusted, Bruin would be there to witness it.

The moon began its slow ascension in the darkening sky. Mason stood on the same ledge from which Jader had watched his infiltration into the fort the night before. In the twilight, the stronghold appeared small and insignificant. He could barely see the town. All of that would change soon, Jader promised. When he took on the Shadowstone.

The ceremony would be held in four nights' time, at the moon's third hour. Jader wanted to wait until Mason had recovered from his harrowing night but had already brought the coveted stone from the Shadowpit. The mere sight of it intoxicated those not ready for it. But Mason was ready—had been for twelve years. Ever since the day he had lost everything until Jader had taken him in and revealed the truth.

Mason allowed his mind to take him back, back to the night that had started him on this journey. He relived that fateful day his brother had fallen before a Steward's sword. The horror of laying on the soaked ground, pelted by cold rain, watching it all play out. He re-experienced it moment-by-moment until that familiar rush of vengeance washed over him.

He clenched his jaw against the sting behind his eyelids. It had taken watching Liam and the other boys murdered by the professed *good*

Stewards to make him see the truth. Baris was right. The Passions were tyrants, willing to kill a bunch of boys for being in their way. And they dared to accuse Jader of being a dictator.

Mason exhaled, rubbing at the bandage wrapped around his wounded arm. The town before him was disappearing into the night, but his vision saw beyond the darkness that fell; his mind was full, reflecting, remembering.

The ceremony would be a turning point for him as a Darkman. Once he accepted the Shadowstone, he would be better equipped to fight for the cause he believed in, sharper and more focused. He was fully aware of this and ready to embrace it.

But it wasn't enough.

His fists tightened. He had to see Seria again, make sure she was unharmed after last night. Had to know if the truth pounding in his head was worth trusting. But she was behind the walls, out of sight and reach.

His heart clenched. There was no way in. No way to see her.

Movement at the border of the empty town drew his attention to a lone figure leaving a cabin outside of Cadence and heading back to the fort. His back straightened, and a weight shifted from his back.

Lena.

61

What joy is there in the fellowship of light and shadow?
For one will consume the other.
-The Sacred Code

"Seria."

At the call, Seria turned from the moonlit path that led from the mess hall to her boarding house and gave her friend a quick hug. "I feel like I haven't had a chance to see you in ages. I've been working late with Nola almost every night lately. I pray you and your mother weathered the storm without harm."

"We're fine." Lena pulled back and searched her face. "I know it's late, but can you come with me?"

"Of course."

Lena handed Seria a dark cloak, similar to the one wrapped around her. "Put this on. It should help us get where we're going."

A ribbon of uncertainty wriggled as Seria swung the cloak on and followed. "Is something wrong?"

"I hope not." Lena said nothing more as she led her to the edge of the residential area. Seria shivered as they walked by the stables, recalling the terror she had lived three nights before. But it was over now. Everyone was safe. Byron had been found later, unharmed, in the mess hall. He refused to talk about what happened, but Seria wondered if he was not the reason Mason found her before Dantus could kill her.

The western wall of the Gateway stood above them, casting its long shadow over the fort. Lena stayed in the shadows and eyed the guard on top making his usual rounds. "Do you trust me?"

"Of course, I do."

"Then be very quiet and stay with me."

The guard took a long look around, his face serious. After a minute, he turned and continued on his way, away from them.

Lena checked both ways, took Seria's hand, and dashed to the base of the wall. Giving Seria a long look, she put her free hand on the stone and leaned against the cold stone, passing right through it and taking Seria with her.

Shock and dizziness swept over her as they moved through the wall. *Through it!* A chill passed over her body, and she stumbled when she made it to the other side.

Lena put a finger up to hush her, but Seria caught a twinkle in her eye. She nodded with a shiver and followed Lena along the second wall, past the quarters for the reserve militia.

Stepping through the second wall was a little easier, though the sensation still left her breathless.

They tiptoed along the wall until they reached the shadow of the Slate Mountains. Then they swung away, leaving the fort behind them. "You all right?" Lena asked.

"How did you do that?" Seria's whisper shook.

"You didn't think the Gifts of the Moon were limited to the men, did you?"

Seria's skin still tingled from the experience. "How in the world do you ever get used to going through walls?"

Lena chuckled. "It makes my mother sick."

"What are we doing out here anyway, Lena?"

"You'll find out when we get to your cabin."

"My cabin? Why on earth are you taking me there?

But Lena would say nothing more as they crept farther into the darkness, toward the empty town of Cadence. They must look like shadows lurking about with the dark cloaks. Seria had never seen material blend into the darkness so well.

All the while, Seria pondered her friend's strange behavior. Lena had always hinted at her sneak-away visits to her grandfather after the gates were closed. That she could pass through solid objects had never crossed Seria's mind, so that was one mystery solved. But what drove Lena to bring her out here so late? And why had Seria so willingly agreed without hesitation? What if they were spotted by the nighttime guards?

You're going to have to start asking more questions, Seria, before you join in on any more late-night adventures.

Her forlorn little shack shoved her puzzlement aside for the moment. It had been her refuge after the anguish of losing her family. Now, it offered painful memories.

As soon as they stepped off the bridge that led to Seria's door, Lena stopped and faced Seria. "There's...something in there you need to see."

Seria cocked her head, trying not to be annoyed. "What's so important that you had to bring me out here so late?"

"You'll find out in there." Lena nodded to the door.

"Fine, but this better be worth me walking through walls to see." Seria gave Lena a poke in the side as she passed her to proceed down the familiar path. The door squeaked loudly as she pushed it open and peered inside. Moonlight poured from the single window, allowing her to make out the worn furniture. It looked so much worse after the time she had spent in her simple but comfortable boarding room. But she did not have much time to dwell on the fact.

Strong hands grabbed her from behind the door, smothering her scream and pulling her back against a hard torso.

Her fight instinct stiffened her limbs, and she clawed at the hands. Then a voice stopped her cold, flooding her with a mix of longing, joy, and dismay.

"Don't scream. It's me."

Mason released Seria as she shoved away, hissing through his teeth when her elbow met his ribs. Lungs constricted, he stepped out of the shadows as she spun around to face him. The moonlight fell over her flushed face.

"What are you trying to do to me?" she demanded, her arms stiff at her sides. "Scare me to an early grave?"

He blinked at her outburst. "That wasn't my intention."

"Then what in the world are you doing here?" A murderous look distorted her usual aura of innocence and wonder. "You controlled Lena to bring me here! How could you?"

"I had to talk to you." Mason ran a hand over his injured arm to hide the way his insides churned. Maybe this was a mistake. He had waited two more nights for Lena to make another appearance so he would have a chance to talk to Seria, but she was already far too upset to be rational. "I couldn't very well walk up to the gate and ask to speak with you."

"I don't know that I have anything to say to you anyway. And you already said all you needed to say the last time we spoke, remember? Right before you betrayed me." Her voice hitched at the last.

"I didn't betray you." He regretted the words the instant they were out.

Her jaw dropped, hurt etched deep in the contours of her face. "You lived a lie every hour you spent in this room, Mason. You used my friend to get into the fort and then to bring me here. You killed the soldiers you *knew* I esteemed right before me. What would you call it?" Her words tumbled over each other.

"I call it survival." His own anger mounted. "You've held on to this childish wonder of the Stewards and their so-called Code." He spat the words out. "You know nothing."

"I know enough." She dug her fists into her hips. "The Stewards are the reason the Old Realm has lived in peace for so long."

"At what cost? Their will has been forced on people for generations until there's no life left in them. Why do you think so many choose to stay in the Gateway, rather than cross into the Old Realm?"

Her mouth opened and closed, without words for once.

Mason gritted his teeth, working to control his temper. "No one should be forced to live under a Code or serve a god they don't believe in."

That stubborn chin jutted out. "You told me yourself that your brother wanted to be a Steward. Surely, you—"

"Don't." Mason held a finger up. "Liam was fooled like everyone else."

"You're the one who's fooled, Mason. The Stewards fight for things the world needs. Goodness, purity, honor, truth."

"*Truth?*" The fury under the surface threatened to boil over. "Nay. You don't want to know the truth. You're afraid of the real truth."

"What truth, Mason? You serve a man obsessed with fear and darkness who wants nothing more than to conquer and destroy all that's good."

He sneered. "That's them talking for you. Jader wants the best for all concerned, and sometimes that means people get hurt. But I can't expect you to believe that, not after falling under the lies of Eric Passion."

She crossed her arms. "Eric is a good man. He helped me when no one else would."

"He's a tyrant." Sickened at her defense, he turned and stalked a few steps. How could he make her understand? Would she ever believe the reality in her blind loyalty? "He's interested in his agenda, and he'll destroy anyone who stands against him."

"That's not true."

"Isn't it?" He advanced toward her, the muscles in his neck tight. "Ask him about the Handan Massacre, Seria. Ask him about the fifteen boys slaughtered by his order, just for being there. Including *my brother*!"

Her face blanched. "That can't be. You're wrong."

"I was there, Seria." An iron band squeezed him, making it hard to speak. "Believe me, he's not a man you want to stand with."

Seria stared off into space, thunderstruck. "And you think Jader is?" She sounded less certain. "He stands against everything the Lambient represents."

A scoff ripped from him. "I stopped believing in the Lambient years ago."

"That doesn't mean He doesn't exist."

"Your faith doesn't mean He does." He shook his head. "You show me proof that He does, and I'll show you a being who cares nothing for the people who serve him."

"What about your Gift? How does anyone get their Gifts if He doesn't exist?"

He turned away, refusing to be baited. "There's a lot that can't be explained. It doesn't mean there's a being up there passing out Gifts."

A sudden, heavy silence stretched between them. When he glanced back at her, she was watching him rub at the bandage around his arm.

Her posture relaxed some, and she clasped her hands together. "I haven't thanked you for saving my life."

Mason shrugged, relieved at the change in tone. "I never meant for you to get hurt."

"I was hurt, Mason."

He stiffened, his mind racing with what might have happened in that barn. Rage lit through him, heating him from the inside out.

Her sniffles brought him back to the moment. "I thought you were my friend. But the whole time, you were mocking me and my beliefs. You despised everything about me."

A rock planted itself in his spirit at the truth staring at him from those weeping green eyes. He was the one who had hurt her, more than what she suffered at the hands of Dantus. His anger drained from him, leaving nothing but that hole. "Seria, I don't despise you." He spoke low and rough. "You've done more for me than almost anybody. But I knew you would hate me if you found out I wasn't what you thought I was. I couldn't take that risk."

"Mason, I knew you weren't a Steward."

The ground tipped beneath him, and he braced a hand on the table. "What?"

She lowered her head. "I mean, at first I didn't, of course. But there were too many signs, too many unanswered questions." Her shoulders curved inward. "By the time I figured that out, I presumed you were a foolish but well-meaning Rackson civilian trying to be a hero. I wasn't happy about the lies, but I thought you were too embarrassed to admit what you really were."

He scowled. "How could you be that naïve in believing I was anything but a Darkman?"

She swallowed and brought her head up again. "Because I believed any man who took the time and risk to put a horse out of its misery had to be a good man. I had no reason to doubt a man who sat by a sick donkey until it could breathe." Her voice caught. "And anyone who would trouble himself with helping me with such a humble task as laundry had to be someone I could trust."

Something dark and heavy crushed him at her admission, and he fought a sudden urge to hold her. His body swayed toward her, but he braced himself against the table with both hands. She stared back at him, her pain raw and gaping for him to see. But she still did not hate him. That truth shook him more than anything.

"Why are you here, Mason?"

He broke eye contact. Why *was* he here? Did this conversation change anything for him? The answer quickly made itself known. Nothing would divert him from the path he had chosen. It couldn't. He had made a promise, and it had to be fulfilled. "I'm taking on the Shadowstone."

She took a step forward. "Mason, nay."

He hardened himself against her dismay. "Tomorrow at the moon's third hour. This is something I've worked at for a long time."

"But it's so dangerous."

"Only to those who stand against it. It's not something to be shunned or feared, Seria."

She clenched her fists. "It was your *Shadowmen,* Mason, who tried to kill me!"

The words smacked him hard. He turned and swiped a hand over his face. "Not all of them are like that, Seria. He carried things too far." He shook his head. "That's not me. I'm taking it for a purpose. I have to."

"But once you take it—"

"I'll be fully committed to Jader and his cause."

She slumped and shook her head. "I don't understand."

"Despite what you feel about me now, I felt you at least deserved to hear me out."

She searched his face until he was convinced she must be able to see every thought he tried to hide. And for the first time, he had no desire to.

"I won't change my mind, Mason. I can't believe darkness is better than light. I don't understand how you can."

Her words, soft and resolute, shattered a fragile piece of a dream he had not known he carried. "Contrary to the lies they've spread, Seria, not everything that dwells in the darkness is evil."

"What good can come from it?"

"What good? How about the stars you look up at every night? Or the moon?"

Seria's jaw slackened.

"What about the black fox or the night owl? Are they wicked creatures that deserve to be destroyed because they prefer the night?" He walked toward her. "And the firefly, whose light shines brightest in the dark. The night rose waits to bloom until after the sun has set. The Gifts themselves are given when the night falls. Does that make them wrong?" He stopped a few feet in front of her, drilling his gaze into hers. "And what about your late-night fishing? Are you evil because you like to fish under the moon?"

She pushed her hair behind her ear with a trembling hand. "Fine, you've made your point. Maybe I don't know as much as I thought. But you don't either. Are you willing to stake your whole life and future on Jader? Your *honor*?"

His brows pinched. "Aye. I am." But it took him too long to say it, just long enough for a flash of hope to flash through her eyes.

She inhaled. "I won't turn from the Lambient. I can't."

"But you can turn away from me?"

Her chin quivered. "Why did you kill him?"

"What?"

"If you feel so strongly about your stance, why did you kill that Shadowman? He was one of your own."

He clenched his jaw and looked at the door, tempted to run from the question. The emptiness inside him seethed, stretching its tentacles to pull him in.

"Answer me, Mason."

"Because I realized something." His breath stuck to his throat.

"And that is?"

He let out a groan and stepped closer, catching her gaze with his. "The Shadowstone won't fill the hole that started when my brother died. Nothing will." He reached out and caressed her cheek. The softness of her skin against his roughened fingertips soothed his frayed nerves. "Nothing but you."

Her expression lifted, and for a moment, hope bloomed. "I discovered something, too," she whispered. She lowered her head as her cheeks tinted.

His hand cupped her jaw and raised it back up. "What?"

Tears gathered in her eyes. "Being a healer didn't bring me the satisfaction I thought it would." She didn't say the rest, but he could see it in her expression.

His other hand came up to frame her face. "I can't give up on my promise to see justice for Liam, Seria."

"So, what are you saying?"

He drew nearer, seething with desire and doubt. "I want both."

Her pulse fluttered beneath his fingers as he dipped his head. The kiss—soft and brief—shot fire through his veins, and an ache settled deep in his soul. But the hole had grown calm, filled with the essence of the woman before him. "Don't leave me," he murmured.

A tear broke free and streaked down her cheek. Mason did not allow himself to read her, could not bear to see her response. Then she shifted toward him, just a little, but it was enough. He covered her mouth with his, pulling her against his chest. Her hands gripped his upper arms, and she leaned against him. He wrapped her tight in his arms, loath to let her escape the boundaries of his embrace or his heart.

She broke the kiss with a whimper, resting her forehead on his shoulder. "I can't."

He gulped against the pain raging through him and held her tight. "I've never felt this way, Seria." His words came out hoarse and thick. "I haven't loved anyone since Liam."

Seria looked up at him, and the depth of grief he saw matched the emotion ripping him to shreds. His statement stunned him. But he couldn't take it back, nor did he want to. Blades, he did love her. Before she could speak, he cupped the back of her head and kissed her again.

Lena was still waiting; their presence would be missed. He had to let her go. For now. "Come back to me. Here, in one fortnight." He swallowed hard. "I'll wait for you. I'll always wait for you."

"You'll change your mind when you take that stone."

"Nay. Nothing will turn me from you." Never had desperation been such a companion as it was now. "I'll be waiting."

"I won't be here. I can't." Her trembling murmur shattered him, but he ground his teeth against it. He refused to believe he'd lost the one good thing he'd found since Liam.

"I'll still be here."

A sob broke from her as she turned away with a violent shudder. The space between them chilled him straight through to the bones. He watched her walk across the room, every step a hammer blow to his broken spirit, and waited for her to look back, to give him some kind of hope that there was a chance.

But she wrenched the door open and ran out, giving him nothing more but the echoes of her cries.

62

The sun shone brightly, promising new light and life. But Seria felt none of it as she stood at her window, looking down at the awakening square. Inside her beat a numb, shriveled knot. Everything she held dear had been wrenched from her.

But that wasn't true. She leaned closer to the opening, soaking in the warmth, willing it to fill the empty places Mason had left behind. One by one, she counted her blessings. A home inside the fort walls, along with a chance to practice the healing arts under the watchful eye of Luron. Her friendship with Lena, a bright spot on her darkened horizon. Living and working among the Stewards she had long admired from afar.

It didn't matter how many times she repeated it. Her spirit still yearned for what she could not have. Or rather, *who.*

A tight band stretched between her shoulder blades, and anger stirred within her. Anger at Mason for being what he was and putting her in the position she was in. Anger at herself for falling for a Darkman. And a whisper of anger toward the Lambient for allowing it all to happen as it did.

That realization scared her, so she turned from the window and pulled her tunic on. She let out a growl when she heard another rip in her gown. At least it would be covered by her equally ratted tunic. Someday, she would have the means to buy new clothes, but for now, she cared little about what her clothes looked like. At least she had a decent place to sleep.

Mallie ran a clean, comfortable boarding house, if not fancy. Seria's second-story room was small, with one window facing the street. An old, empty wardrobe stood in the corner. Her trunk had been brought from her cabin and now sat at the foot of her bed with her few belongings. The bed, though small by normal standards, still outsized the one Mason had slept in for three weeks. Except for that last night when he let her take it, and he slept on the floor.

Right before she learned the truth about him.

Blinking against the stinging in her eyes, Seria flung the door open and hurried down the hall to the wooden steps leading to the main floor, nearly colliding with Mallie coming up.

"Oh, gracious me, dearie, what's the hurry?" Mallie asked with a throaty chuckle.

Just trying to run from my memories. She forced a smile. "I'm sorry, Mallie. Guess I'm anxious to start the day."

"Well, I'm glad I caught you." Mallie thrust a bundle of fabric into Seria's hands. "I came across these, and I have no use for them. See what you can do with them."

Seria readjusted the bundle into one hand and pulled the top piece off to shake it loose. "I can certainly look at them, but where did—" Her words died in her mouth. A deep maroon tunic dangled before her, woven of soft material and without a tear to be seen. "Miss Mallie, what—I can't take this!"

Mallie's gray brows bunched. "Oh dear, you don't like it?"

"Nay, that's not what I meant." Seria clutched it to her, despite her claim. "I mean, this is too fine. Surely, you have need of this."

A smile softened the landlady's lined cheeks as she looked up at Seria. "If you take a good look at the length of those garments, you'll know why they won't work for me."

"Then how did you end up with them in the first place?"

Mallie waved her hand. "Oh, I can't say for sure. Now, why don't you take them to your room, and try them on? And if they suit you, take a spin around the fort. Nothing like a new gown to lift one's spirits." She patted Seria's cheek and shuffled back down the steps.

Seria stared down at the treasure she hugged to herself. Wonder and excitement fought their way through the numbness. New clothes could not touch the deep ache at her core, but how many times had she wished for something better than the rags she wore?

Dashing back into her room, she tore her old clothes off. Besides the tunic, there was a gown of deep cream and another tunic—this one a dark blue. They were a little loose in places but felt like a hug next to her skin.

"Oh my, I can scarcely believe it." Dare she accept this? This was too much, even if they were someone else's castaways. Maybe Mallie had grown tired of her tenant looking like a street waif. Her cheeks burned at the thought, but her old clothes were truly ready for the rag bin.

Seria brushed a wrinkle from the maroon tunic and straightened her spine. She would take them, but she would do all she could to make it up to the dear lady.

What would Mason think if he saw me now?

The pleasure at the thought was washed away by the sorrow of their parting the night before. Mason would not see her in these clothes. Because she had closed the door on that possibility.

What little excitement the gift had generated soured, and Seria folded the rest of the clothes and set them on her bed before leaving. Wallowing in misery never benefited anyone, and she had plenty to do that day.

The morning was spent with Nola, serving breakfast and cleaning up the mess. Seria was thankful the work was such as she could do without thinking, for her mind was still far away. When Nola released her for a while, she headed outside to tend to some other errands. Her first stop was the infirmary, where Gus informed her that he would be released back to his duties soon.

"That's wonderful." She squeezed his arm. "I'm sure you've been missing it."

"Aye, but when am I going to get to see your smiling face?"

"Oh, you'll see me around." Though her smile had been lost in a well of regret.

Gus squinted at her. "You're looking a mite peaked. Mayhap you're working too much."

"Thank you, but I'm fine."

The sun blinded her for a moment when she stepped out. Her attention was drawn once more to the sky, to where the Lambient resided, beyond the sun. The light that lent to the Code its pure and virtuous power. Despite the slight resentment nestling in her spirit, the whole concept still amazed her. How could anyone turn from something so beautiful?

"You're going to get your neck stuck like that if you're not careful."

Seria's head swiveled, her hand going to her throat.

"Sorry." Ollen grinned. "Didn't mean to startle you."

She scowled up at him. "You don't look sorry."

He fell into step beside her when she resumed walking. "How have you been since...?"

She stiffened, clutching her skirt in one hand. "Since what?"

"Since the infiltration."

"Oh. Of course." Ollen had no idea she had had a secret meeting with the Reader who had instigated the infiltration. She forced herself to relax. "I'm enjoying the sunshine."

This was the first time they had spoken since the morning after the storm. The Stewards had stayed busy carrying out memorial services and performing their duties, while she avoided contact as much as possible. It hurt too much to act as though her heart was not crushed to bits. She caught Ollen's sidelong look.

"You didn't exactly answer my question."

She raised a shoulder. "I'm not sure how I feel right now, but I do know that I don't want to relive these past few weeks."

"You and me, both." Ollen pulled his gloves from his belt and pushed his fingers through.

Ready for a subject change, she motioned to his green leather suit. "What is this you've got on?"

"It's our official drill garb. We wear it out on the field for practice or training."

She eyed the getup, noting how it emphasized Ollen's strong build. She had always seen him as somewhat short and slim. Never would she have guessed the well-defined shoulders and muscular arms he hid underneath his basic tunic. She jerked her attention forward. What was she doing admiring his bare arms? Heat flooded her cheeks. "Um, I must say, you Stewards are better dressed than I would've expected."

He chuckled. "Well, thank you, but we're not exactly trying to be the height of fashion. Our clothes represent our rank."

She stopped and faced him again. "Is that so?"

"Sure. I'm sure you've seen Braylee's colorful tunic. That's the frock of a captain."

"And what about yours?"

"Mine's a little more basic: red and white. Because I'm nothing but a mere sergeant." He chuckled. "The militiamen wear black and gray."

"How many officers are there?"

"The captains are the highest office, besides the Grand Marshal. Then there are lieutenants, sergeants, corporals, and privates."

"And you've already made it to sergeant. Impressive."

"Thank you."

His chest swelled a bit at the compliment. She started walking again. "I've learned so much since coming here, and every day there's something new. It's all so fascinating."

"I can tell you more. If you'd like."

Seria darted a glance at him, but he was watching a woodpecker on a nearby tree. His offer sounded casual enough, from one friend to another. But would it be right to spend time with him so soon after Mason?

A lump formed, but she gulped it down. Her time with Mason was over. She would always remember the times they shared with fondness, but they were tainted now with the truth. Mason had made his choice. She had too much here to live for to give up for him. There was no reason she couldn't spend time with Ollen, who had become a dear friend in the last few weeks.

"That would be wonderful. I'd love to learn more about how the Stewards work." The words felt strange and forced, but she made herself say them.

A crooked grin brightened his tanned complexion. "Good, then we'll plan on it." He waved to the green fields ahead. "I'd better get to the training grounds, or Captain Dudley will have my head."

She let out a laugh—weak and brief, but the first one she'd attempted in days. "We can't have that, can we?"

He said goodbye and moved on. She watched him leave, cheered for the moment that she still had his friendship.

But her mood turned pensive as she resumed her walk, her feet dragging. How would Lena receive her now? Mason had used her twice, all because Seria had allowed their paths to cross.

The lady of the house let Seria in and directed her to the attached room Lena shared with her mother. Lena lay in the bed, her arm draped over her head. Seria hesitated. Was she asleep? But then she stirred and glanced up. "Seria! I was hoping you would come by."

"I wasn't sure you'd want to see me." Seria moved further in and took a seat on the single hardback chair.

"I suspected that, too." Lena sat up and squinted at her. "You're wearing new clothes. They look nice."

She smoothed the fabric over her knees. "Mallie passed them on to me. I suspect she was feeling sorry for me, but in the end, I didn't care." She sat back and crossed her arms, relieved at how normal Lena was acting, though it was unusual to find her in bed so late. "So, you have a Gift of the Moon."

Lena chuckled. "I was wondering how long it would take you to bring that up."

"Why did you never tell me?"

"You'd be surprised how many people will ask favors of you when they know you can pass through walls."

"Well, you don't have to worry about that with me," Seria assured. "But now I know how you managed to get into your house during the fire." As she spoke, Lena pressed her fingers against her temple. It hit Seria then. "Oh no...you're feeling the effects of Mason's control."

Lena smiled. "It's not the first time."

Seria squeezed her hands together. No wonder Lena was still resting. "I'm so sorry, Lena."

"It's not your fault, Seria."

"But if I hadn't been responsible for—"

Lena put her hand up. "Stop. I don't blame you."

Seria's nostrils flared. "I can't believe he would do such a thing. He claims to care—" She caught herself. "He shouldn't have done it."

"I agree." Lena swung her feet to the floor to face Seria. "But to be fair, he asked first."

That stopped her. "He what?"

"It's true. He met me coming back from visiting Grandfather and told me what he needed. Then he asked if he could control me into getting you to your shack."

"He asked if he could control you? And you *agreed?*"

Lena chuckled. "Is there any point in refusing a Reader? I think he knew I was willing without his control, but I wonder if he didn't do it to keep any fault from falling on me."

Seria shook her head. "Why would he care?" Her confused brain registered all that Lena had said. "Wait. Why would you have willingly agreed to do anything for him?"

Lena's head lowered. "Because I know not all Darkmen are as evil as others believe."

Seria drew back. Lena could not be hinting at sympathy for Jader's cause, could she? "What makes you think that?"

Sadness lurked in Lena's eyes when she looked back up. "Because my father was a Darkman."

"Your father?" Seria reached out and took her hand. "Oh, Lena."

She gave a dismissive shrug. "It's a story for another time. I still stand against everything Jader offers. But sometimes good men are swept up in bad decisions. Or bad circumstances that lead to bad decisions."

Questions darted about in Seria's head, chased about by shock. "Surely, you're not saying you believe Mason is a victim to Jader's rule. After all he's done."

"I can't say for sure. But he was most adamant, almost frantic, about seeing you."

Doubt began to thread through Seria's resolve. Had she acted too rashly in turning away from him? But one troubling fact chased away what little hope the question aroused. Her spine stiffened. "It doesn't matter, Lena. He's taking on the Shadowstone. Tonight. He told me himself."

Lena grimaced. "That does change things, I suppose."

Quiet dropped for a moment, heavy and pressing. Seria was back in her cabin, held by Mason's strong arms. His desperate pleas were so unlike the stoic reserve he had displayed in the beginning. The pain on his face cut through her like a knife.

She stood to her feet. "Um, I better go," she said thickly.

"Seria."

Lena's call stopped her at the door, and she turned, her vision clouded by tears. "Aye?"

The creak of the cot preceded Lena's slow footsteps. Then Lena pulled her into a hug. "I'm so sorry for all you've been through."

A sob broke through her. "He loves me, Lena. And Lambient help me, I love him. But there's no chance for us. He's devoted to Jader, and I can't support anyone who would destroy everything the Stewards work to preserve."

"I know." Lena did not offer any more pithy words of counsel, but held her until Seria had gained control.

Seria pulled back and rubbed at her cheeks. "Thank you for your understanding."

"You're more than welcome. I know what it's like to love a Darkman."

There was so much more that could be said, so many more questions that could be asked. But the lines across Lena's forehead hinted that she still did not feel her best.

"I'll leave you to rest now."

"Don't stay away, Seria. I'm always here if you need to talk."

"Thank you."

Drying the last of the moisture from her face, she blinked everything back into focus. Grief reigned in the throne of her emotions as she slogged her way back to the mess hall, though all she wanted to do was throw herself in her bed and weep until she had no tears, no emotions left.

It mattered not how many times she repeated all the reasons. Mason did not believe in the Lambient. He was committed to Jader's dark reign of power. He fought and killed the Stewards Seria respected. However, none of those truths reached far enough into the core of her soul to ease the pain.

Maybe someday she would find peace. Maybe someday she would rise above her weakness to feel strong again. Maybe someday she would believe that she had made the right decision.

63

The last golden rays of the sun shrank back in the face of the growing shadows of the forest. Jader stood on a rise overlooking the ground where the trainees worked and watched the swordplay between Mason and one of his students. Mason held nothing back, his hold on his sword firm, his movements rapid but smooth. The duel was over soon after it started. Jader smiled as Mason then proceeded to take on every other trainee in his group, with similar results.

There were still a few hours before the ceremony, but he was almost giddy as he watched the training session. Things were going exactly as he had anticipated and planned for.

Mason was nothing if not driven. Since the infiltration, he had thrown himself into his work. He pushed his trainees hard, accepting no excuses, and took on every task given to him with determined efficiency. Indeed, there were none in the camp like him. He had never been angrier. And this was Mason before receiving the Shadowstone.

Amazing how much good a big dose of revenge can do a soul. A confused, hurting boy when Jader first met him, Mason had developed into a strong warrior with a rage that fueled his every move. That rage would help Jader conquer the Old Realm, its pathetic king, and his self-right-eous prince.

He curled his lips. If Eric Passion displayed a mere fraction of the rage Mason exhibited, he might stand a chance against Jader's Darkmen. But no, he went about spreading his ridiculous message to love everyone and let the light of the Beacons guide your way. It would serve to do nothing but destroy him.

And Mason would play a vital role in that destruction.

"Emperor Jader?"

A young man stood nearby, his head bent in submission.

"Aye?"

"Commander Bruin sent me to inform you of an incoming message."

Jader turned his good eye to observe the session a moment longer. It was impossible to *not* be impressed with Mason's skill. Even Bruin, who, Jader suspected, hosted a good deal of jealousy and distrust toward the young Reader, could not find fault with Mason's skill.

Mason could outshoot every man in the camp with a crossbow. His tracking skills were unmatched. He handled a sword like he had done so all his life. And then there were his remarkable Gifts, which would only prove to be more powerful as time went on. There would be no stopping Jader when that happened.

Smoothing the folds of his dark robe, Jader reined his eagerness back. He was wise enough to know that just because things looked up today, it did not mean that all would go well tomorrow. He needed to gather more men before he could storm the gates of the Gateway garrison. A plan that was even now in progress.

He needed to get that Shadowstone on Mason.

"Very well." Jader moved down the rocky path to Bruin's tent. The messenger ran ahead to open the tent flap for him.

Bruin stood from his table, his humming Shadowstone in hand and a blank scroll already spread out. He handed his stone to Jader, who held it over the scroll, letting its purple light fill every inch. Shadowy letters began to form, blurry at first, but after a moment, they came into focus. Jader smiled as he read the message.

"Good news, Emperor?" Bruin asked.

Jader nodded as he handed the stone back to Bruin. "Very. Feegan has reached the outskirts of Paladin and has already made some recruits."

Bruin hung the Shadowstone back in place around his neck. "Seems not everyone is as dedicated to the Code as their prince."

Jader's scarred eye twitched as his mind moved forward to the day he would overthrow Aden's rule. The day he would curse the Code and the Beacons that powered it. The New Realm and the Old would both know the strength of his power. And the Passions would be no more.

The man who once claimed his light was greater than anything Jader had to offer was now set poised to lose everything.

"Come on, master." The young man puffed. "We've been at this all afternoon. Let's take a break."

The others chimed in their agreement. Even Areem was ready to quit.

Mason scowled. "Oh, you're tired." His voice dripped with condescension. "Is that what you're going to whine to your enemy when you're fighting to the death? 'Can I rest a while? I'm getting *tired*.'"

The boy dropped his head, and Mason gave the whole group a hard look. "If this is the kind of attitude you want to take on, then it's good I know now. Because I'll not waste my time any further." Sliding his sword back into his scabbard with a jerk, he grabbed his shirt off the ground and stalked away. After a few silent seconds, the sound of steel against steel filled his ears.

Good. Let them train without him for a while. Come tomorrow, they would be ready to push themselves.

He pulled the worn blue shirt over his head as he stalked to the camp. Dreeya met him at the edge, her long black hair hanging loose over her shoulders. She had her usual hungry look, and Mason felt anything but obliging.

"I'm getting ready to take a bath in the stream." She sidled up against him. "Want to wash my back?"

"Nay." He brushed past her. "I'm busy."

"Oh, come now." She grabbed his arm with both hands. "It's time you learn how to have some fun."

He jerked away. "I'm not interested, Dreeya."

She blinked, then arched a thin brow. "Well, *pardon me*. Don't let me get in the way of the soon-to-be Shadowman." Her voice went cold. "I won't do it again."

Mason lowered his face inches from hers. "Good."

Dreeya was not given a chance to respond before he moved on, leaving her gaping in outrage behind him.

His mood darker now, he headed for the roped-off corral. Crue jumped to his feet as Mason approached.

"What are you doing, boy?" The words came out in a low growl. "Taking it easy on the job?"

"Just a short break, sir." The lad rubbed his hands against his clothes. "I've already got your horse fed and groomed for the night. A-and I've cleaned your leathers."

"Get him saddled."

"Yes, sir."

Mason frowned as Crue hurried away. Why was he being so hard on him? All in all, Mason had no complaints about Crue. But he was a raw reminder of Seria. Would he have given the kid a thought before he had met her?

He shook his head. It went against everything he believed. People needed to make their own way. They had to rely on their brains and brawn to get ahead. There were no excuses, no handouts. That was what he had told Seria after she defended her actions in helping Byron and his family. And yet, a mere few days after leaving her, he found himself giving Crue the chance to work for him.

"Here you are, sir."

Mason pulled himself back to the present as Crue presented his horse, all saddled and ready to go. Dismissing his previous thoughts, Mason took the reins and gave the boy a brief look. "If anyone asks for me, tell 'em I went scouting the woods."

"At once."

Mason shot him a double take. At the submission in Crue's eyes, he frowned. "Great." In his disgruntled state of mind, carelessness had ruled. Crue would be too drained to do his work in the morning. *Good going, Mason.*

He led the roan away, ready to disappear into the woods until his ceremony. But he had not gotten far before he was intercepted again.

"Mason, hold up!"

Frustration mounting, he put his hands on his hips and waited for Shon to catch up. His horse immediately dropped his head to graze.

"A couple of the men trapped a few squirrels to play with." Shon held up a small pouch. "Want to place some bets?"

Mason could not stop the sneer that twisted his face. "I don't think so."

"Come on. You've been sulking for the last three days."

"And you think torturing animals will fix that?"

Shon's brows slashed downward. "What's going on with you, Mason? You've not been right since you came back from the Gateway."

Mason glowered at him. If one more person told him that, he was going to lose it.

"For someone about to become a Shadowman, you don't act like it."

Resentment stiffened Mason's back, and he took a step closer. "What are you saying, Shon? That just because I don't want to waste my time forcing dumb rodents to kill each other that I'm not a good soldier? Is that all it takes around here?"

Shon frowned back at him, his jaw clenching. After a moment, he relaxed his stance and put his hands up. "All right. You've made your point."

Mason slumped, and the anger drained from him with a loud sigh. What was he doing, flying off at Shon like that? "It's not you. I've already turned Dreeya off and jumped all over my students this morning. I'm not doing well with relationships lately."

"Maybe not. But the fact that you notice at all proves my point."

Biting back a scoff, Mason ran a hand over his face. "Let's not start with that again."

"I'm sorry, but before you couldn't be bothered. Dreeya never got anything out of you, and you couldn't care less whether I talked to you or not."

Mason stilled at the truth in the words, though he wanted to deny it. When did he start caring about his relationships? One in particular took precedence over any of them, though he feared he'd lost that one forever. Regardless, he would still be back at that cabin waiting on her, just like he said he would.

But in the meantime, he also realized how much he'd come to appreciate Shon. In many ways, he reminded him of Baris—bold and brash, but sharp and calculating. He didn't miss a thing, which unnerved Mason at times.

Shon crossed his arms. "Can't help but wonder what's the cause of it. Or *who.*"

Mason eyed him but stayed silent. What could he say? That he had fallen for a Steward sympathizer? How well would that bode for his upcoming ceremony?

"But it's your business. I trust you know what you're doing."

"I do." And he did. Get the Shadowstone and finish his mission. And hope with everything in him that Seria would see him again. He could have both if she would but believe in the possibility.

"Good." Shon gave a short nod. "Well, if I don't see you again, best of luck."

"Where are you going?"

"Commander Bruin's sending me on an assignment in the morning with a missive for the reserves." He cocked his head. "Seeing as I'm the best horseman in camp, it makes sense I'd be the one to go."

Mason scoffed. "Sort of like you're the best shot and swordsman, too, right?"

Shon's eyes lit up. "That's right."

A begrudging smile finally loosened the tight lines around Mason's jaw. "And modest, too."

Shon shrugged and put his hand out. "No hard feelings?"

Mason shook his hand. "None."

As his friend walked off, a trickle of apprehension ran down his back. Why did he feel like he was losing control of his world?

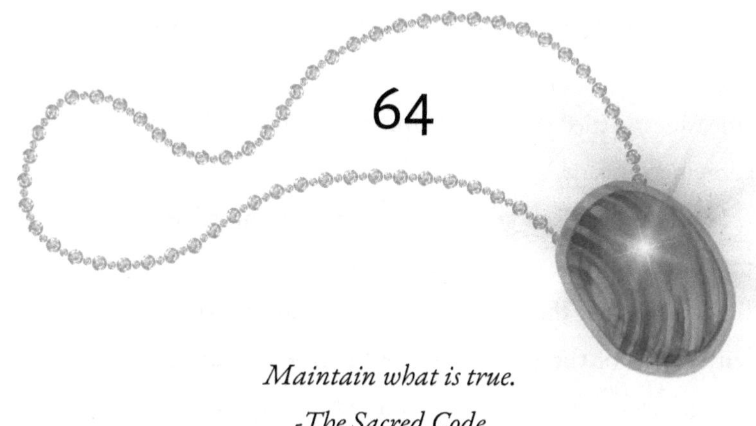

64

Eric gazed down at the small fountain of water into the tired eyes of his white-headed father. Telling the king that Shadowmen had escaped into his kingdom had not been an easy task.

Aden sighed and ran a hand over his lined face. "A Reader in Jader's army. And a rancorous one at that. Thank the Lambient you escaped his hold."

"Though I have no idea how. No one can resist a Reader's command, not without a Beacon."

A soft smile lifted the weariness. "You held Lavrynth, did you not?"

"Lavrynth?" Eric thought back to the moment he succumbed to Mason's power. "Aye. I never lost it."

Aden gave a single nod. "Then that's how you overcame it. Remember, that sword is infused with the power of the Lambient, as well as your ancestors' blood."

Eric remembered the way Lavrynth heated in his hand before he broke the hold of the Reader. It left him in shock now. "I never imagined..."

"Remember, son. When you wield the sword of the Lambient, darkness has to flee. No matter how powerful the Reader might be." His face sagged again. "Though I still hate to think of what this means for the

Gateway and the Old Realm. Especially with rumors of uprisings in the east."

Uneasiness settled over Eric. "Uprisings? That can't be the work of the Shadowmen already."

"Nay. This has been going on for a few months." Aden's tone was grim. "It's the people of the Old Realm."

"Rebels resisting the Code." Eric leaned against his knuckles, one hand on either side of the pool. "No doubt they're figuring out how close Jader's government has brought him to the Gateway."

"They're getting bolder. The other kings have contacted me, asking for help. I've sent what Stewards I could spare, but…"

"You can't afford to send too many." Jader's chaos was already digging its fingers into the Old Realm. And the Shadowmen had not even made themselves known yet. Eric gave a quick shake of his head. "I'll never fathom the level of hatred one must have for the Lambient to bring such destruction to entire kingdoms as Jader has done."

"There is no denying his scorn for everything the Lambient represents, Son, but I fear for Jader this is a matter of pride, as well."

"What do you mean?"

Aden's expression pinched. "Let's just say Jader has reason to make this a personal campaign."

There was more that could be said, but the haggard lines on the older man's face arrested Eric's questions for the time being.

They spoke a few minutes more before ending the connection, though with the future so uncertain, it was difficult to say goodbye. Eric lifted his light rod from the water and watched the image of his father disappear in the ripples. When the pool had calmed, he gave a loud sigh and squeezed the bridge of his nose.

An ache in his side and the weariness in his bones reminded him that he should be in bed, but his mind was too busy. Instead, he braced his arm against his sore side and headed for the mess hall. It was late, but Nola would surely have a hot drink to chase away the chill in his spirit. As he walked, he let his mind wander, though careful to avoid the matter that had kept him awake since the night of the storm.

Things had turned around among the Stewards. For the most part, they had accepted him as their leader, past mistakes and all. There would be times they might struggle with his decisions. He would wrestle with choices as well. But the animosity and distrust had faded, which was fortunate, because now more than ever, they needed a united army. For once, Eric felt confident about their future.

Jader would no doubt be on a triumphant high after his small victory. He wouldn't wait long to act again, so the Stewards had to be ready for anything. The guard had already been increased since the night of the storm, and the call for more knights had been given.

And soon, Eric would take his Stewards beyond the stronghold in search of the Shadowpit that gave Jader his power. He owed it to Lt. Draven and all the others lost. He owed it to himself.

Glancing at the wall of the fortress, Eric pictured the forest surrounding the town of Cadence. Miles beyond those woods, Jader's army was camped, waiting and watching for the opportune time to attack.

And in that camp was the young man who had nearly killed him. The one who had helped the band of Shadowmen get into the Old Realm.

The young man who blamed Eric for Handan.

Pausing on his way, Eric dropped his head and stared at the ground. No matter how he tried, he could not shake the fervor in Mason Grey's voice as he accused Eric. The light of hatred in his eyes. The power he held over Eric in that unguarded moment. His muscles tightened even now at the memory. It haunted him every waking hour.

What a shame. Had things taken a different course, would Mason have had the chance to become a normal, law-abiding citizen, despite his Gift? Could he have had a future with a decent girl like Seria?

Eric rubbed the rigid muscles in the back of his neck. It was too late to wish things differently. Mason was what he was—a Darkman, and, most likely by now, a Shadowman. But much more, he was a Reader who had targeted Eric as the cause for his hatred. Which meant they would surely meet again.

The responsibility Eric bore, protecting Paladin and the other Old Realm kingdoms weighed down on him. He raised his head and searched for the moon, craving its radiance.

"Lambient, I cannot do this alone," he murmured. "Please, walk with me."

He was fighting a noble war, a war that would go down in history, and while he did not wish to be remembered in any special light, determination to see it through filled him.

Jader's Dark Power would fall. The Stewards would prevail, and the Code would stand. The light of the Beacons would shine. Eric would make certain of it.

Even if he had to die to make it so.

"Prince Eric, what are you doing out here?"

Braylee's inquiry shook him from his meditation, and he grimaced. "Halfway regretting it," he said with a wry chuckle.

"Do you need help?" Braylee's dark face tightened.

"Nay, I'll be all right as soon as I sit down for a bit."

Braylee joined him for the remaining short distance to the mess hall. They walked in silence until Eric broke it.

"Give me the truth, Braylee. Am I doing the right thing?" He was glad when Braylee took the time to consider his response.

"You had me worried there for a while. I understood your reservations, but they were holding you back. But I have faith that you will see this through."

"And do we stand a chance against Jader's army? Especially with a Reader on his side?"

This earned a deep breath. "I don't know what the future holds, Prince Eric, and I admit, the Reader gives me some concern. These are dark times, to be sure. But the smallest of lights can disrupt the greatest of darkness. The Lambient will see us through."

The words, spoken with simplicity and sincerity, soothed Eric's battered and worn spirit. His throat tightened, but he managed to thank his faithful captain before they stepped through the doors of the hall.

The room was empty, which came as no surprise. Rather than taking a table, Eric moved to the kitchen on the other side of the hall.

Nola and Seria were both kneading large piles of dough at the massive wooden table as Braylee held the door open for Eric. The dusty smell of flour mixed with the yeasty aroma of fresh bread baking over the open fire.

Seria's jaw dropped when she spotted him. "What on earth are you doing out of bed way over here...Prince Eric Passion?"

Eric stifled a chuckle at her attempt to show respect after scolding him. She sounded much like what he imagined a bossy, younger sister would. Indeed, he was relieved to see her come to life, even if it was at his expense. She had been so withdrawn and pallid when she came to check on him earlier, which was such a contrast to her determined spirit after the storm that he had to wonder why.

"I was hoping some of Nola's hot cider would help me sleep tonight," he told her.

Nola wiped her hands on her apron. "Right away, Your Highness."

A frown bunched Seria's brow. "Is your wound bothering you at night?"

He should have known she'd catch that. "Not really," he assured her. "I've had a lot on my mind, that's all."

She nodded and turned back to her dough, giving it a good punch before flipping it over to knead some more. "Well, you might as well take a seat so as not to aggravate it further."

Braylee spoke up. "I wish I could stay, but my guard is on watch, so I'd best check in with them."

Eric bid his captain good night and watched Seria work the dough over with fervor. She wore some of the new garments he had sent to Mallie. They suited her better than the rags she had before. But Seria's arms were stiff, her face pinched. Something was wrong, but what had changed between the night of the infiltration and now? He doubted it had anything to do with the clothes. Mallie would have been discreet in passing those on to her. If he didn't know any better, he would think Seria had seen Mason again.

"Here you go, Prince Eric." Nola set a steaming mug in front of him. One drink of the spicy cider spread warmth all the way to his fingers and toes. As Nola sat and chatted with him, he could feel his muscles relaxing. Maybe tonight, he'd get some sleep.

He handed Nola the empty mug and thanked her as he stood. He rose too quickly, though, and a sharp jab hit his side. A hiss escaped before he could stop it, drawing Seria's attention.

"Maybe someone should see you back to your room."

Nola waved her off. "Go ahead, young lady. I'm about done here."

Eric's objections died as Seria cleaned her hands with a towel and opened the door for him.

"Well, I'll certainly not object to your company," he said, earning a small smile from her.

She was quiet on the short walk back to the main building, which was highly unusual for Seria.

"I pray Luron has not been working you too hard," he said, hoping to spark her knack for conversation.

"Not at all. I enjoy the work."

"I'm very glad to see you putting those healing skills of yours to good use."

She nodded. "This is what I've always wanted." Her dull tone contradicted her own words.

They arrived at the main building, and she took his elbow as he walked up the steps. By the time they reached the top, sweat beaded his temples.

"Mayhap I did push myself a little too hard," he panted.

She frowned at him. "Mayhap." She left the door open and led him to the bed. It had never looked so inviting. "Do you need me to check the cut?"

He lowered himself to the side and felt the spot where Mason's sword had grazed him under the ribs. It felt achy and warm, but there was no moisture. "I think I'm good until morning."

Seria gave a nod and moved to turn down the covers. Her whitewashed cheeks and downturned eyes were too much for him. "Seria, I wish you would tell me what was bothering you."

"I am fine, Your Highness."

"I think we both know you're not. Something weighs on you today, and I can't help but feel it has something to do with Mason."

There was a long pause as she fluffed his pillow with sharp tugs. He spoke again. "I wonder if, despite the circumstances, you've lost your heart to him."

Her movements faltered. "How can you say that, after what he's done?" The words came out shaky and strained.

Her reaction confirmed his assumption, and pity mounted. "Because we can't always control these matters, and sometimes, we are at the mercy of our own hearts."

She moved to his darkened window, tremors overtaking her form. Compassion and regret pressed hard on him. He had feared this very thing once he learned her story. A girl with a pure heart could bequite vulnerable when it came to conniving, manipulating Darkmen like Mason.

"I am truly sorry, Seria. I wish things had been different. I know you would never consider bowing to Jader's rule, but the man you love has done that very thing. He's let Jader's influence blacken his soul and his conscience so that he will do anything for the man."

Seria grew still. "He wasn't always this way." She turned to face him, slow and deliberate. "There was a time he was no different than the men I've met in this fort. When he was in my cabin, I saw glimpses of a good man. But something drove him to Jader's side."

Silence reigned for a moment. Her steady gaze pierced him, sending dread coursing through him.

"Mason believes you had something to do with the Handan Massacre."

Eric's heart slammed in his chest, and he sat like a statue, unable to tear his eyes from hers. Something cold squeezed around his lungs; the moment he had been avoiding, *dreading,* had come upon him.

"He's mistaken, of course." Seria's statement was heavy with imploration, begging him to confirm her words. "I know you wouldn't have been a part of something like that, but there must be a reason he believes it so firmly."

"Aye, there is." The words tore themselves from his lips. "Because it's true."

Seria blanched. "What do you mean? That was a massacre. You wouldn't have done anything like that!"

The years of silence, of hiding the truth, all of it had been for naught. He had done nothing but alienate his Stewards and put an enraged Reader on the warpath. And now, he had to face this young woman whose life had been turned upside down by the lone survivor of Handan and Eric's cowardice.

"But I did." A weight nearly doubled him over. Regret—the same regret he had lived with for twelve years—rose to smother him.

"I don't understand." Seria shook her head.

Closing his eyes against the memory, Eric began the story he had tried for so long to forget. "I got a report on a small band of Darkmen getting ready to attack a Gateway village. Since the village stood with the Passions, I thought it my duty to protect it. So, I gave the order to attack. No questions asked."

She stared at him, gripping the front of her skirt with bone-white knuckles.

Eric clasped his hands together so that they hurt. "My Stewards carried out their duty and left none alive." His voice broke. "It took but a few hours for us to realize what we had done. We'd killed fifteen orphaned teens from Handan's Home for Boys, along with an apprentice."

Seria swayed and braced a hand on the wall. "So, it's true?" she whispered.

Eric dropped his head. "It's a wound I have lived with ever since. After it happened, I pulled back to my father's palace and swore I would never again take charge and risk another mistake like that. I never knew there was a survivor until I came face to face with Mason."

"You hid it?" A sob punctuated her question.

"I should not have. But...I was ashamed. The Stewards responsible were devastated and honorably dismissed. My father swore them to secrecy, and we tried to move on. But I never could."

"You're the reason Mason hates the Lambient and the Stewards and everything they stand for." The accusation stabbed him. "The reason he turned to serve Jader and the Dark Army." Her voice cracked, and she paused for a moment. "The reason there was never any hope for us."

Oh, Lambient, help me. There was nothing more he could say. He stared back at her, his heart fragmenting as he relived that moment again in his mind. After a long, heavy silence, Seria blinked her tears back and walked past him, leaving him alone in his room.

What had she done? Seria shivered against the soft breeze as she knocked on the door, praying Lena would be home.

Ayna answered. "Why, Seria, is everything all right?" The woman reached out and grasped Seria's arm, making her wonder what she must look like.

"I'm fine, but I need to see Lena. Is she in?"

"I'm afraid not. She went to go see her grandfather, about an hour ago."

Gone! And with her, all chances of Seria leaving the fort. She thanked Ayna and—knowing it was already too late—hurried to the spot where Lena snuck through the walls to leave the fort.

Her heart thumped and bled under her breast. What had she done? She had rejected Mason, fully believing he was wrong about everything he accused the Stewards of. Hearing the truth from Eric's own mouth had destroyed her.

But how much more had it destroyed Mason?

It's true. Eric's words pounded in her ears as she searched the walls for a sign of Lena. She had no idea what she planned to do if she found her, but all she could think of was Mason getting ready to take the Shadowstone. Rejected by the one person who might have been able to change his mind.

Why hadn't she tried harder to talk him out of it when he'd told her what he was going to do? Maybe she could have convinced him against it. Maybe that was why he had shared it with her.

And she had walked away from him.

Lena was nowhere to be seen. She dashed up the steps to the wall, her chest burning with every gulp of air. Tears streaked down her face as she pictured him standing alone in her cabin.

Please, don't do it, Mason.

The crescent moon shone like a white slice in the deep blue sky. Rising higher with every second. Seria gripped the stone wall with trembling fingers, searching through the shadows for what, she didn't know. There was still another wall between her and Mason, not to mention the miles of woods. What did she expect to do if she could escape the fort? She had no idea where Mason was camped.

What am I even hoping for right now?

She pressed her tremoring lips together and drew in an uneven breath. Her body slumped against the wall before her.

Mason loved her. He had told her himself he had not loved anyone since Liam. She had seen the truth in his eyes, those amber eyes that could see every thought of hers. And she walked away from him. If that was the right thing to do, why did she feel like she was dying now?

She could see him, feel his arms, hear his words of strained love, his promise to wait for her. But taking on the Shadowstone would change him. Surely, he would not hold himself to his promise.

The moon continued to rise, mocking the pain slashing at her insides and the tears streaming down her hot cheeks.

She was too late.

65

Mason sat on the edge of his bed, elbows on his knees, his tent dark. Jader would summon him soon, but for the moment, all he could dwell on was how well Seria had fit into his arms. It had taken everything in him not to crush her in his fervor.

He loved her; there was no getting around it. Though he had fought it since first awakening in her cabin, it was stronger than he was. Seria was no longer the peasant girl who talked his ear off and annoyed him to no end. This bundle of spirit, heart, and chatter had gone from nuisance to something deeper than he had ever expected or desired. She was the only woman he wanted. The one woman he could not have.

This wasn't supposed to happen. Not now. He shouldn't love her. She stood in the way of his vow. But he had no more strength to fight it. In a fortnight, he would be waiting for her, as he said he would. But would she be there?

Why had he let her go in the first place? If she meant so much to him, how could he let her slip through his fingers, back to those he fought against with every fiber of his being? He could have controlled her to come with him. But for some reason he could not fathom, he could not bring himself to do so.

Eric Passion. His insides burned with the name. The man had taken everything from him. His home. His brother. His dreams. And now Seria. He had nothing. Nothing but a dark hole that threatened to consume him.

"Sir Mason." A runner called out before sticking his head through the flap. "Emperor Jader is ready for you, sir."

"I'll be along."

The messenger left as quickly as he came. Mason saw Seria with his mind's eye. Her words echoed.

"Please don't, Mason...It's so dangerous."

Mason stood with a heavy sigh. There was no way he could make her understand. Not after Eric had filled her with his lies. Besides, what was left for him now? He had to see vengeance for his brother.

A cloud hovered near the moon as Mason strode through the dark camp, no doubt an added effect from Bruin for the evening. Darkmen and Shadowmen were lined up outside Jader's large tent, where Bruin waited for Mason.

"Are you ready?" the commander asked.

"Aye, sir."

Bruin eyed him. "I won't lie to you, Mason. This won't be easy. Taking on the Shadowstone is a bodily experience as well as a mental one. And for some, it's harder than others."

Mason nodded. "I understand, sir. It doesn't change my mind."

"I didn't think it would." Bruin offered a small smile. "Stay here. Emperor Jader will be out shortly."

Bruin went into Jader's tent, and moments later the emperor emerged, looking regal in his red robe and more than pleased.

"How are you feeling, my boy?"

"I'm well, Emperor Jader." Mason gave him a respectful bow.

Jader stood before him and looked him straight in the face. "I can't tell you how much this moment means to me, Mason. I've seen you grow these past few years, like watching my own son. You've certainly seen your share of hardships, being uprooted from your home and watching your brother die so senselessly."

Mason's jaw clenched at the reminder.

"We share a common bond, Mason. Both of us saw the Passion men for the true monsters they are, though it came at a great personal cost." Jader's fingers traced the scar on his face, his scarred eye twitching while his good eye darkened with unspoken memories. "It's taken a long time for us to get here, hasn't it?" His tone was whisper-soft and soothing as he shifted his scrutiny back to Mason. "And, I fear you have experienced loss at their hands yet again."

Mason shot him an apprehensive look. How much did Jader know about Seria? Surely, he could not know the depth of Mason's feelings for the peasant girl.

Reaching out, Jader placed a hand on Mason's shoulder. "But tonight is a night of victory. All the pain and rage building in you will be turned into a powerful tool. A tool to be wielded against those who have caused you so much turmoil."

The words sank deep into his spirit, and he clung to each one. It was true. After this night, he would be stronger. More able to withstand the lies the Stewards professed. To fill the hole inside him.

Jader raised his head. "Let us begin."

The soldiers stood in half-circle formations behind him. Mason moved to the center of the area, his heart beating fast. Bruin brought out a small trunk from Jader's tent. The one that held his Shadowstone.

Jader straightened and spoke about the merits of taking on a Shadowstone. Mason barely heard him. Seria's resolution played out in his mind.

"I won't be here. I can't."

"Mason has proved himself more than worthy for such a notable honor." Jader continued. "He's taken our men through the fort so that they may do our work in the Old Realm. He risked his own life and faced the prince of Paladin. And from what I hear, left his mark on him as well."

There was a gleeful chortle up and down the assembly. Mason forced a smile, anxious to get on with the formalities. He didn't want to think about the prince, let alone talk of him.

Bruin opened the small box; Jader reached in and withdrew a silver chain. At the end hung a smooth, black stone, emitting a purple glow. Jader held it up for him to see. Instead, Mason saw a pair of innocent, wide-set green eyes, staring up at him with a mixture of fear and longing.

"Taking on the Shadowstone is nothing to be taken lightly," Jader said. "It is a lifelong commitment. There's no going back." He approached Mason with the stone, looking stately and sober. "Once you take this on, Mason Grey, it will *always* be a part of you. Do you pledge to keep it with you for the rest of your days, let it guide you and empower you?"

Mason stared at the rock, trying to see it through the visions in his head. Seria...bent over him, gently caring for him; leaning over the fireplace, stirring their simple meal of vegetable stew; doubled over with laughter over the raccoon fiasco; throwing mudballs at him during their fishing trip; and finally, in his arms, the last time he saw her.

Setting his chin, he forced it all away. His brother's face, young and smiling, flashed through his mind. He had to do this. For Liam.

"I do." The words reverberated in the still night.

A hint of a smile touched the corners of Jader's thin lips. "Take your sword in hand."

Mason pulled his sword and held it tightly in his right hand. Jader lifted the chain over his head and let the stone settle on Mason's breastbone. This was what he had worked for, the culmination of all his plans.

Then Jader raised his hand, extinguishing the light of every oil lamp and torch present. The moonlight itself was dimmed. Nothing could stand in the face of Jader's power. Mason could barely see Jader's face before his in the thick darkness.

"Then this Shadowstone is yours, Mason Grey. May its dark power fill your very being." The older man put his palm over the stone Mason now wore, his expression intensifying. "Darkness begets submission."

Heat radiated from Jader's hand, penetrating Mason's body with such force it robbed him of every last breath. Jader stepped back, into the darkness. Mason gasped at the pain that filled him, shooting from the place where the stone rested on his chest. A strange weight came over him, settling into the soles of his feet, trying to pull him through the ground.

Jader's soothing voice drifted to his ears. "Submission begets power."

Mason's legs buckled, and he doubled over, stunned by the intensity. His chest burned, and his heart raced until he thought it would give out. Struggling to stay on his feet, he groaned and propped himself on a knee with one hand. His sword felt welded to his other hand. He stuck the tip into the ground and braced against it. Without thinking, he grabbed at the stone and screamed at the searing pain that went through him.

He could not see a thing, save a flash of purple light every few seconds. Each flash sent another jolt through his body until he collapsed to both knees. Darkness swirled, starting at the top of his head, and traveling down through his legs.

It's going to kill me! Every time he tried to draw a breath, the blackness pressed closer, suffocating him. And when he thought he could take no more, it got worse. As if his insides were being ripped to pieces by the dark force.

Jader spoke again, the sound cutting through the haziness. "Power begets *victory.*"

Something shot through him, filling him with heat. Mason's lips stretched tight over his teeth in labored perseverance, his eyelids seared shut. He let out another groan as the pressure seemed to crush him.

"Stand up!"

"I can't!" He did not recognize his own voice. So hoarse and strained.

"Stand up!" Jader ordered. "Lift your sword!"

Mason mustered a fragment of willpower to stand. Every move sent red-hot streaks through him. In a last-ditch effort, he shoved to his feet and lifted his sword high. The effort was almost too much, and he let out a guttural cry as he straightened.

Then it was over. Mason dropped his sword and stumbled to keep himself from falling again. He dragged gulps of oxygen into his seared lungs.

All was black. He blinked a few times until he was able to make out Jader's form first, then the soldiers standing around him. A strange, yellow glow stained his vision, sending panic rippling through him. Then it dawned. The Shadowstone tinted his vision in the deep night, letting him see through the thickest shadows. A tingle went over him as the blackness that infused his soul settled deep within him.

"Welcome back, my boy." Jader wore a satisfied smile. "The Shadow-stone is yours."

Author's Note

Dear Reader,

I can't express what it means to me that we are here. This story has been in the making for so many years. I started it with high hopes and the firm belief that I had something special. But sometimes life got in the way and it would sit untouched on my computer for months or even years. Or it was my own distracted nature that halted its progress as I set it aside to work on other projects.

But many times I got discouraged while writing and felt like giving up. Maybe this story was too special for me. Maybe I didn't have what it took to make it live up to its potential. Maybe I wasn't a good enough writer for this kind of story.

Whatever the reason, Shadowcast would not let me give up on it. It called to me every time I tried to move on. It sat in the back of my mind, slowly building and developing and growing until I could not hold it back any longer. Eventually, I finished the first draft.

Since then, Shadowcast has been rewritten and edited countless times. Each time I wondered if that would be the last time, but there was always more that could be done. More to make it better. I prayed over it, worked on it, and stuck with it. Until finally, I knew my story was ready for the world.

And now I get to share it with you. Thank you so much for picking it up and taking a chance on it! I hope it brought a little joy and hope to your heart, as it did for mine.

God bless you, friend!

Until we meet between the pages again,

Crystal D. Grant

Acknowledgments

Mom and Dad: Thank you for all the stories you read and told me as a child. You instilled in all your children a love for reading, writing, and learning. And even more importantly, you raised us to know and serve the Lord. It's because of the foundation you poured into me that I made it here. I love you!

Richard, you were the first one to read my earliest draft and our many conversations sparked a myriad of ideas that lay the groundwork for what Shadowcast became. And thanks for the coolest title ever! Someday we'll be writing the acknowledgments for our secret project. :)

Holly, you became my go-to person as Shadowcast neared completion. Thanks for all the hours you spent reading. (How many drafts did you end up reading?) You always got me thinking of new ways to make it better. I can't wait until the world can read your amazing story!

Emily, you introduced me to Realm Makers and Bookstagram, which opened doors I never would have found otherwise. Thank you for helping me get here. I love how we can get lost in conversation about books and writing. Your stories continue to amaze and inspire me!

AJ, imagine two Potosi girls meeting for the first time online. And now here we are! I can't tell you how much I appreciate you taking a chance on me and my book. Thank you for all the time and work you have put into this project. And for all the late-night chats about anything and everything that popped into my head!

Meghan and Sarah, thanks for all your editing help in polishing Shadowcast up so pretty and shiny!

Brittany and Ava, thanks for your mad proofreading skills and for catching all those "little things" that I missed.

Jessica Gwyn, thank you for all your hard work in launching this book! I would have been lost without you and all the hours you put in to make this release a success.

Kessie Carol, somehow you took the visions I carried in my head of my characters and made them come alive on the page. Lacey Scott, I'm still amazed at how you took my pitiful little scribbles and turned them into a beautiful map of the Gateway! Thank you both so much!!

Anne J. Hill, you put my name in print for the first time in over a decade. I learned so much about publishing and editing working with you.

Sharon K. Connell and Hannah Mae, I never imagined when I joined the ACFW critique group that I'd find lasting friendships! I'm so grateful to you both. Your feedback helped make this story what it is now.

Joy K. Massenburg, you were one of the few people to read Shadowcast all the way through in its early stages and gave me hope that other people might read it, too.

Sara Ella, your enthusiasm for this story did a world of good for this struggling writer's heart. Because of your response, I dared to believe the world might love it, too. Your thoughtful questions and comments inspired new scenes that I adore and deeper character development. Thank you again for all your help!

My Q&F publishing sisters: Vanessa, Anna, Moriah, Brittany, Ashley, Amber, and Hope. So glad we get to cheer each other on this journey!

My Kindle Vella group: Krissi, Callie, Jill, Stephanie, Crystal, Elizabeth A., MJ, Elizabeth W., and Kim—I learned so much about marketing and networking from you. Thanks for all the laughs!

The Bookstagram community and fellow Realmies: there are too many of you to list without being afraid of forgetting someone, so please know that I appreciate every one of you!

And to the Creator of *my* story. Thank You for all of this and so much more.

CRYSTAL D. GRANT

Crystal Grant is a daydreamer who adores freshly-baked cookies and anything with fur or feathers. During the day, she strives to instill a love of books and learning within her young students. As a hearing-impaired, home-school graduate, she found her voice in writing and has had multiple short stories and poems published. When she's not reading or writing stories that sweep her away to another time and place, she watches classic movies and TV shows that do the same. Or she works on jigsaw puzzles. Crystal currently resides in smalltown Missouri, where she is always looking for space for another scented candle.